William Westall

The Princes of Peele

William Westall

The Princes of Peele

ISBN/EAN: 9783337172176

Printed in Europe, USA, Canada, Australia, Japan

Cover: Foto ©Andreas Hilbeck / pixelio.de

More available books at **www.hansebooks.com**

THE
PRINCES OF PEELE

BY
WILLIAM WESTALL

AUTHOR OF

" A QUEER RACE," "THE BLIND MUSICIAN," "THE PHANTOM CITY,"
" MR. FORTESCUE,' ETC.

NEW YORK
LOVELL, CORYELL & COMPANY
5 AND 7 EAST SIXTEENTH STERET

THE PRINCES OF PEELE.

CHAPTER I.

MRS. PRINCE'S PRESENTIMENT.

THE hall of an old-fashioned country house. Background, a massive oaken staircase ; on the walls, several handsomely-framed prints ; a trophy, composed of a fox's mask and half a dozen " brushes " and stags' antlers, arranged as a hat-stand. In the foreground, vases filled with ferns and flowers.

The comely couple standing in the sunlight, which streams in through the doorway, are the master and mistress of the house, Leonard Prince and Dorothy his wife. He is drawing on his gloves, she putting a gardenia in his buttonhole. Mrs. Prince is the stouter, albeit not the taller of the two, a matron of somewhat imposing presence, well-favored, with dark eyes and a fair skin. Mr. Prince, not having thickened with age like his spouse, looks younger than his years, which are far on in the fifties ; his hair and mutton-chop whiskers are turning white, his comely face is bright with health and high spirits, and his keen gray eyes, strong white teeth, and square jaws bespeak a vigorous constitution, a sanguine temperament, and an energetic character.

" Thank you very much, my dear," says Mr. Prince as his wife hands him his hat, " I think I hear Tommy's step on the gravel. Come with me as far as the lodge gates."

Mrs. Prince put on her garden hat, and the two went out together at the open door.

Tommy, Mr. Prince's hack, an old favorite who knew his business so well that he always came to be mounted without escort, was waiting for his master. Mrs. Prince stroked his neck, gave him a piece of sugar, and the three walked slowly down the avenue.

Mr. Prince cast a backward longing glance at the house, as if he were sorry to leave it, even for the day; and well he might be, for it was a glorious morning, and Holmcroft, with its brick walls, tiled roof, clustering ivy and rose-covered porch, and in its fair setting of shrubberies and gardens, never looked more charming and picturesque.

" Yes, it is a dear, beautiful old place," said Mrs. Prince, following her husband's eye, and reading his thoughts. " Yet what a wilderness it was when we came here, nearly thirty years since."

" So it is; and since we were first married. We have a great deal to be thankful for."

" We have indeed. God has been very good to us, and if we are permitted to end our days here——"

" If I had reason to fear we should not, I think it would break my heart."

" And mine. However, we need not talk about ending our days. Neither of us is so very old yet. You are the youngest man of your years in the county; and Mr. Vayle was saying only the other day that you rode as straight as when you were thirty."

" And you walk as straight, Dorothy. While, as for your looks——"

" No more; an' thou lovest me! You might suppose I was fishing for a compliment. Shall you be home late to-night?"

" No, Monday is generally an easy day at the office; and if there isn't much doing I mean to return early and do some jack-fishing before dinner."

" It seems rather a long time since we heard from Jack, doesn't it?"

Mr. Prince smiled; he was amused that his mention of jack-fishing should remind his wife of their eldest son; but answered gravely—

" Well, I don't know. It seems only the other day that you had a letter from him."

" It is nearly three weeks since."

" Dear me! How time flies; I suppose he has been too busy."

" I am sure he has not been so busy that he could not find

time to write to his mother, and—— I hope he is not going wrong again, Leonard."

" Why should you think so ? Peploe speaks of him in the highest terms. He is very steady and regular, and is becoming quite an adept at underwriting, they say. They are quite willing to take him in as a junior partner next year, if I find two thou. I think by that time I shall be able to do it— with a little effort ; and I don't see why I should not. They are a young firm, I know, but Peploe and Pope are both honorable and enterprising ; and it is a chance not to be missed."

" I hope Jack will prove himself worthy of it, but my mind misgives me."

" Because he has not written to you for a fortnight ? "

" Not that only, though it is a bad sign. In his letters lately there has been something that I cannot define, which has made me very uneasy. Moreover, in my last letter to him, written nearly three weeks ago, I put some very pointed questions, which he has not thought fit to answer—another bad sign. And you know how facile and impulsive he is ; and he has gone wrong before. My fear is that he may be running into debt. He was always a spendthrift."

" You are over anxious, Dorothy. True, Jack has gone wrong before, as you say, and given us no end of trouble, but he has many redeeming qualities—he has never done anything dishonorable, nor taken to drink ; he is sharp and clever too, and very affectionate. Moreover, for three years his conduct has been quite irreproachable ; his employers speak well of him ; and I think we may safely conclude that he has sown his wild oats."

" Well, I am perhaps mistaken. Let us say no more about it, and hope for the best ; and if Jack had been like Ned and Charlie we should have been almost too happy. One must have a cross, I suppose. . . . . . Here we are at the lodge gates. I shall expect you about four. Good-bye, dear."

" Good-bye, dear," echoed Mr. Prince ; and then, after kissing his wife, he rode off, slowly and pensively.

" I hope I have not made Leonard unhappy with my croaking," thought Mrs. Prince to herself, as she wended up the avenue. " But I have had misgivings about Jack for some time, and I did no more than my duty in telling Leonard. It is not as if I had no warning for my fears. I know Jack better than he does. His letters have not been sincere this month or more, and if he could have answered my queries he would have done so. Of that I am sure. In spite of our exhortations I fear—nay I am almost sure—that he has been getting into debt. I will write again to-day, and insist on an answer, and if it is not forthcoming his father shall go to Liverpool and see him."

Meanwhile Mr. Prince was mentally accusing his wife of being fidgety, and too prone to look on the dark side of things. "What if Jack has been wild?" he thought. "Many a young fellow who has been wild turns out well. And if there were anything wrong, Peploe and Pope would be sure to let me know. All the same, he should answer his mother's letters; and when I get to the office I will write and tell him so." And then Mr. Prince, dismissing the subject from his mind, and turning Tommy on the turfy side of the road, cantered gaily towards Peele.

Jack, their eldest son, had been a trouble to his parents from his youth upwards. In addition to minor scrapes he was expelled from a public school, and after spending a term or two at Cambridge, ran off, worked his way in a sailing ship to Australia, and a few years later returned to Holmcroft, penitent and ashamed. The experience did him good; his father thought it had wrought a radical change in his character, and after a few months' probation at home, Mr. Prince got the repentant prodigal a place with Peploe and Pope, a Liverpool firm of ship and insurance brokers, where the knowledge of shipping and commerce which he had gained on his voyages and at Melbourne, stood him in good stead, and being bright and intelligent withal, and having that capacity for making friends so common with most scapegraces, he was not long in winning the confidence of his employers, and obtaining a leading position in their office.

His father, though greatly disappointed (he had intended him for the bar), laid the flattering unction to his soul that Jack was on the high road to fortune and would give him no more trouble, an opinion, however, in which, as we have seen, his wife did not share.

Of their two other sons, Edward, the elder, is rounding off his legal education in the office of his father's London agent, and Charlie, in the intervals of shooting, fishing, and hunting, is serving his articles in the paternal establishment.

As Mr. Prince rides up the High Street of Peele, which straggles over a low hill, topped by the ruins of an old castle, he is greeted by all and sundry. Common folks touch their hats to him, others nod familiarly, and say "Good-morning, Mr. Prince," for the master of Holmcroft is the most popular and influential man in the town, leading solicitor, clerk of the peace, clerk to the justices and board of guardians, and agent to Lord Hermitage, the largest land-owner in those parts. He has been several times mayor, and no candidate for suffrages of the "free and independent" burgesses of the borough whom he does not support has much chance of becoming its representative in Parliament.

His friend, Mr. Lincoln (of the great American firm of Lyman, Lincoln, and Jump), who has a country seat in the neighborhood, calls him the "Boss of Peele."

He is, moreover, supposed to be well off ; keeps a stud of hunters, lives in good style, and gives liberally to local charities. His legal business is of the lucrative sort so much desired by solicitors—mainly conveyancing ; he is the trusted adviser of all the squires and farmers in the countryside, and save in litigious cases never had a bill taxed in his life, nor has he ever consented to take up an unclean case or accept a disreputable client.

Mr. Prince reins up before an old-fashioned house in the High Street, throws his right leg over his horse's withers and drops lightly on the pavement. On this, Tommy goes off to his stable, and his master walks briskly into his office, the old-fashioned house aforesaid. The brass plate on the door bears the inscription—

" PRINCE AND PRINCE, SOLICITORS."

The Princes in question were Mr. Leonard Prince's father and uncle, to whose business he succeeded many years previously. They have been long dead, but he likes to keep up the old style, the more especially as he has good reason to believe that his sons will succeed him in turn, and the firm become, in reality as in name, "Prince and Prince" once more.

After looking in at the general office and the estate office, and seeing that all the clerks are at work, and bidding them good-morning, Mr. Prince enters his own room, where he is presently joined by Mr. Lillywhite, his managing clerk.

A queer-looking gentleman was Mr. Lillywhite. People said he had the longest head in all Peele. He had certainly the biggest nose ; and it was the only part of his face which blushed or otherwise showed emotion, the rest of his visage being as sallow and expressionless as a piece of his own parchment. The nose, however, was all expression. It moved when he talked, wobbled when he laughed, and trembled when he swore. Its hue changed with the days of the week. On a Monday morning it was terra cotta red ; by Wednesday it toned down to light purple, on Saturday it was generally light blue. These remarkable variations were conceiveably due to the fact that Mr. Lillywhite made a rule of drinking a bottle of old port with his Sunday dinner, and with his other dinners only beer. The managing clerk was further distinguished by the length of his body and the phenomenal bareness of his face and head, the only hair of which he could boast being a single yellow tuft on the top of his cranium, which he humorously called his scalp lock.

"Anything new this morning, Lillywhite ?" asked Mr. Prince as he opened his letters.

"Nothing particular. Mr. Jumper called. He wants another will making."

"The deuce he does ! Why, that will be the second this year, won't it ?"

"The third. He is a good man, Mr. Jumper, always thinking about his latter end. However, it amuses him and pays us. This is a free country and a man has a right to make as many wills as he likes."

"Well, prepare the draft, and let him have it at once. Has anybody else called ?"

"A gentleman who seemed rather anxious to see you. He was here when I came. Said he would call again shortly, but refused to give his name."

"A stranger then ?"

"He must be ; I never saw him before."

"Probably a commercial traveller, who wants to recover a debt for his house."

"I don't think so. He does not look like one. Besides, in that case he would have told me his business. Shall I send him in to you if he comes again ?"

" By all means."

" Well, I think I'll go and prepare this draft. It will be little more than a copy of the previous will, with a few variations."

Whereupon Mr. Lillywhite withdrew ; but the door had hardly closed behind him when he was back again.

" Here he is, Mr. Prince," he whispered. " Just come in at the front door . . . . . This way, sir. Mr. Prince has arrived."

And then there entered a tall red-haired gentleman in a tweed travelling suit, closely followed by the managing clerk.

" God bless me, Mr. Peploe!" exclaimed Mr. Prince, rising from his chair with a look of blank surprise. " How are you ? "

" As well as can be expected, thank you, seeing that I have been travelling all night. Could I have a word with you, Mr. Prince ? " (glancing at Lillywhite).

The head clerk took the hint and withdrew a second time.

" Peploe, Peploe," he murmured, " Peploe and Pope. One of Jack's masters. What's up now, I wonder ? "

" Pray take a seat, Mr. Peploe," said Mr. Prince seriously, for he thought of his wife, and feared that this visit boded no good. Peploe was a busy man. It was no light cause that brought him all the way from Liverpool to Peele. " How did you leave Jack ? "

" I did not leave him at all. He left us."

" Left you ? How, Mr. Peploe ? "

" In the lurch. You will excuse my bluntness, Mr. Prince. But I have neither time nor inclination just now to beat about the bush. I must come to the point at once. Your son has robbed us—that is why I am here to-day."

Mr. Prince turned as white as a sheet, and fell back in his chair as if he had been struck.

" Robbed you ! No, no, Mr. Peploe ! That is impossible. Jack may have been a little wild and extravagant, perhaps, but not dishonest, don't say he has been dishonest."

" I wish to God he had not. But there, see for yourself."

CHAPTER II.

PEPLOE'S PROPOSAL.

MR. PEPLOE took from his pocket-book two documents and laid them on Mr. Prince's desk.

One was a wildly incoherent letter from Jack, in which, with many expressions of contrition, the writer acknowledged having abused his employers' confidence and " taken " a large sum of money—lost on the Stock Exchange and betting—he must have been mad, but he would pay them back every penny, so help him God, he would. He ended by begging them to say nothing to his father.

The other document was to the following effect :—

" Private and Confidential.
" MESSRS. PEPLOE AND POPE,
" DEAR SIRS,—I have gone through your books and find that the defalcations directly traceable to Mr. John Prince amount to the sum of 19,450*l*, 17*s*. 6*d*.—Yours truly, HENRY TANNER, Accountant."

Mr. Prince gazed at these letters like one fascinated, and his hand trembled so that he could scarcely hold them. He knew from the first that Peploe was the bearer of bad news ; but the reality surpassed his worst forebodings. His eldest son a felon and a fugitive from justice ! He would rather have heard that Jack had died by his own hand. Yet, even in that moment of unspeakable mental anguish Leonard Prince's first thought was of his wife. " What would she say ? How would she bear it ? How should he tell her ? " he asked himself.

" But you—how ? " he said at length in a husky voice.

" I know what you mean," answered Mr. Peploe. " You mean how came we to let him rob us to the tune of nearly twenty thousand pounds ? Well, we were fools, there is no

doubt about that, people are fools sometimes. But he got on
the blind side of us—that's a fact. And it never occurred to
us that such a bright, seemingly straightforward young fellow,
so respectably connected, too, could be otherwise than honest.
The worst of it is that it is not our money that he has
taken."

" Not your own money."

" No, it is clients' money. You know the nature of our
business. We underwrite the names of a number of friends
to policies, and the accumulated premiums form a fund for
the payment of losses. If the premiums exceed the losses
the profit goes to the underwriters, less our commission ; if
the losses exceed the premiums the underwriters have to make
up the difference. We have the handling of the money, which
we invest on the best terms we can obtain, compatible with
good security. Latterly this branch of the business has been
managed by your son, under our directions. I am afraid,
though, we did not look as sharply after him as we should
have done. But as I said just now, we never thought that a
man so respectably connected, and of whom we thought so
highly that we were going to take him into partnership,
would go wrong. He was so diligent, too, and regular in
his attendance at the office—would not even take a holiday.
I know why, now. If he had he would have been found out.

" Well, last Saturday he went yachting with some friends,
and intended to be back on Sunday night or Monday morning,
but the yacht got into trouble off the Welsh coast, and Prince
did not turn up at the office on Monday. Now, it so happened,
that on the same day I received notice of several claims ; also
I heard that a steamer in which we were rather largely
interested had come to grief in the Channel. Knowing we
should want money, and a lot of it—when claims are concerned
it never rains but it pours—I called at a bank where we had,
or rather should have had, ten thousand pounds on deposit,
and gave notice of withdrawal. I was told that nearly half of
it had already been withdrawn in various amounts and at
intervals extending over several weeks. Though surprised I
was not alarmed. I merely thought that Prince had changed
the investment for some good reason, and blamed him only
for not informing me. But when I found that the books
contained no entry of the withdrawals, the possibility of
something being wrong dawned on my mind. As the day

went on my uneasiness increased, and as soon as I could get away from the office I called at your son's lodgings. He had not returned. In the course of the evening I called three times, always with the same result.

"When I called again next morning, I learned that he did not return till midnight, and must have left shortly afterwards. At any rate, he had not been in bed. My visits had alarmed him, perhaps, also, he heard of the loss of the 'Cyclops,' and knew that, in view of our financial requirements, his frauds could no longer be concealed. Anyhow, I have not seen him since last Saturday. That note came by post."

"The wretched, misguided boy," groaned Mr. Prince. "Have you any idea where he is?"

"Well, I am afraid I could not give you his correct address at this moment. But I don't doubt that if I tried I could lay my hands on him."

In saying this Mr. Peploe went rather beyond the mark. He had not the faintest idea what was become of Jack, but it did not just then suit his purpose to say so.

"Do you propose to prosecute?" asked Mr. Prince, in a voice which showed how much the effort cost him.

"Well, that depends on circumstances. We might, you know. Your son has behaved shamefully, there is no doubt about that. We trusted him and he has betrayed us. All the same, we have no wish to go to extremities, and if we could be met——"

"If you could be met. Pray be explicit, Mr. Peploe," said Mr. Prince, looking as if he had no idea what the other was driving at, though he knew only too well.

"Explicit! Oh, yes, I will be explicit. It is very easy to be explicit in an affair of this sort. As I remarked just now, we have no desire to prosecute. But unless we can have fifteen thousand pounds within the next four days—say by next Tuesday, at the latest—we must pull up, and then everything will be exposed, and we shall be forced to hunt your son down and prosecute him, if only for our own justification; and as it is a case of forgery as well as embezzlement, we can fetch him back from America, or anywhere else, if he goes out of the country."

"Forgery! Good heavens!"

"Yes, it is mostly embezzlement, but there are one or two

undoubted cases of forgery. It would be a terrible scandal for all of us. But if we can be met, nobody need be the wiser. Tanner is sworn to secrecy, so to speak, and you may be sure we won't split. If this got wind we should lose half our underwriters, and our credit would be ruined. Can you find us fifteen thousand pounds between this and next Tuesday, Mr. Prince? I am not in a position to make any promises about paying you back; we shall have to lose nearly five thousand ourselves, and we are only a young firm, but we would try to pay you a moderate interest. What do you say, Mr. Prince, will you do it?"

"It is not a quesion of will, Mr. Peploe. I am grieved beyond measure, I am unspeakably humiliated that a son of mine should have done you this wrong. It adds to my grief that his wrong-doing may entail your ruin, but I cannot do what you wish."

Peploe's saturnine face flushed with anger and disappointment.

"That means you won't," he exclaimed angrily. "I know fifteen thousand is a big lump. But just consider the consequences of your refusal. Our ruin is a minor consideration. We should have looked better after our business, I admit; but having regard to the circumstances, I don't think the creditors will be very hard on us. They will let us make a fresh start. But think of your son in a felon's dock, he is sure to get ten years at least; think of the scandal it will cause. You are a great man here, I am told. How will you look your townsmen in the face when they know that your eldest son——"

"Mind what you say, sir, or——," exclaimed Mr. Prince, springing from his chair, as if he were minded to resent the insult with a blow or show the insulter to the door.

Then he sank down and bowed his head. The man had only spoken the truth.

"You feel it keenly. I knew you would. What father would not," returned Peploe soothingly. "All the more reason for letting us have this money. It will be well laid out, and we are asking nothing unreasonable; we will pay you interest. My partner said to me the last thing before I came away —'Be sure,' he said, 'you don't ask the old gentleman anything unreasonable, Sam. It is not hush-money we want, only help.'"

Mr. Prince winced. He prided himelf on the comparative youthfulness of his appearance, and it went against the grain to know that these Liverpool people spoke of him as "the old gentleman."

"Reasonable or unreasonable. I am unable to do it, Mr. Peploe," he returned sharply. "I don't say I would not if I could. But as I unfortunately don't happen to have fifteen thousand pounds in my pocket or at my bankers——"

"I did not suppose you had, Mr. Prince. But there are ways and means. A gentleman in your position could easily raise as much. Anyhow, I should think so."

"Not in four or five days."

"We might, perhaps, make it seven."

"Not in seven, nor in fourteen days."

"In that case there is nothing more to be said," observed Peploe, rising from his chair ; "things must take their course, I suppose."

Mr. Prince made no answer. It seemed useless to prolong the interview, and he wanted Peploe to go. He was beginning to hate the man, and he wanted to be alone.

"Things must take their course, I suppose," repeated the persistent Liverpudlian. "But, perhaps, you may think better of it after all ; and if you do—if you see your way—you will, perhaps, be good enough to telegraph to our office in Liverpool. We won't take any action before Friday, but the sooner the better. One word will do—'Arranged.' We shall understand."

"I can hold out no encouragement, Mr. Peploe, none whatever. Nevertheless, if I should see my way I will telegraph, as you say."

Peploe's countenance brightened. Like drowning men, the financially embarrassed catch at straws, and, though fairly considered, the lawyer's concluding observation offered little ground for hope, Peploe went away comforted, and little doubting that on his arrival at Liverpool he should find awaiting him the telegram whose despatch he had suggested.

When the door closed behind his visitor, Mr. Prince leaned back in his chair, and wiped the perspiration from his brow. He had undergone the most painful experience of his life, and there was worse in store. How should he break the news to his wife ? If he could spare her he would. But it was impossible. Know she must. In a week the secret would be out. For though he had not liked to say so in express terms, it was as much out of his power to find fifteen thousand pounds in four days, or four months, as to find fifty thousand. Contrary to the general belief, a belief which he rather encouraged, Mr. Prince was not rich. He had a good income, and he lived up to it. Beyond the two or three thousand pounds which he employed in his business for temporary advances to his clients, and so forth, and which he could neither well spare nor immediately realize, he had very little laid by. He had always looked on his business as an estate which he could bequeath to his sons as his father had bequeathed it to him. His wife was provided for by a marriage settlement and a policy of insurance on his life. He had not thought it necessary to economize, and though not a thriftless man, it gave him less pleasure to accumulate than to spend. But now he bitterly regretted that he had not been more provident; for he would gladly have paid twice, nay thrice, fifteen thousand pounds, to avert the disaster with which he was threatened.

Only a few days, and, as Peploe said, he would be unable to look his neighbors in the face. The hue and cry after Jack; the story of his defalcations told in every paper in the land; the trial and sentence (for he was sure to be taken); the consternation of friends, the exultation of the envious; the joy of political opponents; all this was torture, even in the thought. What would it be in the reality?

Moreover, the scandal could hardly fail to injure his business and imperil his position, and Mr. Prince valued his position hardly less than he valued his life. Better leave Peele altogether. And yet leaving Peele would be the end of the world. There was no other spot in it where, for him and his, life would be worth living.

A knock at the door.

"Come in," said Mr. Prince, taking a paper at random from the pile before him.

When Mr. Lillywhite entered the room his principal was deep in the perusal of counsel's opinion in the matter of "Towzler *v.* Towzler and another."

"Oh, Mr. Peploe is gone, then," said the managing clerk, with well affected surprise; for he had heard Peploe's departing footsteps.

"Yes, he is gone. What is it? Anything new?"

2

" Only that Hutchins wants ten or twelve thousand pounds on the security of his Tanfield property. It is worth half as much again, and as he will pay five per cent. and execute a mortgage for five years I thought it would be an excellent investment for some of Mrs. Lincoln's money."

" Mrs. Lincoln's money is very well where it is. You cannot beat Consols for safety, and one or two per cent. makes no difference to her."

" That is true. All the same, the transfer would make good business for the office. Hutchins would stand a 'procuration fee,' and investigating titles and drawing the mortgage, and what not, would make a nice penny."

" Right you are, Lillywhite. You have always an eye to the main chance. If I had not you to look after details it it would not be the office it is by a long way. Yes, the transfer would make something nice, and lawyers live on costs I have heard say."

" Two hundred pounds, at the very least."

" All the same, you must bear in mind, my dear Lillywhite, that now Wilmot is dead I am Mrs. Lincoln's sole trustee, and must take the whole responsibility; and really, you know, I hardly like to change the investment, merely to oblige old Hutchins and put money in my own pocket."

" It won't be merely to put money in your own pocket. It will put money into Mrs. Lincoln's pocket, to the tune of a hundred and thirty or forty pounds a year."

" The Lincolns are so rich, Lillywhite, that they think less of a hundred pounds than I do of six and eightpence; and I have no doubt that if I were to mention it to Mrs. Lincoln she would say—'leave the money where it is. A trustee cannot be too particular; and my position is all the more delicate in that I am both her trustee and her solicitor. And so long as I keep the money where it was from the first, nobody can find fault with me. However, I will think about it, and look at the trust deed again before deciding. I have not read it for years, and it rather runs in my mind that I am restricted to Consols."

" Tanfield farm is quite as safe, Mr. Prince."

" Perhaps. Anyhow I am not going to infringe the trusts of the settlement either to make business for the office or to oblige Mr. Hutchins. I suppose it will do if he gets his answer next week ? "

" Oh, yes. He is in no hurry; and if we don't find him the money he can easily get it elsewhere. Anything else, sir ? "

" I think not," and Mr. Prince turned again to the paper before him.

Lillywhite took this as a sign of dismissal, and went away greatly dissatisfied that he had failed to find out the cause of Peploe's visit, and the nature of his business. He liked to know, and flattered himself that he did know, everything that went on in the office, and a good deal that went on outside. There was no end of secrets locked up in that long head of his ; never before had his employer kept anything from him, and, considering his position in the office and his many years of faithful service, he felt that he was being badly used.

What did it all mean ? Why had Peploe come all the way from Liverpool ? What had passed during his long interview with the governor, and, above all, why was the governor so close ? For years there had not been a difficult or delicate case in the office as to which Mr. Prince had not consulted him, and, as often as not, taken his advice.

" Well, if he won't tell me, I must find it out for myself, he thought. " I must find it out, and it is a queer case that Andrew Lillywhite cannot 'bottom.' "

CHAPTER III.

SOWING THE WIND.

DURING the remainder of the day Mr. Prince had little leisure for thought. Several important clients called; he was sent for to the Town Hall; the second post brought him letters which required immediate attention; and when he mounted his nag for the ride home the clock of St. Dunstan was chiming six.

It was a fine evening. The park-like country before him, with its sparkling meads, silvery streams, and hedgerows white with hawthorn, looked exquisitely beautiful. Spring had cast her magic spell over the land; larks were carolling joyously in the upper air; and the red sun was dipping slowly towards the empurpled shades of the distant forest.

But all these sights and sounds, all this glory of nature, were lost on Leonard Prince. There was no sunshine in his heart. It was heavy with grief and pain. For the first time in his life he was battling in deep waters. Never before had he gone home reluctantly, never before looked forward to meeting his wife with apprehension and fear.

For the hundredth time he asked himself how he should tell her the evil news, tell her that their eldest son was a forger, thief, and a fugitive from justice, and that in a few days his shame and their own would be published on the house-tops? And how would she bear it—she who was more sensitive on the point of honor than himself, whose pride was even greater than his own, and who had lavished so much love and tenderness on this unworthy boy?

"It has to be faced," he murmured; "the sooner I get it over the better."

So soon as he was cleared of the town he touched Tommy with his heel, and the gallant little horse stepped out to such purpose that in less than twenty minutes he was at the Holmcroft lodge-gates.

As Mr. Prince pulled up at the hall door, his wife crossed the lawn with a bunch of freshly-gathered flowers in her hand.

" How about the fishing? " she said, smiling pleasantly. " I thought you were coming home early to try for some jack ! "

" Fishing ! Well, do you know I forgot all about it—never thought of it since."

" You have been busy, then ? "

" All day. Every minute occupied. Had to see the Mayor and the Watch Committee about an impending lawsuit ; long conference with Thornwood touching that disputed water-right, and I don't know what besides."

" You look fagged, and your eyes are troubled. You are more than fagged, you are worried. What is it, Leonard ? Nothing has gone wrong, I hope."

" Yes, Dorothy, something has gone very wrong. But come into my room, dear. We can talk there more at our ease, and without being observed or overheard."

He led the way, and she followed him in silent surprise. The style and furnishing of Mr. Prince's room were in harmony with its owner's tastes and pursuits. On the writing-table law papers neatly tied and docketed, on the walls trophies of the chase, and engravings of celebrated horses and scenes in the hunting-field ; fishing-rods in one corner, a gun rack in another.

Mr. Prince drew up a chair for his wife, then seated himself by her side, and took her hand.

All this preparation and the gravity of her husband's manner naturally alarmed Mrs. Prince.

" Good heavens, Leonard ! " she gasped. " What is it ? The boys ! Has—— Are they well ? Tell me quickly."

" I believe so. I have heard nothing to the contrary. But there are worse things than not being well. You have high courage and you will need it."

Mrs. Prince drew a deep breath.

" Go on, please. Don't keep me in suspense. I can bear anything but that."

" You remember what you said this morning about Jack, that you feared he was going wrong. I did not share in your fears. But you were right. He has gone wrong, fearfully wrong——"

" Oh, Leonard !   What has he done? "

" Robbed his employers of nearly twenty thousand pounds and absconded."

Mrs. Prince neither exclaimed nor turned pale ; she looked dazed and bewildered, as if the stroke had stunned her, and she was unable to grasp the full significance of her husband's words.   Then drawing a long breath, and putting her hands before her eyes she remained silent several minutes. Mr. Prince, who had expected a scene, watched her anxiously.

" Did you understand, Dorothy ? " he said at length, again taking her hand.

"Oh yes, I understood, perfectly.   This boy of ours—the first I bore you, Leonard—this boy by whom we set such store, whom we have helped so generously and forgiven so often, has played the thief, and will engulf us in his own ruin. Is this all, Leonard ? "

" All, Dorothy !   Good God, what would you have ?   Yes, it is all."

" He has not been arrested ? "

" Not yet."

" You think he will be, then ? "

" I am sure.   Peploe says that unless I can find fifteen thousand pounds within the next five or six days they will put the police on his track, and if they do the odds are a thousand to one against his escape."

" Tell me all about it."

Mr. Prince told her of Peploe's visit and his demand.

" The money must be found, Leonard."

" Must !   Must ! " he said bitterly.   "It is easy to say must.   But how?   Tell me how?   You know that I have not fifteen thousand pounds in the world, or anything like it."

" Cannot you borrow it ? "

" No.   What security can I offer ?   The bank would let me have two or three thousand, I daresay, but that would be of no more use than two or three hundred.   These people want fifteen thousand by next Friday, at the latest."

" Mr. Lincoln ? "

" I doubt whether Mr. Lincoln would lend me a thousand pounds, rich as he is, and he starts for Liverpool to-morrow morning, *en route* for New York.   I don't see how I could raise this money though I had a respite of six months instead of six days.   It cannot be done.   I wish it could."

" It shall be done. It must be done. . . . Have I been a good wife to you, Leonard Prince ? "

" Why do you ask so strange a question, Dorothy ? You know that I love the very ground you tread on."

" Have I been a good mother to your children ? "

" Ask them. Even Jack ; but why——"

" Well, I would rather give up my life, I would rather follow you to the grave, I would rather see Jack lying dead at my feet than that this disgrace should befall us. Do you realize the horror of it ? "

" To the full. A great misfortune has come upon us, and we are threatened with a disaster which I see no way of averting."

Mrs. Prince wrung her hands, and her white lips twisted convulsively. " It must be averted. There is a way," she exclaimed wildly. " You are a man of business. I would do anything, anything. If you love me, think of something, for if the worst happens I shall either die or go mad."

He leaned his head on his hand, made a desperate effort to compose himself, and obey his wife's injunction to " think of something."

When he looked up she placed her hand on his shoulder.

" You have thought of something," she said eagerly, " what is it ? "

It was a terrible moment for Leonard Prince. He had inherited from his father a healthy body, a sane mind, and a nature so happily organized that it cost him no effort to do right. And he had always been dominated by a desire to do right. Never in his life had he paltered with his honor or abused the confidence of a client, nor was there any class of men for whom he had so great a contempt as chicaning lawyers and defaulting trustees. He was a strong man, too, with a clear head and a rare capacity for facing and over-coming difficulties. But there was a weak point in his armor—he loved his wife with hardly less ardor than when they were first wed—and though she was the weaker of the two, love gave her a power over him which he was unable to withstand. Left to himself, or less passionately entreated, he would never have thought of so fatal an expedient as that which had occurred to him. He would have braved the storm and lived down the scandal which the revelation of his son's misconduct would have caused. But with that pale, drawn face before him, with those dear beseeching eyes raised to his in agonized suspense what could he do, how help himself?

" You have thought of something," she repeated. " What is it? Tell me, Leonard. Tell me at once."

" I have thought of something, only——"

" What? "

" It would not be right."

"But what is it? "

Again Mr. Prince hesitated, and then slowly, and almost in a whisper, as if he feared the walls might hear him, he answered—

" It is this. I am the sole surviving trustee under Mrs. Lincoln's marriage settlement. The entire fund, fifteen thousand pounds, is invested in Consols. It stands in my name, and I could turn it into cash within twenty-four hours."

" Thank God! Oh, Leonard, why did not you tell me this sooner? It would have saved me—words cannot tell the agony it would have saved me."

" Because I did not think of it sooner. Remember this is not my money, Dorothy."

" I am sure Mrs. Lincoln would lend it to you."

" She has no power to lend it. The corpus, the principal, cannot be dealt with till she is dead and her youngest child is twenty-one. Remember, too, that my position is very peculiar. I am both her solicitor and her trustee. When Wilmot died, she might have appointed another in his place. But she put so much trust in me that she would not. It is owing to her generous, her excessive confidence, that I have the sole control of the fund, and if I were to use it for my own purposes, what would she think of me; what should I think of myself? "

" I would not wrong Mrs. Lincoln for the world. We should pay her back every shilling," broke in Mrs. Prince, impetuously. " Every shilling! And though it is a little irregular, consider the alternative."

" I have considered the alternative; and as for reinstating the fund, that would not be so easy as you think. Fifteen thousand is a great deal of money."

" We will economize. We can save several hundreds a year without perceptibly altering our style of living. Edward is keeping himself; there is only Charlie on our hands, and

with care and good management we can make the amount
up in a few years."

"You forget one thing, Dorothy. We are all mortal, and
if anything should happen to me, you and the boys would be
in a terrible difficulty. Mrs. Lincoln would then be obliged
to appoint another trustee, and exposure and disgrace would
be inevitable. You would have to confess that I had misappropriated the trust fund. Everything would come out."

If Mr. Prince thought that this argument would induce his
wife to renounce the scheme which he had so unfortunately
suggested he was mistaken.

"You might insure your life, and then Mrs. Lincoln would
be safe in any event," she said after a short pause. "You
will do it, Leonard, won't you? Say you will do it, and
relieve me from this dreadful suspense. It is to save the
family honor. Where should we hide our heads if it were
all made known, and Jack put on his trial. You said only
this morning that it would break your heart to leave Holmcroft. For my sake and Edward's and Charles's, if not for
your own, you will do it, dear. And Jack himself, he is our
own boy, after all, and dear to me still. Think of him under-
going a term of penal servitude! It would be his ruin, here
and hereafter. Oh, think of it! Why should you hesitate?
While you live the money will be at your disposal, and when
you die it will be paid by the insurance—unless we save it in
the meantime—and I feel sure you will live so long that we
shall. You are not an old man yet. You will, won't you,
dear?" And she took both his hands in hers, and looked at
him pitifully with tear-filled eyes.

"Adam and Eve over again," thought Mr. Prince. "But
it is my own fault; I gave her the idea.

"Very well, Dorothy, it shall be as you wish," he said sadly.
"I only hope the remedy won't prove worse than the disease."

"I am sure it won't, Leonard. Thank Heaven! I can
breathe now. I should have gone mad. You will insure your
life?"

"My own life and the lads' lives. They are to be my
partners; and it is a common thing for partners to insure
each other's lives. It will add to the value of the security.
In that way Mrs. Lincoln will, as you say, be practically as
safe as if the money remained in Consols, provided, of course,
I keep up the payment of the premiums, and that I must and

can do, though it will come very heavy. I shall try to make
Peploe and Pope pay five per cent. even though they never
repay the principal—and, yes, I will give up my shooting in
Scotland. I can easily say that I have not time for both that
and hunting. It is irregular, very irregular, there is no denying that, but the emergency is a desperate one, and if Mrs. Lincoln does not suffer—and with the arrangements I shall make
I don't see how she can—we shall have nothing much to
reproach ourselves with."

This was rather an expression of hope than conviction ;
he knew that if anybody else had done what he was proposing
to do he should have characterized the proceeding by a very
ugly word, and though he was trying to make the best of it,
and to make believe that no harm could come of it, he had
an uneasy feeling that harm would come of it in some way not
then apparent either to himself or his wife. She, however,
had no misgivings. Albeit so honest that she would not have
plucked a flower in Mrs. Lincoln's garden without asking permission, it did not seem to her that in urging her husband to
take that lady's money and use it for his own purpose, without her knowledge, she had done anything reprehensible.
Leonard was merely borrowing it, she argued ; the measures
he was taking would ensure its eventual repayment, and all
would be well.

" When will you send the money to Liverpool ? " she asked.

" I shall not send it—I shall take it. I must have a
thorough understanding with Messrs. Peploe and Pope, and
if possible, get some security from them before I part with
any money."

" But suppose they have Jack arrested before you get
there ? "

" I shall telegraph them in the morning that I am coming."

" I wonder what has become of him, Leonard? Where
can he be ? "

" That does not concern me at present. I only hope he is
far enough, and that we may hear nothing of him again for a
long time—if ever."

" Oh, Leonard ! you hope never to hear of Jack again !
Why ? "

" Because we are not likely to hear any good of him. When
a man goes so utterly to the bad as he has done, he is generally past praying for. Before this last affair I had more faith

in him than you had ; now I have none whatever. The best
thing for him to do, though I doubt whether he will have the
sense and resolution to do it, is to go to America or one of
the colonies, begin a new career, earn an honest livelihood,
and stay there until his misdeeds are forgotten. I hope it
won't turn out that he has victimized other people besides
Peploe and Pope."

"God forbid, Leonard ! Why should you think so ? "

"Because a man who is capable of robbing his employers
and deceiving his parents is capable of anything. It is one
of the points I must inquire about when I am at Liverpool."

"Will you tell the boys ? "

"Not Charlie—except that Jack has behaved badly and
gone away, we know not whither, and the less that is said
about him the better. But Edward must know everything."

"Why Edward and not Charlie ? "

"There is no need to lay on the lad's shoulders so heavy
a burden. Let him enjoy his life while he is young. But
either Edward or Lillywhite must know, and faithful though
Lillywhite is, I don't want to put myself in his power. I shall
have to deal with Peploe and Pope on the one hand and Mrs.
Lincoln on the other. Her dividends will have to be paid
just as if the trust fund was still invested in Consols, the interest from Peploe and Pope will have to be collected as may
be arranged, and the insurance premiums regularly paid.
All this must be done without hitch and unknown to everybody in the office but ourselves. It is only by taking Edward
into my confidence that I can make sure that in the event of
my illness or absence there will be no difficulty, for a hitch
might be fatal. And Ned has an old head on young
shoulders."

"Yes, Edward is very good. But all this is very, very sad.
Oh, Leonard," said Mrs. Prince, sighing deeply, "shall we
ever know content again ? "

"We may. Anyhow, I know people who have very ugly
skeletons in their cupboards, and yet laugh and joke, dine
with appetite, and ride as merrily to hounds as if they had
nothing on their minds. Use is second nature, they say ;
and we shall perhaps get so used to our particular skeleton
that its presence in the cupboard won't trouble us—very
much."

This assurance, though it may have answered its intended

purpose of comforting Mrs. Prince, neither allayed her husband's apprehensions nor quieted his conscience.   No
amount of sophistry could reconcile his trained intelligence
and essentially upright mind to the gross breach of trust
which he contemplated, or render him oblivious to the fact
that he was about to lay on his soul a burden of which only
death could relieve him.   But the alternative: a broken-
hearted wife, a frightful scandal, and a convict son, had
even greater terrors, and he chose, as he thought, the lesser
evil.

On the following day, after telling Lillywhite that he had
decided to decline Hutchins' proposed mortgage, Mr. Prince
went to London, and thence to Liverpool, where he arranged
matters with Peploe and Pope as satisfactorily as so bad a
business could be arranged.   Shortly afterwards, however,
what he had feared came to pass.   It was discovered that Jack
had not confined his depredations to his employers.   He had
discounted a forged bill with his private bankers.   But as
there was reason to believe that he had left the country for
parts unknown, the bankers decided not to throw good money
after bad by trying to hunt him down.   Nevertheless, they
were very wroth, declined an offer from Mr. Prince to make
the amount good, and intimated that in the event of the cul-
prit returning to England they should consider it their duty
to prosecute him.

But none of these things oozed out at Peele.   The people
of that rather sleepy old town were quite satisfied with the
only explanation which the Princes vouchsafed to them:
that Jack, having got into debt and lost his billet at Liverpool, had betaken himself to America, there to make a fresh
start.

CHAPTER IV.

THE BROTHERS.

ONE of the last days of October, a still air and a dappled sky, a veil of silver mist mellowing yet not obscuring the sunlight, two horsemen riding along a deep lane, over-shadowed by trees, from whose half nude branches russet-colored leaves, heavy with dew, are falling noiselessly to their mother earth.

The two men wear costumes suitable either for road or field —breeches, leggings, gray coats, and felt hats—one has spurs but no hunting crop, the other a hunting crop but no spurs.

The rider with spurs is three or four years under thirty—tall, slightly built, swarthy and clean shaven. He has dark intelligent eyes and good looks, but his skin is sallow, his face that of a man who does not live much in the open air.

His companion, younger by several years, and not quite so tall, has laughing brown eyes, brown hair, and a brown face, to which a silky moustache with naturally curled points gives a somewhat rakish, devil-may-care air.

This young fellow is Charlie Prince; the other, Edward—generally called " Ned " by his family and familiar friends.

" Do you expect any sport to-day? " asked the elder brother.

" Not much, but we shall at any rate have the pleasure of riding about in the forest, which is never so beautiful as at this time. I would rather go with the foxhounds, of course. But regular hunting hasn't begun yet, and this week's cubbing fixtures are all long ones. You can never tell what may happen with Mr. Vayle's harriers. This should be a good scenting-day, and if we have the luck to find a straight running fox——"

" A fox."

" Why not? The foxhounds always fight shy of the forest—if they once get in they never get out—and if the harriers chance to rouse a long tail they will do good service by running him. Last season we found a fox in Silverwood. Spinney ran him——"

"Spare me, Charlie," interrupted Edward with a laugh. "It is a thrice-told tale. The day we dined at Cherry-Tree Hall that run was discussed a full hour by the clock. And do not imagine that I am pining for an heroic run. I am not a keen sportsman like you and father; and I have ridden so little lately that I should be all abrasions. I shall be quite content with a little tittuping through the rides, or a canter across Thornwood Plain—if by good fortune we do get into the open—and whatever happens, I shall leave off in good time. I must do two or three hours' work at the office before dinner; and to-morrow I may have to go to town."

"In *re* Lyman, Lincoln, and Jump?"

"Of course."

"I say, what a fine pot-boiler that case is proving for the office. It would almost keep us going, though there was nothing else. Is there any likelihood of its being settled, do you think?"

"Not the least, I should say. There is a big estate; the partners and Mrs. Lincoln are all at sixes and sevens, and you may be sure the lawyers won't let them settle until they have had a lot more picking out of it."

"The pater advised Mrs. Lincoln to settle, though, didn't he?—if she had a chance."

"Yes, the pater always advises his clients honestly, sometimes against his own interests. But the partners are combative and won't listen to reason. Litigants seldom do listen to reason. If they did we lawyers should lose our reason for being. And a friendly settlement is out of the question now, whatever it may have been a little while ago. Suits are going on both here and in America."

"Yes, I know. And that reminds me that I have a question to ask you. Has anything been heard of Jack? I am aware it is a tabooed subject, and I should not think of mentioning it to father or mother. All the same, he and I were very good friends—though after I went to Marlborough I saw very little of him—and I cannot help wondering what has become of him. Poor old Jack."

"You need not waste your pity on him, Charlie. He is not worthy of it. Jack behaved very badly."

" You mean he was always getting into scrapes."

" Always. And he gave father and mother no end of trouble. At first they thought it was all boyishness and high spirits, and that he would steady as he grew older. But the last thing he did was the worst."

" Running away from Liverpool ? "

" Yes, and before running away he ran heavily into debt, and it cost the pater no end of money to put things straight —this is entirely between ourselves, Charlie—and if you add to that what it cost when he went wrong at Cambridge it comes to a nice penny."

" Bad enough, in all conscience. All the same, there are worse things than running into debt, and I don't quite see——"

"Jack did worse. It was not merely getting into debt, though in his case there was not a shadow of excuse. Just consider ! When he came back from Australia, penniless, he was kindly treated and freely forgiven. Father found him a good place in Liverpool, where he might have done well. But almost from the first, as we afterwards ascertained, he went to the bad, and worse still, played the hypocrite. He hoodwinked his employers completely, made them believe he was as steady as a growing tree, and wrote letters home, telling how well he was doing. Then, when exposure became inevitable, he just disappeared without writing a line to any of us to say he was sorry, and left father to pay the piper. And naught has been heard from him or of him since. What could be worse than that, I should like to know ? "

" As bad as that, was it ? No wonder father won't talk about it, and hasn't been the same man since."

" Who says he has not been the same man since ? " asked Edward sharply.

" Isn't it evident ? And Lillywhite was saying so only the other day."

" So it was Lillywhite that gave you the idea. Did he say anything about Jack ? "

" He merely asked whether anything had been heard of him ! "

" I wish Lillywhite would mind his own business. And you are both wrong. I don't think father has altered in the least, except in being three years older, and he is still one of the most active men for his age that I know."

In making this assertion Edward spoke rather diplomatically than truthfully. Leonard Prince had not been the same man since the disappearance of his eldest son. His hope that he should get used to the skeleton in the cupboard had only been realized in part. The deceit which he was obliged to practice fretted him, a deceit of which he was reminded every time he paid Mrs. Lincoln her dividends, every time he remitted the Assurance Company the premiums on his life policies, and every time he received a check or a "put off" from Peploe and Pope. Then, again, the sense of the heavy pecuniary liability which he had assumed, and the fear, never long absent from his thoughts, that the fraud might be discovered when he was least expecting it, weighed on his mind and damped his naturally high spirits. He gave more time to business and less to sport, rode less boldly to hounds and seldom went from home—never when Edward was away. His friends ascribed these changes to increasing years, and as he always contrived to be cheerful at home they passed almost unobserved by his wife. And then there came to pass an event which by adding to Mr. Prince's professional engagements made his personal anxieties easier to bear.

This was the death of his friend and neighbor, Mr. Lincoln, on which, for some doubtless sufficient yet not very apparent reason, his partners fell out amongst themselves and went to law. Mrs. Lincoln being compelled in self-defence to join in the fray, the proceedings on her behalf were conducted by Mr. Prince, who entrusted the active management of the suit (which speedily drifted into Chancery) to Edward, and as the interests at stake were important, and frequent consultations with counsel necessary, the young man had to spend the greater part of his time in London.

We may now return to the two brothers.

"Which way are we going?" asked Edward, as they came to a place where three roads met.

"By Wroughton Shaughs, of course. It will save us a mile and a half at least."

"How about the gates, though."

"I have not been this way since last season, but now that hunting is beginning, they are sure to be open."

Turning from the high-road into a narrow lane, they went on until they came to a gate leading into a bridle-path.

"Let me, I rather like opening gates," said Charlie.

Edward made no objection; he did not like opening gates. But Charlie found the task more difficult than he had expected. His mare would not be still, and the gate, though unlocked, was ingeniously fastened with a chain, a ring, a staple, and a hook.

" Get off," said Edward.

" No, thank you. I never get off to open a gate, and if there were not so many broken stones on the road——"

" Allow me, sir," said a wayfarer, who, while Charlie was struggling with the gate, had come up unperceived; " allow me, sir," and with that the wayfarer loosed the chain and drew back the gate.

He was a particularly disreputable-looking tramp, with a grim, unshaven face, a patch over one eye, and nothing much on but a sailor's jumper and a pair of ragged trousers.

" Thank you. I say, Ned, have you any coppers? "

Ned answered " No," and rode on, without giving the tramp a second glance.

" Well, there's a sixpence for you. And, look here; would you mind letting out that curb chain a link, while I light a cigar? "

The tramp looked at the cigar longingly.

" God bless you, sir," he said, " but might I make so bold as to ask if you have a bit o' baccy about you. I have not had a smoke for twenty-four hours (producing a short clay pipe), nor yet broken my fast."

" Poor fellow! Here are a couple of cigars; and take this shilling and go and get a good meal. Go at once! " and Charlie, touching his horse with his heel, cantered off.

But the tramp did not go at once. He lighted one of the cigars, and as he smoked it leaned on the gate and looked after the two horsemen.

" That's Charlie," he soliloquized. " The same kind-hearted, generous lad, he always was. How he has altered! If he hadn't been with Ned I shouldn't have known him. No wonder he did not know me. And Ned—but he hardly so much as looked my way. He is too superior a person to notice a poor devil of a tramp—and we were never real friends. Anyhow, I need expect no help from him. But the old man would give me a lift, if he knew—or Charlie. To which of them shall I apply, and how? A few pounds—just enough to take me to London and buy me a kit. . . . But it would never do to go to the house any more than for Charlie to come to me at a boozing ken. And whatever I do I must keep close. There are constables at Peele, and some fellow might—by God ! my back tingles at the mere idea. . . . I have it—a note ! Yes, I think I can fake a scribble that will fetch him—and without exciting suspicion either. And now for some grub ; and it shall be a skinful. I have not had so much money in my pocket since I left Colchester."

"What did you give that fellow ? " asked Edward, when Charlie came up with him.

"Eighteen pence and two cigars."

"Eighteen pence and two cigars ! Say two shillings—nearly as much as a laborer in these parts earns by a day of honest work—and for opening a gate ! "

"He was starving."

"How do you know ? "

"He said so—and he looks it."

"Of course he said so—tramps always do—yet I'll be bound the rascal has as much money in his pocket as you have. I never give anything to beggars—on principle."

"And deuced little to anybody else—also on principle," said the other *sotto voce*.

"You have been taken in, my boy, and not for the first time. You are too impulsive. If you give to everybody who pleads poverty you will end by being poor yourself ! "

Charlie, irritated by his brother's reproof and painfully conscious that he had acted impulsively and, in all probability, been victimized by an impostor, held his peace.

After passing through two more gates, that were easily opened, they crossed a big field and came to yet another gate armed with spikes which opened, or rather should have opened, into a grassy lane.

On one side of this gate and nearly as high was a stiff flight of posts and rails.

"It is not locked, I hope," said Edward.

"Worse, it is nailed."

"By Jove ! We shall have to go back, then."

"That would be two miles out of our way and throw us late for the meet. We can jump this rail ; there is turf on both sides."

"In cold blood, and that drop ! Not if I know it."

" Merry Boy will do it easily. Come, I'll give you a lead. Kitty likes a bit of timber."

The next moment Charlie was over. Edward, who, though a fair horseman, was not a bold rider, did not seem to like it, but liking still less to turn tail he let Merry Boy follow, and albeit the old horse hit the top rail with his hind legs, he alighted safely in the lane, round a bend of which Charlie had already disappeared.

" God bless me, another gate ! " exclaimed Edward, as he turned into the road. " Nailed up, of course."

" Also locked," said Charlie, coolly, at the same time backing his horse.

" Good heavens ! you are surely not going to jump it ! It's a foot higher than the other, and as strong as a brick wall. If Kitty hits it with her fore-legs she will turn a somersault and break your neck and her own back."

" There is nothing else for it. We cannot jump the rails from this side : the drop is too big."

" Nothing else for it ! I would rather wait here all day. Why on earth you came this way I cannot imagine. We had far better have gone round by the road."

" It is a regular bridle-path. How could I know that the rascally old farmer had hung new gates and nailed them up ? "

" What shall we do, then ? I have it ! One of us must run to Oxbridge for a blacksmith, or a hammer or something, while the other waits here. You are the better run-ner——"

" I am not so sure about that. Would not it be fairer if we tossed up ? " returned Charlie, laughing. The reproof was still rankling in his mind, and Ned's discomfiture amused him. " However, I think we can do better than that. We must make a circumbendibus and do the fence."

" What are you thinking about ? It is impossible ! "

It certainly looked so. The fence was a high bank, topped by an impenetrable blackthorn hedge, and with a ditch on both sides.

" I think, though, I noticed a practicable place in that corner," said Charlie, turning his horse round.

At the corner in question the fence turned at almost right angles, and the blackthorn hedge was weaker, and the ditch narrower than elsewhere.

"This will do. You go first, Ned, and make a gap for me and Kitty. It is just the sort of place old Merry Boy likes. He is as clever as a cat, and Kitty is such a beggar to rush. As likely as not she would go slap into the thickest part and stick fast."

" It is the most beastly place I ever saw. No, thank you, I prefer to play second fiddle on the present occasion. You go first."

" Certainly, if you will let me ride Merry Boy. But why not lead him over ? You go on ; I'll send him after you."

" A happy thought, I'll act on it at once," replied Ned, dismounting with great alacrity.

" But hold him till I climb the bank. I don't want to be jumped upon."

" All right ! Go ahead ! Say when you are ready to catch him."

" Now ! " shouted Edward as he disappeared on the further side of the fence.

Charlie, dropping the bridle, gave Merry Boy a touch with his whip, whereupon the old hunter sprang over the ditch, scrambled up the bank and pushed through the gap, which he greatly widened. But Edward somehow missed catching him, and the next moment Merry Boy was justifying his name by cantering merrily round the field.

Meanwhile, Kitty was dancing about on her hind legs and Charlie vainly trying to make her take the jump quietly. In the end he was obliged to let her take it as she liked, with a rush that carried her triumphantly over the ditch, and through the gap, only to fall ignominiously on her head in the field beyond.

" Serve you right, you impetuous hussy ! " said the young fellow as he scrambled to his feet. " You'll not be in such a hurry next time."

And with that he remounted and galloped after Merry Boy, whom Edward was vainly trying to catch. But the old horse yielded himself a willing captive to Charlie, who held him while his brother "got up."

" Call this a short cut ! " said Edward, as soon as he could speak. " Call this a short cut ! It is a cut I shall cut no more, I can tell you. I would rather go five miles round any day."

"Oh, it is good fun, and all in the day's work," returned the other, laughing.

"Fun! A fig for such fun!" exclaimed Ned in a tone of deep disgust.

After this they had no further trouble. An easy jump over some sheep hurdles and a ten minutes' trot brought them within sight of Cobster Green.

CHAPTER V.

THE MEET.

"THERE they are ; we are just in time," said Charlie, point-ing to the hounds, which were gamboling in a grassy glade, while the huntsman and whip stood guard over them. The horsemen on the ground did not exceed a dozen, for the Master detested a big field—unless the fair element greatly preponderated—only one degree less than a blank day. Though his hard riding days were over, Mr. Vayle sat his bob-tailed gray like a centaur, and was as keen a Nimrod as when he first carried a horn half a century before. Near him rode a young girl, to whom he paid great attention, for Mr. Vayle was still a gay cavalier and, as was said, could refuse nothing to fair ladies who favored him with their company and ad-mired the forest which he so dearly loved, and of which he knew every nook and corner, and almost every tree. Among his other peculiarities was a habit of saying, quite uncon-sciously and irrelevantly, "Dear me ! Dear me !" and speak-ing his thoughts in a soft (and fortunately generally inaudi-ble) undertone.

The name of the young girl was Olive Lincoln ; her years were about seventeen. As touching her person she was slim and well-shapen, slightly built, and rather tall than short. She had a fair, soft skin, peach-like cheeks, clearly-cut features (nose a little *rétroussé*), dark hair, and large violet eyes, with long lashes, which were merry, mischievous or tender as the humor took her.

As touching her costume, Olive wore a dark-green habit and a jockey cap, which became her to admiration, and she rode a corkey blood cob, hardly less good-looking and high-spirited than herself.

"We are rather late, I fear," said Edward, after his brother and himself had greeted Miss Lincoln and the Squire. "I hope you have not been waiting for us."

" No, indeed, I have not. I never quarrel with people for
not coming, and I am like time and tide, I wait for no man.
(Dear me! dear me! what a conceit that young man must
have of himself)."

Miss Lincoln, who alone heard Mr. Vayle's " aside,"
laughed merrily.

" The Squire means that he waits only for ladies, Mr.
Edward," she said. " He would not wait for you though you
were really a prince. We are waiting for ladies now—Mary
Windle and Kate Convers, and the Spankaway girls."

" There they come down the Earl's Path," said Charlie,
who had sharp eyes and kept them open.

" That is right. I am glad of it," observed the Squire.
" They will be here in two minutes. We will draw Earl's
Wood, Horner."

The huntsman (a stout, short-legged old fellow mounted
on a horse the right color for a hearse and big enough to
draw one with a coffin inside) blew his horn and trotted off,
followed by the pack. Next came Bill the whip, who rode a
common-looking yet marvellously clever bay cob, whose name,
" Noah's Ark," had been bestowed upon him because he was
considered eminently safe and never shirked water.

Mr. Vayle (who possessed a sense of humor) had christened Horner's horse " Pagan," partly on account of his
color, but chiefly because nobody had ever seen him on his
knees. When he did fall at a fence it was always backwards,
which was very convenient for Horner, who (being fat and
heavy) found it much pleasanter to slip over the animal's tail
than come a " cropper " over his head.

Earl's Wood was reached in a few minutes, and the hounds
(all small foxhounds) were no sooner thrown in than their
eager cries proclaimed that " something was afoot." Said
something proved to be a hare, which gave a very fair half-
hour's run in the wood and out of it. Edward Prince got
his gentle tittuping, the girls had " good fun " jumping the
drains and dodging the trees ; and when the hare was killed
the old Squire dismounted from his bobtailed gray, waved
his hat and shouted " Whoo-whoop " with the best.

While this was going on, Charlie had spoken to the huntsman, and a forest-keeper, who was watching the sport, and
made a confidential communication to Miss Lincoln, which
bore fruit later on.

"Where shall we try now?" asked Mr. Vayle.

"Let us try the Warren," said Olive.

"Why the Warren?"

"We may find a fox there. The keeper saw one only this morning."

"Oh, that is it, is it? And would you really like us to find a fox?"

"So much; and so would Mary Windle and Kate Conyers, would not you, girls?"

"So much!" echoed the young women in question. "Do draw the Warren, Mr. Vayle."

"Well, I suppose we must. Dear me! Dear me! What do you say, Horner?"

"I'm willing, sir. If we don't find a long-tail we shall, mebbe, find a hare, and the fox-hunting gentlemen cannot complain. They never come hereabouts," said the huntsman, whom a cap, collected by Charlie, and a long pull from Charlie's flask had put in excellent humor, and made him feel—for the moment—as bold as brass.

So Horner blew his horn again, and the cavalcade made at a round trot for the Warren.

"It's your fault, Charlie," whispered Miss Lincoln, who had dropped behind in order to have a word with him. "If you had not heard about the fox and put me up to it I should not have asked the Squire, and——"

"He would not have done it for anybody else. Never mind, I'll take all the responsibility."

"But suppose I get my neck broken or lame Daisy, or——"

"You won't do either one or the other. I'll pilot you."

"Thank you. I'll do my best to follow. But what will mother say? She won't let me go with the foxhounds for fear of accidents, and now——"

"You are not going with foxhounds."

"But we are going to hunt a fox."

"That remains to be seen. We have first to find a fox, and it will be no easy matter to bustle him out of the Warren, I can tell you."

"I think we shall find a fox, Charlie. I am sure we shall. The Squire says it is an ideal hunting day, and I am sure there is a scent."

"Not a doubt of it. But that does not prove we shall find a fox."

"We shall find a fox. I have a presentiment. If we don't I will never ask Mr. Vayle to draw the Warren again. So it will be all your fault. But what shall I do about Potts? He is riding old Tinker, one of the carriage horses. I don't think it can jump a bit, and Potts would fall off if it did— and as mother told him to take good care of me, he considers it his duty to go wherever I go."

"Oh, never mind old Potts. We will drop him into the first ditch, and leave him to vegetate."

"Charlie, you are really too bad," and then she laughed and said, "Poor Potts! I hope the ditch will be soft, he is a good old man," and laughed again.

Just then Edward came alongside, with so grave a mien that Olive rallied him.

"Why so serious, Mr. Edward. Aren't you enjoying yourself?" she asked.

"I have enjoyed myself exceedingly, so far; but this is a serious matter."

"What is?"

"Drawing the Warren for a fox. I doubt whether it is the right thing. I quite admit that the Squire is lord of the forest, so to speak, by general consent: but it is a question in my mind whether the Warren can fairly be considered a part of the forest."

"I don't think anybody will mind the question in your mind, Mr. Edward, if we find a fox in the Warren, and, if we do, mine be the blame, for it was I who asked the Squire to draw the Warren."

"In that case there is nothing more to be said," returned Edward, his grave face relaxing into a smile, "for where is the man who could refuse when Miss Lincoln asks?"

"I forgive your previous doubts in consideration of your pretty compliment. But here we are at the Warren. Where shall we go, Mr. Charles?" (It was always "Mr. Charles" when Edward was present.) "I have heard something about upwind: which is upwind?"

"You mean that foxes generally run upwind; but to-day there is no wind——"

"So there can be no up. What shall we do then?"

"Well, it is a safe rule to stick to hounds, above all in a big cover like this, where they may slip away unseen and unheard."

" All right. Mr. Charles, you stick to the hounds, and we'll all try to stick to you, won't we, Mr. Edward ? "

" Certainly, Miss Lincoln, if you will it. I am not sure, though, that Charlie is to be trusted. He must be careful not to lead you into danger."

" Or you. At any rate, where he goes I shall go ; and unless you keep with us you will be thrown out," answered Olive, rather sharply. It displeased her to hear Charlie disparaged, and she did not " care " for Edward.

CHAPTER VI.

THE RUN.

THE WARREN was a large wood, technically a part of the forest, but separated from the main portion of it by a broad stretch of turf. It was intersected by two rides and several bridle-paths, the trees and undergrowth being elsewhere so thick as to render progress on foot difficult and on horseback well-nigh impossible.

When the field reached the wood Mr. Vayle marshalled his forces. The main point was to prevent reynard (if perchance he should be found at home) from stealing back into the forest, in which event a run in the open would be out of the question. To this end he posted several men between the wood and the forest, with instructions to head back the fox if he should attempt to break in that direction.

Bill, the whip, took his stand at the top of the principal ride ; a long-legged brewer, on a roan gelding, with a bit of red ribbon flying from its tail as a danger signal, and a sporting butcher, on a thorough-bred screw (which he wanted to sell), undertook to watch on one side of the covert ; and the ladies and the keeper were asked to keep a look-out on the other.

Horner was then ordered to throw in his hounds and draw towards the higher ground, and away from the forest.

" If we don't take care, we shall all be left lamenting," said the Squire when these dispositions had been made. " The covert is so thick that you can neither see hounds nor hear a hallo. Twenty years ago, when the foxhounds used to come here, they once slipped out with a fox unseen by anybody, the huntsman got bogged, and the hounds had a fine run of an hour and forty minutes all to themselves. (Dear me ! Dear me !) Where are you going, Charlie ? "

" Into the Warren with Horner. I can whip up to him."

" Yes, yes ; go. Quite right, and if you find, shout your

loudest. (Dear me! Dear me! I wish I was as young as Charlie, or even that conceited jackanapes, his brother)."

Miss Windle and Miss Conyers, overhearing this soliloquy, laughed consumedly.

"What is the matter? Why are you laughing? (Dear me! Dear me! Youth is the time for laughter; why shouldn't they laugh?) Are you going too, Olive?"

"Yes, Squire; I should like to be as near the hounds as possible, if there is going to be any fun."

"Quite right. Yes, go. But beware of trees and holes, and take care of your hat. (Dear me! Dear me! I wonder whether it is the hounds or Prince Charlie she would best like to be near.)"

Fortunately, none save the object of it heard this *sotto voce*, and, blushing brightly, she followed her pilot, and was followed in her turn by Edward Prince and coachman Potts.

Nobody else went into the wood, and they had not gone far before two of the party began to wish they had stayed with the others. They were forced to ride in single file, twisting and turning, dodging the boughs and threading their way through the brambles, their horses slipping where the ground was smooth, and stumbling where it was rough.

"Stoop low and shut your eyes, Olive," said Charlie: "never mind Daisy, she will take care of herself, and I will take care of you." Which he did so effectually that not a bough touched her.

"Can anybody see the hounds?" inquired Horner. "If they was to get on a line now we shouldn't be in it."

"I wish we were not in it," growled Edward. "I knew Charlie would lead us into some mess. Confound it! I believe I have cut my nose."

"So you have," said Olive, glancing round. "It is bleeding dreadfully. You look like a red Indian in his war paint."

Whereupon Edward, muttering an imprecation, applied his handkerchief, thereby adding greatly to his difficulties: with the same hand he had both to guide his horse and ward off the branches, one of which flying back, crushed Potts's castor and bonneted him completely.

"Oh Lord!" shouted the coachman. And dropping his reins he made frantic efforts to extricate himself. But the lining of his hat having fouled on his rather large nose he found this no easy task. In the end, however, he emerged, very red in the face and uttering strange oaths.

All laughed, even Edward, who was beginning to think that the tip of his nose would go on bleeding forever.

"Oh by—that hurt, that did," howled the huntsman. " Ooo, oo, oo !" While he was laughing at Potts his shin-bone had collided against the bole of a tree and got the worst of it. " I won't come into this 'ere hole again, not for ten long-tails. And where's the hounds? They may be a mile away by this time. Thank goodness, here's a path at last. We can get along a bit now."

All put their horses into a brisk trot, Horner still leading, for he best knew the way.

" Hark !" he cries, stopping short so suddenly that Kitty nearly cannoned against Pagan. " Cannot you hear summut ? "

" By Jove ! I do believe it's a whimper."

" Ay is it " (listening intently), "it's Ringlet, and when Ringlet speaks you must be sure there's summut. There it is again. It's a line. Mr. Charlie, it is a line. Hike to Ringlet ! Hike to Ringlet ! For-rard ! For-rard !"

And the old fellow, bending over his saddle-bow to avoid impending branches, goes off at a canter, followed by the others, all in a state of high excitement, for Ringlet's solitary note has now swollen into a full chorus.

Charlie, mindful of the Squire's injunction, shouts his loudest ; Olive cheers on the hounds ; Edward pockets his handkerchief and lets his nose take care of itself ; and Potts squaring his elbows and using his heels, succeeds in putting old Tinker into a high and ponderous gallop.

" This way," cries the huntsman ; "we can't see 'em, and we don't know what it is—mebbe a hare, after all—we must just ride to the music till we get out of the wood."

Presently they emerge into a broad path, riding, as before, to the music, for the hounds still keep to the thick of the wood.

" Bill should be somewhere about here," says Charlie. " And hark ! There's a hallo ! A fox ! by all that is glorious, a fox ! Hike hallo ! Hike hallo ! Forrud away ! Forrud away ! "

" How do you know it's a fox ? " asks Edward.

" Because it's Bill's voice, and he knows better than to tally-
ho a hare. Hike hallo! Hike hallo! I hope Mr. Vayle and
the others will hear. Blow again, Horner.

At the top of the wood, which they reached at the same
time as the hounds, are the brewer, the butcher, and the
whips, holding up their hats and halloing till they are black
in the face.

" He's only just gone! he's slipped through the gateway
into that field. There! Beauty has it. That's the line.
For'rard to Beauty! Well done, old girl!"

" Hike for'ard! Hike for'ard!"

" I hope the Squire has heard the row and will be able to
catch us up," says Charlie. "Shout again! Forrud, forrud,
forrud! to Beauty. Sound another blast, Horner."

Meantime Bill has opened the gate, and all ride after the
hounds, which are racing across a big pasture to a breast-
high scent, the butcher leading on his thoroughbred screw.
Next come Charlie and Olive, Bill and the brewer, followed
by Horner and Potts.

The first fence is a low bank with a widish ditch on the
near side. To the surprise of everybody, himself probably
included, Tinker takes it in his stride, and the coachman
sticks on.

" Bravo Potts!" shouts Charlie : " if you go on like that
you will be in at the death. . . Not quite so fast, Olive!
If we don't save our horses now they will not live through the
run. Never mind though the hounds do get a bit ahead.
They cannot keep up this pace over that plough."

Nor do they. The scent grows colder, and two or three
freshly ploughed fields with openable gates are traversed at
a trot, the hounds hunting beautifully, checking only once
and recovering the line without any help from the huntsman.

Then more grass and faster going; small enclosures and
blind fences, with few jumpable places.

" The butcher seems inclined to make the running, let him
go first and make gaps for us," says Charlie, whose native
daring was tempered by a sense of his responsibility for the
safety of his fair companion.

At the third fence, after leaving the plough, Tinker blundered into a blind ditch, throwing Potts clean over his head
and completing the destruction of his rider's hat.

" He is done to a turn ; you had better go home," said

Charlie, after ascertaining that Potts was none the worse. "And tell Mrs. Lincoln, with my compliments, that I will take good care of Miss Olive."

The field, now reduced to seven, continue the chase, the hounds for the most part running mute to a burning scent. A few yards behind them ride the brewer, the butcher, and the whip, closely followed by Olive and Charlie, while Edward and Horner bring up the rear.

The chase has lasted nearly an hour, and shows no signs of coming to a close when the hounds run on to a highway where two roads meet (one of them bounded by a wide brook), throw up their heads and stop short. They have lost the scent.

Horner makes a couple of casts without result, and things are beginning to look serious when a faint hallo in the distance, and a hat at the end of a stick, gives a timely hint as to the direction taken by the fox.

" He has crossed the brook," says the huntsman, sounding his horn. " Hike hallo ! Hike hallo ! Yoh over ! Yoh over ! "

" Hike hallo ! Hike hallo ! " echoes Bill, whipping the hounds up the brink. " Yoh over ! Yoh over ! Beauty has it again. Faw-rud to Beauty ! Faw-rud ! Faw-rud ! "

The hounds swim the stream in the wake of Beauty, and after " feathering " a few seconds on the further side, go off full cry.

" All very fine," says Edward, " but how are we to get over ? "

Seeing that the opposite bank, besides being high, is crowned with a three-barred rail, a pertinent question. The brewer, the butcher, and the whip answer it on the instant. Crossing the girth-high stream, they leap their horses on the bank and then, dismounting and breaking down the topmost rail, lead them over the others.

" Dare you ? " asks Charlie of Olive.

" Go, and I will follow."

Charlie goes.

" Let Daisy have her head," he shouts, as Kitty scrambles up the bank, and then, though there is hardly standing room, leaps his mare over the rails without dismounting. Olive does the same, and the next moment they are galloping after the hounds, which, like the horses, have been greatly refreshed by the check and the bath.

"Are you going to have it, Mr. Prince?" asks Horner, looking ruefully at the obstacle.

Though neither a bold rider nor a keen sportsman, Edward had, so far, gone very well—partly, perhaps, out of a spirit of emulation, partly, it may be, because he did not like to lag behind when a lady led the way, and that lady Olive Lincoln. But the brook looks ugly and the bank dangerous, to say nothing of the rail; and it requires a strong effort to screw up his courage to the sticking point and let his horse go. But at the critical moment his nerve fails him. As Merry Boy rises at the bank, Edward clutches at the bridle and pulls him back into the stream, whereupon the bewildered and indignant animal plunges down the middle of it, flounders into a hole, and only after a desperate bout of swimming and scrambling succeeds in getting back on to dry land.

"I don't think I should try that again, sir, if I was you," observes the huntsman. "You'll be drowned if you do. That is a main dangerous place, that is, though when I was young like your brother and Mr. Macadam, and Bill and the butcher, I should ha' thought naught on it—naught. But I'm an old fellow now. Come along o' me. I think I know the fox's point. We'll be at it as soon as them."

"You can go where you hanged please, Horner. I am wet through from the waist, and shall go straight home. I wish we had not found that brute of a fox. I never go out with my brother that I don't get into some beastly mess," answered Edward savagely. He was not naturally sweet tempered, and an involuntary cold bath on an October day with a ten-mile ride in wet clothes and water-logged boots before him, would try the patience of a saint.

"Call him a sportsman," soliloquized Horner, as he went his way. "Why, he is not fit to be named in the same day as his brother. Mr. Charlie's the boy for me. He both rides straight and takes a pleasure in seeing hounds hunt. Hark! Is not that 'em? His point is Welsby coppice I do believe. Hold up, hoss. You're not a getting tired already, surely."

"Isn't this glorious, Charlie?" cries Olive, as they reach the crest of a hill, over which the hounds have disappeared a few moments previously, and up which the four men have walked to ease their horses. "Is not this glorious?"

She might well say so. Below them was a breezy, wide-stretching common, which sloped gently towards a verdant, well-wooded valley, dotted with quaint cottages and red farmhouses, and bounded far away by a shining river.

"Yes, that is Harold's Common, as big as a parish, they say. And see how the hounds are going—all in a cluster! Well, we are not likely to lose sight of them, that is one comfort, and, by Jove, there he is!"

"The fox do you mean—where?"

"Don't you see that dark object, a mere speck—about half-a-mile before the hounds?"

"And that is the fox! Poor fellow! Do you know, Charlie, I almost hope he may escape."

"I don't think he will: the scent is too good. But if we don't go on the hounds will escape us. Come along!"

And they went—helter-skelter down the hill, Macadam and Charlie leading, for the butcher had taken a good deal out of his thoroughbred, and speed was not the strong point of Noah's Ark. But the going was good, and, after a two-mile gallop, all overtook the hounds, just as the latter left the common for the fields, and exchanged grass for plough. And then the pace slackened—fortunately, for it is no joke to face wide ditches and formidable fences with fagged horses. Even the hard-riding brewer was glad to let the whip lead the way and keep a keen look-out for gates and weak places.

But jumps were not always avoidable, and at the very last obstacle—a rail and ditch—which had to be taken flying, Daisy came to grief. Charlie went first, and then, with keen anxiety, turned to see how it would fare with Olive.

"Send her at it," he cried, "it's rather a big place." The little mare did her best, but being well-nigh spent, hit the rail hard and went into the ditch instead of over it. Olive luckily fell clear, and before Charlie and Macadam could dismount to help her, was on her feet. As for Daisy, she seemed minded to repose for a while in the ditch, and it was with some difficulty that they got her out of it.

"Whether we lose the hounds or not, we must have no more jumping," said Charlie, as he helped Olive into the muddy saddle. "Remember, I am responsible for your safety, and you would not like any harm to befall Daisy."

"Not for the world. But I should be very sorry to spoil your sport. Ride on after the hounds. I can take care of myself."

4

"Certainly not. What would your mother say? And the hounds have stopped running. Don't you see them feathering in the middle of that stubble?"

"Have they killed?"

"I don't think so. You would hear Bill shouting 'whoo-whoop' if they had. The scent has either failed or the fox run to ground. Let us go on and see."

The hounds were baying at the mouth of a drain.

"He's in here, sir," said the whip, who was prone on the grass, listening intently. "I can hear him. Shall I run to yonder farmhouse, get a spade and try to dig him out?"

"Don't, Charlie, don't! He is a gallant fox and has given us a splendid run. Let him live," pleaded Olive.

"Very well.—Yes, I think he deserves to save his brush—an hour and forty minutes with only two checks. What do you say, Macadam?"

"I am quite of your opinion. And it is Hobson's choice. This drain is deep, and we have no terriers. You may as well call them off, Bill. How far are we from Peele?"

"If that house across the fields be the King George, and I think it is, nigh on fifteen miles. It's been a clinking run, Mr. Charlie, it has that."

"You are right, and you have ridden well up, Bill. Here's a crown for you! And now let us go to the King George and refresh our horses and ourselves, and then we will hie us home. What has become of my brother and Horner, I wonder?"

"They did not like that brook, I think. But never you fear, sir. Horner will turn up. He does not ride as straight as you and Mr. Macadam, but he's generally somewhere about at the end of a run."

The whip proved a true prophet. As hunters and hounds drew up at the door of the inn Horner came jogging up the road.

"What have you done?" he asked.

Bill told him.

"I felt sure he was making for Welsby Coppice, and he'd ha' got there, too, if the hounds hadn't pressed him so hard. The Squire will be as well pleased as if he had ridden the run himself. But he'd ha' been all the better pleased if you'd ha' taken the brush home in your hat, Miss Lincoln. He likes a kill, the Squire does."

" But I don't, and I am sure the brush is much better where it is than in my hat. Here is something to put into yours " (handing him half-a-sovereign), " and will you see, please, that the horses are properly attended to, and then you can go into the house and get something for yourselves."

" Thank you, miss, thank you kindly," said the old fellow, pocketing the tip and touching his cap. " But I'll stop where I am. If I was to get off it would take me half an hour to get on again, I'm that stiff and rheumatical. I'll have some cheese and bread and sixpenn'orth o' whiskey, Bill. And slip the bit out of Pagan's mouth and bring him some gruel. He'll not run away, I'll warrant."

CHAPTER VII.

GOING HOME.

THE ride home was long and, so far as pace went, slow, yet very pleasant withal. The declining sun shone brightly on a charming landscape, which still retained much of its autumnal glory; and the run and its incidents, besides being pleasant to think about, made a subject for conversation which it seemed impossible to exhaust.

Horner, as was meet, rode first, at the head of his pack. Next came Bill and Mr. Macadam—the latter acting as amateur second whip—to whom followed Olive and Charlie. The butcher, whose horse had gone dead lame, brought up the rear, and was soon left hopelessly behind.

"We had better keep together; horses like company, and this jog-trot is quite fast enough," had said Charlie to Miss Lincoln.

"By all means. It will be so much more cheerful for us, besides being better for the horses," answered Olive, with a sigh.

"Are you tired, Olive, that you sigh?" asked Charlie softly.

"A little. But it was not that."

"What, then?"

"I was thinking about my mother. She will be frantically anxious. What time shall we get home?"

"You, at six, I, half an hour later. I don't think you need distress yourself on that account. I suppose Potts would deliver my message?"

"I have no doubt he would, also a few observations of his own. He thinks nobody can take care of me but himself, and will tell mother that without him I should be sure to come to desperate grief."

"Well, your appearance at home safe and sound will prove the contrary."

" For which thanks to you, Charlie. If you had not piloted me so carefully and told me what to do I should never have seen the end of the run—and I have enjoyed it so much. So much that I am almost ashamed of myself, for I fear it is very cruel."

" What is ? "

" Hunting."

" There's no doubt it is, in a sense ; but what is not ? You cannot eat a mutton chop without killing a sheep, nor drink a glass of water without swallowing a lot of microscopic organisms. And remember that if there were no hunting all these hounds would have been drowned when they were whelps."

" So we may regard ourselves as philanthropists. Instead of being a cruel amusement, hunting is a humane pursuit. Foxes die in order that hounds may live. I vote for the hounds," returned Olive brightly, for though she rather suspected that there lurked a fallacy in Charlie's theory, she was not disposed to scrutinize too severely his ingenious argument in support of so pleasant a pastime.

" That's it, Miss Lincoln," put in the brewer. " If there was no hunting there would be no hounds, and if we killed no foxes there would be no hunting. And you may do a lot of hunting without killing—to-day for instance. The betting is always ten to one on the fox. I suppose you have nothing of the sort in America, Miss Lincoln ? "

" Do you mean fox-hunting ? "

" Yes."

" You are quite mistaken, Mr. Macadam," said Olive, who, though she liked hunting and England exceedingly, was too patriotic to admit that her country played second fiddle in anything whatever. " You are quite mistaken. I believe there is very good fox-hunting in Virginia, and we have something far finer—buffalo-hunting on the prairies and grizzly bear-hunting in the Rockies."

" But they hunt buffaloes without hounds—just ride up to them and shoot them down. The poor brutes have no chance," said the brewer.

" I don't call that sport at all," said Charlie ; " hunting without hounds is like dancing without music—and then there is no jumping."

" And what is that like ? " demanded Olive, tartly.

" Fox-hunting without jumping is like war without fighting."

" Or beer without hops," suggested the brewer.

" Or love without kisses," added Charlie.

" All the same, America is——"

" Your country, and you are quite right to stick up for it. I admit your superiority as to buffaloes and grizzlies, and I daresay it is good fun hunting them. But I am quite content with Old England and fox-hunting ; I want nothing better."

" Hear, hear !" said the brewer ; " Old England forever, and may we never have worse sport than we have had to-day."

" That is a sentiment in which I can concur without reserve," observed Olive. " It is the best day's sport I ever had ; and I don't think I shall have a better until I hunt the buffalo and the grizzly in their native wilds."

And then they all laughed. When people are in high spirits a small joke goes a long way.

An hour's alternate jog-trotting and walking brought them to Rodwell Cross, and there they parted company, the hounds and the brewer going one way, Miss Lincoln and Charlie another.

" My mother and I were talking about you the other day," said Olive, after a short interval of silence.

" I hope you were speaking well of me."

" I am not sure that you would think it well. My mother said that you were not cut out for a lawyer, and I rather agree with her."

" So do I. To tell the truth, I don't like the law, and I am not a lawyer by choice."

" You would rather have been something else ? "

" I would rather have been a soldier. I wanted to go into the army, but, as my father and mother objected, I yielded to their wishes, and became an articled clerk, a good deal against the grain. My father is very good, though. He does not tie me to the desk. ' Enjoy yourself while you are young,' he says. ' Care will come soon enough. If you are not ploughed more than once at your exams. I shall be content.' "

" And have you been ploughed ? "

" Never. My pride would not let me, and the exams. are not very difficult."

" But you don't spend much time at the office ? "

"No more than I can help."

"And is that the way you intend to go through life—doing no more than you can help?" asked Olive, rather contemptuously.

"I did not say I do no more work than I can help," returned Charlie, with some asperity. "I said I spent no more time in the office than I could help, which is a very different matter. And there is no particular reason why I should work hard. Ned does. He likes it, and old Lillywhite is a host in himself, to say nothing of my father; and, though he is fond of field sports, no man in the county works harder at his profession."

"Yes, your father is a very fine man. Everybody respects him. He has been very good to us. My mother says that there is nobody in the world in whom she has such absolute confidence. He is integrity itself."

"Yes, and he is kindness itself. I would rather lose my right hand than vex my father. It was to please him that I gave up my idea of going into the army."

"It was not to please your mother, then?"

"It pleased them both. If the pater had been left to himself I think he would have consented. But she would not hear of it—she comes of a Quaker family, and has some Quaker notions about soldiering and that—and if you want to please my father you must please my mother. . . I am afraid you think me a very idle fellow, Olive."

"No, I would not say that. You hunt and fish, and play cricket and football with great energy and success. No, you are far from idle. But you don't seem to care about getting on. Now, in America, a young man in your position would throw all his energies into business."

"Make a fortune, you mean? By the time I should have made a fortune I should have lost the capacity to enjoy it. I would rather go on as I am. I shall have enough for my wants."

"But could you not try to make a name?"

"What chance has a country solicitor of making a name, I should like to know?"

"Oh, there are ways. You might get into Parliament, for instance. Anyhow, if I were a man, I should not be content to be a nobody. I would either make a fortune or a name, or, in some other way, win distinction."

" I lost my chance of winning distinction when I went into my father's office instead of going into the army, and I shall never have another—unless the French come and the yeomanry cavalry are called out," said Charlie, laughing lightly, yet not without a touch of bitterness. " But here we are at your lodge gates, and just at the time I expected. The church clock is striking six. Shall I go in with you ? "

" Of course you must, and give an account of your stewardship, and help me to make my peace with my mother.'

" All right. Let us trot up the avenue, and then she will know we are coming."

As the two belated ones reined up before the house a footman threw open the door, and a plump, little woman, with a round, fat face, lively black eyes, and wearing widow's weeds, appeared at the threshold.

" At last ! Thank heaven, you are safe, Olive. If you only knew how anxious I have been ! When I heard the sound of hoofs in the avenue, I feared it might be the huntsmen coming to tell me you were killed. Why didn't you return with Potts ? "

" Because I should have had to leave off at the very beginning of the run. I would not have done it for a thousand Potts. He got home all right, I suppose ? "

" He did get home, but I cannot say he was all right. His hat was battered all to pieces and fastened on with a handkerchief, his face scratched all over and encrusted with blood, his coat torn and covered with mud, and Tinker lame. Potts returned in a sorry plight, I assure you, and he said you two were careering over the country like mad people, and he doubted whether either of you would come home alive. He frightened me dreadfully, and I don't think I shall ever let Olive——"

" Potts is an old tea-pot," interposed Charlie. " It was one of the finest runs ever known, Mrs. Lincoln, and no dangerous jumping, and Olive rode like an Amazon. If the fox had been killed, instead of running to ground, she would have got the brush."

" Yes, Olive does ride well," said Mrs. Lincoln, mollified by the young fellow's praise of her daughter. " But that is no reason why you should lead her into danger."

" He did not lead me into danger, he led me into safety," answered the girl warmly. " If you had only seen—he kept

with me all the time, he went first over all the difficult places
and told me what to do. But for him I certainly should
have come to grief."

" Well, well, we will say no more about it. All is well that
ends well. Won't you stay and dine with us, Charlie? We
will excuse your costume."

" You are very kind, Mrs. Lincoln ; but they are expecting
me at home, and Kitty has had a hard day. I must get her
made comfortable for the night as soon as possible."

And then they shook hands, and the young fellow hied him
homeward, musing, and not in the best of humors. It was not
the first time Olive had hinted—though never before so plainly—that he was not taking life sufficiently in earnest, and
that he ought to have higher aims and nobler pleasures than
being merely a country lawyer, captain of the Peele Eleven,
and riding straight to hounds. His conscience told him that
the imputation was true, and he did not like it ; less, however,
out of regard for his conscience than Olive's good opinion,
which he greatly desired. He had known her since she was
eleven or twelve years old—that was why they called each
other by their Christian names—and he was her senior by
three years. But being as precocious as travelled American
girls generally are, and having seen a good deal more of the
world than he had, she treated him much as a strong-minded
elder sister treats a wayward brother—ordered him about,
made him fetch and carry for her, and occasionally admonished
him for his good. Charlie, on his part, made no objection ;
he did not find it unpleasant to be ordered about by a pretty
girl, and he liked Miss Lincoln so well that he would have
suffered much rather than forfeit her good-will or forego the
pleasure of her society. He had never seriously asked himself whether he loved her. A little flirting was all very well,
but the conscience aforesaid told him that he was too young
to become engaged, and existing arrangements were so entirely to his satisfaction that he had no wish to change them
for a state of things that might interfere with hunting and
cricket.

Nevertheless, Olive's strictures on his want of purpose
were very galling, the more especially as, albeit in one sense
true, they were not altogether deserved. She did not give
him credit for the sacrifice he had made in renouncing his
desire to enter the army. It had been the dream of his life

to go to the wars, and he knew that he had it not in him to shine as a solicitor. The study and practice of the law were only made tolerable to him by being largely intermixed with sport, and out-of-door work in connection with Lord Hermitage's estate.

"If I can only please Olive by making my fortune as a lawyer, I may as well give it up as a bad job," he thought. "And I would rather please her than anybody else. But what can a fellow do? I might enlist; but after the way Jack has behaved that would break their hearts entirely, and I am not sure that Olive would like me to be a private soldier."

So it came to pass that, notwithstanding the good day's sport he had enjoyed, Charlie went home pensive and despondent.

Meanwhile Olive and her mother were making him the subject of another discussion.

"What have you and Charlie been talking about?" asked Mrs. Lincoln, as they sat in the drawing-room, waiting for dinner to be announced.

"All sorts of things—the run and the hounds—and, lastly, about himself. I took the liberty of telling him what you said the other day—that he was not sufficiently in earnest, that he ought to have a purpose in life and try to make some show in the world."

"How did he take it?"

"Very well. He never resents anything I say. The trouble is that he does not like law a bit. He wanted to go into the army."

"It was very well he did not. All idle young men want to go into the army, I think."

"Charlie is not idle, mother; anything but that. He works with great energy at anything he likes, and it is not his fault that he has been put into a profession which he detests."

Mrs. Lincoln smiled.

"What would you have, my dear?" she said. "A minute since you were blaming the young man, now you are praising him."

"Well, I am afraid of him sinking into a nondescript and a nobody—half sportsman, half lawyer, and he has it in him to do a great deal better than that—he is generous, cour-

ageous and high-spirited and in many things really very clever
—much more so than some people imagine."

" You have observed him very closely, I think."

" Naturally. We were children together ; and I always
observe people.   It is amusing."

" All the same, Olive, there is a grave defect in Charlie's
character.   I fear he is unstable and will never excel—except
in sport. What if he does not like the law? He has gone
into it, and it is his duty to conquer his dislike. Many a
man has made a fortune and a name in a profession which he
did not find congenial at first.   Let him take example by his
brother. Edward will get on. He works at this unfortunate
suit of ours night and day. His knowledge of the law is
simply immense. He seems to know everything and forget
nothing."

" Yes, he is the model young man, which is perhaps the
reason I don't much like him."

" You mean you don't like him because other people do."

" That is not it. I dislike him because he is priggish and
conceited, after the manner of models.   Then he doesn't
ride straight, and I detest his laugh."

Mrs. Lincoln smiled again.

" That is a new fad of yours, Olive, judging people by their
laugh," she said, " and if riding is to be the test I admit
that Edward is hopelessly inferior to his brother. But it is
not a test of a man's moral worth, and judged by any other
standard, Edward is the better man.   He is industrious
and clever, as high-principled as his father, and altogether a
most promising young man.   I greatly prefer him to Charlie,
and so I think must every sensible person."

" Then I am not a sensible person, for I am sure I don't,"
returned Olive defiantly.

" Well, well, there is no accounting for likes and dislikes,"
said Mrs. Lincoln with an air of amused resignation, " and
perhaps if I preferred Charlie you would prefer Ned. Some
people go by the rule of contrary. But let us go in to dinner ; the bell has rung and you must be very hungry."

CHAPTER VIII.

"THE BLESSING."

" Got some gruel ready, Tom?" asked Charlie of the head groom, as he rode into the stable-yard.

" Yes, sir."

" Well, take good care of Kitty. We have had a clinking run and a long hack home. What are you doing with a fire in the harness-room ? "

" Drying Mr. Edward's boots and saddles and things. He got into a brook or summat, and came home sousing wet."

"Give Kitty a linseed mash—but no corn, mind, and no bran, and when she is cool sheet her well up and bandage her legs."

And with that the young fellow hurried into the house, for it was quite dinner-time ; but it took him only a few minutes to change his hunting suit for evening dress, and he entered the dining-room with the second course.

A large low ceiled room it was and oak wainscoted : at one end burnt a bright fire of logs, at the other shone resplendent a fine black oak cabinet and sideboard, lighted with wax candles, in its way quite a work of art, to the building of which Mr. Prince, who was curious in such matters, had given much time and thought. The windows were hung with crimson curtains, the walls adorned with choice oil paintings, and all the arrangements were suggestive of good taste and easy circumstances.

" Had good sport, my boy, eh ? " said Mr. Prince pleasantly, as Charlie took his seat.

" Capital ! Found a fox and ran him an hour and forty minutes with only two checks. Hasn't Ned told you ? "

" He could not tell me more than he knew. He got into trouble at Cobbin Brook and came home. Gad ! I would not have come home."

" I think Edward did quite right to come," observed Mrs. Prince gently, and with a slight lifting of her beautiful arched eyebrows. " It would have been very foolish of him to go on with wet clothes and his boots full of water."

" Ah, well, there's no accounting for tastes in these things. And Ned never was much of a sportsman."

" I never pretended to be, father. *Chacun à son gout*, you know "

" All the same, you rode like a sportsman to-day, Ned," put in Charlie. " If you had not got into the brook you would have seen the end of the run as well as the best—and an accident may happen to anybody."

The mother smiled. She knew that her sons were not always sympathetic, and the junior's generous defence of the elder, even in so small a matter as this, touched a responsive chord in her heart.

" Well, one cannot help getting a bit excited when hounds are running," said Ned, smiling in turn, " and, if Merry Boy had not blundered into the deepest part of the brook, I don't think I should have been far behind you."

" Blundered, did he ? " said Mr. Prince, with a gesture of surprise. " The old horse does not often do that, unless—— However, it is perhaps as well you did not take much out of him. He will be fit for me to ride with the foxhounds on Thursday—if you will help Lillywhite to look after the shop, Charlie ! Ned is going to town for a few days."

" Of course I will, father ; and if the weather holds out you ought to have good sport."

" I hope Olive came to no harm," said Mrs. Prince. " I have never been able to reconcile myself to the idea of girls riding to hounds ; and I know that her mother is never quite happy when she is out."

" She did not come to the least harm, and straight she rode, too ; never shirked a single jump," returned Charlie.

" Did not boggle at the brook, I suppose ? " said Mr. Prince, with a side glance at his elder son.

" Nor anything else."

" If you mean that for me, father," he said, " if you mean that I boggled at the brook, just let me tell you that I did nothing of the sort. If Merry Boy had not refused the bank and plunged into mid-stream, so wetting me through, I should have gone on ; but I am not so fond of huntings as to be indifferent to the consequences of a ducking."

" You see what you have missed, Ned," said the father,

mischievously, "the best part of a clinking run, and a ride home with a pretty girl."

Edward, who took himself too seriously to like being chaffed, did not deign to reply.

Before dinner was quite over the butler told Mr. Prince, in an aside, that Thomas Roots, from Windy Gap, would like to have a word with him.

"Bother Thomas Roots. Why cannot he come to the office in business hours?   However, he is an important tenant, and always up to time with his rent.   It is about that new barn he wants building, I suppose.   See him, Charlie—it is in your line—and say that Lord Hermitage won't let us spend any more money in improvements this year; but, after Lady Day, I daresay we can manage it.   Show Roots into my room, Hartly, and give him a glass of grog."

Charlie had got rid of the farmer, and was on the point of returning to the drawing-room when one of the maids gave him a note, which on opening he found to run as follows:—

"The waif, whom you so generously relieved this morning, craves the favor of an interview with Mr. Charles Prince. He has a very important communication to make, but being in rags would rather not show himself in the house.   He will wait for an answer at the stable-yard gate."

"He must be a queer tramp," thought Charlie; "this letter is well written and not badly expressed.   Shall I see him? Ned would say he was a begging-letter impostor, and want to send for a constable.   As likely as not, though, he is a decent fellow down on his luck.   Anyhow, there is no harm in hearing what he has to say."

So, after lighting his pipe and putting on a felt hat, he went leisurely into the stable-yard, unsuspicious of evil, and anticipating nothing more serious than a tramp's story, possibly true, but more probably false, ending with a request for money.

He found his man lounging against the gate-post with his hands in his pockets, and his hat slouched over his eyes.

"Well," said Charlie, stopping before him.

"I should like a word with you, sir, if you would be so kind as to give me a hearing.   But we might be overheard here, people are coming and going.   Could we go somewhere?   I shall not detain you long."

The tone, voice, and manners of the man were so different

from those of the tramp who had opened the gate for him, earlier in the day, that Charlie could hardly believe it was the same.

" Is it so very particular, then, what you have to say ? " he asked.

" Very, sir, as you will be the first to admit when I tell you."

" Let us go into the harness-room. There is a fire, and the men are sure to be away by this time."

Charles led the way to the harness-room, opened the door and went in, the tramp following. Edward's saddle was drying before the fire on an old wooden case, turned upside down. Charlie removed the saddle and told the tramp to take a rest on the box, then he put a log on the fire and stirred it up. As he stooped to do this his face came near the tramp's.

" You have been drinking," he said sternly, turning round with the poker still in his hand.

" Yes, sir, I have had a glass of brandy, but not out of your money, for on my way to Peele I earned sixpence by helping a carter to get his cart out of a ditch. And if you are ever as tired and hungry and used up as I was this morning, you'll be glad of a drop of something to put a bit of life and courage into you. And I'd have no objection to another glass if you'd give me one. Might a fellow smoke ? "

" Might a fellow smoke ! Do you know you are getting confoundedly familiar. You have not only been drinking ; you are drunk."

" No, I am not. One glass of brandy does not make a man like me drunk, and that is all I have had. As for familiarity, I have a right to be familiar."

" You impertinent scoundrel ! I've a good mind——"

" Don't use bad language, my dear sir. You'll be sorry for it afterwards."

" 'Pon my word, this is intolerable. Say at once what you have to say or I'll send for a constable."

" I don't think you will, sir."

" Why not ? You are either an impostor, or worse."

" Well, perhaps I am—in one sense. All the same—don't you know me ? "

" Know you ? How on earth should I know you ? "

" Look at me."

The tramp rose, doffed his hat, removed the patch from his eye, and then threw back his head.

"Look!" he repeated.

Charles shook his head.

"By this fitful light," he said, again stirring the fire. "By this fitful light I should not know my own brother."

"I am your own brother."

"My own brother! Good Heaven! You don't mean to say you are Jack?"

"Yes, I am your vagabond, ne'er-do-weel brother, the same, though I can hardly believe it, who, when you were a little chap, so high, used to romp with you in this very room and ride you round the garden there on his back."

Charlie's first impulse was to exclaim, "Dear old Jack," and take his hand. Then, remembering the evil Jack had wrought (though he did not know the worst) he drew back.

"What are you doing here, and what has brought you to this pass?" he asked coldly.

"I will tell you. But not so loud, not so loud—the servants—somebody might hear. But let me ask you first of all, did the governor square Peploe and Pope?"

"I believe so. At any rate, he paid a good deal of money."

"Then they did not burst up; there was no scandal?"

"Peploe and Pope did not burst up; there was no scandal."

"Then he must have squared them. I wonder how much it cost him? But did he square the bank as well?"

"What bank?"

"Jardine and Jameson."

"I cannot tell you; I never heard of them before. Now, answer my questions—where have you been, and what do you want?"

"Where have I been? Well, when I found the game was up I jumped a ship——"

"You ran away from your debts, you mean. That was cowardly."

"My debts? Yes, I ran away from my debts," answered Jack with a hard laugh, "and a good job I did. I put on a suit of sailor clothes, went down to the docks, jumped on board a ship as she was being towed out, got a berth as ordinary seaman, and sailed in her to China, and a rough voyage we had, I can tell you. At Hong Kong I left her and got a billet in a merchant's office, and if I had been a steady-going chap I might have saved money and got on. I did save some, but I spent it in a spree and lost my billet at the same time. There was nothing for it but to go to sea again, so I shipped on board a brig bound to Queenstown for orders. We got orders to go on to Liverpool, and that being about the last place in the world I wanted to go to, I slipped overboard and swam ashore, and as I had not a copper in my pocket and hardly a shirt to my back, I 'listed. By the time I had finished my drill, the regiment was sent to Colchester, and there I got across with an infernal brute of a sergeant-major. One day last week he provoked me beyond endurance, and I knocked him down. I was placed under arrest, of course, but the same night I escaped from the lock-up, went to a boozing ken, a common lodging-house, and exchanged clothes with a tramp while he slept, then set off on the tramp myself."

"You are a deserter, then ? "

"A deserter—and worse ; he is——"

Jack seized the poker and sprang to his feet. Charlie turned sharply round. There was a dark figure in the doorway.

"You, Ned ? " he exclaimed.

"Yes, you dropped this note in the hall, and, recognizing the handwriting, and guessing what had happened, I came here just in time to hear this vagabond's confession—or so much of it as he chooses to tell. How dare you show your face here, Jack ? "

"What is that to you, Ned ? You are not my keeper. I have done you no harm."

"Done me no harm ! You have harmed us all. Are we not partners in your disgrace. To make good your defalcations and prevent a frightful scandal, father had to borrow money and incur a liability of which he will not get rid while he lives. Is that no harm ? Is it no harm to us—to Charlie and me—think you, that our eldest brother should be guilty of forgery and fraud and become a drunkard, a deserter, and a tramp ? "

" Forgery and fraud ! " exclaimed Charlie. " No, no, Ned. Surely, it is surely not so bad as that ! "

"You were so young at the time that father did not want you to know, so, for God's sake, keep it to yourself, but it is true, ask him if it isn't."

"It is true," murmured Jack, bowing his head.

" And the bankers refused to be squared. If they find out that you are in the country they will prosecute you. Why on

earth didn't you stay in China or go somewhere else? If
you possessed the slightest vestige of a conscience, you would
have cut your throat or blown out your brains rather than
come back here."

"Don't say that, Ned," interrupted Charlie. "It is almost
as if you told him to commit murder. And he is our brother,
after all. It is not for us to throw a stone at him. If we
don't forgive him, who will?"

"Well, I might have forgiven him if he had not come back.
But this is the worst thing he has done yet. If he is taken
up as a deserter, and he may be any moment, for I have not
the least doubt the police are on the look-out for him—if he
is taken he is sure to be recognized, and then——It makes
my very blood run cold to think of it. . . . . What is your
object in coming here, Jack? I suppose you have an object?"

"I thought I might get a little help. There is not a beggar
on the road who is poorer than I am."

"And you shall be helped, Jack," broke in Charlie impetuously. "I cannot do much, but whatever I can do I
will."

"He does not deserve to be helped, Charlie, and if it was
not for the disgrace it would cause the family, I should say
leave him to his fate."

"No, you would not, Ned; when it came to the point you
would not have the heart to turn your own brother from your
door, without raising a hand to help him, though he is a black
sheep."

"You are right, Charlie," said Jack, gloomily. "I am a
black sheep, and I fear I always shall be; but is it entirely
my own fault, think you? A man is pretty much as God
makes him. At school I was always getting into scrapes;
Ned was never in a scrape in his life. I could never do right;
he could never do wrong, and it has been so ever since. How
I wish my father had let me go to sea when I wanted. I
should have got licked into shape while I was a cub. What
was the use of trying to make a barrister of a fellow like
me?"

"Not a word against the pater, Jack, if you please," said
Charlie. "He has been only too good."

"I am not saying a word against him: merely expressing
a regret that I was not allowed to go to sea. I regret still
more that he did not drown me while I was a whelp. I wish

I had never been born. Don't you think I feel my degradation? Ned accused me of being a drunkard. I am not; at
any rate I am not a sot; but sometimes I get utterly reckless. I think of what I am, and what I might have been, and
then I am ready for anything. I try to drown dark memories
in drink—and, I won't deny it, the habit grows. . . . But I
won't trouble you, why should I? You are among the fortunate of the earth, while I, like Cain, am a vagabond on
the face of it. Let me go. What if I am lagged? It will
only be fifty lashes. I can stand that, and I did not enlist
in my own name."

"That would not do at all, Jack," said Edward, speaking
kindly for the first time. "You would have to be brought
before the Bench, and somebody would be sure to recognize
you: and I cannot bear to think of you wandering about the
country like a common tramp. Have you any money in your
pocket, Charlie?"

"Three or four sovereigns."

"And I have no more."

"That will do, thank you," said Jack, humbly. "Five
pounds will make me rich beyond the dreams of avarice."

"No. You should have enough to take you out of this
country, and start you in another—forty or fifty pounds at
least—and you must be away from Peele before daylight to-
morrow—by the 5.30 train. . . . I have it. I am going to
town to-morrow by the 10.30 express, *in re* Lincoln. I can
get the money there, and you can meet me—it won't do for
you to come to Wood's Hotel—at the Black Bull, in Holborn,
between five and six o'clock. Where will you go?"

"To New York, in a sailing ship from the Thames. I
must fight shy both of Liverpool and Queenstown."

"You will really go, now? You won't spend the money
in drink?"

"I assure you, Ned——"

"Well, it is your last chance, remember; and I don't mean
to give you all this money at once. Fifteen pounds or so
will be enough to keep you a few days in London, and pay
your passage in a sailing ship to New York. I will remit the
balance to the care of some banker to wait your arrival.
What may be your latest *alias?*"

"It was John Jones the other day. It is anything you like,
now."

" Let it be grandfather's, then, Mark Darnley. And now we must go in, or we shall be missed. Charlie will bring you some clothes and a rug presently. You cannot go to London in those rags ; and you must be off before the men come in the morning."

" Couldn't I see *him* and my mother and ask their forgiveness ? It might help me to do better."

" No. It would be too cruel. It would reawaken painful memories ; their hearts would bleed afresh—and—there are other reasons."

The " other reasons " were Edward's dread of a scene, and a fear that the scapegrace might obtain from his father a great deal more money than the modest sum which he himself proposed to give him.

" Anyhow, he may see them," Charlie said. " We have evening prayer about ten o'clock. When the stable clock strikes the hour go round to the dining-room window, Jack. I will arrange the blinds so that you can look in without being seen. But take care they don't see you. I will bring you the things as soon as I can, and I shall come again in the morning to see you off and say good-bye."

When his brothers were gone Jack put his elbows on his knees and his head between his hands, and gazed gloomily at the flickering fire.

" Evening prayer ! Evening prayer ? " he moaned. " They keep it up, then. How long is it since ? To think of that time and what I am now is enough to make a fellow hang himself, as my dear brother advised me to do. How proud I was when mother took me in to prayers for the first time, and held me on her lap while father read, and then I would kneel at her side and say my own prayer, ' God make me a good boy ! ' . . . . Not much use, that prayer. He has made me a deuced bad boy—or the devil has—worse than I dare tell or anybody knows. . . . . I'll ask Ned to pay my passage and see me safely on board. If he gives me all that money I shall go on the loose and get lagged, to a dead certainty. . . . . They are very good, 'pon my soul. Charlie is really kind ; he means it. Ned is good because he wants to get rid of me. He is nothing if not respectable. Gad if he saw me marched off with those things on my wrists, between a couple of fellows with fixed bayonets, he would have a fit. . . . . I am on the down grade and no mistake.

If I could only keep off drink! Unless I do I shall go to the deuce fast, and utterly—faster I dare say in America than here. However, as nobody knows me there and nobody cares for me here, it don't much matter. Life is but a thought, and I have seen more of it than most men twice my age."

And so his vagrant thoughts ran on until the clock struck ten. Then he went out and crept furtively, by well-known paths, to the dining-room window and looked into the house from which he was an outcast and might never enter again. The room was empty, but there presently came a servant and laid a Bible and a prayer-book on the table. Next, a bell rung, and Mr. and Mrs. Prince and their two sons, followed by several domestics, entered the room and took their places, just as they had done in days gone by. For the most of those present it was a ceremony without any particular meaning—Mr. Prince taking part in it mainly to please his wife, and because it was the right thing to do—but the vagabond's interest in it was intense ; he lost neither a word nor a gesture ; it was his last glimpse of home, the last time he should look on his father and mother, for whom, despite his sins and degradation, there was, deep down in the heart, an undying affection.

When Mr. Prince had read a few verses and a short prayer the servants withdrew, and Mrs. Prince, sitting down at the piano, asked her sons and her husband to join her in singing the old Evening Hymn :—

> " Glory to thee, my God, this night,
> For all the blessings of the light ;
> Keep me, oh keep me, King of kings,
> Under thine own almighty wings."

When it was finished she rose from her seat.

" Are you going to bed already, mother ? " asked Charlie.

" Yes, I feel rather tired."

The two young men kissed her.

" Good-night, and may God bless you," she said with emotion, " and may He also bless poor, erring Jack, wherever he is this night. I have thought much about him to-day."

" Aye. God bless him," added Mr. Prince, in a choking voice. " He needs a blessing, if anybody does. It is nearly three years since his name passed my lips. He has done us a cruel wrong. But he is our own lad still. That is a fact one cannot blot out; and for aught we know he may be leading a better life. I often wonder where he is, and how occupied. All the same, I hope we may never hear of him again —unless it be something good. Better that he should perish in a foreign land than come back and disgrace us."

All this fell on the listening vagabond's ears and burnt into his soul. His whole body trembled with suppressed emotion, and his face was bathed with tears.

"I have their blessing," he murmured; "they love me still, drunken reprobate though I am. Please God, I'll never touch drink again; and when they hear of me it shall be something good—it shall—it shall."

And then he crept back to his hiding-place, by the way he had come.

A few days later Jack was at sea, on board a ship bound for New York; and during the voyage, which was long and stormy, he never turned in without murmuring: "Keep me, oh keep me, King of kings, under thine own almighty wings," and saying to himself: "It shall be something good, if I live."

CHAPTER IX.

MRS. LINCOLN'S PLAN.

THOUGH Mrs. Prince was neither a match-maker nor a schemer, it would have been strange if the idea of mating her son Edward with Olive Lincoln had not occurred to her. The advantages of such a match would have been obvious to a much less intelligent matron. Olive was an heiress, and, albeit somewhat wayward and self-willed, a very charming girl; and Edward, who was a model son, could not fail to make an exemplary husband. Moreover, in the probable event of the misappropriation of the trust money coming to light, the fact of Olive being Edward's wife would disarm Mrs. Lincoln's resentment and prevent scandal. The secret would be kept in the two families; and the intercourse between them had latterly become so frequent and friendly, that she anticipated no difficulty in the realization of her designs. Formerly the Lincolns were generally from home—if they could be said to have a home—dividing their winters between Paris, Italy, and the Riviera, making occasional visits to America, and spending only their summers at All Hallows. But since Mr. Lincoln's death his widow and his daughter had lived there exclusively and in strict seclusion, making few calls, and receiving scarcely anybody save the Princes.

Mrs. Prince opened the campaign by sounding her son.

"Olive is a charming girl," she said, "and will make a very fine woman. Don't you think so?"

"Yes, I think she is. All the same, she would be more so if she were a little less wilful and capricious; and not being a prophet I am unable to say whether she will make a fine woman," answered Edward, who (probably owing to his legal habit of mind) had a provoking way of never assenting to a proposition without cavilling.

"I did not say she was faultless," observed Mrs. Prince rather impatiently. "A girl brought up as she has been is sure to be a little wilful; and she has seen so much of the

world that she is older than her years. But I think I know
her as well as you do, and I assure you she is a girl of noble
nature, whose love any man might be proud to win."

"Unquestionably—always, of course, provided——"

"Oh, don't give me any of your always provided. You
need not talk to me as if you were afraid of committing yourself. I am very much in earnest. Tell me without equivo-
cation whether you would not be proud to win her, whether
the advantages, both to yourself personally and to the family,
which would accrue from a marriage with Olive have not
occurred to you ? "

"Of course they have, and as you press for an answer, I
admit that I should be very glad—but there are difficulties in
the way which you do not seem to have taken into account."

"What are they ? "

"Well, in the first place, I might have to keep her."

"Naturally, but as you have now a share in the office, and
as she is an heiress, that is surely not much of a difficulty."

"You forget that Mr. Lincoln, in his will, expressed a
strong desire, amounting almost to a command, that his
daughter should not marry until she was at least twenty-one ;
and in the event of her marrying without her guardians' consent before she is twenty-five the whole of her fortune, except
two hundred a year, goes to another branch of the family
(after her mother's death), a provision intended, no doubt, to
prevent her being snapped up by a mere fortune-hunter."

"But her guardians have nothing against you ? "

"Perhaps not, but they would certainly object to her marrying before she comes of age. In no case can she touch a
penny of her fortune pending that event, and my share in the
business would not enable me to give her such an establishment as she has a right to expect. Besides, I know for a fact
that Mrs. Lincoln would object to any engagement whatever
during Olive's minority. She would regard it as a violation
of the spirit, if not the letter, of her husband's injunction ;
and in my opinion it would be impolitic even to raise the
question."

"That does make a difference, certainly," said Mrs. Prince
pensively. "All the same, I do not see why you should not
make yourself agreeable to Olive in the meantime. There
are a hundred ways in which a young man may let a girl know
that he loves her, without actually proposing. And the sooner

you begin the better, for, though Olive is fancy free now, she is at an impressionable age, and there is no knowing how long she may remain so. It will be quite enough to propose in two years or so, and, if you have secured her affection in the meantime, I am sure Mrs. Lincoln would not object. Why should she? Where will she find a man more likely to make Olive happy?"

"All very well, but suppose I fall in love with Olive and she does not reciprocate, how then?"

"That is the risk you must run, my dear, and remember that faint heart never won fair lady."

"I don't think I have a faint heart, mother, though I do confess to a cautious temperament. And, to tell the truth I have begun your plan already; I have tried to make myself agreeable to Olive, as yet, however, without much tangible success. I seem to get no 'forruder.' She gives me the go-by for Charlie, and, do you know, I have sometimes had a suspicion that those two are slightly spoons on each other. Has that possibility entered into you calculations, mater?"

Mrs. Prince laughed.

"You are really too absurd with your doubts and suspicions and misgivings, Edward. Mentally, Charlie is little more than a boy. They saw a good deal of each other when they were children, that is the reason why they are so friendly. Besides, he is both too young and too much taken up with hunting and that to fall in love. He thinks more of Kitty than Olive, and he is not Olive's ideal. These Americans are very practical. Mrs. Lincoln is a farmer's daughter, and Mr. Lincoln made his own way. They think nothing of a man who does not put all his energies into his profession and make money. I do wish father would insist on his spending more time at the office."

"Charlie is a lad after father's own heart," answered Edward with a supercilious smile.

"Yes; he says he was much the same at the same age, and that Charlie will buckle to when he has had his fling. We shall see. . . . You will think of what I have said, dear?"

"I will, mother; and, to be quite open with you, I care for Olive very much—perhaps more than, considering the circumstances and having regard to my own peace of mind, is quite prudent—and I am glad you think I have a chance."

" A chance ! You have every chance—good looks, a good position, good manners, a stainless character, a fair future and no rivals—what could you want more ? "

If Mrs. Prince had known that at the very time she and Edward were concocting this ingenious scheme for the capture of Olive's heart Mrs. Lincoln was beginning to question whether it was not in danger from another quarter, the former lady might have seen reason to modify her opinions and revise her plans. Mrs. Lincoln could have told her that despite Charlie's faults and the other's virtues, Olive's preference was for the younger and (matrimonially) less eligible brother.

Nevertheless, Mrs. Lincoln had no reason to suppose that her daughter's happiness was compromised as yet, much less that Charlie had spoken words of love ; but young people were young people, and the latent spark might easily be kindled into a flame which it would be difficult, perhaps impossible, to control. This contingency Mrs. Lincoln greatly deprecated. Even though Charlie were a desirable *parti*, it would be her duty to respect her husband's wishes as well in the spirit as the letter, and the surest way of doing so was to prevent Olive from forming any attachment whatever for several years to come.

On the other hand, it would be the height of indiscretion to talk to Olive in this strain, or warn her against Charlie. Indeed, Mrs. Lincoln shrewdly suspected that she had talked too much about that young gentleman already, and that her somewhat exaggerated reflections on his faults, instead of making her daughter think worse of him, had made her think better of him.

Had it not been for the exigencies of the lawsuit, the difficulty might easily have been got over by a voyage to America or a trip to the Continent. But neither of these expedients being admissible, she adopted a third, which, as she believed, would prove equally effective.

This was to renounce the seclusion in which she had lived since her husband's death, entertain freely, and encourage the visits of young men and maidens, who might, she hoped, prove a counter attraction to Charlie.

As a beginning, she resolved to give a breakfast to the hunt, of which the late Mr. Lincoln, though he never rode to hounds, had been a liberal supporter.

Mr. Prince, who thought she had mourned quite long enough, and delighted in anything which gave *éclat* to the noble sport which the famous Mr. Jorrocks happily described as the image of war, without its guilt and only 25 per cent. of its danger, warmly approved of his client's design, and rendered her every help in his power. Negotiations were opened with the Master and Secretary of the Hunt, and a fortnight later the local papers announced that the Riversdale Hounds would meet at All Hallows on the following Monday at 10.30 (for breakfast). The words in brackets, it is hardly necessary to observe, referred exclusively to the biped members of the hunt, the dietary of hounds on hunting mornings being strictly limited to fox—when they can catch one.

The occasion afforded a fine opening for Edward Prince. He was a good caterer, an adept in the management of picnics, outings and parties, and made himself very useful to the ladies of the house. Mrs. Lincoln left all the details to him ; and the butler and the cook were ordered to place themselves at his disposal. The result justified her confidence, the breakfast was all that could be desired, and Edward won great praise.

On the eventful morning All Hallows, a fine old country house commanding a wide prospect of green valley and sylvan heights, was as merry as a fair. Gay cavaliers were cantering across the park, dashing dog-carts driving up the avenue, hounds reposing on the lawn, led horses pacing to and fro before the house. The portico, the hall and the dining-room were ablaze with scarlet, and brilliant with white breeches, shining boots, and resplendent spurs. The gathering was large, for Mrs. Lincoln had invited several of her neighbors to see the show, and some had come to breakfast whose hunting would be finished when the first fox broke cover.

At one end of the principal table sat Mr. Prince (who was doing the honors for Mrs. Lincoln), at the other Bertie Brown, the master of the hounds and the captain of the county eleven, a long-limbed, broad-shouldered gentleman, whose handsome face was radiant with health and high spirits, as well it might be, seeing that its owner hunted four days a week in winter and played cricket as often in summer, and between whiles did a fair amount of shooting and fishing. The banquet was graced with the presence of sev-

eral elderly ladies and a few fair girls; and Olive's bright
eyes, scarlet jacket and broad-brimmed low-crowned hat
turned the heads of at least half a dozen of the younger
members of the hunt.

Time being limited, everybody worked at high speed, and
most of the guests, so soon as they had finished, gave place
to later comers who had not been fortunate enough to find
seats. Among them was Charlie, but while the majority of
the others went out of the room he went no further than the
back of Olive's chair—a fact which did not escape the notice
either of his brother or Mrs. Lincoln.

When the clock on the mantelpiece cuckooed eleven the
master stood up and signified that he had something to say.
But his erstwhile radiant face had become pathetically
solemn, for speech-making was more abhorrent to him than
a dodging fox or a hard frost, and even his warmest friends
were fain to admit that oratory was not his forte.

"Ladies and gentlemen," he began in faltering accents,
"Ladies and gentlemen, I have to thank you—no, I don't—
I mean that it would not be right for us to separate without
expressing our high sense of Mrs. Lincoln's kindness in
inviting the Riversdale hounds to breakfast this morning,
and on their behalf——"

"Is thy servant a dog that he should do this thing?" interrupted the waggish secretary in a *sotto voce* sufficiently
audible to set the table in a roar.

"Hang it, Rookwood, don't cross a fellow in that way,"
exclaimed the master with a bewildered look, and pulling up
short. "What the dickens? Ah, I see, I must hark back.
I beg your pardon, ladies and gentlemen, hounds was a slip,
I meant members of the hunt——"

"Gad! I think the hounds are the most important members of the hunt," muttered the irrepressible secretary.

"If you don't shut up, Bob, I shall—On behalf of the
hunt, I thank Mrs. Lincoln for her hospitality, also for the
interest she takes in our sport. Her covers are always a
sure find; Charlie Prince, who has almost as keen a nose
for his namesake as a veteran hound, tells me that an uncommonly fine fox was seen in Whitethorn Wood this morning. I hope he is there yet and will give us a good run.
Gentlemen, fill your glasses and join me in drinking the
healths of our highly respected hostess and her lovely daughter."

Mrs. Lincoln bowed, Olive smiled and blushed, and after the healths had been drunk Mr. Prince responded in a neat little speech, which was very much applauded. He had scarcely sat down when a sporting farmer, whose breeches and boots looked as if they had been heirlooms in his family for several generations, went up to the master and whispered something in his ear.

"Gentlemen," said Mr. Brown excitedly, "a fox, probably the fox I alluded to just now, was viewed away from White-thorn Wood five minutes ago. If the hounds are laid on at once we may have a good run. Perhaps Mrs. Lincoln will kindly excuse us."

The words were hardly out of his mouth when there was a general stampede for the door; and the next moment men were rushing wildly about in all directions, looking for their horses, calling for their grooms and mounting in hot haste.

Charlie leant over to Olive.

"Let us mount quietly in the stable-yard, and get out the back way," he said. "Come."

CHAPTER X.

WELL SAVED.

MISS LINCOLN followed her pilot and their horses, which had been waiting on the pillar reins, were brought out at once. Daisy being amiss, Olive was going to ride a thorough-bred chestnut, belonging to a dealer, which her mother had promised to buy for her if the horse behaved to her satisfaction.

Charlie had tried the animal a few days previously, and pronounced him to be a fine goer and a good jumper.

" But you will have to be careful at first," he said as they rode out of the yard. " He is quiet enough by himself, but he may get excited with hounds, and chestnuts are sometimes rather hot."

" Oh, I think I can manage him. He seems very gentle, and you will keep near me, won't you? "

" Of course I shall. Don't I always? "

Olive smiled. She was quite conscious of the fact that Charlie generally did keep near her, whether in the hunting field or elsewhere.

The " back way " was a short cut which brought them to Whitethorn Wood in advance of the crowd and just as the hounds were laid on. But the scent had grown cold almost to nothingness, and as Quickly, the huntsman, did not believe in pottering about to no purpose, he blew his horn and went off at a canter to Lorton Springs, a cover about two miles distant, which was probably the fox's point. The way thither led across some large grass fields and through a line of gates.

So far, the chestnut, which rejoiced in the name of Rataplan, had been quite under control, but with the hounds before him and a hurrying crowd of horses behind him he grew excited and began to pull.

" Not so fast, Olive," said the watchful Charlie, " if he gets fairly into his stride you won't be able to stop him."

"I am doing my best," returned Olive, straining at the bridle, "but the harder I pull the faster he goes."

Right before them was a ditch, bounded on the further side by a quickthorn hedge, which, though high, seemed too thin to be either difficult or dangerous ; but Charlie knew it of old.

"This way," he said, "there is a gate yonder, and that hedge is topped with wire ; it would be certain grief."

"He will neither stop nor turn," cried the girl, tugging at the reins with all her might.

Charlie rode close up to her, and, grasping the bridle, tried to pull the horse round. He might as well have tried to turn a steam-engine. Rataplan had got his head down, and seemed bent on charging the bullfinch.

"He will come an awful cropper. You must get off, Olive. Quick, slip your foot out of the stirrup ; see that your skirt is clear, and when I put my arm around your waist, throw yours round my neck. Now ! "

The next moment Olive was on Kitty's back, with Charlie's arm round her waist and as the young fellow turned his mare from the fence Rataplan rose at it, but he was going too fast to jump high, and hitting the almost invisible wire with his fore legs made a complete somersault in the air and landed in the next field on his back.

"Dear Olive, thank God you are safe ! " exclaimed Charlie passionately.

"And I owe my life to you."

"It was nothing. Any other fellow would have done the same."

"But no other fellow did ; and, oh Charlie, I would rather owe my life to you than anybody else in all the world."

Her face was very pale, but her eyes were bright, and there was a light in them which Charlie had never seen there before.

Just then the secretary and several other men, who had observed the incident from a distance galloped up to offer their help. The secretary jumped from his horse and assisted Olive, who was half fainting, to dismount.

"That was a deuced near thing, and very well saved," he exclaimed. "The beggar bolted, I suppose. Take a drink from my flask, Miss Lincoln : it will do you good."

Olive drank and felt better. Meanwhile, Macadam and

the butcher, who had scrambled through the bullfinch, shouted
that Rataplan was all right—he had fallen in a soft place—
and they would lead him round to the gate.

"But you will surely not ride that bolting beggar again,
Miss Lincoln," put in the secretary. "He may bolt when
Charlie Prince is somewhere else, and you would be in the
wrong box then."

"She shall have Kitty, and I will ride Rataplan," said
Charlie, "then she wont lose the day's sport."

"But wont he bolt with you?" asked Olive anxiously.

"I think I can hold him, I am a little stronger than you
(smiling). Besides, that tumble will have taken the devil out
of him."

It seemed so, for when the butcher brought him round to
the gate the horse looked as quiet as a lamb.

The saddles were changed and the secretary (who was the
pink of politeness where ladies were concerned) having
helped Olive up, they resumed their interrupted journey.

Presently Edward overtook them, looking not very happy.
Albeit he had resolved not to lose sight of Olive, even though
he should break his neck, he had made a bad start, owing to
the temporary disappearance of the rustic to whom he had entrusted his horse; and had the hounds found at the first draw
would have been left hopelessly behind. When he heard
that Charlie had saved Olive from a great danger—probably
from death—by a brilliant feat of horsemanship, he did not
feel any happier. Nevertheless, he could not help congratulat-
ing her and complimenting him—in a fashion.

"I hope you have quite recovered from the shock, Miss
Lincoln," he said, with slightly exaggerated anxiety.

"Quite, thank you; but I confess that when I saw that
wire, and Rataplan would not stop, I was horribly frightened."

"Of course you were; I should have been myself," returned
Edward, sympathetically. "It was very well done of my
brother, very well done,. How fortunate he was with you.
All the same, Charlie, I am rather surprised you did not discover that the horse was a bolter when you tried him the
other day."

"When I tried him the other day he was as easy to hold
as a parson's hack. You forget, too, that Bristowe said he
was quiet with hounds and a perfect lady's hunter. Besides,

I am by no means sure that the horse is a bolter. He was very fresh, and when he heard the field clattering behind him got excited. Exercise him regularly, and ride him to hounds twice a week, and he will be as safe a mount as Daisy."

Olive was about to say that Charlie had acted nobly, and to protest that he deserved unqualified praise, when a thought, suggested by a new-born prudence, arrested the words on her lips, and, turning to Edward, she inquired how he had left his mother, rather to his bewilderment. But as he always assumed—unless there was strong evidence to the contrary —that other people took him as seriously as he took himself, he answered with becoming gravity that his mother, though not fully recovered from her cold, was much better.

When they reached Lorton Springs the hounds were being "blown out." Reynard was not there. After a word with the master, Quickly led the eager pack to a third cover, Raklow Park, at so fast a pace that the hindmost hunters imagined that the hounds were running, and did not discover their mistake until they overtook the main body.

A big cover was the so called park, with deep winding rides, and so difficult to get away from that even hard riders were sometimes left sorrowing in the fastnesses of its impenetrable thickets.

By the advice of the urbane secretary, who, having been brought up in the way he should go, knew every brake and bush in the country, Olive, the Princes, and several others took up a strategic position at the north-east corner of the cover.

"Here," he said, "we command a view of two sides. Whether the fox breaks this way or that we shall see him. If he breaks yonder we shall hear the whip's view hallo, if on the other side, Quickly's horn. Now silence in the rank! if you please."

The secretary's prescience was justified by the event.

"What is that, Charlie?" asked Olive, a few minutes later, pointing to a dark object which was gliding across a stubble field some two or three hundred yards from where they stood.

"That is the fox, Miss Lincoln," answered the secretary. "He has stolen out of the cover unbeknown, as Mrs. Gamp would say. But keep quiet until he is fairly away, or those loitering fools in that old lane will either head him back or get before the hounds."

6

But when reynard was in the next field and had put a brook with rotten banks between himself and the loitering fools in question, the secretary and Charlie gave a series of view hallos that made the horses prick their ears, and nearly frightened to death a poor hare which had been hiding in her form. Before the echo of them died away, Quickly, followed by his pack, leaped from the wood, and soon the baying of the hounds proclaimed that the chase had begun.

"Over the brook by the bridge," said Charlie, leading the way. "We shall nick in on the other side."

Which they did, just as the hounds, closely followed by the master and Quickly (who had done the brook despite its rotten bank), were streaming over a big pasture, bounded by a flight of posts and rails, which was easily done by the timber jumpers; the others rode for a gate.

For fifteen minutes or so the pace was fast and furious; then, after a short check it became slower, yet not too slow for enjoyment—more enjoyable indeed for folks who liked to look about them and had an eye for the picturesque. They were in the best of the Riversdale country, a country which though mostly under plough rode light and carried a good scent, slightly undulating and intersected by ditches so wide that the man and horse who went in were seen no more until they got out—yet quite practicable for resolute jumpers and riders of nerve. No use looking for gaps or riding for places; those who did not take things as they came had to stop behind or make ignobly for the nearest road.

As the chase swept on, the sun, which had been hiding all the morning, came out, nobly investing the far-away hills and brightening the brown fields and dark woodlands with the wondrous witchery of his smile; and all this beauty, blending with the sights and sounds of sylvan war, red-coats and galloping horses, the cries of men, and the music of hounds, gladdened still more the two young souls who had just made the supreme discovery of their lives—that they loved and were loved.

They talked in snatches: it is not easy to keep up a conversation when hounds are running.

"Are you enjoying it, Olive?" he asked.

"Can you ask? So much."

"You look so. Your eyes are as bright as the sun."

"Oh, Charlie! But mind what you say—somebody might

—and your brother is close behind. How well he is going."

Edward was going well. He had made up his mind to keep close to Olive, and as he was riding the cleverest horse in his father's stud he had no difficulty in sticking to his resolve. He needed merely to stick on, and though he had no stomach for the sport and never took a jump without fearing a fall, the thought that he was gaining credit with Miss Lincoln for his bold riding and preventing her from getting too thick with Charlie steeled his nerves and converted what would otherwise have been a penance into the semblance of a pleasure.

After a run of two hours, the latter part of it rather dragging, the fox was handsomely killed in the open, and the brush awarded to Miss Lincoln. Then the hounds went further afield to draw again ; but as Olive said she was tired and Charlie declared that Rataplan had had enough, and Edward said he had, they decided to hie them home, as did most of the others who had no second horses out, they turned their backs on the field and their faces towards Peele.

Olive rode between the brothers and was very gracious to Edward, complimenting him warmly on his riding, though not quite as judiciously as she might have done.

"You went as well as anybody," she said. "With a little more practice you will soon be as good a man with hounds as Charlie."

"It is very kind of you to say so, Miss Lincoln, but I am sure I shall never be Charlie's equal in horsemanship. He gives his mind to it, I don't," answered Edward, in a tone which implied that he held horsemanship in light esteem.

"Well, if you want to excel in anything you must give your mind to it, mustn't you? You give your mind to law, therefore you excel as a lawyer. But would it not be possible for a man to excel in both—like your father, for instance."

"I am not sure that my father does excel as a lawyer. But there was no examinations in his time. He owes his success rather to native shrewdness, sound judgment and capacity for business than profound knowledge."

"No matter, he excels. And you forget his high sense of honor and his pleasantly genial manner, so important in a lawyer."

"It is not for me to praise my father, Miss Lincoln. But

you are quite right. Character, and manner which inspires confidence are more essential to success—at any rate in a country lawyer—than mere knowledge of the law," he answered, wondering at the same time what she would say if she were to know about the broken trust.

Charlie listened in silence, but he guessed that some of Olive's remarks were intended for him.

"She wants me to take the pater for my example," he thought, "and I will."

The brothers saw Olive home.

"I am sorry I cannot ask you to stay," she said as they reined up at the door, " my mother is gone to town and won't be back till dinner-time. Will you change saddles here, Charlie ? "

" No, I will ride round to the stables. You go on, Ned. I'll overtake you before you get to the lodge gates."

Whereupon, after shaking hands with the two cavaliers and bidding them good-night, Miss Lincoln tripped into the house.

As Charlie was mounting his horse in the stable-yard a man put a note into his hand.

" From Miss Olive," he said.

It contained these words : " At four to-morrow afternoon, in the King's Path."

CHAPTER XI.

"THEIR FIRST TRYST."

ON the next day Charlie was early at the office, and, having an object in view, worked with unwonted diligence. He draughted a rather complicated lease so well that Lillywhite declared he could not have done it better himself, and Mr. Prince said the same.

Shortly before three o'clock, Charley, having finished his lease, went into his father's room.

"I am going to Fountains," he said; "one of the chimneys is in a very bad way, and Pringle wants somebody to look at it."

"Yes, you had better; but take care what you promise. If we let the account for disbursements get too high we shall have his lordship complaining again. I suppose you will be back in time to go home with us in the dog-cart?"

"No, I think I shall walk home by the fields. One gets so little walking in the hunting season."

"Anyhow, you won't be late for dinner."

"Trust me for that; I have always a frightful appetite the day after hunting."

Fountains was a farmhouse in the neighborhood of All Hallows, and thither, after leaving the office, the young fellow went with swift strides. The chimney was, of course, only a pretext. A few days previously he had met Mr. Pringle "promiscuous in the street," when that gentleman casually observed that his kitchen chimney was tumbling down, and suggested that the "mending of it" was rather a landlord's job than a tenant's.

Pringle seemed surprised that Charlie had taken his joke seriously, and after showing him the chimney and his prize bullocks, invited him to step inside and have a glass of home-brewed. Charlie being, as he said, pressed for time, prayed to be excused, and after taking leave of the farmer made a bee line for All Hallows, whistling blithely as he crossed the fields, vaulting all the gates, and feeling generally as if he were walking in air. For was he not going to his first love tryst? Little recked the high-spirited lad just then of prudence and caution, of impending difficulties and possible trials.

"Olive! Olive! Dear Olive! She loves me. She loves me," was his sole thought, a thought which quenched every doubt and silenced every misgiving.

And was it not better so? Youth is the time of illusion and love, the time when life seems endless, and the future has no terrors. Let those to whom it is given enjoy it while they may.

As Charlie drew near All Hallows he sobered down somewhat, and looked sharply about him. The house, which occupied the site of an ancient hunting-lodge built by Henry VIII., stood on the brow of a gentle acclivity, overlooking a spacious park, dotted with noble trees and begirt with broad woodlands. The King's Path (so called after the much-married monarch), where Olive had asked Charlie to meet her, was a sequestered walk winding between laurel bushes and leading to a small lake, nestling in a grove of copper beeches and weeping willows, invisible from the house.

Though the time was winter, the weather was mild, and the air balmy. The setting sun was raining gold on Whitethorn Wood, and as he sank below the horizon a crescent moon mirrored itself in the still waters of the tiny lake.

It was an ideal trysting-place.

Charlie, guessing that Olive did not want him to venture too near the house, leaned against the bole of a lordly beech tree and waited. He was too happy to be impatient, and his thoughts were of the pleasantest, and he knew she would come.

Presently a light hand touched him on the shoulder. While he was looking one way, Olive had come another, and the soft carpet of fallen leaves deadened her footsteps.

"Dear Olive! How good of you to come," he exclaimed, turning to her.

He would have clasped her in his arms, but young love is often timid, and not yet daring to do more, he took both her hands.

"Dear Olive! How good of you to come," he repeated ardently.

" I am not sure that it is quite right ; but after yesterday it seemed necessary to have an explanation—I feared
you would be committing some imprudence, and there may
be no other opportunity for a long time. But, first of all, let
me thank you again for saving me from a danger which, if it
had not been my death, would almost certainly have made
me a cripple for life. I am really very grateful, Charlie ; so
is my mother, as she will tell you when you call. How can
I thank you enough ? "

" By letting me kiss you and saying you love me."

Then Charlie, taking silence for consent, and growing
bolder, drew her to him, and looked into her love-bright eyes,
and took love's tribute from her yielding lips.

" You love me ? " he said, still holding her in his arms.

" Do you think I should be here if I did not ? " she returned
with a happy laugh. " But until yesterday I knew not myself
how much. I thought my affection for you was no more than
sisterly. But when I felt that I was safe in your arms, and
I looked up at your face, and heard you call me dear
Olive, it was like a revelation. I learnt the truth. What did
I say ? I am afraid it was something very foolish."

" That you would rather I had saved you than anybody
else ; which meant, I thought, that you loved me better than
anybody else."

" You might have made a worse guess, my Prince. But
it must be all love, remember."

" Naturally, my sweet Olive. Is not love lord of all ? "

" I did not mean in that sense, you foolish boy. I meant
that we must not be engaged."

" In love and not engaged ! How can that be, Olive ?
You talk in riddles. What is the difference ? "

" Immense. We cannot help being in love ; love comes of
itself, but we may help being engaged. In the one case we
can keep it to ourselves, in the other we should have to tell
everybody. You would have to ask my mother's consent,
which you would not get, and tell your own people, and that
might lead to trouble."

" So ! You think your mother would not consent."

" I am sure. My father disapproved of early marriages.
I am forbidden to marry before I am twenty-one, and my
mother disapproves of long engagements, and I fear she
would also disapprove of you."

" Personally, do you mean ? "

" Personally, in the sense that she thinks you take life too easily and your character is unformed. But that is not the point. She would not consent to an engagement now, though you were all she could wish ; and if you were to ask and be refused you could not come any more to our house ; we should not be allowed to meet, and that would not be nice, and if I marry without the consent of my guardians, who would, of course, be guided by my mother, I forfeit my fortune."

" I don't care anything about your fortune."

" But I do, I have heard my father say that only fools despise money, and I think he was right. It would be dreadful to marry on narrow means. Fancy not being able to buy pictures and have things, and go on the Continent or to America whenever you wanted. You must let it be as I say, if you please, dear."

" I see," said Charlie thoughtfully, " we are to regard ourselves as being in love, but not engaged. Being in love is a state of mind ; an engagement is a quasi-contract. But how long ? "

" Until I am of age. I shall be eighteen next month."

" So long ? "

" Well, perhaps my mother might consent to our being engaged when I am twenty, or so—if you wish it very much, and please her in the meantime. But what does it matter so long as we love each other. Engaged couples are so stupid. Three months will be quite long enough to be ridiculous. And there is another reason for not saying anything—Edward."

" I think I know what you mean. Well, we must keep him in the dark—as long as we can. I say, Olive, what a wise little head you have got."

" It is an American head, Charlie, that is the reason. Now you must promise not to be jealous if I seem to prefer Edward to you sometimes, and let other men pay me little attentions —only, of course, to hoodwink the censorious and suspicious."

" All right ! I promise. Am I to consider myself at liberty to pay little attentions to other girls—to hoodwink the suspicious, you know."

" Certainly not. The idea ! Other girls, indeed ! All

you have to do is not to pay me marked attention—in public ;
or look at me too often or too ardently. If you do I shall
flirt outrageously, so mind."

And then as if to enforce the admonition, she gave him a
playful tap on the cheek, which Charlie resented, as a Chris-
tain should, with a kiss.

" But surely, Olive, you will meet me here sometimes, or
elsewhere," he said ruefully.

" If you are good and discreet ; and if we play our parts
properly and keep them in the dark we shall have many opportunities of exchanging a word. So long as we don't seem
to care for each other you will be a welcome guest at All Hallows. And now I am going to read you a lecture. You
won't be vexed ? "

Charlie warmly protested that he would not be vexed whatever she said, and putting his arm round her waist and taking one of her hands in his he bade her begin.

" You are a foolish boy," she said, smiling and nestling up
to him, " and I have a great mind to——"

" What ? "

" Leave you right away. Let me go."

" Not until I have had my lecture."

" We will take that as read, then, as they do at meetings,"
she said with a smile. " You had the substance of it as we
rode home after that good run with the harriers. But then I
was talking to you merely as a friend, rather telling you what
my mother said than I myself thought ; and perhaps she exaggerated, hoping thereby to make me think less of you."

" And she did not succeed."

" No, dear. All the same, I want my mother and my people in New England to think well of you—when they know—
and if they hear that you are merely a lawyer's clerk, and
that you give all your energy and your time to sport I am
afraid it will be just the other way. In America—I mean in
New England, for I know nothing of the South—everybody
works, the rich as well as the poor. My mother says she
would not give a fig for the man who has no occupation, or
who, having one, does not put all his energies into it. You
have now a great chance of securing yourself in her good
opinion. She is grateful for what you did yesterday ; and
thinks even that there is some advantage in fine horsemanship.
It is not a question of money. You will have some ; I shall

have a great deal; it is a question of having a purpose. And
I need not say how anxious I am that my Prince should be
well thought of by all who are dear to me."

"Is that all?" asked Charlie, after a minute's thought.

"Yes I have said my say."

"And a very good say too. What terribly earnest people
they must be in New England; and I really don't see the
good of being rich if you have to work as hard as if you were
poor. However, I am not rich, and I quite agree with you
that I ought to work harder than I have done. I knew that
you would expect me to turn over a new leaf, and I began
this morning, and did so well as to win high praise both from
my father and Lillywhite. And I mean to go on. I will win
your mother's good opinion, and when you meet your toiling
kinsfolk in New England you shall have no reason to be
ashamed of your young man. For the remainder of the season
I shall hunt only two days a week. I am through with my
articles. Next year my father will give me a small interest,
and I shall become a member of the firm. As for a purpose,
I have a threefold purpose—to be as smart a lawyer as Ned,
as honorable a gentleman as my father, and to make myself
worthy of the love of the best and dearest and sweetest girl
in the world."

"Oh, Charlie, you have made me so happy!" she cried
joyously. "And you are so clever that you can be anything
you like."

"Didn't you know that before?"

"I knew you were good and brave, but I was not so sure
about the cleverness. And—afterwards—my fortune will be
yours, you know—you must run for Parliament—I am sure
you could get in for Peele—you must run for Parliament and
become a great statesman—perhaps Prime Minister."

"Hadn't I better go to America, and run for the Presi-
dency?"

"You couldn't. You are not a born American. You
might get naturalized and go into Congress. But no, that
would not be good enough; the best people don't go into
Congress; our politicians, I am sorry to say, are, for the most
part, scallawags."

"That sounds very dreadful, dear, though I have not the
least idea what it is. Still, on the whole, I think I would
rather be an English Premier than an American scallawag.

I once thought of being a general; in dreams I have been an M. F. H. But I daresay the Premiership would suit me almost as well. Yes, I decide for the Premiership."

After the laugh which this sally provoked had subsided, and Olive had observed that more unlikely things had happened, she bethought her that it was time for them to part. Her mother would be wondering where she was ; and if she should send one of the maids to look for her the result would be too awful to contemplate. Charlie appreciated too keenly the necessity of prudence to press his sweetheart to prolong her stay.

He went with her to a point where the path bent towards the house—she would not let him go further for fear he should be seen—and there they parted as lovers (engaged or otherwise) are wont to part.

Charlie jumped no gates as he wended homewards ; for though happy and exultant, his exultation was not altogether free from apprehension. He had accepted new responsibilities, and the position of an accepted yet unbetrothed lover was not entirely to his mind. And if Ned were kept in the dark and Olive led him to think that he was not indifferent to her, he would have just cause for complaint, and when he knew the truth there would be a bitter quarrel, much unpleasantness and, perhaps, lifelong enmity between his brother and himself, to the great distress of his father and mother. The possibility was undeniable, and Charlie could not help asking himself whether it would not be better for him and Olive to avow their love and take the consequences? But Olive thought differently; her will was his law, and when he remembered that the avowal would be followed by an interdict on their lovemaking and, probably, by Mrs. Lincoln's departure from the neighborhood, he felt that he had not the courage to advise, or adopt, so bold a course.

" There will be a row in any case," he soliloquized ; " what is the good of meeting it half-way? If we can put it off a couple of years that will be so much to the good."

" How about Pringle's chimney ?" asked his father when they met at dinner.

" I had my walk for nothing. The chimney only wanted pointing and a new pot, and Pringle had it done himself."

" Just like Pringle ; he always calls out before he is hurt."

" Pringle ! You must have been close to All Hallows. Did
you call ? " asked Edward suspiciously.

" No ! But I suppose it will be our duty to call in the
course of the week. Will you go with me ? "

Edward would rather have gone alone, but seeing that if
he went alone, Charles would also go alone, he said " yes,"
and it was agreed that they should call on the following
Thursday.

Both he and his mother had been a good deal exercised in
their minds by Charlie's rescue of Olive.

" I am glad he showed so much courage and presence of
mind, and it is a mercy dear Olive was not killed," said Mrs.
Prince. " But I wish you had been the rescuer. It is just
the sort of thing that makes an impression on a young girl's
mind—dramatic and romantic and that. However, as Charlie
cares nothing about girls, and is not her ideal, I don't think
any harm will come of it."

Whatever misgivings Edward might have had were set at
rest by his visit to All Hallows. Mrs. Lincoln thanked Charlie
warmly for his rescue of Olive and lauded his gallantry, and
while he talked with the mother Edward talked with the
daughter, who seemed pleased with his company and was
more gracious to him than she had ever been before. But
while her smiles were for him, the responsive pressure of her
hand was for Charlie, and both brothers went away happy,
the one in the belief that he had made an impression, the
other in the assurance that he was the favored swain.

As owing to bad weather and stress of circumstances the
King's Path was not always available the lovers had to do
most of their courting in the hunting field. It was the only
place where they could talk freely ; and as Mrs. Lincoln had
asked Charlie to act as her daughter's pilot he was doing no
more than his duty in looking after her. Nevertheless, when
Edward was out she rather affected his company, and gave
him frequent opportunity of paying her the little attentions
to which his mother attached so much importance. This
was generally when they were riding to the meet or drawing
the first cover ; for, after the fox went away, he had to give
place to his younger brother, and, as often as not, was either
left behind or thrown out, the result being that three times
out of four Olive and Charlie found themselves together at
the close of the day, and had a delightful ride home together.

On the whole, however, Edward was well satisfied with the way in which things were shaping. The hunting season would not last forever, and when it was over his innings would begin. Meanwhile, as the result of close observation, he had arrived at three very definite and comforting assurances—that his attentions were beginning to tell, that Olive's liking for Charlie, never more than a feeling of *camaraderie*, was fast changing into indifference, and that Charlie had not yet turned his thoughts to love. Rather was he turning them to business, buckling to, as his father and Lillywhite always said he would, and working almost as industriously as his elders.

From all of which it may be inferred that the lovers were playing their parts well. They, too, were satisfied, so were Mrs. Lincoln and Mrs. Prince,—the one because she felt sure that her fears touching the relations of her daughter and Charlie were groundless ; the other because she was equally confident that her plan for a marriage between Olive and Edward was working to a successful issue.

CHAPTER XII.

THROWN OUT.

IT was one of the last days of the season : the winter was past and spring was coming forth in all her glory. The erstwhile dark wheat fields had donned their livery of green ; farmers were busy harrowing their meadows and making up their fences ; hedgerows were beginning to bud, birds to build their nests, and gentleman foxes to ramble from their native wilds and be out o' nights.

It was one of the last days of the season and the Riversdale hounds were meeting at Blackthorn. Not a favorite fixture by any means, Blackthorn being a great wood, as big as a small forest, where it was easy to go astray, and which it was difficult to make a fox quit. On the other hand, Blackthorn was a sure find, and when the hounds got away with one of the right sort the result was generally satisfactory to the fortunate few who happened to see him break cover or hear the halloes of those who did ; to the residue and remainder confusion and disappointment.

Nevertheless, there was a full muster, for the weather was propitious, and devotees of the sport were eager to put in all the hunting they could before Diana for a season bade the world farewell.

Among those present were Olive Lincoln and the two Princes, who, with their horses, had "railed" from Peele to a station some three miles ride of Blackthorn. *En route* Edward had been very fortunate ; he sat opposite to Olive, and talked to her, and feasted his eyes on her all the way ; for that had come to pass which he once expressed himself to his mother as fearing—he was smitten, and so deeply withal that the material advantages which a marriage with Miss Lincoln would bring him faded into insignificance as compared with the fair girl herself. At the station he superintended the unboxing of Olive's horse, helped her to mount, and rode with her to cover, Charlie pairing off with the second Miss Spankaway, one of a trio of red-haired, hard-riding sisters.

At the cover side counsels were divided, even the knowing ones hesitating whither to betake themselves. Some tried to follow the hounds into the thick of the wood, others kept in the rides or stole round to points where they thought the fox might break; the majority, of whom were our friends, took post to windward of the wood.

While Edward, who had a weakness for big-wigs, was being introduced by the secretary to Sir Somebody Something, a distinguished stranger from a distance, and Lydia Spankaway was talking to Mrs. Rivers, Charlie exchanged signals with Olive, and then turned his horse quietly into a contiguous ride. She followed, and presently came up with him.

"Do you think we are going in the right direction?" she asked. "Have they found a fox?"

"I have not the remotest idea, I wanted to give Ned and Lydia Spankaway the slip and have a talk with you, dearest. Don't you think I care more for you than for all the foxes in the country?"

"I hope so. All the same, there is something in your tone—you speak as if you were not quite happy."

"How can I be quite happy? Did not Ned monopolize you all the way, and the last time we were out you flirted with Teddy Spankaway all the time."

"How horrid you are, Charlie," returned Olive with her prettiest pout. "Didn't you promise not to be vexed if I pretended not to care for you, and let other men pay me little attentions?"

"I call them big attentions, and you flirt as if you liked it," muttered the young fellow.

"Well, I do, just a little. It is great fun. Your brother was quite wild when I was flirting with your friend Teddy the other day, and I dearly like to tease Edward. He thinks so much of himself. All the same, I almost think I did him an injustice in saying that my fortune was the exclusive object of his affections. I begin to think he is half in love with me."

"Of course he is; everybody is."

"Not quite so bad as that, I hope, Charlie dear. You must not imagine that everybody is as infatuated as yourself. And don't be jealous and absurd. Rather give me credit for

tact and fine management. Nobody either suspects us or
talks about us ; and you know that I love you. What would
you have more ? "

Charlie saw that it was time to climb down.

" You are quite right. You are always right," he said,
penitently. " I am an ass, a dolt, and you are wise and
clever. But I love you so dearly that I begrudge every smile
that you give to another. It is one the less for me."

" You avaricious wretch ! Cannot you console yourself
with Lydia Spankaway ? She is always smiling on you."

" Hang Lydia Spankaway ! She is always smiling on everybody. Her life is a perpetual giggle."

The words were hardly spoken when the young woman in
question and her brother came tumbling out of the wood a
few yards ahead of them.

" Where are the hounds ? " asked the brother.

" That is just the question I was going to ask you, Teddy,"
said Charlie.

" We tried to follow them into the hollow and got bogged."

" Of course."

" By Jove, I believe I heard a hallo. Come along, Lydia.
Won't you come, Prince ? "

" No. We are just as well here, and if you ride to every
semblance of a shout you hear, your horse will be used up
before the fun begins."

" It's a view hallo. I'll swear it's a view hallo," exclaimed
the youth excitedly. " Come along, Lydia. If they have
gone away I'll give a screech, and if they come this way, you
do as much for us, there's a good fellow."

And with that Mr. Spankaway and his sister went off at
full gallop.

" Do you think they are gone away ? " inquired Olive,
anxiously.

" As likely as not."

" Then why ?——"

" Why don't we ride after the Spankaways ? Because I
would rather ride home with you, darling ! "

" Ride home with me ? What ? Listen ! I am sure that
is Teddy screeching."

" Let him screech. I'd rather ride quietly home with you
than have a galloping run of forty minutes without a check.
It is almost our last chance. The season is as good as over,

and I doubt whether we shall be able to contrive a *tête-à-tête* of more than a few minutes all summer. Now the days are so long the King's Path is not safe—too many people about."

"But isn't it a very long way, and won't it seem strange?"

"Only fifteen miles, and our horses are fresh, and we can gruel them and get a cup of tea at the Beehive. And there is nothing strange in losing hounds in Blackthorn high woods. Half the field will be in the same fix; and having lost them, it will be better for us to go straight home than potter about here for the remainder of the day, or wait in the village for the 4.30 train."

"I am not sure that it will be quite wise," said Olive passively. "All the same; if it will give you pleasure——"

"Give me pleasure? Oh, Olive, if you only knew. This way," and with that he turned his horse in the direction of Teddy Spankaway's last screech.

"You are going to look for the hounds, then?"

"We must find out what has become of them. They may be in the wood yet. It would never do to leave without having a proper tale to tell when we get home."

Olive smiled. It pleased her to think that, impetuous though he was, her lover had not altogether lost sight of prudence.

As they went on they were joined by many others, and presently the master himself came up in a great heat and asked the question everybody else was asking, "Where are the hounds?" and like everybody else got no answer.

"I do believe they have slipped away," he said.

And so it proved. On reaching the confines of the wood they found there several yokels and second horsemen, from whom they learnt that the hounds had gone away ten minutes previously, Quickly and some two score gentlemen with them, very fast, and as it seemed, running towards Sandford.

"What a sell!" chorused twenty voices.

"I shall go on and try to nick in; they may check or run a ring," said the master, and off he went, followed by a dozen of the belated ones, whose number was continually increasing.

"Not a bit of use," said another. "Ten minutes' start and a fast thing. They will only hammer their horses' legs to pieces on the hard high-road. I shall chuck it up and go home."

" I suppose we had better do the same," observed Charlie to Olive, as if the idea were occurring to him for the first time. " If we try to overtake them we shall only use up our horses to no purpose."

" You think it would be a vain pursuit, then ? "

" Decidedly."

" Very well. Let us go home, then. Which is the way ? "

Several of the others set off with them ; but they soon parted company, and Charlie had Olive all to himself for the rest of the ride, and a delightful, long drawn out ride it was—through green lanes and pleasant bridle-paths, past ancient halls nestling among trees, farmhouses with red roofs and high gables, and barns such as are not built nowadays —big enough for cathedrals—and quaintly picturesque churches, whose ivy-mantled towers looked down on the dust of twenty generations.

At the Beehive, an old timbered inn, which had been a house of entertainment since the dissolution of the monasteries, the travellers halted to bait their horses and refresh themselves. Tea was served in a snug little parlor with black oak wainscoting and diamond shaped window panes, looking into a venerable garden ; and as there was nobody in the garden, and the lovers were sole occupants of the parlor, they were quite happy, forgetting for a while everything but themselves and their love, and lingering perhaps longer than was altogether wise. Nevertheless, they reached home an hour sooner than they would have done had they returned by rail.

" What will Edward say ? " asked Olive, as they reined up at All Hallows lodge gates.

" I do not see that he has a right to say anything. I am your duly appointed pilot ; and I have taken you home many a time before."

" The circumstances were very different, though. We have been alone nearly all day, and he will be vexed at being left to train home by himself—perhaps say something to mother which may reawaken her suspicions. Anyhow, for the next few weeks we shall need to be extremely circumspect, and I will be very gracious to Edward. No, don't come up to the house with me. If mother thinks you are neglecting me, so much the better. Good-night, Charlie, dear."

"Good-night, darling. This has been the happiest day I ever had in my life."

"I hope we may not have to pay a heavy price for it," thought Olive as she trotted up the avenue, "but something tells me that Edward will be very angry—and I distrust him more than I like to let Charlie know. Dear old Charlie! How strange it is that two brothers should be so different."

CHAPTER XIII.

JEALOUS.

EDWARD did not miss the lovers until some time after
they had stolen away. Then, after making several fruitless
inquiries, he went to look for them. He might as well have
looked for a needle in a haystack ; but while he was seeking the lovers he found the hounds, and the hounds found a
fox. Feeling sure that he was now on the right track, he
rode to the first whip's in view hallo, and was one of the
first out of the wood ; and having no doubt that he should
presently encounter Charlie and Olive (who were generally
in the first flight) went boldly on. But the field being rather
scattered and the country rather heavily timbered, he looked
for the fugitives in vain, and had to console himself with
the reflection that he should find them with the hounds
checked—or, at any rate, at the end of the run, which he
devoutly hoped would not be long. It lasted a good hour;
the latter part of it, however, being rather slow, and ended
in the middle of a covert, where Reynard ran into a drain
and could not be persuaded to come out and be killed.

Edward, who thanks to easy fences and a line of gates,
was well up, looked round, and when he saw nothing of those
whom he sought his first feeling was a sense of elation. He
had beaten his brother for once. But when the last of the
laggards appeared on the scene, and the said brother and
the young lady were still invisible, he began to feel uneasy.

" Have you seen anything of my brother and Miss Lincoln ? " he asked of Teddy Spankaway, who was standing at
his horse's head, devouring a ham sandwich and drinking
whiskey and water from an electro-plated flask.

" The last time I saw them was in Blackthorn Wood and
very thick they seemed."

" Thick ! What do you mean ? "

" They were in close converse, and very near together—
heads almost touching, in fact—and though I told them I

had heard a hallo, and when I knew the hounds were running gave a screech which I am sure they must have heard,
they did not come on. Anyhow they are out of it, and I
expect that is where they want to be. That brother of yours
is a sly dog, Prince, and Miss Lincoln is a deuced nice girl."

And then Mr. Spankaway, who was himself rather sweet
on Olive, and jealous of Charlie, laughed maliciously and
offered Edward his flask. Edward tried to look unconcerned,
muttered something about the possibility of anybody losing
hounds in Blackthorn Wood, and asked whether they were
going to draw again.

"Of course we are, as soon as the master turns up. He
has been thrown out—not often that happens, though—and
I expect Quickly will take the hounds back on the off chance
of falling in with him. Do you know your horse has lost a
shoe?"

"Confound it! So he has. Where is there a forge?"

"Down the road to the right; near the windmill."

The loss of the shoe delayed Edward half-an-hour, and
when he set his face towards Blackthorn, hounds and hunters
were nowhere to be seen; but presently he met a groom
with a lame horse, who was able to tell him that Mr. Brown
had fallen in with the hounds, and that his brother and Miss
Lincoln were gone home.

"But there is no train till 4.30."

"I think they are hacking all the way, sir."

"The deuce they are!" and Edward Prince went on, looking as black as thunder and in a very evil frame of mind.

Teddy Spankaway's words had reawakened the suspicion he
had once entertained, that Olive and Charlie had a sneaking
kindness for, and, perhaps, a secret understanding with each
other.

"It looks like a planned thing," he thought. "It looks as
if they had stopped in the covert on purpose. Anybody
may lose hounds in that horrid wood; but why did not
they come on with Brown, and why, oh why, have they
gone home by road without waiting for me, or making an
effort to find me? It is not fair, it is not right, it is scarcely
courteous."

Edward was furiously jealous; the idea of being supplanted
by his brother, whom in his heart he rather despised,
was gall and wormwood to him, and he had made so sure

that Olive liked him and cared no more for Charlie than Charlie cared for her that the disappointment was doubly bitter. He had been deceived, played with, made a "spoon handle of," and he said in his anger that he would let "those two" see that he could not be befooled with impunity.

But when he cooled down somewhat and considered the matter further, he perceived that he had really very little ground for complaint; the existence of a secret understanding between Olive and Charlie had still to be proved. Spankaway, a mere sporting man, who regarded coarse jokes as high wit, was quite capable of straining a point to provoke a laugh. He had no doubt grossly exaggerated, if not actually invented; and, after all, there was nothing very alarming in Charlie and Olive being left behind for once in a way, and hacking home instead of waiting for a train. In like circumstances he would probably have done the same.

Notwithstanding this commendable effort to weigh both sides of the question Edward was suspicious still. Though the circumstances were consistent with either theory, the thoughts and memories which came unbidden to his mind fed the flame of his jealousy, and he felt intensely anxious to know the truth. But how was he to know it? He could not openly ask Charlie without risking a rebuff and showing his own hand. He was neither his brother's keeper nor Olive's guardian. Charlie had just as much right to fall in love with her as he had, and would certainly refuse to disclose anything which might compromise her, or which he desired in his own interest or hers to keep secret.

After long cogitation Edward made up his mind to dissemble his jealousy and keep his suspicions to himself. Until he had evidence that Olive and Charlie were carrying on a clandestine courtship he would not say a word to anybody—even to his mother. But he would seek for evidence, leave no stone unturned to obtain it, and when he had obtained it, act. How, he could not, as yet, decide; that would depend on circumstances; only he was fully resolved that Olive should be his and not Charlie's. The mere thought that he might lose her angered him almost past bearing. He had known for sometime that he loved Olive, but never until then had he realized the intensity of his passion, and how necessary to his happiness she was become.

Charlie, indeed! Charlie's partiality for Olive—if it existed—was mere calf love, the fugitive fancy of an overgrown boy, who took no thought for the morrow ; his, the strong love of a mature man, who had formed definite views of life and meant to get on. If the matter were fairly put to Olive there could, he felt sure, be no question as to her choice. Meanwhile, the fair putting being neither feasible nor expedient, there was nothing for it but to wait, and, as Edward said to himself, everything comes to the man who knows how to wait—and watch.

His first question to the groom who met him at Peele station was whether his brother had returned.

" Yes, sir ; he hacked."

" He got home early, then ? "

" Not very. About half-past five, I think. It is a longish way from Blackthorn."

" Fifteen miles ; they took five hours to ride fifteen miles, and their horses quite fresh," thought Edward. " What could they be doing all the time ? " And the demon of jealousy gnawed harder at his heart than ever. But when he got home and met Charlie in the hall he smiled pleasantly.

" A nice fellow you are, to run away and leave me to come home alone," quoth he.

" Nay, it was you who ran away and left us. When we got out of the covert you were *non est*, and you had been gone so long that there was no chance of overtaking you. So we just hacked home, Olive and I."

" You did not stop anywhere, then ? "

" Only at the Beehive to gruel. Had you a good run ? "

" A regular clinker. A good sixty minutes, first twenty as fast as we could leg it, and lost the fox in a drain at Slasher's Mill."

" And we were out of it ! But make haste and get changed. The pater wants you in his room."

" What's in the wind now ? "

" A family council. You are required to make it complete, so hurry up."

Edward, though particular about his person, and generally slow over his toilet, did hurry up, and, on entering his father's room some fifteen minutes later, found the other members of the family in deep consultation. The matter was this :—

The firm of Lincoln, Lyman, and Jump (whose affairs were in Chancery) had made heavy advances to one of their correspondents in Trinidad, on the security of various properties there. The correspondent in question having failed, and the amount involved being large, and the business complicated, it was considered necessary to send somebody out to protect the interests of the house and realize the hypothecated properties; and in the opinion of the Vice-Chancellor no gentleman could so well perform this duty as Mr. Leonard Prince; he was a lawyer, a man of business, and had all the facts at his fingers' ends. Would he accept the commission, and on what terms?

"The letter came after you were gone, this morning," said Mr. Prince to Edward, "and, as you see, it requires a prompt answer. Mother and Charlie are rather for it. They are pleased to think the trip would do me good. What is your opinion?"

Edward was also rather for it. Like the others, he thought the trip would do his father good; moreover, during his absence he would naturally take his father's place in the office, and represent him in the town, and the idea pleased Edward. But he was not the man to answer an important question by simply saying ditto to somebody else.

"What is your opinion?" repeated Mr. Prince.

"What is my opinion?" said Edward, knitting his brows and looking wondrous wise. "This is a very serious matter, and requires a good deal of consideration. Mother and Charlie think the trip would do you good. I hope they are right; but what is their authority? These West India Islands are not generally supposed to be the most healthy places in the world."

"Mr. Lincoln had been several times to Trinidad, and I have heard him say that the island was healthy and the voyage there pleasant."

"Then we may regard that point as settled. The next is, can you be spared?"

"That is rather for you to say. Charlie has been doing very well lately, and I don't see why you, and he, and Lilly-white should not be able to do without me for three or four months; and the pay I get for going out would be all to the good."

"Less the extra premium on your life policy."

Mr. Prince's countenance fell. Something was always happening to remind him of that terrible skeleton. Only the

week before Peploe and Pope had written to say that they
doubted whether they should be able to pay any more
interest.

"I had not thought of that," he said gravely. "It is not
indisputable, yet."

"It does not become indisputable for two years. In the
meantime you are limited to Europe and North America.
But the company would give you a license."

"Of course they would. But upon what terms? You had
better go to town to-morrow and ascertain. If they make
any charge at all it should be something quite nominal; as
my policy permits me to cross the Atlantic the mere voyage
involves no extra risk, and the trip out and home, and the
change and that, can hardly fail to benefit my health."

"That is a good point. I will urge it," said Ned, making
a memorandum in his note-book. "If this can be arranged
you will go, of course."

"I think so. It will be an agreeable trip, and a new experience; and they cannot give me less than five hundred
and my expenses."

"Five hundred is not enough, father. Shall I arrange
that for you also while I am in town?"

"By all means, Ned. You are a better hand at a bargain
than I am, and will probably get more than I should dare to
ask. And now, having finished our business, let us go in to
dinner."

The next morning Edward went to London, and justified
his father's opinion of his business capacity by making two
satisfactory bargains. By persuading the assurance company
that the contemplated voyage could not fail to benefit his
father's health he obtained the license on very favorable
terms, and by taking the opposite tack with the Chancery
people—dwelling on the perils of ocean travelling and the
manifold dangers of a tropical climate (especially for a man
at his father's time of life)—he obtained a hundred and fifty
pounds more than the sum which Mr. Prince had named, and
with which he would have been content.

Edward called this diplomacy, his father would have called
it sharp practice—if he had known the facts—but Mr.
Prince was too well satisfied with the result to be inquisitive
about details, and the money would be very useful.

The license granted by the Insurance Company (in consideration of a payment of twenty pounds) was for a voyage to Trinidad and back per Royal Mail steamer, and the perils incident thereto, and a residence in the island not exceeding three months—unless Mr. Prince should be detained there longer than that period by circumstances beyond his control.

For a hundred and thirty pounds more the Company would have anticipated the time by which the policy was to become indisputable and made it "good for all the world." But as this seemed to Edward like paying so much money for nothing, he elected for the conditional license, and plumed himself on having scored a great success. But it is possible to be too clever, and in the issue Edward discovered that the proverb about a penny saved being a penny gained is not of universal application.

CHAPTER XIV.

LILLYWHITE'S DEMAND.

MR. PRINCE'S main (though unconfessed) reason for desiring to go to the West Indies was that he might get away from the skeleton for a time. With three or four thousand miles of ocean rolling between them, it would (metaphorically) be out of sight, and, as he hoped, out of mind. The fresh scenes he should behold and the new and varied impressions he should receive must needs divert the current of his thoughts, and he would enjoy a short interlude of peace, which he sorely needed, for latterly the skeleton had been unpleasantly obtrusive.

After paying the agreed interest in full, though intermittently, for three years Peploe and Pope had suddenly ceased their remittances and intimated pretty plainly that it was unlikely they would ever be resumed. This meant a loss of six hundred a year ; and the premium on the triple life policy brought up to a thousand pounds, per annum the cost of keeping the skeleton under lock and key. But for the profits arising out of the Lincoln lawsuit the burden would have been almost more than Mr. Prince could bear without making such retrenchments as would seriously affect his position in the town. For Mrs. Lincoln's sake he wanted the suit to end ; for his own, it was better for it to go on—a conflict of interest that sometimes rendered it difficult for him to advise his client with that singleness of purpose which for three generations had been the rule of the office.

Edward, on the other hand, was rather disposed, for financial reasons, to protract the suit, and father and son had occasionally " words " on the subject. The young man had, moreover, an unpleasant way of referring to the skeleton as that " terrible business," and hinting that in using Mrs. Lincoln's trust fund to square Peploe and Pope, his father had committed a fatal mistake. This Mr. Prince knew only too well ; but he did not like being told so. It was as bad as rubbing bay salt into an open wound. Nor did he in his heart approve in his wife's project for making a match between Edward and Olive. There was something underhand about it; he had a great regard for Olive, and felt sure that Edward and she would not pull well together. But Dorothy had set her mind on it, and if he could not successfully oppose her alone much less could he do so when she was supported by Edward, who was a host in himself, and to whom the knowledge of the secret gave additional power.

Oppressed by all these cares, and feeling as he had never felt before the weight of years, there were times when Mr. Prince wished himself dead. His death would settle everything, the assurance money make good his breach of trust, and though he could not leave his sons a fortune he should leave them an excellent business, and a name free from reproach. These fits of depression were, however, infrequent, and he was forgetting his worries in the work of preparing for the approaching voyage, and beginning to contemplate the future more hopefully, when an incident occurred that revived his fears, and gave him the most severe shock he had sustained since the discovery of Jack's defalcations.

Two or three days before his departure he was in his room, looking over papers, and making notes for Edward's guidance during his absence, when the door opened and in walked Lillywhite. In this there was nothing unusual, but the deliberation of the managing clerk's movements, and the solemnity of his visage, bespoke the importance of his errand.

"What is it, now, Lillywhite?" said Mr. Prince, looking up. "Has our best client run away without paying his bill of costs, or does Mr. Trumpler want a new will making?"

Instead of greeting his employer's joke with a smile, Lillywhite looked more solemn than ever.

"It is not office business this time, Mr. Prince. It's touching a matter personal to our two selves that I want a word with you."

"Can he want his salary raised?" thought Mr. Prince. "All right, Lillywhite. If there is anything I can do for you, I am sure I shall be very happy——"

"You set sail on Friday?"

"God bless me! Is that what you had to say?" quoth Mr. Prince with a laugh. "Yes, I set sail on Friday."

"I hope you will come back, sir."

" 'Pon my word, Lillywhite! Of course I shall come back. Why not?"

"Well, there's a sight of water between this and the West Indies; and where there is water there is danger. I never liked it—neither inside or out. I don't want to discourage you, sir, but I cannot help thinking that it is a very hazardous undertaking for a gentleman at your time of life. And as you may never come back, though I sincerely hope you will, I should like to have a proper understanding."

"As to what? For heaven's sake come to the point, Lillywhite. For you know how busy I am."

"My position in the office."

"Your position will be what it has been—that of managing clerk."

"Under Mr. Edward?"

"Of course. You surely don't suppose that he will be under you?"

"He might do worse. He has not all the sense in the world, though he evidently thinks so; and his manner to me is often very discourteous, almost offensive, indeed; and if I am to be under him during your absence, he must promise to treat me with becoming respect, also I should like a slight increase of salary."

"Anything else?" asked Mr. Prince, sarcastically. "You had better open your mouth wide enough while you are about it."

"Not at present. I think that will do till you come back."

"Not at present! Gad, you speak as if you were surprised at your own moderation. You have been with me a long time—more than twenty years."

"Twenty-two on the tenth of next month."

"Twenty-two, then; and served me well and faithfully, and I have treated you handsomely, giving you my entire confidence, and letting you have pretty nearly your own way in everything. In point of fact, I have spoiled you. It is as Edward said the other day. You cannot stand corn. You are getting above yourself."

"Edward said that, did he? I am obliged to him," interposed the managing clerk, with an angry shake of his portentous nose, which, after blushing violently, had become almost blue.

"You are getting above yourself," repeated Mr. Prince, heedless of the interruption, "and as your demands are unreasonable and cannot be complied with, I fear we shall have to part—unless you choose to withdraw them. Think about it, Lillywhite. I should be sorry for you to decide hastily."

"I have thought about it already, and my mind is made up. But before you finally make up yours, sir, there is one observation I should like to make. You say you have given me your entire confidence. So you have—with one exception —and a very important exception."

"What is that, Lillywhite ? "

"The matter of your son John and Peploe and Pope."

Mr. Prince turned as pale as if the cupboard had opened of itself and the skeleton had walked into the room.

"My son John—Peploe and Pope ! What do you mean ? " he exclaimed, trying to keep his countenance.

"I guess you know, sir," returned Lillywhite grimly. "I can perhaps put two and two together, and likewise see as far into a stone wall as anybody else. When Peploe came here three or four years since I thought something was wrong—he would not come all the way from Liverpool for nothing—and when I heard that Mr. John had got into debt and run away I felt sure something was wrong. I took Peploe's measure. He would not have cared a button top how much Mr. John got into debt—so long as it was not to him. So I put two and two together and from certain things that happened at that time and afterwards I came to the conclusion that you had sold out Mrs. Lincoln's——"

"Lillywhite, I did not expect this of you," interrupted Mr. Prince in a voice of bitter reproach. "You have been playing as spy, prying into affairs that do not concern you, and I very much fear opening my private letters."

"No, sir ! no, sir ! no, sir ! " thundered the clerk, emphasizing each denial with a resounding thump of his fist on the table. "I never opened a private letter of yours in my life. I would scorn to stoop to any such rascality. I am curious, I know, but I am not a scoundrel. But those who run may read, Mr. Prince. The outward appearance of a letter, like the outward appearance of a man, often gives a clue to what is inside. The way of it was this, sir ; when that unfortunate affair took place, and I saw that you could not or would not trust me, I felt hurt, and I resolved to fathom the mystery —by strictly honorable means, of course. Peploe comes, unexpectedly, stays a long time, and leaves you much disturbed. The next day you go off and don't return for three or four days. You decline to sell out Mrs. Lincoln's stock and lend the money on mortgage as I proposed. Nevertheless, there comes a letter from the Bank of England, which unless I am much mistaken, was an intimation that application had been made for power of attorney to sell out stock, and I knew, of course, that Mrs. Lincoln's was the only trust money we had in Consols ; also, before that her dividends passed through my hands, whereas, afterwards, you took the management of the trust entirely into your own. From these, and other circumstances, which I need not mention, I drew certain conclusions."

"Ah ! You drew certain conclusions. What were they ? You may speak fully; but bear in mind, please, that inferences are not evidence, and 1 admit nothing."

"I did not suppose you would, sir—at first. It is a safe rule not to admit anything. Well, my conclusions—or if you like it better, my suspicions—amounted to this ; that your son got into trouble about a bit of paper, or something of the kind, and to prevent him from being prosecuted you made up the deficiency by—shall we say borrowing ?—the whole or the greater part of Mrs. Lincoln's trust fund. When Mr. John appeared here a little while ago, disguised as a tramp, these suspicions became absolute certainty. People don't run away and return in disguise for nothing more serious than contracting debts which they are unable to pay."

"Jack here ! Jack in disguise !" exclaimed Mr. Prince, after a long stare of bewilderment and surprise. " Preposterous ! It is absurd, impossible. This is an invention of your own, Lillywhite, a wicked invention."

"It is no invention, sir, though I judge by your manner that you were not aware of the circumstance," returned the clerk quietly. "I saw Mr. John with my own eyes."

"You did, really, Lillywhite? You are sure you are not deceiving me ?" said Mr. Prince, in a husky voice, as he wiped away the sweat which stood in big beads on his forehead.

"I did, sir, and I am not the only one that saw him. One evening, about the end of October or the beginning of

November—I have the exact date in my diary—I met a tramp
in Church-lane, in whose appearance, though his clothes
were ragged, and he had a patch over his left eye, there was
something strangely familiar to me. All the same, I could
not make him out, but I'm naturally of a curious turn, and as
I never like to have an unsatisfied doubt on my mind, I
just followed my young gentleman, which the growing dark-
ness enabled me to do without attracting his attention. He
took the road to Holmcroft, and when I saw him enter your
grounds the mystery was solved. I knew that the tramp was
John Prince."

Mr. Prince's face broke into a smile of relief. It was not
as bad as he thought. Lillywhite was either trying to impose
on him or had found a mare's nest.

"What nonsense!" he said. "How could you know anything of the sort? Not a day passes that half-a-dozen unrec-
ognizable tramps don't come begging to Holmcroft."

"Wait a minute, sir, I have not done yet. On the following night I happened to drop into the 'Blue Bear,' and there
met Turnbull, the leather-seller, who was just back from
London. He went by parliamentary train the same morning,
and saw a man with a patch over his left eye, who got in at
Peele and got out at London, for all the world like John
Prince."

"It was not John Prince. It could not be John Prince.
Do you think that if he had been here and come to Holmcroft
I should not have known? You are mistaken and Turnbull
is a fool. And now let us come to the point. I have no
time for more talk. You think you have found something
out and want paying for your silence. Mind, I don't admit
you have found anything out of importance, and if you were
to say outside what you have been saying to me now I should
either treat it with silent contempt or prosecute you for slander. But I detest scandal and I don't want to have my
family affairs discussed in every tap-room in the town.

"So let me know, please, at how much you value your
silence, which, allow me to remind you, it is your duty to observe in any circumstances. To divulge anything you may
have learnt here would be—a gross breach of trust," Mr.
Prince was going to say, but remembering that he had himself committed a still grosser offence of the same sort and
fearing a *tu quoque*, he stopped short.

"Oh sir, you do me a great injustice," protested Lillywhite, in a tone of injured innocence, which Mr. Prince thought was put on, but which may well have been sincere. "You do me a great injustice. All that comes to my knowledge professionally I regard as sacred; but what I discover is surely my own property, in the sense that I may keep it secret or not at my pleasure. And I ask no price for my silence—merely such a modest increase of my salary as my long and faithful services deserve—say a hundred a year—and the assurance that during your absence Mr. Edward will treat me with ordinary courtesy and respect."

"I engage that he shall do so. You shall also have the increase you ask for, but you will please to remember that if you do not observe the most absolute discretion we shall have to part. When Mr. Edward comes in be good enough to tell him I would like to speak to him."

The clerk, who was evidently rather taken aback by the firmness of his principal's manner, rose from his chair, bowed and retired.

"D—— Mr. Edward," he muttered when he was outside. "I'll be even with that jackanapes one of these days. The governor put a better face on it towards the last than I expected. But he could not deny it: he could not deny it—and if he had given me his confidence at the beginning he would have saved himself a hundred a year."

"My God, what a life," murmured Mr. Prince, leaning his head on his hands. "Why did I let Dorothy over persuade me? Why didn't I have the courage of my opinions and face the thing? It would have been forgotten by this time. . . . How I have been deceived. And Lillywhite! He professes to be hurt because I did not give him my confidence. That would not have mended matters at all. I should be more in his power than I am now; and I fancy he cares quite as much for power as money. If he had asked for two hundred I should have had to give it him."

Presently Edward came in. His father told him what had happened.

"Dear me! Dear me!" he exclaimed. "That terrible business again. What will be the end of it?"

"That is the question I often ask myself. I often think it will be the end of me, and that would perhaps be the best of all. The insurance money would put everything straight.

One man can steal a horse, while another may not look over a gate. It seems hard that I should be harassed in this way for a single dereliction of duty—the only one, as I can truly say, which I ever committed."

"It was worse than a dereliction of duty, father. It was a blunder. And I am rather afraid, it was another blunder giving in to Lillywhite. He knows nothing; it is all surmise. In your place I should have set him at defiance."

"No, no, Ned, that would not do at all. If I did that I should make an enemy of him at once. He would talk. Think what a fine handle such a rumor would be for the Radicals. Mrs. Lincoln would be sure to hear of it, and though she should regard it as a base calumny she might propose to lessen my responsibility by appointing another trustee; and a trustee in my position should be above suspicion. . . . . Do you know, I think Lillywhite really believed that the tramp he saw going to Holmcroft was Jack!"

"Very likely. Nothing is easier than to confound one person with another—especially after dark. The leather-seller's story also belongs to the category of illusions. You may depend upon it that Jack is thousands of miles away from Peele."

"I hope he is. All the same—poor Jack!" and the father's eyes filled with tears.

Edward had very promptly decided to treat Lillywhite's statements as illusory, partly out of a commendable desire not to add to his father's anxieties on the eve of his departure; mainly because his father would be sure to tell his mother, and he feared her reproaches for keeping her in ignorance of the scapegrace's return and sending him away without giving her an opportunity of seeing him.

When Edward left his father's room he took Lillywhite aside.

"My father has told me what passed between you a little while ago," he said. "You want to be treated with more courtesy it seems. Well, I will treat you with more courtesy. Not because I am afraid of you, mind; merely because of my father's promise. But if I had been in his place, I should have promised nothing. I should have told you to do your worst."

"Then you would have done a very bad thing, sir. Your

father is a wiser man than you are ; though I daresay you don't think so."

Edward certainly did not think so. He looked on his father as old-fashioned, and lacking in judgment and resolution, and felt quite sure that he could have managed things a great deal better.

CHAPTER XV.

HER AMERICAN COUSIN.

WHEN it was fully decided that Mr. Prince should go to Trinidad and his passage was taken, and the day of his departure drew near, Mrs. Prince began to waver in her opinion as to the expediency of the undertaking; and cruel doubts assailed her mind. The voyage might do him good, the resulting gain would be very satisfactory—all to the good, as Mr. Prince had several times observed—but the way was long, the seas were treacherous, and shipwrecks, alas! only too common. It was hardly possible to open a newspaper without reading of some fresh disaster. What if disaster were to overtake him? What if the ship in which he was to sail should be lost? She would never forgive herself for allowing him to go. The mere thought thrilled her with anguish, and if she had not confided her fears to Mrs. Lincoln it is quite likely that she would have made an effort to prevent her husband from implementing the agreement which she herself had sanctioned.

Mrs. Lincoln, who had a cheery manner and a sympathetic nature, comforted her friend with kindly words.

"Danger!" she said. "Do you know, I believe there is no more danger at sea than on land. I have crossed the Atlantic twenty times, and I don't believe I was ever in more danger than I am at this moment. And there is less danger in a voyage to the West Indies than to New York. In going south you encounter neither icebergs nor fogs (she wisely said nothing of earthquakes and cyclones). Once out of European waters you are sailing in summer seas. You leave winter and hard weather behind you, and have nothing to do but read novels and bask in the sun. The voyage will do your husband all the good in the world : he will have a real good time, and come back looking ten years younger. He

needs a change. He has been looking very fagged lately,
don't you think?"

"I don't think he is looking quite so well as he used to
do."

"It is a long time since he has looked as well as he did
when I first knew him. It is all this dreadful lawsuit.
Merely to think of it makes my head ache. No wonder,
with such a weight on his mind, he looks ill. But don't
worry. The voyage will set him right. And don't damp
his spirits by losing your own. Let him go away cheerful,
whatever you do."

Mrs. Prince, who had an uneasy feeling that the cause of
her husband's fagged looks lay much deeper than any lawsuit, took this advice in good part. She also allowed Mrs.
Lincoln to dissuade her from accompanying her husband to
Southampton as she had intended. It would only make
them both "feel bad," said her friend, and serve no useful
purpose. So Charlie accompanied him instead, and after an
affectionate though not painful parting with his wife, Mr.
Prince "went away cheerful"—at any rate, looking cheerful.

But he was worn out with anxiety and work, and the train
was no sooner in motion than he leaned back in his corner
and slept; dreaming of Jack, who since the interview with
Lillywhite, had been much in Mr. Prince's mind. Despite
the incredulity which he had avowed, and at the same time
felt, touching the clerk's statement he could not rid himself
of a suspicion that it might be true after all. It was conceivable that Jack had returned to Peele, disguised as a tramp,
and that, his courage failing him at the last moment, he went
away without making himself known.

When Mr. Prince awoke he began to talk to Charlie on
the subject which was uppermost in his thoughts.

"Do you ever think of Jack?" he asked him abruptly.

Charlie, startled by the unexpected question, and feeling
rather guilty, admitted that he did sometimes think about his
eldest brother.

"He behaved very ill; nearly broke our hearts, in fact,"
said Mr. Prince, sadly, "but that is no reason why he should
be entirely forgotten."

And then he told the strange tale of the tramp whom
Lillywhite, taking for Jack, had followed to Holmcroft, and

his supposed recognition by Turnbull, the leather-seller, asking Charlie, in conclusion, whether he had ever heard of a more palpable case of mistaken identity.

This put Charlie in a dilemma. He had agreed with Edward to keep Jack's visit secret; but not telling something was a very different matter from telling a lie, especially to his father, who had always treated him with loving confidence, and to whom he had never lied even when he was a small boy.

" Did you ever know a more palpable case of mistaken identity ? " repeated Mr. Prince.

Still Charlie hesitated.

" Why don't you answer ? You surely don't think——"

" I cannot tell you a lie, father. The tramp Lillywhite saw was Jack. He came to Holmcroft."

" Came to Holmcroft! How ? Good heavens ; how did it happen, and why were we not told ? "

" We thought it would only make you and mother unhappy and do no good, and if we had taken him into the house the servants might have suspected something. He was in such a state—just like a common beggar, so we took him in the harness-room. He slept there."

" Well, perhaps you acted for the best," said Mr. Prince gloomily. " It would have been bad if the thing had got wind in the town. All the same, I should have been glad to see the lad, and I take it very unkindly of Ned that he kept me in the dark when I spoke to him the other day. It was not straightforward. Tell me all about it, Charlie—how he looked, where he had been, and what doing."

Charlie told him ; also that Jack had seen them at prayers through the dining-room window ; also of his vow that he would never touch drink again, or rest satisfied until he had repaid his father every penny that his defalcations had cost him.

" Jack makes vows with as much facility as he breaks them," said Mr. Prince bitterly. " When a man takes to drink he is generally past praying for. God ! What a wasted life."

" I don't think he was a confirmed drunkard," put in Charlie eagerly. " When he wrote to Ned acknowledging receipt of the money he said that since leaving Peele he had tasted nothing stronger than water, and never would. I believe Jack will be as good as his word this time, father."

" You are more sanguine than I am. If you only knew——"

Here Mr. Prince paused. He had been on the point of letting out the secret.

"Yes, father," said Charlie.

"If you only knew how much your mother and I have suffered because of him you would understand our feelings. But enough about Jack. Let us talk about yourself. You will stick to the shop while I am away and give Ned all the help you can."

"Of course I will, father, I give you my word."

"I know you don't take kindly to the law, and I am sorry we did not let you go into the army; and still more so that we did not let Jack go into the navy. But your mother thought differently and she had her way. However, use is second nature, and I have no doubt you will end in liking the profession, as I did myself. And now I am going to give you a word of advice—perhaps the last I ever shall give you."

"You are surely not growing nervous, father, or having presentiments, or anything of that sort," interrupted Charlie with a smile. "Everybody says that the risk of a voyage to Trinidad is well nigh infinitesimal."

"I was not thinking of the risk—merely of the uncertainty of life in general. Whenever a man goes away for three or four months there is always a possibility that he may never come back."

"And the advice?"

"Is this. It may happen to you in life to have to choose between following the dictates of your conscience and your judgment—acting, let us say, as if left to yourself it would be your duty to act—and pleasing somebody else, somebody, it may be, whom you are desirous to please and would make almost any sacrifices to serve, one who will put great pressure on you. In that case, dear boy, do the right thing, and, if you have any doubt, give conscience the benefit of it. It may be hard at the time, but you will be glad afterwards, and you will have nothing to reproach yourself with, and right can never be wrong, nor wrong right."

All this was uttered so earnestly, and with so much feeling, that if the speaker had been anybody but his own father Charlie might have surmised that he spoke from bitter experience, and in time past had sinned grievously against the light. He thanked him for his advice, and said that if occasion should arise he would do his best to follow it ; and then the subject dropped.

The arrival at Southampton, the trip from the shore to the ship, which lay at her moorings off Netley, the bustle and excitement on board raised Mr. Prince's drooping spirits. The day was beautifully fine, and it seemed certain that the voyage would, at any rate, begin well. Charlie went below, inspected his father's stateroom, and helped him to arrange his things.

Then they turned into the saloon and drank success to the voyage in sparkling moselle.

" I wish I were going with you, father," said Charlie. " I should like to go to the West Indies immensely. I have seen next to nothing of the world outside Peele."

" I wish you were, lad," returned Mr. Prince, heartily, "but I fear you will have to stay at home this time ; and Peele is not half a bad place. You might go further and fare worse. Be sure, now, to tell mother I shall write from St. Thomas's, and by every mail afterwards ; and let you know when I shall return—and, if you like, you and she may meet me here. They say the Royal Mail steamers arrive almost as punctually as they depart ; so you may know almost to a day when to expect me."

Charlie remained on board to the last moment, and waited alongside until the *Otranto* cast loose from her moorings ; and as the great paddles turned round, the father from the taffrail of the steamer, the son from the bows of his boat waved to each other a last farewell, little doubting that in a few months they should meet again, and foreboding naught of the momentous consequences which Mr. Prince's voyage would entail on him and his.

As it was too late to get back to Peele the same night Charlie slept in London, and resumed his journey on the following morning.

He was in good time at the station and entered a compartment whose only other occupant was a traveller so deeply absorbed in a newspaper that he did not seem to notice Charlie's arrival.

" Tickets, please, gentlemen," said a guard, opening the door. " Where for ? Both for Peele. All right ! "

Charlie glanced at his companion, who in order to get his ticket had laid down his newspaper. The first glance was followed by a second and a third, for the stranger was a man worth looking at. Charlie guessed him to be twenty-five years old, and six feet high. His shoulders were broad, his limbs long and muscular ; he had bright humorous eyes, which, together with his chestnut hair, fresh color, smooth skin, and beardless face, gave him, considering his proportions, a singularly youthful appearance. In dress this gentleman was almost a dandy. His clothes, gloves and boots fitted to perfection, and his shirt front was lustrous with diamond studs.

"We are bound for the same port, it seems," he said, as the train moved out of the station, "and as we are likely to have this box to ourselves all the way, we may as well make ourselves comfortable. You smoke, of course?"

"Yes."

"Let us smoke, then."

Whereupon each produced a cigar case.

"Allow me to offer you one of mine," said the stranger, whose manner was easy and self-possessed. "They are superb. Part of a lot of regalias I bought myself in Cuba and have smuggled through half-a-dozen Custom-houses. I enjoy a little smuggling. It comes as a pleasant relief after the tedium of a voyage ; a little excitement, you know."

Charlie accepted the offer, and had no reason to regret his choice. It was the finest cigar he had ever smoked.

"You have been to the West Indies, then. I have just been seeing a relative off to Trinidad," he said.

"I have been there, too. A pleasant enough place for a short stay, and gloriously picturesque. I don't think I should like to stay there for the term of my natural life, however. I'm one of your rolling stones."

"Not with the proverbial result, though, if I may judge by your appearance."

"Well, I think I have gathered a little moss in more senses than one (glancing complacently at his brawny arms and glittering studs). Six years ago I was nothing but skin and bone, and as poor as a church mouse. And now I am going to ask a question which I hope you will not deem impertinent. Do you live at Peele?"

"I live in the neighborhood, and most of my days are spent in the town."

"Then you will know a place called All Hallows."

"Very well."

" And the people who live there—Mrs. Susan Lincoln and her daughter Olive."

" They are dear friends of ours."

" In that case we may as well make friends.　Mrs. Lincoln is my cousin, and Paul Coniston is my name."

" And America your nation ? "

" You might have made a worse guess, Mr. Prince, thank you.　Don't I look like an American ? "

" My experience of Americans is limited ; but if I may hazard an opinion I should say decidedly not."

" I see.　Your idea of an American is a lantern-jawed lamp-post, with high check bones, a sallow skin, and a nasal twang."

" Not quite so bad as that," returned Charlie with a laugh.

" But something like ? "

" Well, yes, something."

" And yet, unless you have been in the States, I'll be bound to say that you have not met a score of live Americans in your life."

" If you mean men, I have not met more than three or four, yourself included."

" I thought so.　You should not make old women's deductions, young man."

" Young man, indeed," quoth Charlie, firing up, " I am not much younger than you are."

" In that case you are nearly thirty."

" You surely don't mean——"

" I mean that I am in my thirty-first year.　You think I look younger.　Well, I daresay I do, and I can tell you the reason why.　When I was seventeen I ran away from college, and volunteered for the Mexican war.　After that I went overland to California, and for ten years I have lived out West, in one of the finest climates in the world, mostly in the saddle, my drink water—when I could get nothing stronger—my food beef, without vegetables.　If I had stopped in Boston, run a store, and chewed tobacco, I daresay I should have borne a faint resemblance to the Yankee of your imagination."

" You have been a soldier, then ; you have seen active service," said Charlie, with sparkling eyes.　" What was your rank ? "

" Full private ; then sergeant.　Afterwards when we were fighting the Apaches the boys made me captain."

"In the Mexican war! Fighting Indians! You have been fortunate."

"I thought so at the end of it all, when I found myself alive, and with my hair on my head," said Coniston dryly. "And now I should like to ask you a question or two. One good turn deserves another, you know. The Lincolns, are they well?"

"Quite."

"I was sorry to hear of Lincoln's death. Anyhow, he made his pile and left his wife and daughter in easy circumstances. When a man does that he may be forgiven for dying, and those he leaves behind have no excuse for being inconsolable. And Olive? The last time I saw her she was as pretty as a peach. How is she now? Has she fulfilled the promise of her childhood?"

"Quite, I should say. You will have to go a long way before you find so charming a girl as Olive Lincoln."

"Has she a sweetheart?"

This was a poser, but necessity is the mother of invention, and though Charlie colored up and felt rather warm he got out of the difficulty better than might have been expected.

"Has she a sweetheart?" he repeated, with a surprised look, as if the question had startled him by its exceeding novelty. "I have not heard so, and as she is only just out of mourning for her father I don't think it's likely."

"Well, she ought to have; and I'll see if I cannot find her one before I go back."

"Confound the fellow, what does he mean?" thought Charlie.

"Why, if she were out West," continued Mr. Coniston, "if she were out West she would have been the deaths of two or three tall fellows by this time. A few years ago, when I was on the Rio Colorado with an outfit, a Mexican *nina*, with a nut-brown skin and big black eyes,—as beautiful as Cleopatra, she was,—used to come over the river in a dugout, singing and playing the banjo, and with her coquettish ways and her Spanish love-songs she just drove the boys wild; and though I warned them to give her a wide berth, for those Greasers are as treacherous as panthers and as jealous as Turks (they will greet you, smiling, with one hand, and knife you with the other), they must go one night to a fandango where they knew she was to be present. Well, I heard next

morning there had been trouble, and when I went to the
casino I found four of them stretched out like sardines in a
box."

" And what became of the young lady ? "

" Never saw her again.   I expect the caballero spirited her
away—perhaps cut her throat.   *Quien sabe ?*   It is dangerous
work courting a Mexican *nina*, I can tell you.   There is only
one way.   You must have your bowie handy and your six-
shooter loaded ; and if a Greaser sneaks up to you with his
hat in his hand and a smile on his face shoot him down before he has time to draw, and then get the drop on his *amigo*,
for Greasers don't often attack unless they are two to one.
This is a beautiful country we are travelling through.   What
is the name of that pretty village with the ivy-clad church ? "

Charlie told him, and then Mr. Coniston inquired how
soon they should arrive at Peele and how far it was from the
" deepo " to All Hallows.   Charlie, guessing that he meant
station, answered " two miles."

" That's a long way," observed Mr. Coniston, " I suppose
there are teams to be got ? "

Charlie, who was being rapidly initiated into the niceties
of the American language, said that there were always flies
in waiting at Peele station.

" Let us fly it, then.   The only thing I object to is walking.   And now, Mr. Prince, I have a great favor to ask of
you—I want you to go along to All Hallows and introduce me."

" Introduce you !   You don't require introducing.   You
have only to send in your card, you know." ·

" That would let the cat out of the bag, and I want to see
whether they will recognize me.   Now if you go along you
can perhaps take me in as your friend, without giving my
name."

Charlie knew that Edward would expect him to call at the
office before going home ; but the chance of seeing Olive and
the reception of her surprising cousin being too good to be
lost, he agreed to accompany the gentleman in question to
All Hallows.

So at Peele they exchanged the train for a cab.   But the
horse left a good deal to be desired.

" Call this a fly ! " said Mr. Coniston, as they jogged on
at the rate of five miles an hour.   " Call this a fly ?   I call it
a hearse, and slow at that."

However, they arrived in the end.

"Are the ladies at home?" asked Charlie of the servant who came to the door.

"They are in the south garden, sir, under the mulberry tree. Shall I announce you and this gentleman?"

"No, Thomas, we will join them. This way, Mr. Coniston."

It was a fine old-fashioned English garden, with shrubs cut into shapes, shady walks running at right angles to each other, like the streets of an American town, flower beds brilliant with tulips and rose-trees; and an emerald lawn, in the middle whereof grew a wide-spreading mulberry tree, laden with purple fruit. Under its branches were two rocking-chairs, in one of which sat Mrs. Lincoln knitting a stocking, and in the other Miss Lincoln reading a novel.

Olive wore a soft creamy gown and a low-crowned sailor hat trimmed with blue, and at her breast were a red rosebud and a sprig of stephanotis. Her lover thought she was the loveliest thing in all that garden fair, and Mr. Coniston owned to himself that Charlie had in nowise exaggerated her charms.

As the two men made towards the mulberry tree, mother and daughter looked up in surprise, and asked each other who was the stranger.

"I have taken the liberty of bringing with me a friend, who is wishful to make your acquaintance, Mrs. Lincoln," said Charlie.

Coniston took off his hat with a flourish, and, after bowing, raised his head and threw back his long hair, as if to invite inspection.

"I am sure I shall be very glad, but——"

"Dear me! What am I thinking about? I have not told you his name," interrupted Charlie. "Mr. Paul Coniston, from the wild West, Mrs.——"

"Paul Coniston, and I did not know him!" exclaimed Mrs. Lincoln. "And no wonder; he is quite another man. His own mother would not know him."

"Oh, what a shameful take in. This is your doing, Charlie," said Olive reproachfully.

"Not at all; it is my doing entirely. I wanted to see whether you would recognize me," and with that Mr. Paul took Mrs. Lincoln's hand and kissed her dutifully, which done he put his arm round Olive's waist and kissed her with

evident relish, a proceeding which Charlie admired so little
that he made as if he would take his leave.

"Oh, don't go yet," said Mrs. Lincoln. "Stay and have
a cup of tea. We don't dine till seven, Paul, and as you
must be hungry we will have tea here, under the mulberry
tree."

Paul made a slight grimace at the word "tea," but said
"With all my heart;" and a table and chairs were brought,
and the tea things set out amid a perfect storm of questions
and answers.

"So you have not a sweetheart, it seems, Olive?" observed
Coniston, after he had given an account of himself.

"Who says so?"

"Mr. Prince. I asked him as we came along."

"Do you think if I had one I should tell him?" returned
Olive, glancing archly at her lover.

"Olive, I am surprised," exclaimed Mrs. Lincoln, bridling.
"I must really beg of you not to put such ideas into the
child's head, Paul."

"I don't think I have, Susan. You may depend they are
there already by the light of nature."

"I should hope not. Olive has been very carefully brought
up, let me tell you. She is much too young   It would be
quite against her dear father's wish, as expressed in his will;
and I could not permit anything of the sort for at least three
years to come."

"And yet you were engaged at seventeen and married at
nineteen! But you were not an heiress. Snakes! how
circumstances alter cases. Come now, Susan, I'll lay you a
thousand dollars to twenty that Olive has a sweetheart
before the year is out."

Mrs. Lincoln made a deprecatory gesture, and asked her
daughter for another cup of tea.

CHAPTER XVI.

CHARLIE'S SOMERSAULT.

ONE day, during Charlie's absence, Edward called at the Beehive to bait his horse and refresh himself. The landlady, a comely woman with a foolish tongue, thinking to do her guest pleasure, made a polite inquiry after Mr. Charles and his sweetheart.

"Sweetheart! What on earth do you mean, Mrs. Marigold? He has no sweetheart."

"I ask your pardon, sir. I meant the young lady as he called with in April, after the hunting—Miss Lincoln, you know. They had tea in my back parlor, and walked in the garden and stopped nearly two hours, and he seemed so loving and she so kind that I felt sure they was courting. But maybe I was mistaken."

"Of course you were mistaken. There is nothing of the sort, I assure you, Mrs. Marigold. Two hours, did you say?"

"Yes, sir, I should say quite two hours."

Mrs. Marigold meant well, but she could no more help exaggerating than she could help talking. Olive and Charlie had not stayed in her house more than an hour, but Edward, though not generally prone to accept uncorroborated statements, fully believed her, and he felt very sore. His worst fears were confirmed. Unless they had an understanding— unless, in fact, they were secretly engaged, they would never dawdle two hours over afternoon tea in the parlor of a country inn.

"He was loving and she was kind."

When Edward thought of the love-making that doubtless went on in that same parlor he gnashed his teeth. It was a positive scandal; it must be put a stop to. But how?

He was always brought up with the "how." To tell Mrs. Lincoln might do more harm than good. It would certainly injure him with Olive; and as he had only hearsay to go upon, the story might be discredited, reference to Mrs. Marigold being in the circumstances quite out of the question.

The best plan—if he could only hit upon one—would be to bring the facts to Mrs. Lincoln's knowledge without incurring the reproach of tale-bearing, or, better still, without appearing in the matter at all.

The idea of sending her an anonymous letter was conceived only to be rejected. He would either have to write it himself or get some other body to write it. In the latter event he would put himself in the other body's power ; in the former, his writing might be recognized, and then his second condition would be worse than his first.

There seemed nothing for it but to persevere in his policy of watching and waiting.

With this unsolved problem in his mind Edward was naturally not in the best of humors, and when Charlie turned up, shortly before dinner-time, his brother asked him somewhat sharply how he came to be so late.

" I called at All Hallows," was the answer.

" What on earth for? You are always calling at All Hallows, I think."

" I don't call as often as you : and, as it happened, I had a very good reason for calling," returned Charlie with some heat.

" How did you leave your father, Charlie ? Tell us all about him, and then you can tell us why you called at All Hallows," interposed Mrs. Prince.

After giving an account of his father's departure and delivering his message, Charlie explained why he called at All Hallows.

His description of Paul Coniston appeared to interest his mother and Edward greatly.

" Strange that we never have heard of him before," observed Mrs. Prince. " From what you say he must be very good-looking."

" He is one of the best-looking men I ever met, and very bright and amusing."

" Is he a bachelor ? " asked Edward, thoughtfully.

" I did not ask him, but I should say he is, decidedly. At any rate, he acts and talks like one," said Charlie, thinking rather ruefully of the more than cousinly affection with which Olive had greeted her stalwart cousin.

Edward smiled. The American might prove a useful foil to Charlie, perhaps set him and Olive at variance, and it would be strange if the complication thus arising did not turn to the elder brother's advantage. When certain people fall out honest folk get their own.

After dinner, as they were smoking in the garden, Edward told Charlie about Lillywhite having seen and recognized Jack, and inquired whether his father had referred to the incident.

Charlie said he had, and related all that had passed.

" Well, that is what I call an infernal shame," exclaimed Edward, " after I had denied it, too. It is a positive breach of our understanding. Didn't we agree that they should be kept in the dark?"

" We agreed not to tell them. But father asked me point-blank, and I could not tell him a lie."

" You might have evaded the question, as I did."

" He put it in such a way that I could not evade it—honestly."

" You mean that I was not honest."

" I know nothing about that. I did not hear what passed between you. I only speak for myself."

" Anyhow, you did not behave honestly to me."

Charlie retorted, and there was a quarrel which left a sore feeling behind it, and the breach between the two brothers, instead of healing, widened almost daily. Edward, who was a good organizer, managed the office well. He drew the bonds of discipline tighter, got more work out of the clerks, cut down expenses, and did other good things. But he was too arrogant and dictatorial, and rubbed people the wrong way, thereby provoking remonstrances from both Lillywhite and Charlie ; and the relations between the brothers grew at last so strained that, except before their mother and on business, they seldom spoke to each other.

Meanwhile, Paul Coniston was proving a great social success. Though he went occasionally to London, he made All Hallows his headquarters, and spent the greater part of his time there. Mrs. Lincoln introduced him to all her friends ; and Olive was evidently proud of him as a typical American, racy of the soil. In thews, sinews, manly presence, and good looks, Peele could not show his equal ; and though, as might be expected of a man who had passed a great part

of his life in fighting Indians, ranching cattle, and seeking
gold, he lacked polish, his manner was frank and open, his
talk fluent and picturesque. Being, moreover, supposed to be
rich, he soon became highly popular, and the ladies of All
Hallows and himself were always either making visits or
receiving visitors, giving dinners, or dining out.

As Paul one day remarked to Olive, he was having a high
old time.

These festivities, however, though he took part in most of
them, did not greatly exhilarate Charlie Prince.   In truth, he
was just then tormented by two demons, envy and jealousy.
Albeit only some nine years his senior, Paul Coniston had
distinguished himself in war and made a fortune, and lived,
and would live again, the wild free life of the far West.   No
wonder Olive was fond of him, and Lydia Spankaway quite
"gone" on him.   No wonder men crowded round him to
hear his anecdotes and enjoy his jokes.   What chance had
a mere quill-driver with this hero and fire-eater ?   It was not
that Olive had given her sweetheart the cold shoulder.   She
still responded to the pressure of his hand, and when they
could exchange a word unobserved was as kind as ever.   But
she was equally kind to Coniston, whose attentions were so
marked and so well received that some people set them down
as an engaged couple.   There could be no doubt, thought
Charlie, that he had lost her love—perhaps in spite of herself—and as he did not care to have the name without the
reality, he resolved—after enduring much agony of mind—to
give her back her promise, and, on the first opportunity, tell
her that if she preferred Paul Coniston he would not stand
in the way.   But this resolve rather aggravated than relieved
his torments ; he fell into a condition of extreme despondency,
alternating with fits of jealous rage, and presently arrived at
the conclusion, usual in like circumstances, that life was a
mistake, and he should never know happiness again.

The desired opportunity came in the shape of a garden
party, to which were invited most of Mrs. Lincoln's friends
and acquaintances in the neighborhood of Peele, also several
members of the Riversdale Hunt and their womenfolk.

Charlie arrived at All Hallows rather late, and found Captain Coniston (as it was the fashion to call him) the centre of
an admiring throng, among whom were Lydia Spankaway and
Olive.   He was telling an anecdote which, judging by the

laughter it provoked, was highly amusing. But, after nodding nonchalantly to Paul, and doffing his hat to the ladies, Charlie passed on and joined Kate Conyers and Mary Spankaway in a game of croquet, lawn-tennis being not yet.

The game finished, they strolled through the grounds, and, on the proposal of Miss Spankaway, who had the equine tastes common to her family, went to the paddock to look at the horses; and there found Coniston, Olive, Edward Prince, and two or three others, who were come on the same errand. Their talk was naturally horsey, and the captain was expressing his regret that he should be obliged to leave England before the hunting season began.

"I don't think it can beat buffalo-hunting," he said, "but I have heard so much about the jumping prowess of your English horses that I should like to see how they do it."

"What sort of jumping have you on the prairies?" asked Teddy Spankaway.

"Buck jumping, and plenty of it, as high as you like to go. But no gates and ditches or anything of that sort. You may ride hundreds of miles and meet no obstacle bigger than a match box. How would you get over that, now?"

"That" was a fence enclosing the paddock—a bank topped with a rail and bounded by a ditch, a fair, though rather formidable, jump, when hounds were running, but not to be undertaken with a light heart in cold blood.

"We should jump it," said Charlie quietly.

"You would need a big horse."

"Not at all. Rataplan is hardly fifteen hands, and he would do it easy enough."

Coniston glanced significantly at the horse, which was grazing in the paddock, and then at the fence.

"You doubt it!" exclaimed Charlie, who was dying to eclipse the captain. "Well, I'll bet you a fiver I'll ride him over it bareback now—if Miss Lincoln will allow me."

Olive hesitated, and then answered rather coldly:

"Very well—if you promise neither to hurt Rataplan nor yourself. I think he can do it."

"I am sure he can."

And with that Charlie went towards the stables and called to a helper to bring a bridle. The bridle was brought, and the helper gave him a leg up. Charlie cantered Rataplan round the paddock to get his blood up; then, leaning well back, and gripping tightly with bent knees, he put the horse at the fence.

Rataplan went over at a bound, without touching ; whereupon everybody shouted, "Well done !"

"It was very well done indeed," said Coniston. "I see that Mr. Prince can ride."

"Of course he can, and Rataplan can jump," added Olive, with a gratified smile. It pleased her to think that her lover and her horse had equally distinguished themselves.

Meanwhile, Rataplan, being very fresh, and having a good deal of way on, was galloping across the next field ; and Charlie had to pull hard in order to stop him.

"How will he get back?" asked Coniston.

"By the gate, of course," said Teddy Spankaway ; "I'll run and open it."

Charlie, however, had no such intention. Having turned Rataplan round he made straight for the fence, which this time was not a fair jump. The ditch being now on the taking-off side and the field lower than the paddock, it was a far more difficult feat than before.

"Don't try it, Prince. It is too much," shouted Teddy, while Olive and the other girls waved him back.

Charlie, whose blood was up, gave no heed to their warnings. He rode on as straight as a bullet. Rataplan rose nobly at the obstacle, but hitting the rail with his fore-legs, turned a complete somersault, as he had done on a previous occasion, and landed in the paddock with his heels in the air, his rider, as it seemed, under him.

The girls gave a terrified shriek, and the men rushed to the spot in dire dismay, but Charlie had fortunately fallen clear, and with admirable presence of mind rolled away as the horse turned over in the effort to rise.

"This beats buck-jumping," said Coniston. "Many a man knows how to ride ; but it is not everybody who knows how to fall."

Olive was very pale, but no paler than were Mary Spankaway and Kate Conyers.

"I never saw anything more foolish. Didn't you see that it was an impossible jump?" she said, severely.

"Anyhow, I got over it," replied Charlie, who, though rather white, was smiling. "And I have kept my promise— neither of us is hurt—and won my bet."

"And nearly lost your life," put in Teddy Spankaway. "If you had fallen under instead of on one side you would have been crushed as flat as a pancake."

"And we should have got the insurance money and reinstated the trust fund, and a troublesome rival would have been out of my way," thought Edward.

The idea came unbidden, and Edward was fully conscious of its wickedness; but once conceived it was not easily dismissed: it recurred to him again and again; even in the night watches it would thrust itself into his thoughts:

"If Charlie had fallen under instead of on one side we should have got the insurance money, and I should be sure of Olive!"

CHAPTER XVII.

"MY LITTLE HUNTER."

"COME into the house and have a drink, Mr. Charles," said Coniston, kindly. "That fall must have shaken you."

They returned to the garden, and presently the guests began to leave; but Mrs. Lincoln invited all who would to stay for dinner, and have a dance in the cool of the evening.

Among those who accepted the invitation was Charlie, and when the dancing began he danced with Olive.

"I want to speak to you," he whispered.

"And I want to speak to you. Go into the shrubbery behind the fish-pond. I will come to you as soon as I can."

When he had conducted his sweetheart to her seat, Charlie slipped out of the room unobserved, and betook himself to the trysting place, a path winding between tall shrubs, and so overshadowed by trees that even on that fair summer evening it was almost as dark as a moonless midnight.

Presently he heard a footfall on the gravel.

"Hist! Is that you?" he asked, as a shawled figure came noiselessly towards him.

"Yes, and what we have to say must be said quickly, or we shall be missed. I thought you loved me, Charlie?"

"I do love you. You know I love you—with all my heart —and yet——"

"Why are you so unkind, then?"

This took the wind out of Charlie's sails completely. He had meant to reproach her, and here she was imputing to him the very fault of which, in his thoughts, he accused her; and it began to dawn on his mind that he had perhaps been making rather a fool of himself.

"I, unkind to you!" he stammered. "It is impossible. I never thought of such a thing. I even imagined——"

"What?"

"That you had ceased to love me."

"Oh, Charlie, do you want to break my heart?" she murmured, with a half sob, and made as if she would go away.

What could he do but cry *peccavi*, and protest that he was a brute, and kiss away her tears and entreat her forgiveness?

Having brought him to this pass Olive laughed, and called him a foolish boy, and said that she really believed he had been jealous of her cousin Paul.

"Weren't you now?" she asked.

"Well, just a little. You seem so fond of him, and are nearly always with him."

"Naturally. He is our guest and my cousin, and a very fine fellow, as you must admit. But my liking for him makes no difference in my love for you. Was it jealousy that made you take that mad leap to-day? The truth, now!"

"Yes, I think I must have been mad."

"I am sure you were. Suppose you had been killed! Oh, when I think of it I tremble all over."

"Dear heart! But you forgive me, don't you, darling?"

"Yes, on one condition."

"What is it? But never mind. I accept it, whatever it is."

"That you don't do so any more, and have limitless confidence in me, and keep nothing back from me that is in your mind; and put the best, not the worst, construction on anything I may do. Be sure I have good reasons, and if I give you all my love you must give me all your confidence."

"I agree."

"Fully?"

"Fully."

"And now I have something to tell you. We are going to Switzerland next week."

"You and your mother?"

"Yes, also Paul. He asked us to go with him, and, as the long vacation is close at hand, and the law courts will be closed, mother can be spared two or three months. Afterwards, Paul will return to America, sailing from Havre, I think."

"And you will be two or three months away?"

"Perhaps."

"That will be dreadful."

"Yes; it will be rather trying. But, in consideration of

your penitence, and your promise not to be jealous and unkind any more, I shall write to you."

"Dear Olive!"

"Shall I address my letters—I don't think it will be wise
to write more than one or two—to Holmcroft or the office?"

"The office. . Never a letter comes to me at home that
my mother does not ask whom it is from. How shall I
address mine to you?"

"I am not sure that it would be prudent to address any.
I will tell you when I write. And now you must let me go.
No, I cannot stop longer, I have the guests to look after, you
know. Mother will be wondering what has become of me."

As they turned out of the shrubbery whom should they
meet but Paul Coniston!

"Hello!" he exclaimed. "You two here! But never
mind; I won't tell. I guessed as much some time ago—saw
it in this gentleman's face when I mentioned your name to
him in the cars, Olive. However, your secret is quite safe
with me."

"I am sure it is, Paul. You are as good as gold. But I
must really run away. Tell him about Myra, Paul."

"Who is Myra?" asked Charlie, as Olive hurried towards
the house.

"A little girl at Boston I am going to marry and take out
West. That is my secret. At any rate it was before I told
Olive."

"I congratulate you heartily," said Charlie, feeling now
quite sure that he had made a fool of himself.

"Thank you. Perhaps you will be coming to America
one of these days."

Charlie shook his head.

"You are sure to do if all goes on right—and then I hope
we shall meet again, and you will afford me an opportunity of
introducing you to the young woman in question. Frankly,
Mr. Prince, I like you, and I think Olive has made an excellent choice. The way you turned a somersault over that
fence excited my unbounded admiration. Why aren't you a
cowboy? Yes, when you come to the States you must seek
me out and we will have a high old time. Meanwhile, I
shall be glad to do anything for you in my power. Can I
serve you in any way?"

"You are very kind. Well, if you should chance to meet

—it is not likely, I know, but it is possible—if you should chance to meet a man of the name of Mark Darnley, you might give him a message from me."

" Where is he ? "

" All I can tell you is that he landed in New York last November and went West."

" That is very vague, Mr. Prince. The chances are about ten millions to one against my coming across this gentleman before I die—afterwards, perhaps."

" The impossible happens sometimes."

" What is he like ? "

Charlie described Jack.

" What shall I say to Mr. Darnley if the impossible does happen ? "

" Say that you have been to Peele and seen us all, and give him my love."

" Good ! I will make a note of it; and if I do meet him you may be sure I shall not forget to deliver your message."

When the two men rejoined the other guests in the house they found that music had been substituted for dancing, and at Olive's request her cousin produced his banjo and, to his own accompaniment, sang a Spanish love-song, which, though nobody understood it, appeared to give general satisfaction. Then Charlie, also at Olive's request, followed with a hunting-song known as " My Little Hunter," which ran as follows :—

MY LITTLE HUNTER.

I've as nice a little hunter as e'er you'd wish to see,
So high she lifts her fore-foot, so proudly bends her knee;
Her fiery head and nostrils red assert her noble blood ;
Deep is her girth, and hocks she has that send her through the mud.—
My gallant little hunter, my dashing little bay.

Now see her at the covert side, responsive to my hand,
While other horses fret and fume how quietly she'll stand;
But when hounds proclaim a find, and "forward " is the cry,
She'll fling the dirt behind her, and o'er the pastures fly,—
My gallant little hunter, my dashing little bay.

The scent is good, the pace is fast, the crowd's soon left behind,
A minute's check, a view hallo, and onward like the wind ;
At rotten bank and yawning ditch the funkers turn away;
" The best thing," quoth the master, " we've had this many a day,"—
Oh my noble little hunter, my dashing little bay.

Forty minutes now we've run, and the best begin to flag,
Yet Kitty still goes free and fast, the sturdy little nag :
The ground is deep, the jumping big, yet still I keep my place
Among the foremost riders in this right glorious chase.—
    My noble little hunter, my dashing little bay.

There was more of the same sort, but the foregoing is probably quite enough for the reader, although the Spankaways and some others were loud in their plaudits, and demanded an *encore*. The song was popularly ascribed to Charlie's own muse, but, as a matter of fact, it was an old hunting song re-touched and partly re-written by Olive and himself, and, as they thought, greatly improved.

CHAPTER XVIII.

LILLYWHITE SMELLS A RAT.

DURING Mr. Prince's absence, Edward, as acting head of the firm, took possession of his father's room, Charlie meanwhile occupying the room which had been his brother's. Lillywhite was always first at the office, generally entering with the postman, from whom he took the letters. After carefully scanning the outsides of them, and forming shrewd guesses as to the nature of their contents, he would put the firm's letters and Edward's on the latter's desk and Charlie's on his desk.

One morning, about a fortnight after the garden party, the managing clerk came across a letter with a foreign stamp and the Geneva postmark, addressed to Charles Prince, Esq.

" Geneva—Switzerland—the Lincolns are in Switzerland —a woman's handwriting—not Mrs. Lincoln's—I know it as well as my own—*ergo* it must be Miss Lincoln's," muttered Lillywhite. " I smell a rat, I smell a rat. I have thought for some time that Edward was sweet in that quarter ; but if Charlie is the favored swain, so much the better. If he wasn't, would she write him a long letter like this ? " (feeling it with his finger and thumb, and holding it to the light). " Not she, not she. And a very sensible young woman I call her to prefer Charlie to his conceited jackanapes of a brother. This is a new development. I must watch it. And now I'll put the letters on their desks. They will be here presently."

A few minutes later Edward arrived.

" My brother won't be here for an hour or two," he said, after greeting Lillywhite. " There was a fire at Longmire's last night, and he has ridden that way to ascertain the extent of the damage. (The Princes were agents to the Rhadamanthus Fire Insurance Company.)

Shortly afterwards Edward had occasion to consult a law

book, which formed part of the collection in his old room, and hither for that purpose he went, going through the general office. As he passed Charlie's desk he noticed the letter which had aroused Lillywhite's curiosity.

"A foreign letter for Charlie! Whom can it be from?" he thought, taking it up. "Olive, by Jove."

There could be no doubt about it. He knew that the Lincolns were going to Geneva, and he recognized the hand-writing. Here was a chance of ascertaining the nature of Charlie's relations with Olive not to be lost, all the more so as he had almost persuaded himself (the wish being father to the thought) that Olive's flirtation with Coniston indicated a growing indifference to Charlie.

So, slipping the letter into his pocket, he returned to his own room.

Having gentlemanly instincts and a regard for the pro-prieties, Edward Prince was fully alive to the meanness and treachery of the deed which he contemplated. But curiosity and jealousy were too much for his scruples. After a moment's hesitation he wetted a sheet of thick blotting-paper, placed it on the back of the letter; then, putting both between two sheets of oiled paper, screwed them up in the letter copying press.

In five minutes the adhesive matter of the envelope was so softened that the letter could be opened without diffi-culty.

Edward opened it, and took out and read the letter. It began "My dear Charlie," and as touching the greater part of it might have been written by a sister to a brother, or by one friend to another. Olive gave a lively description of their journey, of an excursion they had made to the Col de-la Faucille, of a never-to-be-forgotten "Tour of the Lake," and of the sayings and doings of Cousin Paul, who seemed to have been very amusing. The significance of the letter and, for Edward, its sting, lay in its conclusion. It ran thus:—

"And now that you have nobody to be jealous of, I hope you have ceased to worry, you foolish boy. As you know that I love you dearly, and shall never love anybody else, I will protest no more, except that I am yours, and yours only, Olive."

Then there came a P.S. suggesting that Charlie should

write to her at the Schweizerhof, Lucerne, enclosing his letter in an envelope addressed to Cousin Paul.

" Confound them both," said Edward, dashing the letter on the table. " It's as I suspected at first ; they are secretly engaged, and that cursed American cow catcher is a party to the fraud. That flirtation was a piece of make-believe, and I actually let it take me in. What shall I do ? Suppress the letter, and show it to Mrs. Lincoln when she comes home ? "

But when Edward cooled down a little he saw that this, besides being highly dangerous, would do him no good. It was not every day that a foreign letter came to the office. Lillywhite had doubtless observed Olive's missive and might mention it to Charlie. Neither could he bring it to Mrs. Lincoln's knowledge without admitting that he had committed a shabby action and broken the law. So, reluctantly and *faute de mieux*, he restored the letter to the envelope, and returning to Charlie's room with the law book under his arm, put book and letter where he had found them.

As it happened, however, Lillywhite had been there a few minutes previously, to place on the table a document which concerned Charlie's department of the business. Naturally he missed the foreign letter, and as naturally concluded that Edward had taken it.

" Gone, by George ! " he mentally exclaimed. " What's his game, I wonder ? Does he mean to keep it, or merely to look inside ? And what can be his motive—curiosity, or something else ? "

The managing clerk returned to his desk, and while he still pondered these questions Edward went into Charlie's room a second time. So, after a short interval, did Lillywhite.

The letter was in its place again.

Lillywhite examined it deliberately and with deep interest, and his practiced eye, sharpened by suspicion, told him that it had been tampered with. The envelope was damp, one of the edges slightly torn, and it appeared to have been touched up with fresh gum.

" A true bill," he soliloquized. " Edward has read it. He is mad that Miss Lincoln has written to Charlie instead of to him, and wanted to know what she said. It almost seems as if these brothers were rivals. Well, I'm for Charlie. He is rather free and easy sometimes, but he has always treated me with becoming respect, and I'll do my best to forward his views, if only to spite the other."

At eleven o'clock Charlie came in, fresh from his ride, his hat slightly on one side, himself looking happy and careless.

"Good-morning, Mr. Lillywhite," he said pleasantly. "You have heard of Longmire's fire, I suppose. It does not amount to much. Fifty pounds will cover the entire damage. I don't think the Rhadamanthus will consider it necessary to send a surveyor. They will accept my report. Any letters this morning?"

"You will find several on your desk, one of them a foreigner, I think. Also——"

But Charlie did not stay to hear more. He whipped into his room, shut the door, pounced on the foreigner, slit open the envelope with his desk knife, and devoured Olive's letter, dwelling ecstatically on the concluding portion. He was reading it a second time when there came a knock at the door, followed by Lillywhite.

"I beg your pardon, sir," said the clerk, "but I was just about to observe, when you left me, I was just about to observe, that I had put the draft brief, *in re* Powderley, on your desk."

"All right, I'll look at it," returned Charlie, rather impatiently.

"Your foreigner is on the floor. Oh, it is only the envelope (picking it up). I hope you have good news of Mrs. Lincoln, sir."

"Mrs. Lincoln?"

"Yes, I see that the envelope bears the Geneva post-mark, and as the Lincolns are in Switzerland I thought you had perhaps news of them."

In his mind Charlie characterized this observation as "a piece of cheek," but considering the circumstances and Lillywhite's age and position, he answered, with a show of indifference, that Mrs. Lincoln was quite well.

"And the young lady?"

"Is also quite well," answered Charlie, reddening.

"I am glad to hear it. Miss Lincoln is a very nice young lady—to my thinking, one of the nicest in these parts."

Here Lillywhite paused and looked keenly at Charlie, but as the latter made no sign he went on: "Would you mind letting me have the stamp, sir? I have a nephew who collects them, and this would please the little chap immensely."

"Certainly; let him have it. I'll go through this draft at once and make any emendations that may occur to me, and then you can have a fair copy made. I suppose nobody has been in my room besides yourself this morning?"

"Only your brother, for a volume of 'Copeland's Digest,' I think, which he afterwards brought back."

"Yes, most of his law books are here. An uncommonly useful book, 'Copeland's Digest.' I say, Lillywhite, if there is another foreign letter for me, don't put it on my desk; keep it till I come."

"All right, sir, I'll not forget. I thank you for the stamp, Mr. Charles," and with that the managing clerk pocketed the envelope and left the room.

"He need not have taken the envelope for the sake of the stamp," thought the young fellow discontentedly, "but never mind, it is only the shadow, here is the substance (looking fondly at the letter). I wonder whether Old Sly Boots suspects anything. He looked very knowing when he asked after Miss Lincoln. However, that would be better than for Ned to spot one of Olive's letters. I wonder whether he saw this? I don't think so. He only came in for a book. But he might another time. He won't have the chance, though. Lillywhite will take care of the next: and he isn't a man who talks except to ask questions .... Dear Olive! I must read her letter once more, and then for a grind at this infernal brief."

Meanwhile "Old Sly Boots" was mending his pens (he always wrote with a quill) and rejoicing hugely over his morning's work. He had scored again—added to his store of secrets, and, as he believed, got a hold over both the brothers. Beyond a doubt Charlie was carrying on an amatory correspondence with Miss Lincoln. He had received one letter and expected others, which he did not want anybody to see, especially Edward. If he only knew that Edward had read his precious missive before he read it himself! A word from him (Lillywhite) would set the brothers by the ears, and he wagged his portentous nose in delight as he thought of the clever way in which he had secured possession of the compromising envelope. It might prove a valuable piece of

evidence. The mere sight of it would be enough to show
Edward that his treachery had not passed unobserved.

But "Old Sly Boots" knew how to bide his time. Whether
and in what fashion he should utilize his newly-acquired
knowledge depended on circumstances. He hoarded secrets
as misers hoard money, for the mere pleasure of possession,
and seldom used them—save either as a means of capturing
others, or, on rare occasions, to show his power.

Charlie, of course, answered his sweetheart's letter, and the
correspondence went on until Captain Coniston left Europe
for America, and the ladies betook themselves to the Italian
lakes, when Olive, prescient and thoughtful as ever, deemed
it expedient to put an interdict on her lover's letters ; nevertheless, she continued to write to him, and her missives,
thanks to Lillywhite's watchfulness, were received without
being seen by anybody else.

And so the summer days wore away, and the younger
Prince, as happy as they were long, dreamed of a still brighter
future; while Ned, nursing his wrath in silence, indulged in
thoughts inimical to his brother's peace, even at times to the
extent of hoping that Charlie would break his neck next
hunting season.

Mrs. Prince, happily unsuspicious of her sons' rivalry,
was gladdened every fortnight by a letter from her husband.
Mr. Prince found the business which took him to Trinidad
more complicated than he had been led to expect, and his
stay there was likely to be longer than he had originally anticipated. For the rest, however, all was well with him. He
spoke in the highest terms of the beauty of the island and
the hospitality of its inhabitants. His health left nothing to
be desired, and the change and freedom from small worries
(which meant great anxieties) were doing him "a power of
good." He still hoped to be back in time for the October
cub-hunting, and in the course of a mail or two would be able
to say by which packet he should return.

The letter containing this information was received early
in September, and greatly rejoiced Mrs. Prince.

"We shall have your father back in a month," she said to
her sons.

"Hardly.   If he lets us know by the next mail but one that
he is leaving by the following packet, he won't be here for
six weeks or so. For my own part, I do not expect him until

about the middle of October, which will be just within the limit allowed by the insurance company," returned Edward, who suspected that his father was making the most of his holiday and could, if he had liked, have got through his business in a month.

" You always were a kill-joy ; I think you make it a rule never to agree with anybody," said his mother, rather resentfully.

" If you mean that I neither cherish illusions nor shape my opinions according to my desires, you are right. A lawyer has no business to cherish illusions."

" Well, perhaps you are right, dear. All the same, I hope I am not cherishing an illusion in believing that your father's next letter will fix the day of his return, and that we shall have him with us by the end of the month."

Edward shook his head, and smiled dubiously, and Mrs. Prince, perceiving that he did not agree with her, let the subject drop.

The result justified his scepticism, albeit in a way which he little anticipated. The following mail brought no letter whatever, to his mother's great disappointment.

" What can have happened ? " she said. " He has never missed writing before."

" Perhaps he has not missed writing, merely missed the mail. That is a possible chance, and I rather wonder it has not happened before," quietly observed Edward, who, when the ordinary seemed to afford an adequate explanation for aught obscure, never admitted into his calculations the extraordinary.

" I wish I could think so. But how do you know that he was not too ill to write ? "

" I don't, any more than you know that he was. But I think that if he had been ill, at any rate seriously ill, we should have heard. The agents would have informed us. To my mind the wonder is that my father's letters have come so regularly—so slight a cause may make a man to miss a dispatch—the carelessness of a clerk, the stupidity of a servant ; and from Trinidad there are only two dispatches a month, remember ; miss a mail and you lose a fortnight."

" That is true—yet, I cannot help thinking that if all had been well with your father we should have had a letter from him as usual; and I shall be very anxious until the next mail comes in."

Charlie, who was present, held his peace. He did not want to discourage his mother, and his opinion, if he had expressed it, would have confirmed her in her fears. For, Edward's arguments to the contrary notwithstanding, he had an uneasy feeling that all was not well with their father.

CHAPTER XIX.

" EVIL TIDINGS."

THE morning-room at Holmcroft was neither too large to be cozy nor so small as to be cramped. The furniture was substantial without looking heavy ; two French windows opened into a beautiful bit of garden, and the oil paintings on the walls, the flowers on the table, and a merry fire burning in the grate gave it a bright, homelike aspect, which made it one of the pleasantest rooms—in the opinion of Mr. Prince, whose portrait surveyed the scene, the very pleasantest in the house.

Here, on a certain morning in the latter half of September, the members of his family, whom he had left at home, are having breakfast. Edward is the only one who appears to be eating with appetite. His manner is as quiet, his face as impassive, as usual. But Mrs. Prince's face is gray and worn, and there are dark circles round her eyes, as if she has passed a sleepless night. So tremulous is her hand that she can scarcely pour out the tea, and when her sons offer her anything she silently refuses. Charles makes a show of eating, but after every mouthful pauses and looks nervously towards the door.

The letters nearly always come while they are at breakfast ; the West India mail is due, and the shipping intelligence of the *Times* reports that the *Tamar* arrived at Southampton early on the previous day. A .few minutes will decide whether Edward is justified in his confidence or his mother in her fears.

Presently there is a knock at the door, and a servant enters with a tray, on which are letters and a newspaper or two. He passes the lady of the house and offers the tray to her elder son.

" It there nothing for me ? " she demands in a tone of eager anguish.

" No, madam, all for Mr. Edward."

Mrs. Prince falls back in her chair with something like a groan, and then, recovering herself and leaning forward, inquires whether the servant has not made a mistake.

"There must be news from father by this mail," she says. "One of those letters——"

"Has the Port-of-Spain post-mark. But the address is not in his handwriting. However, if the letter is not from him it will tell us something about him."

Edward opens the letter smiling, but he no sooner begins to read it than his countenance changes ominously.

"What is it?" cries Mrs. Prince. "There is something wrong, I can see it in your face."

"Father is ill," he says in a faltering voice.

"Give me the letter, let me see it."

"Wait a minute, mother, till I have read it through. I—I can scarcely make it out."

"Give it me, I say," and leaning over she snatches the letter from his hand.

The first words on which the poor lady's eyes light are these :—

"*I deeply regret to inform you that your father is no more. He died on the thirteenth instant from the effects of a snake bite.*"

"Dead! Dead! Leonard dead, and it was I who let him go," moans the stricken woman, and then sinks back in a swoon.

The young men take her in their arms, lay her on the sofa, and ring for help.

"Is it really true—is father——" gasps Charlie, who feels as if he were playing a part in some frightful nightmare.

"Too true. It is terrible. Read the letter."

"The letter, though sympathetic, was brief. The writer had evidently been pressed for time. He told that Mr. Prince, while on a yachting expedition in Venezuelan waters, had been killed by the bite of a snake. A full account would be found in the newspapers, which the writer was sending by the present mail. The body had been buried in the Port-of-Spain cemetery. Further particulars, together with all the deceased's papers and certificates of his death and burial, would follow by the next opportunity.

When Mrs. Prince regained consciousness her condition was so pitiable, and she talked so wildly, that the brothers did not think it would be right to leave her even for a short time. It was therefore agreed between them that Charlie should stay with her while Edward went to the office, calling on his way at the Rectory to ask Mrs. Manners (the Rector's wife) to come and keep their mother company.

Charlie, although he strove bravely to keep up, was so undone that he could scarcely speak, and in no condition to offer consolation to anybody else. Besides, how could words, mere words, mitigate the measureless sorrow which had come upon them? The dear father whom he had so tenderly loved, who as long as he could remember, had been good and kind to him, his best friend and faithful companion and counsellor, was gone, gone forever. Never more would he hear that cheery voice, meet that kindly smile, feel the pressure of that reverend hand; and, as the poor lad looked up with tear-be-dimmed eyes at his father's portrait, it seemed to him as if all the gladness were gone out of his life and he should never know happiness again.

And the manner of his father's end increased the sharpness of his own grief. The thought that he had died a terrible and painful death in a strange land made Charlie almost frantic. He wanted to know more, to know all, and, when Mrs. Manners came and took his place by his mother's side, he opened one of the papers (Edward had taken the other) and read the account mentioned in the letter.

It appeared that towards the end of August, being about a month before the time which he had fixed for his departure from the island, Mr. Prince accepted an invitation from several of his friends to join them in a short cruise in the Bay of Paria, in a hired steam-yacht. It was to be a sort of marine picnic. The day was fine, the air balmy, and there was barely enough wind to ripple the surface of the tideless sea, which Columbus, or his successors, christened the Gulf of Sadness. The party included a fair proportion of ladies; there was music on board, and for a while all went as merry as a marriage bell.

After skirting the north-eastern coast of Trinidad, touching at Goose Island, and looking at the Bocas, the yacht was steered for the Spanish Main, the idea being to "let go " in an inlet known as Chachacara Bay, and afford any who were so minded an opportunity of landing and spending an hour on Venezuelan soil. Three or four of the party, however, among whom was Mr. Prince, having their lives insured under conditions which precluded them from landing on the continent, stayed where they were.

But owing to some mismanagement—probably neglect of sounding, for the bay was not buoyed—the steamer ran on a mudbank, stuck there and heeled over. She did not appear to be any the worse, and so long as the sea remained smooth was in no danger ; yet as the wind might get up before morning and the position of the steamer rendered staying on board at night very uncomfortable, if not altogether impossible, the passengers, on the advice of the captain, went ashore. Meanwhile, a falucha, then lying at anchor in the bay, was despatched to Port-of-Spain for a tug, which, as the captain thought, would get the yacht off without difficulty. But the wind being contrary for the falucha, the tug was not likely to arrive before noon on the following day.

There was very little to see ashore—a few fishermen's huts —roofs on stilts—a plantation owned by a coatless peasant (who called himself Senor Don Ramon Estramadure, and politely placed all his possessions at the disposal of his uninvited guests), and a background of primeval forest.

Bedding was got ashore, hammocks were slung in Don Ramon's *patio* and elsewhere, and the excursionists, fanned by a gentle breeze, which cooled the air and dispersed the mosquitoes, passed a pleasanter night than might have been expected.

At daybreak most of the men set off to bathe in a freshwater creek, which Don Ramon had pointed out to them, and where, as he assured them, there were no alligators. Indeed, according to his account, the place enjoyed a complete immunity from what the Spaniards call *plaga*—meaning thereby noxious creatures generally.

The part of the creek chosen for the bath was secluded and picturesque, overshadowed by trees, but close to an ugly bit of swamp, which one of the party protested that he would not cross for a thousand dollars in gold.

After swimming and splashing about in the creek for some ten or fifteen minutes, Mr. Prince landed at a spot a few yards from the point where he had left his clothes. On his way thither he was seen to step on what at first sight seemed to be a log of wood. But quick as lightning the log up-reared an evil-looking head and fastened on Mr. Prince's leg.

In his surprise and horror Mr. Prince screamed, and one of his companions—the same who had said he would not cross the swamp for a thousand dollars in gold—ran to him just as the snake, loosing its hold, glided away.

" My God ! A water moccasin," he exclaimed.

" Is it dangerous?" asked Mr. Prince. " It felt like red hot needles, but the wound does not seem much."

It was hardly perceptible, indeed. Only two slight punctures, from which two drops of blood were slowly oozing.

" Dangerous ! Come here, Masters. Quick, come at once ! "

Masters was one of the party and a surgeon. He came running.

" Mr. Prince has been bitten by a water mocassin."

The doctor turned pale.

" A water mocassin. Are you sure ? "

" Quite. I know them only too well. I have seen scores. And that swamp is just the place for them. What is to be done ? "

" If I had my pocket-case with me I would cut the piece out right away. There is only one chance. We must try and suck the poison out."

" The bite is dangerous, then ? " said Mr. Prince.

" It is. I could not say otherwise without telling you a lie. The water mocassin is one of the most venomous snakes known ; but we may perhaps succeed in sucking out the poison. Lie down, please. Fetch Mr. Prince's clothes, Power, and one of you go at once to the steamer for my pocket-case. Bring also brandy—and the captain has some medicines, I think. If he has any laudanum, or morphia, or chloroform, bring them too."

And then Dr. Masters began to suck the wound, Power and the others occasionally relieving him. When the brandy and the laudanum came he gave the patient strong doses of both.

These measures, though they may conceivably have prolonged the span of Mr. Prince's life for a few hours, did not, unhappily, suffice to save it.

When the steam-tug arrived they carried him on board the yacht, and there, shortly before sunset, he died.

At the outset he suffered much, but whether from the effects of the venom or the brandy and laudanum, or all three combined, he presently sank into a state of semi-consciousness, and at the last appeared to be entirely free from pain.

On the following day his body was laid in the Port-of-Spain cemetery.

The writer of the account had obviously personal knowledge of the events which he described, and the editor of the paper, in bringing it to the notice of his readers, observed that the catastrophe had caused a most painful sensation in Port-of-Spain, where during his short sojourn Mr. Prince had made for himself many friends and gained the confidence and respect of all with whom he had come in contact.

When Charlie had ended his reading he consulted Mrs. Manners as to the expediency of showing the account to his mother. He thought it might rouse her from the tearless apathy into which she had fallen. Mrs. Manners agreed with him, and handing her friend the paper, pointed out the portentous headlines :

"A TERRIBLE FATALITY.

" THE DEATH OF MR. LEONARD PRINCE."

Mrs. Prince took the paper and read the account, read it again and again, weeping.

"Oh, God," she murmured, "that he should die thus, away from us all, without a word of farewell, and be laid in a grave I can never see. Why did I let him go ! Why did I let him go ! "

In truth, Mrs. Prince was suffering from stings of conscience as well as from grief for the loss of her husband. She saw now, as she might have seen before, had she not wilfully shut her eyes, how the breach of trust which he had committed, mainly at her instance, had weighed on his mind and embittered his life. She allowed him to go to Trinidad, against her better judgment, for money. Or, to put the matter more accurately, she would have used her influence to prevent him going if money had not been needed ; and the need was created by that first fatal step which she had persuaded him to adopt.

Yet when she was somewhat recovered from the shock and could think calmly, it was not difficult to convince herself

that she had acted for the best. Nobody could have foreseen the fatal issue of the enterprise. Leonard himself was
eager to go, and everybody thought that the voyage out and
home would do him good. Yes, she had acted for the best,
and terrible as was the blow it had its compensations.

Her dear husband had not died in vain. The insurance
money would make good the misappropriation, and the world
would never know that her eldest son was a thief and her
husband a defaulter. True, the rest of her life would be an
abiding sorrow; but Leonard Prince's memory would be
honored in the place where he was born, and Edward and
Charles could look their neighbors in the face without
shame.

This was the way in which Mrs. Prince looked on her husband's death after some days, when the stress of her grief
was beginning to abate.

And Edward, though neither a man of strong affections
nor noble nature, was as much affected by the terrible news
as his mother and his brother. His father's tragic death
gave him intense pain, and for awhile, albeit he had pressing affairs on hand, he could think of naught else. But this
was not for long. The sun had hardly gone down on his
grief before he said to himself that, regarded as an incident,
his father's death was by no means a misfortune without
alloy.

The next day he said to himself that it was a very good
thing, and before long Edward had come to the conclusion
that it was the best thing that could have happened—in his
own interest and that of the family.

He would step into his father's shoes, become the head of
the firm, and for several years to come take the lion's share
of the profits. It was, moreover, an immense relief to know
that the family skeleton had been buried in his father's grave.
The insurance money would put right that awkward matter
of Mrs. Lincolns trust, and the annual premiums, if he decided to continue the policy in Charlie's name and his own,
might be greatly reduced.

And he could not help thinking that his accession of fortune, and the importance he should derive from being head
of the firm and boss of Peele (as he fully intended to be)
would influence Olive in his favor, and induce her to cease
her philandering with Charlie. She was a girl who valued

position ; and by the time she was free to marry he should be able to offer her a position which she would not disdain. For Edward believed that he could greatly increase the already considerable profits of the office, and in dreams saw himself M.P. for the borough, and a man of mark in the county.

CHAPTER XX.

AN UNPLEASANT SURPRISE.

THREE or four days after receiving tidings of his father's death Edward read the will to his mother and brother.

The testator appointed his wife and his son Edward as his sole executors and trustees. The business, subject to the payment of five hundred a year to the widow during her lifetime, was left to Edward and Charles in the proportion of two-thirds to the former and one third to the latter, until the younger should attain his twenty-sixth year, when he would take an equal share with Edward. Mrs. Prince was to remain in possession of Holmcroft, and have the use of the furniture in common with her two sons. After her death the house and its contents were to be offered to the elder of them at a fair valuation; if he declined the offer, then to the younger. In the event of both of them declining to purchase the property, it was to be sold to the highest bidder, and the proceeds to be divided equally between them. The personalty was also to be equally divided, except the carriage-horses and the carriages, which were left to Mrs. Prince. All the other horses were left to Charlie.

Jack's name was not mentioned. Nor was there any allusion to the secret.

The will having been executed several years previously, when Charlie was under age, he took his exclusion from the executorship as a matter of course. Moreover, two executors were quite enough, and he had full confidence that Edward, with whom his relations were now as seemingly fraternal as they had ever been, would administer the estate honestly and well.

"How much was father's life insured for?" he asked.

"Fifteen thousand pounds. We are all in the same policy, you know; and if either of us was to die the same amount would be payable to the surviving member of the firm."

" How good of father to make so great a sacrifice for our
benefit ! He must have paid two or three thousand pounds
in premiums. We shall be quite rich."

" Yes," said Edward dryly, " we shall not be badly off.
Your third share will make more than a thousand a year,
nett."

" I would give it all, give everything, if we could have him
back for one short hour," exclaimed the young fellow passionately, and then, too full to say more, left the room.

" Shall we tell him now or not?" asked Edward of his
mother deferentially.

He did not say whom or what, but Mrs. Prince understood
him perfectly.

" We will tell him neither now nor at any other time,"
she answered emphatically, though her voice was low and
troubled. " Why should we? What would be the good? "

" That is not exactly the question, mother. We must tell
him, sooner or later."

" But why?"

" Don't you see? He is a beneficiary, and we shall have
to account to him for his share of the fifteen thousand
pounds we are going to receive from the Insurance Company. Suppose he asks how I am going to invest it? It
will be quite within his right."

This was a new idea to Mrs. Prince, and it evidently caused
her great annoyance. She made an impatient gesture, and
before answering thought deeply for several minutes.

" You say he must know sooner or later," she said at
length, " let it be later then. If poor father had wanted him
to know he would have told him, and we must respect father's
wishes. It is a duty, a sacred duty. Besides, I don't want
him to know,"

" But what shall I say if he asks how I am disposing of
the money?"

" Say you are investing it in Consols. You will have to
do, won't you? Mrs. Lincoln's fortune was in Consols."

" So far you are quite right, and the expedient might answer for a while. But he must know, eventually, and to tell
the truth, mother, I don't like taking the responsibility of
keeping it from him," said Edward uneasily. He feared that
by letting Charlie think the insurance money was available

for distribution he might at some future time have it in his power to demand payment in full of his share therein. As Edward had often told his clients, the path of trustees is beset with snares and pitfalls, and they cannot be too careful.

" I will take the responsibility. When I am gone—and I do not think I shall long survive this fearful trial—when I am gone you can please yourself. But for the present, at least, Charles must not know. You will not tell him, Edward, without permission. Promise me."

Mrs. Prince generally got her way, and Edward, feeling that it would be unseemly—at any rate just then—to set his mother at defiance, gave the required promise, albeit reluctantly and with a bad grace.

" I have my reasons," she said.

He guessed as much, and having a shrewd idea what they were felt all the more vexed, for Edward had no sympathy with sentiment when it conflicted with common-sense. Charlie had been Mr. Prince's favorite, and he Charlie's model and faultless exemplar, and the mother shrank almost with horror from letting the lad know that his father had made free with Mrs. Lincoln's fortune. He might not see, as she did, that in this instance at least the end justified the means. It would be quite time enough to tell him—if he must be told—when the new trustees had been appointed and the defalcation made good. The wrong—the unavoidable wrong, as she put it to herself—would then be redressed, and nobody, much less Charlie, would have any right to complain.

The day after the reading of the will Edward informed the Insurance Company of his father's decease, at the same time intimating that on receipt of the certificate of death from Trinidad he should prove the will and make a formal claim for the amount payable under the late Mr. Prince's life policy.

The Company's Secretary " had the honor to acknowledge the receipt of the letter and awaited his correspondent's further communication," which he assured him, would have the prompt attention of his Directors.

" That's all right," thought Edward, as he docketed and filed the Secretary's letter. " Payment is due three months after notification of decease ; but it's a rich Company and I have no doubt will settle on production of the probate. That's the good of dealing with a first-class firm. Rather a pity, though, that the premium was paid only last month. If it had fallen due this month or next we should have saved £500. However, we cannot have it every way. . . . I think we had better continue the policy on our joint lives. Charlie is sure to break his neck one of these days, and fifteen thousand and nothing to pay out of it would be a fine haul."

The news of Mr. Prince's death caused an even more painful sensation in Peele than it had caused in Port-of-Spain. As the local paper observed, it cast quite a gloom over the town. Everybody of note in the neighborhood left cards at Holmcroft, and Mrs. Prince received so many letters of condolence that she was obliged to answer them by lithographed circulars.

The Town Council held a special meeting, at which an address of condolence to the widow and family was unanimously adopted, and a resolution taken to place a marble bust of their late colleague in the vestibule of the Town Hall. The local justices adopted a similar address, and the County Court Judge delivered from the bench an eloquent eulogium on the deceased gentleman and expressed the warmest sympathy with his family in their bereavement.

The theme of the addresses and of the speeches by which they were supported was the late Mr. Prince's public spirit, unfailing urbanity and unswerving integrity. Above all, his integrity.

" Although for forty years member of a profession which affords more scope for equivocal practices than any other, and is popularly yet erroneously supposed to be incompatible with high honor and fair dealing, nobody has ever ventured to question Mr. Prince's honesty and straightforwardness. His best epitaph will be that he never took up a questionable case or engaged in a transaction that would not bear the light." Thus the Judge.

All this was very pleasing to Mrs. Prince, and made her bereavement more tolerable. But it suggested a possibility which, when she thought of it, terrified her beyond measure.

" If they should get to know," she said to Edward.

" They won't get to know, mother. There is less likelihood of their getting to know than ever there was. In a month or so I shall draw the insurance money, and put the right amount in Consols, in our joint names, as trustees under the will of the late Leonard Prince. Then we shall be as safe as houses."

" But doesn't Lillywhite know ? "

" He only guesses. And if he were to say anything, nobody would believe him. I should only have to open the safe and show the certificates to convict Lillywhite of a base slander. Besides, he is very much cut up about father's death ; and to do him justice, I do not think he has the least desire to play the traitor. ⸱ What would it profit him ? "

Mrs. Prince gave a sigh of relief.

" Well, get the money and buy the Consols as soon as ever you can, dear," she said, " I shall be on pins till you do."

A few days afterwards Mrs. Prince received a letter from Mrs. Lincoln, who was at Pallanza. She had read an account of Mr. Prince's death in the *Times*, quoted by that paper from a Trinidad contemporary. She could not have been more shocked and distressed, she said, had Mr. Prince been her own brother, and warmly sympathized with Mrs. Prince in the grievous misfortune which had befallen her, all the more, as it was a grievous misfortune for herself. Since her own husband's death Mr. Prince had been her best friend ; she was under the greatest obligation to him for acting as her trustee and discharging the duties of the office so faithfully and well. She presumed she would now have to find another trustee—perhaps two—but as to this she would confer with Edward on her return to All Hallows.

Mrs. Lincoln observed further that she doubted whether she should remain at All Hallows during the coming winter. It was an expensive place to keep up and the chancery suit had made serious inroads on her income. She felt disposed to take a house on the coast, within easy reach of London. But of this more when they met ; she expected to be at All Hallows for a few days in the course of the following month.

" That means," said Mrs. Prince, reflectively, after Edward had read the letter, " that means she has made up her mind to leave All Hallows."

" It certainly looks so."

" I shall be very sorry. Mrs. Lincoln is a pleasant neighbor and a kind friend—and you would not have nearly so many opportunities of meeting Olive."

" If I remain Mrs. Lincoln's legal adviser, and I think I

shall, and if this chancery suit goes on—and I am sure it will—I shall meet Olive pretty often."

" And Charlie will meet her very seldom," he thought. " It is a most excellent idea, and I hope Mrs. Lincoln will carry it into effect."

" Has it ever occurred to you that she may make you her trustee ? "

" It has, and I trust she will—one of them. That will keep the business in the office."

"Need she appoint two ? "

" There is no law compelling her to do so ; but you may depend on it that she will."

" Why ? "

" Because it is the right thing to do, and Mrs. Lincoln knows it. She appointed two in the first instance, and only refrained from appointing a successor to Wilmot because of her unbounded confidence in father. She cannot be expected to have the same confidence in me—yet."

" Well, I hope she will provide you with a pleasant colleague, dear."

" I hope so. One who will sign whatever I put before him, without reading it, and never bother his co-trustee with idle questions."

The same post that brought Mrs. Prince the letter from Mrs. Lincoln brought Charlie a letter from Olive, full of deep feeling and expressing the warmest sympathy and love. It must be terrible to lose such a father as his had been, she said, and her heart bled for him ; indeed, it did. His sorrow, was her sorrow, his loss her loss, not only because she felt for him and with him, but because she had loved and honored Mr. Prince more than she could tell. He was one of the best and sunniest men she had ever known. It was a great blessing to have had so good a father, and she counted it as a priceless privilege to have had such a friend.

And then Olive went on to speak of themselves, mentioning the probability of her mother giving up All Hallows, and regretting the concealment they were obliged to practice. But she held out a hope that when the time of mourning for his father was past, her mother might be prevailed upon to sanction an informal engagement, an engagement, that was to say, not to be made public until Olive came of age.

Charlie read this letter with mingled feelings. It gave

him a strange sense of sweet pain. Olive's appreciation of his
father's noble qualities, the assurance of her sympathy and
love were unspeakably grateful to him. But the thoughts her
words suggested and the consciousness of the irreparable loss
which he had sustained wrung his heart with anguish. With
his father gone and All Hallows empty, Peele would be like
a strange land. The dear old days, so full of pleasure and
enjoyment, when the present had no sorrows and the future
no terrors, were gone forever. Fair as were his prospects,
and albeit he had come into a goodly heritage, and Olive
was loving and true, he was still cast down; and at times he
had a vague foreboding that his father's death would prove
the harbinger of further misfortunes, as well for himself as
for others.

But only at times, for he was too busy for much brooding.
It almost seemed as if Mr. Prince's demise had created
business. It poured in from every side, and Charlie got his full
share of it. Then the books had to be balanced, and other
preparations made for proving the will. At the same time,
Edward was making interest to obtain the public appointments
so long held by his father. The brothers had already received
a kind letter from Lord Hermitage, in which he spoke in high
terms of the late Mr. Prince, and requested them to act as
his agents on the old terms.

The papers from Trinidad did not come quite so soon as
Edward had expected, but within a few days of their arrival he
and his mother paid the succession duty and proved the will.

"When will you write to the insurance company?" asked
Mrs. Prince, when the transaction was completed.

"This very day; I have only been waiting for the probate,
which I shall of course let them see."

"And how soon are you likely to get the money?"

"In a few days. The directors meet on Tuesday, I think,
and as everything is in order I don't see why they should
not send us a check at once. The Ægis make a specialty
of prompt settlements."

"That is well. What a relief it will be! Before your
father died it did not trouble me much. But now, I know
how much he must have suffered."

On the Wednesday next after this conversation Edward
found on his table a bulky packet, bearing the seal of the
Ægis Life Assurance Office.

"They have returned the probate," he said to himself; "and sent a check, I wonder? If they have not I will offer to allow them two months' interest at bank rate. Mother worries so, and I want to get the confounded thing off my mind." (Opening the packet.)

"A letter—of course—but no check. . . . What—why —they—villains, idiots—what do they mean?" and Edward Prince, after turning as pale as if he had seen a ghost, reddened with rage and dashed the letter on the floor.

Then he picked it up and read it again. Thus the portentous missive ran :—

"DEAR SIR,—I am instructed by my directors to inform you that as facts have come to their knowledge which lead them to believe that Mr. Leonard Prince did not observe the conditions of his license, they are unable to make any payment in respect of his joint policy (No. 43,751).

"I have the honor to return herewith the probate of your late father's will, the receipt of which be good enough to acknowledge.

"Your obedient servant,
"MYLES CUTTER, Sec."

CHAPTER XXII

EDWARD'S DILEMMA.

THE refusal of the insurance company to comply with his demand was a greater shock to Edward than his father's death. The latter event, though it befell so suddenly and tragically, was at least in the course of nature. It had been foreseen, and, in a sense, provided for.

But that an office like the Ægis should decline to pay up was an undreamt of contingency, a bolt from the blue, and Edward was so fiercely indignant at what he deemed the company's flagrant dishonesty, and so sick with disappointment, as to be rendered for a while unfit to consider the matter fairly.

" My directors declined to pay, do they ? " he muttered. " Well I'll make them pay, then. I'll sue them ; I'll expose them, I'll smash them. Haven't we paid the premiums regularly all the time ? Didn't I get a license and pay for it ? . . It's fearfully awkward. What will my mother say, and what shall we do about the broken trust ? Mrs. Lincoln will be here in a fortnight, and if she appoints new trustees before I get the money out of these rascals—that would be ruin. But I must get it ; there is no other word for it— must, must. . . From facts that have come to their knowledge they have reason to believe that father did not observe the conditions of his license. By going ashore when the steamer went aground, I suppose. They have seen the account in the papers. They argue that if he had not landed he would not have been bitten by the snake. But he was obliged to land ; if he had stayed on board and it had come on to blow he might have been drowned. He acted for the best. He could not prudently have done otherwise. . . . . No ! There is nothing in it. It's just a miserable attempt at chicane, unworthy of a great office like the Ægis. They think I am in want of the money, and that they can frighten me into offering a compromise. I'll see them —— first. I'll not take a penny less than the full amount. . . . Shall I confer with Lillywhite? The old fellow is very shrewd. . . No, I'll write to the secretary and ask what he means, and keep my own counsel till I get his answer."

So Edward, bottling up his wrath, constrained himself to write a studiously courteous, yet curt and slightly sarcastic letter, asking Mr. Cutter "kindly to state for his information the precise ground on which the company refused to pay the amount for which his father had insured his life, and paid the stipulated premiums regularly, and to the last fraction."

Mr. Cutter's reply came in due course. It was to the effect that, after reading the account of the late Mr. Prince's death in the public papers, an account which was implicitly confirmed by the certificates his executors had submitted to them, the directors could come to no other conclusion than that he had invalidated the policy by violating its provisions. The license was for a voyage to and from Trinidad, and the perils incident thereto, and a limited residence in the island. It did not include the perils incident to a cruise in the Bay of Paria and a landing on the Spanish Main. In these circumstances the directors could not, in duty to their shareholders, pay the amount of which the late Mr. Prince had insured his life by the joint policy (43,751).

"There seems to be something in it after all," soliloquized Edward when he had read the letter. . . . "The accident was clearly not incident to the voyage between England and Trinidad. But surely a license to reside in Trinidad implies a right to do whatever an ordinary resident in the island would do—cross a river, climb a mountain, or cruise in the bay, which is almost completely landlocked and as much a lake as a sea. However, I will have Lillywhite in and hear what he says—two heads are better than one—and I may as well tell Charlie at the same time. It will save trouble."

So the two were called and the matter laid before them.

"What do I think about it?" exclaimed Charlie, impetuously. "Well, I call it a piece of infernal rascality. The grounds on which these people want to repudiate their liability appear to me quite frivolous, and I should pitch into them without further notice."

Edward smiled.

" What do you say, Lillywhite?" (turning to the managing clerk).

" Well, I cannot quite agree with Mr. Charles that it is a piece of rascality. There are two ends to a stick, break it as often as you will, and it seems to me that these people have a case, though not one to run away with; and they are surely taking a very narrow view of their obligations in refusing to pay. But it is a nice point, a very nice point, and one as to which two good lawyers might easily arrive at opposite conclusions. Was your father, according to the strict letter of his license, justified in taking that cruise? That is the question. I should say he was, and I can promise you one thing, Mr. Edward: if it comes to a fight, and the case is tried in this county, you'll get a verdict, whatever the lawyers say. But perhaps the company don't mean fighting, after all. How would it be to show your teeth—write that, in view of the position they have taken up, you have no alternative but to proceed for the recovery of the sum due under the policy, and inquire who will accept service for them?"

" That is exactly what I thought of doing, Lillywhite, and I will do it to-day—nothing like striking while the iron is hot."

This ended the conference. Edward turned to his desk, and the other two left the room.

" A very unpleasant affair this, Mr. Charles," observed the managing clerk, sympathetically, when they were in the outer office.

" Very; and rascally, too, on the part of the Ægis people, I call it. But you don't think there is any chance of their winning, do you?"

" Not with a Peele jury. But when you go to law you never know what the issue will be. A surprise may be sprung on you at any moment; and fifteen thousand pounds is a large sum, either to gain or lose."

" Yes. I wonder why my father insured his life for so much. It was very, very good of him; but there was really no need. My mother is provided for by her marriage settlement, and the office will bring in quite enough for Ned and me."

" One of you might get married, and that would involve another establishment, you know."

"It would not involve an outlay of fifteen thousand pounds. However, that is no reason why the company should not pay up, and I am glad that Ned is going for them."

"Humph! They have not told him, then. I thought as much," mused Lillywhite, as he returned to his desk. "They ought to have done. It may be my duty to enlighten him one of these days."

Mr. Lillywhite, as Edward had informed his mother, was a good deal "cut up" by Mr. Prince's death. He knew that he had not been very kind on the occasion of their last interview; letting pique get the better of propriety, and rather returning evil for good than good for good (Mr. Prince had always treated him handsomely), and being at the bottom by no means a bad fellow, he greatly regretted the fact; "it stuck in his crop," to use his own expression; and, by way of making amends, the managing clerk resolved to do all that he could for his late employer's family. This meant Mrs. Prince and Charlie, particularly Charlie, for though Edward had observed the conditions of their compact, and since his father's death had been surprisingly affable, the managing clerk did not love him.

Though Lillywhite had not been told so, he inferred with certainty that the insurance money was destined to replace Mrs. Lincoln's trust fund; he also foresaw that failure to recover the amount from the company would lead to a serious crisis in the fortunes of the family and the firm.

It would be his business to protect Charlie.

Edward might look to himself.

"If he likes to get into a mess—make himself a party to the fraud, and run the risk of being struck off the rolls—that is his affair," thought Lillywhite.

By return of post came an answer to Edward's second letter to Mr. Myles Cutter. It was provokingly laconic, and ran as follows :—

"I have the honor to acknowledge the receipt of your esteemed favor of yesterday, and in reply, beg to inform you that Messrs. Bartrum, Fox, and Crafty, Chancery-lane, are prepared to accept service on our behalf."

"They do mean fighting, then," muttered Edward between his set teeth. He had cherished a lingering hope that when

" my directors" saw that he was in earnest they would climb down.

" So be it. I will hurry on the action with all speed ; draw up a case for counsel's opinion and retain Going and Somers. There is no reason why the cause should not be tried at the winter Assizes."

When Edward went home he told his mother.

" The insurance company won't pay," he said bitterly.

" Won't pay ! Why ? "

" There, read for yourself," showing her Cutter's letters and the copies of his answers.

It is given to few people to consider judicially cases in which they are personally interested, and Mrs. Prince was not one of them. In the refusal of the Ægis to pay she saw only a vile attempt to ruin herself and her children, and denounced the company with passionate indignation.

" You must make them pay. Don't dally, make them," she cried.

" You may be sure I shall do my best, mother."

" Your best won't do, Edward. You must make them. What is law for, if not to redress wrong and punish fraud ? You are a lawyer, are you not ? "

He tried to explain, but she interrupted him with angry exclamations, until, and at length, he, too, grew angry.

" Do you suppose I have not as much interest in getting the money as you have ? " he said. " If you think I am not competent to conduct the case, put it into the hands of some other solicitor. I won't stand in the way. But at least listen to reason, and please to understand that though I will strain every nerve to succeed, it is beyond my power to guarantee success. As for the law and fraud, and wrong and so forth, perhaps the less we say about that the better."

Mrs. Prince rose from her chair, her nostrils quivering, her hands clenched, and fierce words rose to her lips ; but restraining herself with a great effort she asked her son quietly, albeit in a voice trembling with suppressed wrath, what would happen if he did not succeed.

" Frankly, mother, I don't know. It will be time enough to consider that contingency when it arises, and I think we shall succeed ; and chances are at least in our favor. I only want you to understand that the company have a case, and we must not reckon on success as a certainty."

"When, then—how soon ? "

"When is the case likely to be tried ? In two or three months I hope. At any rate, before Whitsuntide."

"God help me ! " she murmured. "Until then I will try to possess my soul in patience. . . . But Mrs. Lincoln is coming to confer with you about the appointment of fresh trustees. She will be here in a few days. What will you say to her ? "

"I shall temporize. The appointment will be made by deed, which I will promise to prepare as soon as I have a little spare time. Mrs. Lincoln's matter is not urgent ; she is too good-natured to hurry me, and one way and another I can easily put her off three or four months."

"Very well, I leave it to you," returned Mrs. Prince gloomily. "Anything but exposure. It would kill me—and not a word to Charlie, mind. You see I was right in not letting you tell him the other day."

"I am not so sure about that. You know my opinion—and circumstances will force us to tell him—mark me if they don't."

"But not yet, not yet. Spare him a little longer—and me," murmured Mrs. Prince faintly, as if the mere idea were more than she could bear.

Edward said no more, but if he had not dreaded another scene he would, probably, have insisted on telling Charlie the whole truth without further delay, for he perceived that if the impending action against the company went against them he should have to bear the brunt. Up to the time of his father's death Edward had neither incurred blame nor taken responsibility. He had simply been the recipient of a secret. But his father's mantle had fallen on his shoulders, and whether as Mr. Prince's executor or Mrs. Lincoln's solicitor, it was his duty to inform that lady of the disappearance of her settled fortune—unless he could restore it—and if he failed in his suit restoration would be impossible. In that event he would be regarded, and rightly, as *particeps criminis*, and though his offence might be less flagrant than his father's, exposure would react injuriously on his character and mar his professional prospects.

The thought that Charlie was out of it all, and should the "worst come to the worst," would be able to say to Mrs. Lincoln and Olive, "I knew nothing of this dreadful business; if I had known I should have told you," made him almost wild, and he made up his mind that if counsel's opinion were unfavorable he would tell Charlie all, whatever his mother might say.

But counsel's opinion was not unfavorable.   It was to this effect :   From a strictly legal point of view the insurance company were probably right in their contention that the late Mr. Prince had violated the conditions of his license. On the other hand, there could be no question that the landing on the Venezuelan coast was unintentional, and, in the circumstances, unavoidable.   Moreover, juries did not always take a strictly legal view of the cases which they are called upon to decide.   They seldom sympathized with wealthy corporations, and in this instance the sympathies of the jury would almost certainly be with the plaintiffs, for at the worst Mr. Prince had erred from inadvertence ; the grounding of the yacht and the bite of the water mocassin being accidents pure and simple, and no fault of his.   Taking all these facts into consideration there was every reason to believe that the executors were well advised in taking action against the company.

After this Edward, regarding success as certain, decided to say nothing to Charlie till after the trial.

CHAPTER XXI.

OLIVE'S DESIGN.

As the Princes had no interest in making a secret of their difference with the insurance company, it soon became a matter of common knowledge in the borough of Peele, and the burgesses naturally sided with the family of their " late eminent and respected townsman," as the local paper described Mr. Prince.   Equally natural was it that the subject should be warmly discussed wherever men met, and the "shameful conduct " of the Ægis nightly denounced in every tavern in the town.

The *Mercury* did a leading article on the subject, in the course of which it expressed great regret that a certain highly-respected lady should be called upon, so soon after the death of her late lamented husband, to undergo another trial, assured her of its sympathy, and wished her a happy issue out of her afflictions.

This and the many other assurances of sympathy which she received were very gratifying to Mrs. Prince.   She regarded them as well-deserved tributes to the respectability of the family and the memory of her husband.   But Edward, who took wider views than his mother, would have been much better pleased had the sympathy of his neighbors been somewhat less demonstrative.   He feared that it might do him more harm than good, and the result justified his apprehensions.   The defendants, getting wind of the strong feeling which prevailed against them at Peele, and believing with reason, that no Peele jury could be trusted to render an impartial verdict, applied for a change of venue, and the application, though energetically opposed by the plaintiffs' counsel, was granted, and an order made for the case to be tried at London by a special jury.

"A bad job, this, Mr. Charlie," observed Lillywhite

gravely, when they received the news from Edward, who was in London, "watching the case."

"I don't see it, Lillywhite. One jury is as good as another. We have right on our side, and an insurance company that contests a claim always fights at a disadvantage. The legal presumption, as well as popular feeling, is against them."

"That is true. All the same, I don't much like London juries. They are conceited chaps, those Londoners. Then the omen is bad. It is just as if you were going to fight a duel, and your opponent had won the toss for the choice of ground."

Edward, also, was discouraged by the result of this first passage of arms. Like Lillywhite, he regarded it as a bad omen. But a consultation with Sergeant Somers, his leading counsel, who never, under any circumstances, allowed himself to be discouraged, restored his confidence.

"I am not sure that you don't gain more than you lose," observed the great advocate. "Though a Peele jury might be more friendly, a London jury is sure to be more intelligent. On the facts before me, Mr. Prince, I have little doubt as to the result. Not that I think our legal position is absolutely unassailable—it has one or two very weak points —but I shall be able to make a strong appeal to the jury on their sentimental side, and when sentiment and prejudice go together they are bad to beat."

So Edward went home comforted, for the sergeant was a great verdict winner.

Meanwhile Mrs. Lincoln and Olive were returned to All Hallows, and the now senior partner of the firm of Prince and Prince presently waited on his client to inform her as to the progress of the chancery suit (if it could be said to progress) and consult her touching the appointment of new trustees under her marriage settlement.

His report was disheartening. To all appearance the suit might go on forever, or, at any rate, until the partnership estate was exhausted and there was nothing left for anybody, save the lawyers, and Mrs. Lincoln, appalled by the prospect, urged her adviser to try whether he could not put a stop to further litigation by arranging a compromise. To effect this object, she was ready to make any sacrifice short of absolute surrender.

Edward quite agreed with his client as to the expediency
of the course she suggested, and said he should use his utmost efforts to carry out her wishes. He would have said so
in any case, if only by way of keeping in the lady's good
graces; but in this instance he spoke with more than professional sincerity. True, the chancery suit was a good
thing for the office; but it is doubtful wisdom to kill the
goose that lays the golden egg, and Edward reflected that
in view of certain eventualities it were a still better thing to
deserve well of Mrs. Lincoln. Moreover, as he had not
abandoned the hope of marrying Olive, it was clearly his interest to save the remnant of her heritage from the harpies
of the law.

Mrs. Lincoln next mentioned that she was resolved to
leave All Hallows. It would go very much against the grain.
But she felt that she must; the expense of "running it" and
fighting a chancery suit at the same time was greater than she
could afford; and Edward received instructions to advertise
the house to be let furnished. Mr. Marsh, an old friend
of her husband's, whose business took him frequently to
America, owned a pleasant little house on the coast, not more
than two hours' railway journey from Peele, which, having no present use for, he had offered her, at a nominal rent.
There she and Olive would abide until they were "out of
chancery," and could see their way more clearly.

"And now about my trustees," observed Mrs. Lincoln.
"I suppose I should appoint two."

"That is as you like. You have power under the settlement to appoint two."

"And I shall do so. It is more regular; and it is not fair
to saddle one friend with the entire responsibility. Everybody is not like your dear father. He was one in a thousand.
The money is still in Consols, I suppose?"

"Yes, certainly, of course," answered Edward with a nervous start; and his eyes fell somewhat, and a fugitive flush
of shame mantled his brow, for he was not yet so case-
hardened that he could lie in cold blood without a sense of
humiliation and shame.

"Well, keep it there. It is a comfort to know that, whatever happens, I shall have twenty-five hundred dollars a
year, of which nothing short of the collapse of the British
Empire can deprive me. But I must have two trustees—

would you kindly consent to be one of them—in succession
to your father?"

"With all my heart. I shall only be too glad," was the
quick and almost eager answer.

Mrs. Lincoln looked pleased. It was not often that the
self-contained Edward Prince showed so much warmth.

"I knew you would. Thank you very much. You lay
me under a great obligation, which I hope some time to
have the opportunity of discharging. And now, as to your
colleague. I cannot think of anybody more suitable than
Mr. Marsh, the friend of whom I spoke just now. He is a
man of business and means, and very nice in every way.

"Will he act?"

"I have not the least doubt he will. I shall ask him the
next time we meet; or shall I write? Is there any hurry
about the appointment?"

"Not the least. And I have so many irons in the fire just
now that I hardly know which way to turn. Our action
against the Ægis takes a good deal of my time, not to speak
of other matters; and then there is your chancery suit, and
the proposed compromise, as to which I mean to run up to
town and see Topper, Sandboy, and Perrywinkle right away."

"You are very good. Well, never mind about the appointment just now. I won't write to Mr. Marsh. I will wait till
I see him, and as he is going abroad, that will not be for
some time."

Edward breathed again. The immediate appointment of
Mr. Marsh would be fatal. He knew him by repute as a
very shrewd man of business, not likely, Edward felt sure, to
accept the trusteeship without ocular demonstration that
Mrs. Lincoln's Consols stood in their joint names. At all
hazards the appointment must be delayed until the Ægis
paid up.

When her solicitor was gone Mrs. Lincoln gave her
daughter an account of what had passed, lauding Edward to
the skies for his kindness and business aptitude.

Olive was in a captious mood, due mainly to the necessity
(which there was no denying) of leaving All Hallows; and
praise of Edward seemed to imply dispraise of Charlie.

"Where does the kindness come in?" she asked abruptly,
when her mother paused for a reply.

"Come in? What a question. It comes in everywhere, First of all in agreeing to be my trustee."

"That is not much. I remember hearing father say that when a trust fund is invested in Government stock a trusteeship involves no risk and very little trouble. Besides, Edward Prince being a lawyer will make a charge for his trouble, I suppose? Why don't you ask Charlie or Mr. Lillywhite to be a trustee? They would consider it an honor, and be quite as efficient as Mr. Marsh, I should say."

"Not a bad idea, Olive; and if Mr. Marsh does not return from the Continent in a few weeks, or shows any disinclination to act, I shall ask Charlie."

"You think he would be better than Mr. Lillywhite?" asked Olive carelessly, as if it were a matter of indifference to her which of the two her mother might prefer.

"Charlie, of course, if only because he is the younger."

"Mr. Marsh is not young."

"No, but he is an old friend. However, I am not nearly so wedded to the idea as I was before you suggested Charlie. There is no hurry, Edward says, and—we shall see."

From which Olive inferred that the decision would be in accordance with her desires. As may be supposed, her motives for wishing Charlie to be chosen were based rather on sentiment than reason. If possible she would have had him appointed and Edward discarded, but that being out of the question she wanted him to be at least equal with his brother; she also thought that if Charlie were made a trustee he would be brought into more intimate relations with her mother, and that business arising out of the trust might afford him an occasional excuse for visiting them at their new home by the sea.

To all seeming a harmless enough design, yet fraught with momentous consequences, as well for Olive herself as for the Princes.

CHAPTER XXIII.

EDWARD SCORES AND OLIVE SCHEMES.

EDWARD PRINCE had no great hope of success in his mission of compromise. Nevertheless, the attempt was worth making. If he succeeded he should make a fast friend of Mrs. Lincoln, and by serving both mother and daughter increase his chance of winning the latter. If he failed, the chancery suit would go merrily on, bringing grist to the professional mill—for there still existed a considerable residue of the partnership estate to cut and carve at.

So "equal to either fortune" as touching the matter in hand, and confident as to the outcome of his action against the Ægis, Edward went to London in high spirits. His first proceeding was to call at the office of Topper, Sandboy, and Perrywinkle, of King-street, Cheapside, the legal advisers of Mr. Jump, who was supposed to be the most irreconcilable litigious of the half-dozen parties concerned in "*re* Lincoln, Lyman, and others."

Edward had a slight acquaintance with Mr. Perrywinkle, who managed the Chancery department of the firm's business, and after cooling his heels for an hour in the general office, he was allowed to see Mr. Perrywinkle, a short, slightly-built man of thirty-five or so, with a quick, vivacious manner, a sallow skin, lantern jaws, and beady black eyes.

Although Edward was exceedingly riled at being kept so long waiting, he put on his pleasantest smile and most urbane manner, and opened the campaign with an apology to Mr. Perrywinkle for trespassing on his valuable time.

Perrywinkle was equally expansive.

"Don't mention it, my dear sir," said he. "I am delighted to see you. Pray take a seat. And now what can I do for you?"

"Well, we are both busy men, and I will come straight to the point. I am concerned for Mrs. Lincoln, as you know, and my object is to ascertain whether you don't think it would be advisable for us to cease litigating and arrange our difference amongst ourselves."

Perriwinkle's cadaverous countenance lengthened portentously.

"God bless me! I surely haven't made a miscalculation," he exclaimed. "The Pactolean stream is not dried up at its source? There is still corn in Egypt—an estate I mean?"

"Of course there is, or I shouldn't be here."

"I see. Of course you wouldn't. Yes, I see. You are from the country, and your client is a widow. Being tired of litigation—which I admit is rather a costly luxury—she has instructed you, or you have advised her, to hoist the white flag, with a view to a suspension of arms and a treaty of peace?"

Edward nodded. Perrywinkle's manner was growing slightly unpleasant, not to say offensive.

"You have been in the general office?"

"Rather! I waited there an hour."

"Well, as I daresay you observed, it is crowded with clerks, and there are as many more in other parts of the building—and then the rent of these offices! How much do you think we have to make before we get anything for ourselves?"

"I have no idea."

"Five thousand a year—rather more than less. We are not a country office, and business is business."

"I understand. You have got hold of a good thing and mean to stick to it."

"I did not say so, but of course you are at liberty to infer what you like. However, I may as well tell you that our client won't hear of a compromise. He thinks he has been badly used, and resents, as an imputation on his good faith, Mrs. Lincoln's demand for an account of the firm's transactions during the twelve months immediately preceding her husband's death. He has large independent resources, and means to go on fighting as long as there is a shot in the locker."

"In that case I have got my answer, and may as well take my departure. Good-morning, Mr. Perrywinkle."

"Good-morning, my dear sir, *good*-morning," repeated Perrywinkle, bowing his visitor to the door with effusive politeness.

As Edward, highly indignant, rose to take his leave, he noticed on Perrywinkle's desk a letter addressed :

> " Jabez J. Jump, Esq.,
> Thatched House Club,
> St. James's-street."

This gave him an idea, on which he forthwith acted. Making for Cheapside, he hailed a passing hansom, and bade the driver take him to the Thatched House Club.

" It's highly irregular, and as likely as not I shall meet with another rebuff," he thought ; "but I'll make the attempt, if only on the off-chance of getting even with that cad of a Perrywinkle."

Mr. Jump was not in, said the hall porter, but he generally lunched at the club, and the most likely time to find him disengaged was about 2.30. On this Edward went elsewhere for a while, and, presently returning, met with his man, whose acquaintance he had made a few years previously at All Hallows. Albeit Jabez J. Jump hailed from Vermont, he bore not the least resemblance to the Yankee of comedy and the comic papers. He was an essentially " all round man." His body was round, his face was round, and his limbs were round. He had rosy cheeks, shrewd gray eyes, and a genial smile. His whiskers were of the orthodox British cut ; he neither chewed tobacco nor sported a goatee ; and, strangest of all, had almost lost the nasal twang of his native land.

Mr. Jump received his visitor cordially.

" Glad to see you, Mr. Prince," he said. " Won't you sit down ? What can I offer you ? A cup of coffee ? All right. Two cups of coffee at once, John Thomas. You smoke, of course. Here is a cigar I can recommend."

Edward took the proffered cigar, and settled himself in the very easy chair which Mr. Jump wheeled round for him.

" A great many changes since we last met five years ago at poor Toby's (one of Mr. Lincoln's Christian names was Tobias). And sad ones. Toby and your father both gone to their long homes ; the house of Lyman, Lincoln, and Jump gone to pot ; and ourselves at loggerheads, fighting with the ferocity of Kilkenny cats. But such is life. How is Mrs. Lincoln ? "

" Well in health, but low in spirits."

"Owing to this cursed chancery suit, no doubt. Well, I don't wonder at that damping anybody's spirits. I know it often damps mine; and it takes a good deal to do that, you bet. Why doesn't she come down from her high horse and settle, then?"

"I am not aware that she ever rode the high horse. Anyhow, she is quite ready to come to terms."

"The deuce she is! Why, it was only last week I said to Perrywinkle, 'Why doesn't somebody propose a compromise?' It is about time, I guess. If we quarrel much longer there won't be a red cent left to serve as a bone of contention. Hadn't you better see Perrywinkle?"

"I have seen him, and as the interview was not precisely satisfactory I came here to see you."

"You surely don't mean to say that he told you I did not want to end it?"

"If he had said you did I should not be here now, Mr. Jump."

"I see. He does not want to end it, and no wonder, considering how he is fattening on our folly. I was a fool not to think of that before. I wish all lawyers were at the devil —I beg pardon (laughing heartily), I was forgetting you were one of the tribe—all London lawyers, let us say. And now about business. What are your ideas? Have you anything definite to propose?"

Edward had something definite to propose, and he put the matter so clearly and fairly, and was so "well up" in all the complicated details of the case that Mr. Jump complimented him on his smartness. After some further conversation the American assented, "in principle," to Edward's proposals, and undertook to submit them to the other parties to the suit, and recommend their adoption. But as two of the litigants were in New York, and for other reasons, this would require time; and use what diligence they might several months must needs elapse before "the business could be put through," but that it would eventually be "put through" Mr. Jump had no doubt whatever.

"I don't think I shall change my lawyers," he observed. "It is a bad thing to swop horses when you are crossing the stream; and Perrywinkle knows the ropes. But if I remain his client he will have to dance to my tune; I have danced to his quite long enough."

All of which greatly pleased Edward. He had scored in every way; done a good thing for himself and his client, and put a spoke in the wheel of Mr. Perrywinkle; and he returned to Peele full of admiration of his own cleverness, and in a serene and self-satisfied mood.

"I have as good as settled it," he said complacently to Charlie and Lillywhite, "and that means a saving to Mrs. Lincoln and Olive of something like two or three score thousand pounds out of the fire. Perrywinkle gave me a shirty answer, and sneered at me as a country lawyer. But I was not going to be bowled over in that way, so I went straight to Jump. It was rather a bold thing to do; but it turned out all right. I showed him how desirable it was—in his own interest—to come to terms, and he not only accepted my proposals—in principle—but undertook to get the other parties to the suit to accept them. That is why I regard the affair as being practically settled."

Charlie warmly congratulated his brother on his success.

"Seeing Jump was simply a master stroke," he said; "I should not have thought of it. I should just have punched Perrywinkle's head and come home."

Edward bore himself rather more modestly when he made his report to Mrs. Lincoln. Yet, even with her he did not hide his light under a bushel, and felt that he fully deserved the profuse thanks which she gave him and the praises she bestowed on his fertility of resource and presence of mind. Olive also thanked him, and so graciously and heartily withal (for had he not rendered them a great service and lifted a load of care from her mother's mind?) as to raise his hopes still higher and make him hardly less confident of winning her love than beating the Assurance Company.

Before he went away Mrs. Lincoln inquired after Charlie, especially as to whether he was taking more kindly to the law.

"Oh, he does his best, and makes himself useful—after a fashion; but he is not clever, Mrs. Lincoln, and I fear will never make a lawyer."

Although this observation, and the manner of it, which was flippant and almost contemptuous, vexed Olive, she could not disguise from herself that there was much truth in Edward's opinion of his brother's character, and she regretted more than ever that destiny had made Charlie a second-rate lawyer instead of a hero, or a poet, or something equally dis-

tinguished. A few days later the lovers met at the old trysting-place for the last time. On the morrow she and her
mother were leaving All Hallows, probably never to return, for
even though Edward's proposed compromise were accepted
without serious modification there was grave reason to doubt
whether Mrs. Lincoln's future income would enable her to
keep the place up. The unliquidated costs of the suit were
sure to be heavy, and nobody could tell how much the assets
of the defunct firm were likely to realize.

No wonder, therefore, that the lovers were not in the best
of spirits. Charlie was the more melancholy of the two. Edward's success in the matter of the chancery suit had kindled
his natural arrogance, and he was again making things unpleasant at the office. Home was not what it had been. His
father's death had worsened his mother's temper ; she kept
her younger son at a distance, and, as it would seem, gave
all her confidence to Edward, and Edward affected to treat
him as a boy. This was quite bad enough ; and now Olive
was going away. Correspondence with her would be difficult, if not impossible, and he could only hope to see her at
long intervals.

Olive tried to cheer him.

"We are not going to the end of the world, you foolish
boy," she said, smiling. "Whitebeach is only fifty miles
away."

"What does it matter where you are if I cannot see you ?"
asked Charlie moodily.

"Oh, but you can see me. You must come to Whitebeach."

"All very fine ; but what would mother say—and Ned ? "

"You must have an excuse, of course, and I think you will
have one. I am almost sure my mother will ask you to be
one of her trustees, along with Edward. You will, won't
you ? "

"Certainly. I would do anything in the world to oblige
her and please you, darling."

"Take care what you say. I shall, perhaps, be putting
you to the test one of these days."

"I wish you would—any test you like. I shall, of course,
be glad to act as one of your mother's trustees, but I don't
quite see how that will afford me a pretext for visiting you
at Whitebeach."

" You could come to her to talk about business, you know."

" I cannot imagine what there would be to talk about—unless you put her up to ask me to bring her dividends now and then."

" Well, I shall see whether I cannot. I shall have to mind what I am about, though. But you are all to be invited to spend a few days with us at Whitsuntide ; and your mother has asked me to visit her at Holmcroft. Oh, we shall have opportunities, and I shall write to you occasionally, though you must on no account write to me. Mother is so very curious about letters. And when the chancery suit is gone to the bourne from which no traveller returns, which I hope will be soon, and mother can think about other things, we will tell her all. So keep up your courage, Charlie dear. You said just now you would do anything to please me. Do that ; be of good cheer ; it will please me immensely."

" God bless you, Olive, you are the best and dearest girl in the world."

" Of course I am—but that is no reason why—see how you have upset my hair. And now I must really run away. We shall meet again at Whitsuntide ; and you shall hear from me in the meantime. Good-night."

And then they parted, and rather to his surprise Charlie went away in better heart than he had come—the outlook was not so bad as he had thought it, after all.

CHAPTER XXIII.

TRIED AND FOUND WANTING.

SOME two months after the Lincolns left Peele Edward received a letter from his client to the effect that Mr. Marsh being still on the Continent and the time of his return uncertain she had decided not to trouble him in the matter of the trusteeship. She was writing to Charlie, asking him to be good enough to accept the appointment, and in the event of his acceding to her request (as to which she made no doubt) Edward would perhaps kindly prepare the necessary deed, and they could all sign it when the brothers and Mrs. Prince came to Whitebeach at Whitsuntide.

"Charlie will accept, of course, and a good thing, a very good thing. His appointment will make us safe in any event." thought Edward to himself : and he felt much as a general would feel who on the eve of battle was told that an important pass in his rear had been occupied by a detachment of his own troops. For as the day of the trial drew near Edward grew less confident. He protested to himself and everybody else that they were sure to win ; but the possibility of failure was undeniable, and followed by the appointment of Mr. Marsh would have spelt ruin.

He hinted as much to his mother, when he told her of Mrs. Lincoln's proposal, to appoint Charlie, saying what a good thing it was and how much it had eased his mind.

Mrs. Prince looked as if she did not quite understand him.

"I am glad Mrs. Lincoln wishes to appoint your brother," she said. "It is a compliment to him and the family. Still, I don't quite see——You are surely not in any doubt as to the result of the trial."

"I think we shall win, of course : but everything is possible, and there is always the glorious uncertainty, you know."

"Don't talk to me in that way. I know nothing of the sort,

in this case," returned Mrs. Prince, severely, almost angrily, indeed. "I refuse to admit the possibility which you suggest. And if—if the verdict were to go against us, I think I should doubt the goodness of God."

Edward, dreading a scene, said no more. Besides, it was obviously impossible to reason with a woman who flatly refused to consider a certain contingency because its occurrence would conflict with her ideas of the divine goodness.

Charlie, whom Olive had already apprised of her mother's decision, wrote to Mrs. Lincoln by return post, saying how glad he should be to accept the appointment ; and Edward, writing at the same time, expressed his sense of the honor conferred upon them, and assured her that he and his brother would use their best endeavors to justify her confidence.

The trial came off the following week, in the Court of Queen's Bench. It was marked by no sensational incidents, nor, save at Peele, did it excite any particular interest. There was no dispute as to the facts ; for nobody doubted that Leonard Prince had died from the effect of a snake-bite on the coast of Venezuela ; and in order to avoid the expense of bringing witnesses from Port-of-Spain, or sending thither a commission, the solicitors concerned had agreed to accept, as evidence, the account of the occurrence given by the Trinidad papers, and confirmed by private correspondents.

Sergeant Somers and a junior appeared for the plaintiffs, the Attorney-General and a junior for the defendants.

The sergeant, who was a fluent and powerful speaker, carried the war into the enemy's camp with great vigor, stigmatizing the Assurance Company's refusal to pay the amount for which Mr. Prince had insured his life as a mean evasion of a solemn obligation, and contending at considerable length that the deceased had not broken his contract by going ashore at Chachacara Bay. The license for a limited sojourn in Trinidad, a license for which he had paid an extra premium, surely carried with it the privilege of doing what ordinary inhabitants of the island were in the habit of doing. A cruise in the Bay of Paria was an ordinary incident of Trinidadian life ; the landing and the result of an accident, for which Mr. Prince could no more be held responsible than for inadvertently treading on the water mocassin that caused his death. He disembarked because, in the captain's opinion, he would be safer ashore than aboard. In this he exercised a wise

discretion, and the learned counsel felt quite sure that in
analogous circumstances any of the "gentlemen of the jury"
would have done the same.

Sergeant Somers concluded with an eloquent appeal to the
jury to give his clients the benefit of any doubt they might
entertain—if, contrary to his belief and expectation, they
should entertain any doubt—as to the right of the widow and
children to receive the sum for which the late Mr. Prince had
assured his life, and for which he had honestly and regularly
paid the stipulated consideration.

When Sergeant Somers sat down, the Attorney-General got
up, and as in duty bound made very light of his adversary's
arguments, even going so far as to protest that the plaintiffs
had no case. A great company like the Ægis, he said, never
disputed a claim unless it were flagrantly and obviously
unjust, as in the present instance. But if they were to admit
this claim, they might as well make all their policies absolute
at once, and let their policy-holders live where they liked,
even in the most pestiferous parts of the earth. The license
was expressly for a voyage to and from Trinidad, and the
perils incident thereto. It included a residence in the island
for a limited time, and, of course, all that "residence" in the
ordinary acceptation of the word fairly implied. His clients
had no wish to construe this condition in any narrow sense.
If Mr. Prince had lost his life while voyaging in Trinidadian
waters they should have paid the sum for which it was
assured without demur. But the Attorney-General called the
particular attention of the jury to the fact that the license
did not cover the perils incident to a voyage in Venezuelan
waters, and a landing, voluntary or involuntary, on the
Venezuelan coast.

If it were competent for Mr. Prince under his license to go
to one part of Venezuela it was competent for him to go to
all parts, and some parts of that country were amongst the
most unhealthy in the world.

This would be practically converting a conditional license
into an all-world policy, and the correspondence between the
Secretary and Mr. Edward Prince (which he proceeded to
read) showed that the company's offer to make it an all-
world policy on very moderate terms was distinctly declined.
In taking this course Mr. Edward Prince had clearly made
a grievous mistake ; he had been penny wise and pound

foolish, but it would be hard indeed to visit on the company
the unwisdom of a policy-holder. If there were any element
of doubt in the case, he, the learned counsel, would be the
first to urge the jury to give the plaintiffs the benefit of it;
but there was none, not a scintilla, and he besought the jury,
as men of business and the world, to render a verdict in
accordance with the principles of equity and the dictates of
common-sense.

The judge's summing up was decidedly in favor of the
defendants. He cautioned the jury not to let their natural
feeling for Mrs. Prince and her sons, and the common prejudice against wealthy corporations, either warp their judgments
or influence their verdict. All they had to do was to construe
a contract as set forth on the policy on Mr. Prince's life, and
the license for the voyage to Trinidad; both of which he read
and commented upon in some detail. If the jury were of
opinion that a license for a voyage to Trinidad and the perils
incident thereto included a voyage to Venezuela and its
incidental dangers, they would give a verdict for the plaintiffs,
if not, their verdict would be for the defendants.

After a short deliberation the foreman of the jury informed
the Judge that they had found for the defendants.

"It was your refusal to make the policy 'all-world,' that
did the mischief," whispered Sergeant Somers to Edward
Prince. "In the face of that, I really don't see how they
could have come to any other conclusion."

The Attorney-General, who had been conferring with the
company's Solicitor and Secretary, asked and obtained permission to make a statement before the jury separated. The
directors had instructed him to say that, in the event of the
verdict being in their favor, they would not ask for their
costs, and he, on his part, should advise them to pay to Mr.
Prince's executors the surrender value of his interest in the
policy at the time he went abroad, either in cash, or in the
shape of a reduced premium, should the sons decide to continue the policy on their joint lives."

"Very liberal, very liberal indeed," observed the judge;
and murmurs of approval were heard in the jury box and
echoed in the bar.

"That's two for themselves and one for you," observed
Sergeant Somers to his client. "It would be a shame if they
kept all those premiums and gave nothing in return. They

could not do less, and this public announcement of their liberality will get into the papers and be a splendid advertisement for them."

Edward made some sort of a reply—he hardly knew what —and the sergeant, seeing that his client was indisposed for conversation, said no more—to his client's great relief. For Edward was terribly disappointed. He had hoped against hope, and to the very last believed that they should win. Now, the scales were fallen from his eyes, and he saw that he had been living in a fool's paradise from the first—worse still, that public opinion at Peele would hold him responsible for the result. People would say that to save a hundred and fifty pounds he had thrown away fifteen thousand.

The Attorney-General's taunt cut him to the quick. It wounded him in his most sensitive part—his self-esteem—he felt the imputation all the more keenly that it was entirely undeserved, and he could not resent it as publicly as it was made. He had not made a mistake. He had acted on sound business principles. The veriest fool could be wise after the event. What would have been the good of making the policy "all-world" when his father proposed to go only to Trinidad? The fault was his father's. But for his father's fatal indiscretion, all would have been well. Unfortunately, however, this was a line of defence he could not undertake without incurring the reproach of disrespect for his father's memory : and at Peele respect for that memory was an article of faith.

"Well, I must just grin and bear it—and alone, too," he thought bitterly. " Mother is very trying—she won't listen to reason—and Charlie is as happy as the day is long, confound him. However, that is nearly over. When he learns the secret and executes the deed of appointment his immunity will cease. We shall both be in the same boat then, and he will have to do as he is told. But what is to be done next ? That is the question."

To which question Edward promptly addressed himself, and, being a man of energy and resource, was not long in deciding on a plan of action. When he had done thinking he wrote to his mother apprising her of the result of the trial, which he ascribed to the one-sided and almost malignant summing up of the judge. Yet though it was a terrible misfortune, he implored her not to be cast down. The secret

was still intact, there was not the least reason to fear exposure, and he had thought of a scheme which would enable
them to meet the difficulty arising out of the loss of the insurance money. Of this he should give her full particulars on
his return ; business of importance would keep him in London
another day. He wrote in the same sense to his brother,
omitting, however, any reference to the secret and the
scheme.

Edward's object in remaining in town was to avoid breaking the bad news to his mother in person. He thought that
by the time he got home she would have recovered somewhat
from the shock, and spare him the reproaches in which she
might otherwise have indulged.

In this he was not disappointed. He found his mother looking pale and stern indeed·; and the dark circles round her
eyes told of a sleepless night, but she was quite composed,
and, as it might seem, in a reasonable frame of mind.

"What is your plan?" she asked abruptly. "I want to
know nothing more of this iniquitous trial. Let us not talk
about it—your plan?"

Edward's plan was to surrender the policy out and out
and get all they could from the company. There was no
object to be gained by keeping up the policy on Charlie's
life and his own. They were both young and likely to survive Mrs. Lincoln, and the payment of the premiums was a
heavy drain. He had seen Mr. Cutter, and the company
were disposed to deal fairly with them. The full surrender
value, reckoned on a liberal scale, would probably amount to
fifteen hundred or two thousand pounds. As to this, he
should hear further from the Secretary in the course of a
few days.

The sum recovered from the company would form the
nucleus of a fund for the liquidation of the liability to Mrs.
Lincoln's trust. Meanwhile, the money could be used for
temporary advances to clients at a high rate of interest,
thereby bringing grist to the mill both directly and indirectly. Edward had also a plan for notably increasing the
profits of the office, and he thought, by limiting their draw-
ings and living carefully, they might wipe off the debt in
seven or eight years. In all probability an over sanguine
estimate ; but besides being as ignorant of figures as women
generally are, Mrs. Prince was just then too anxious to be
critical.

" Thank God ! It is not so bad as I feared," she said with a sigh of relief, and the care-worn face lost some of its gloom.

" How clever you are, dear ! I like your plan ; it seems so practical. We must all economize. I think I can keep house on my marriage settlement and the five hundred a year; so that you and Charlie will only need to take from the business what you require for your personal expenses. In seven years, you say ? "

" Seven or eight—with ordinary luck."

" Of course. And as Charlie is to be your co-trustee, nobody will know anything—the secret will be kept in the family."

" Exactly. And if I happen to be ill or away from home when Mrs. Lincoln's dividends fall due Charlie can do what is necessary."

" You will tell him then ? "

" Of course. There is nothing else for it, he is my partner. Without his consent I can neither surrender the policy nor go on paying Mrs. Lincoln her interest."

" Poor boy! I would have spared him a little longer," murmured Mrs. Prince sadly. " It is a terrible weight to lay on his young shoulders, Edward."

" Well, they are pretty strong shoulders ; and it is quite time for him to learn the family secret and help in carrying the family burden," returned Edward.

" The family secret," said Mrs. Prince with a slight shudder, and in a low, intense voice. " Do you know, dear, I sometimes think it has been the family curse ? But for it your father would never have gone to the West Indies. See what trouble it has caused you ! It has lain on my mind like lead all these years—and now Charlie—yet we acted for the best. It was impossible to let Jack be prosecuted. The disgrace would have been more than I could bear, and utterly ruined your prospects. We should have had to leave Peele. I would do the same again, Edward. When shall you tell Charles ? "

" Let me see ! We go to Whitebeach next Friday. I will tell him the day before."

" Poor boy ! Break it as gently as you can. It will be a great shock to him, and a heavy burden afterwards. He is very like his father, sensitive on the point of honor."

CHAPTER XXIV.

A FAMILY DIFFERENCE.

ON the following Thursday the brothers were in the room at Holmcroft, once their father's, where they wrote and smoked, kept their fishing-tackle and fowling-pieces, and used generally as a bachelors' den. They had just dined ; their mother was in the drawing-room. Both were smoking Ned a cigarette, Charlie a briar-root pipe.

Charlie, looking forward to seeing Olive on the morrow, was in high spirits, all the more so as Ned, owing to an unexpected demand for his presence at some committee meeting (he had succeeded to all his father's appointments) could not leave for Whitebeach before Saturday. Wherefore, Charlie, as he hoped and confidently believed, would have his sweetheart pretty nearly all to himself for the greater part of two days.

But Edward, vexed at having to stay behind, and surmising the cause of his brother's brightness, was in an evil temper, and his thoughts were not pleasant.

"You have got the deed of appointment, I suppose?" he said, *à propos* of nothing in particular.

"It is in my bag."

"Mrs. Lincoln knows you will accept?"

"Of course. Didn't we both write to her?"

"Well, as you are to be my co-trustee—I have something to tell you, Charlie—something very important."

"All right, old man. Go ahead!"

"Pray be serious. It is no laughing matter, I assure you."

"I was not laughing."

"At any rate, you smiled."

"How long has it been a sin to smile? I smiled because you looked so glum."

"I look glum, do I? So would you—what I have to tell you is something in which you, like mother and myself, are deeply concerned. It is a family secret, long kept back from

you, first by father's wish, since by mother's, for your own
good ; but things have happened which render it imperative
that you should be told."

"Go on, I am all attention," said Charlie, sobering down
and looking serious.

"Before I go on I must ask you not to reveal or hint to
anybody, directly or indirectly, what I am about to tell you."

"As it is a family secret, that goes without saying. I give
you my word to keep it inviolate."

"Well, it concerns Mrs. Lincoln's trust. There is nothing
in it."

"Nothing in it ! What do you mean ? "

"Money. There is no money in it."

Charlie looked quite bewildered.

"But—why—how ? " he stammered. "Mrs. Lincoln's
money is in Consols, and she gets her dividends regularly. I
have seen the receipts. You are chaffing, after all."

"Chaffing ! This is too serious a matter for chaff, Charlie.
I tell you Mrs. Lincoln's settled fortune is non-existent. It
is gone—vanished—though Mrs. Lincoln does not know it."

"Gone ! How ? "

"Father sold out the stock and used the proceeds to square
those Liverpool people, when Jack robbed them and ran
away."

"But that was—a breach of trust," exclaimed Charlie,
aghast.

"Of course it was, but it was either that or letting Jack be
prosecuted for embezzlement and forgery—to the tune of
nearly twenty thousand pounds—which would have meant
penal servitude for him and a fearful disgrace for the family.
We should have had to leave Peele. Not that I approve of
what father did. I would have let Jack hang before I would
have used trust money, and saddled myself with that huge
liability, and risked unspeakable consequences. I did not
know of it till afterwards."

The young fellow bowed his head, and his heart sank
within him. His idol was overthrown. The father whom
he had so deeply loved and revered, whom he had always
regarded as a model and exemplar of every manly and
Christian virtue, that father had committed an act of delib-
erate dishonesty and violated the trust reposed in him by a
friend, and that friend a woman. And then, remembering

his essentially noble nature and high sense of honor, and that memorable conversation on the way to Southampton, he realized how intensely his father must have suffered, how terrible had been the temptation to which he yielded, and pitied him with all his soul. His poor father!

"It was to provide for restitution of the trust fund that father insured his life," observed Edward, after a long pause, which Charlie did not seem disposed to terminate. "The trial was a terrible blow. I really durst not face mother with the news. That was why I stayed in London another day. But she bears up bravely, much better than I expected."

"My God! What shall we do, then? We have not fifteen thousand pounds."

"Nor anything like it. We must keep it quiet, go on as we have been doing, and wipe off the debt as best we can."

And then Edward explained his plan, and showed Charlie the calculations on which it was based.

"I told mother we could pay it in seven or eight years—that was to keep her quiet, she worries so—but if we can do it in nine or ten, without crippling ourselves overmuch, I shall be very glad."

"And meanwhile?"

"Meanwhile?" repeated Edward snappishly. "Don't you see? Didn't I say that we must go on as usual, pay Mrs. Lincoln her dividends as they fall due, and keep our own counsel?"

"And execute the deed of appointment, and make believe that the principal sum is intact and invested in Government stock?"

"Exactly. I think, though, you might have put it a little less bluntly."

"Well, you may do as you please, but as for me, I shall not be a party to the—deed."

"The devil you won't!"

"I shall not accept the appointment unless Mrs. Lincoln is first informed of the facts. She is a good woman; she won't be hard, she will give us time."

"Oh, this is the most infernal nonsense I ever heard," exclaimed Edward, impatiently. "What has Mrs. Lincoln's goodness to do with it? You cannot bind her to secrecy; indeed, I doubt whether she can keep a secret. She would tell two or three other women—in strict confidence—and it would be all over Peele in a week. Besides, I told her distinctly that her money was still in the 'three per cents.'—I could not help it, she asked me—and mother would rather die than give her consent."

"All the same, Ned—No, the deception would be too gross. I will do anything in reason, but put my name to a statement which I know to be untrue! That I cannot do, to please anybody."

Edward was getting very angry. His brother's refusal to accept the trusteeship was the last thing he expected.

"So that is the line you take, eh?" he said, sneeringly. "You have a higher sense of honor than the rest of the family, and yet you won't stretch a point to save the family from disgrace. I suppose you think I am quite capable either of telling a lie or signing a false statement?"

"And if I do think so I only judge you out of your own mouth," returned Charlie whose temper his brother's insolence had thoroughly roused. "Didn't you say just now you had told Mrs. Lincoln that her fortune was still in the three per cents? What do you call that?"

Edward now almost beside himself, sprang to his feet. "If we weren't brothers you should smart for this," he exclaimed fiercely.

"What do you mean?" asked Charlie, also rising.

"What do I mean? I mean that I should thrash you."

"You couldn't, Ned. I am stronger than you, and you were never much of a fighter." Though excited and angry, Charlie was much cooler than his senior. "But we are brothers, and it is wicked to quarrel in this way."

"Why did you insult me, then?"

"Why did you?——"

At this point the door opened, and Mrs. Prince came in.

"Haven't you done smoking?" she began, and then seeing that something was wrong, stopped short. "Why—what—you are standing up; you both look pale and angry," she went on. "Surely you have not been quarrelling? How was it? What is it about?"

"Ask Charlie," said Edward.

"Ask Ned," said Charlie.

"You are the elder, Edward; I ask you."

"I told him about that—as we agreed—and now he won't accept the appointment, and refuses to sign the deed."

Mrs. Prince's countenance darkened.

"Is this so, Charlie?" she demanded sternly.

"I don't think it would be right, mother—unless Mrs. Lincoln is told."

"Tell Mrs. Lincoln!" exclaimed Mrs. Prince, aghast; "tell Mrs. Lincoln! Are you mad, boy? Do you know?"

"I know. Ned has told me everything. Let us do the right thing, mother. We shall never have a better chance. Jack is far away, poor father gone—forever. We can explain to Mrs. Lincoln how, but for the loss of the trial, which is no fault of ours, the money, used under the stress of a great emergency, would have been restored; and proposes to make it good by instalments, as Ned says—of course paying the interest regularly in the meantime. I am sure she will agree and think all the better of us for our honesty and frankness and keep our secret. And think what a weight it would be off your mind, mother!"

Mrs. Prince seemed to hesitate. Charlie's appeal had evidently made an impression.

"What do you think, Edward?" she said, turning to her elder son.

If his mother had been simply a client and himself disinterested Edward would doubtless have urged her to follow Charlie's advice. But he had told Mrs. Lincoln that her fortune was intact; and the disclosure must needs lower him in that lady's estimation—and Olive's, and exalt his brother, who would shine as the only immaculate member of the family. Anything were better than that.

"I cannot agree with Charlie; I wish I could," he said earnestly, and in his usual self-contained manner. "It would simplify matters immensely, as he says, and take a great weight off your mind—and mine. But how do we know that Mrs. Lincoln would undertake to keep the matter secret, and whether, though she did, she could? In her annoyance—and she is sure to be more or less annoyed—she might let out whatever we confide to her—and we shall have to tell everything. There can be no half confidence. And as for giving us time to pay up—isn't it at least on the cards—in my opinion it is almost certain that Mrs. Lincoln would change her mind about appointing Charlie and me? And whomsoever else she might appoint would be in duty bound to enforce immediate restitution of the trust fund by all the means in their power. Unless I am mistaken, mother, you and I as father's executors, could be made personally responsible ; the office would be broken up ; I should lose my appointments, and if the new trustees were hostile—which is quite possible—the estate might have to be wound up in bankruptcy also."

"That is quite enough, Edward," cried Mrs. Prince, appalled by this catalogue of contingent calamities, "you need say no more. Mrs. Lincoln must not be told, and you must accept the trusteeship, Charles."

"I cannot, mother. I don't presume to judge you ; but from my point of view it would not be right."

"Would it be right to besmirch your father's name and drag Edward and me into the Bankruptcy Court ? That is the alternative. It cannot be wrong to obey your mother, and I ask you to do this for my sake, if not for your own. I will take the responsibility."

It was hard to withstand his mother, but the young fellow, recalling his father's parting counsel, given, as it might appear, in view of the very eventuality which was now come to pass, repeated his refusal.

"I am very sorry ; you distress me beyond measure, but I cannot, I really cannot. I would rather lose my right hand than sign that deed without telling Mrs. Lincoln."

"Oh, Charlie, do you want to break my heart ?" and with that Mrs. Prince threw her arms around his neck and laying her head on his shoulder fell a-weeping.

No wonder Charlie wavered and showed hesitation, which his mother quickly perceiving redoubled her efforts, not commanding, but entreating and beseeching.

"My dear boy, my own Charlie, don't be so hard. Your acceptance of the trusteeship is the only way of preventing disaster and disgrace. I am getting into years, these troubles are telling on me. I should die, Charlie, and oh, to think of it, you would be the cause."

Charlie kissed his mother tenderly ; and it was evident that, for the moment at least, he was silenced, if not vanquished.

"It is all right ; he will do as you wish," interposed Edward. "He would not let me dictate to him just now, and quite right, too. I lost my temper. I am sorry if I hurt you, old fellow, but we will say no more about it, and let bygones be bygones. Come, I will take you to your room, mother. You must lie down, or you will have a headache after all this excitement."

"Let bygones be bygones!" murmured Charlie bitterly, when they were gone. "Does he mean it, I wonder? If he had not frightened mother with his exaggerations she would have agreed to my proposal. Oh, why didn't I stand to my guns? They may say what they like, but it would be an infamy to sign that deed and keep Mrs. Lincoln in the dark."

Again Charlie recalled his father's words almost the last he had heard from his lips: "If you have any doubt, give conscience the benefit of it. . . . You will be glad afterwards, for you will have nothing to reproach yourself with, and right can never be wrong, nor wrong right."

"Which is it to be?" he asked himself. "Shall I obey my father and do right, or my mother and do wrong?"

"I had no idea Charlie would prove so restive and stubborn. He has always been so easy-tempered and obedient," observed Mrs. Prince to her elder son as they passed to her room.

"Well, he surprised me, but it was a good deal my own fault. I was out of temper and rubbed him the wrong way. I suppose that got his back up. It was well you tried entreaty. I tried the other thing and it did not answer."

"Yet he did not say he would sign the deed, after all."

"He did not say he would not, and that comes to the same thing. Silence gives consent. Take for granted that he will and say no more. And when you come to think about it, he has no alternative. He has promised Mrs. Lincoln to accept the trust and given me his word not to split. You need not worry, mother; he will sign fast enough when it comes to the point."

CHAPTER XXV.

"AT WHITEBEACH."

WHEN Charlie considered the alternative of compliance with his mother's wish he saw, as Edward had seen, the difficulty of his position. He was between the devil and the deep sea. To sign the deed would be to make himself participator in a fraud, a fraud that, in view of his present and prospective relations with the Lincolns, would be doubly infamous, which, were it to come to Olive's knowledge, she never would pardon. On the other hand, refusal would embroil him with everybody. His mother and brother would overwhelm him with reproaches; Mrs. Lincoln would be deeply and justly offended, and Olive unappeasable. It was her pet scheme, a scheme on which she had set her heart, and of which he himself had warmly approved.

How could he get out of it? What excuse could he offer? That he was too young, that the responsibility would be too great for him, that it was inexpedient for brothers to be trustees under the same settlement? None of these pretexts would hold water, and if made would simply be laughed out of court.

He could not even think of a plausible, harmless lie, and if he did take to lying he might as well sign the deed and have done with it. That would clearly be the simplest course and by far the easiest,—if he could forget honor and honesty, his father's sage advice and his duty to Olive and her mother.

These thoughts kept Charlie awake the greater part of the night, and morning found him still halting between two opinions, still wandering in a maze of perplexity and indecision.

When he met his mother at breakfast no reference was made to the scene of the night before. Mrs. Prince, who since her husband's death had been subject to fits of despondency, was unusually cheerful. Edward urbane and in good spirits. He had received a letter from the Ægis people to

the effect that they were prepared to pay two thousand pounds
for the surrender of the life policy. This was more than its
actuarial value, but for reasons which would readily suggest
themselves they were desirous to offer the most liberal terms
in their power.

"I suppose you will accept?" said Mrs. Prince.

"Of course. I shall write and say so at once, though as
we are going away the transaction cannot be completed until
ofter the holidays."

Later in the day Edward had a characteristically happy
thought. It occurred to him that he might as well try to get
a little more. So he wrote a polite letter to the company,
thanking them for their offer, which he and his brother were
disposed to accept. He would communicate with them
further after the holidays. Meanwhile, he put it to the
company whether, considering the heavy sums which the late
Mr. Prince had paid in premiums, and the unfortunate
circumstances of his death, it would not be a graceful act on
their part to meet *all* the costs of the recent suit.

This drew a prompt and curt reply from the Secretary, to
the effect that his directors declined to modify in any sense
the terms which they had proposed, and unless these were
formally accepted and the policy surrendered in the course
of the ensuing week the offer would be withdrawn and not
repeated.

The Secretary's letter followed Edward Prince to Whitebeach, and was answered a few days later in a way which
took the first-named gentleman's breath away and gave his
directors a bad quarter of an hour.

Five-and-thirty years ago Whitebeach had not begun to be
popular; it was neither infested by cheap trippers nor patro-
nized by people of fashion. The village consisted of a post-
office, an inn with an ivy-covered porch, and a dozen fishermen's and laborers' cottages with thatched roofs. The
parish possessed, further, three or four farmhouses, and half-
a-dozen or so of a better sort occupied by people who preferred the rural charms of Whitebeach to the rampant row-
dyism of Ramsgate or the ostentatious vulgarity of Brighton.
There were neither donkey-boys nor bathing-vans, and trains
were so few and far between that the station-master had time
to cultivate roses, and his garden was one of the sights of the
place.

When the Princes arrived at Whitebeach station, they were greeted, rather to their surprise, by Mrs. Lincoln and her daughter.

"So kind of you to meet us," said Mrs. Prince, as she exchanged kisses with her hostess.

"So good of you to come," murmured Charlie as he shook hands with Olive.

"We are so quiet here that the arrival of visitors is an event of which we naturally make the most," said Mrs. Lincoln. "Sometimes we come down merely to see who is coming or going. The phaeton is outside. We can either drive round by the road or go by the footpath, an easy walk of a mile or so."

"The footpath, by all means, I feel quite cramped with sitting so long," returned Mrs. Prince.

Charlie also elected for the footpath, the bags and rugs were deposited in the phaeton and the Lincolns and their guests climbed a rustic stile by the roadside and took to the fields. The day was perfect, the way delightful—now passing over a daisy-pied meadow, now through a field of waving corn, anon dipping into a glade, where a gurgling stream, crossed by a moss-grown bridge, flowed gently between the entwined boughs of overhanging trees. Larks were carolling in the sun, swift-winged swallows chasing in graceful flight their tiny prey; and a quiet sea breeze wafted inland the odor of pine woods and the perfume of flowers.

Albeit still preoccupied and perplexed, Charlie Prince could not be insensible to the subtle influence of these sights and sounds, so propitious to enjoyment and love. The brightness of the day, the beauty of the landscape, and the presence of his sweetheart were not long in conjuring away his cares. Before they were over the first field he had become talkative and gay.

For prudential reasons the lovers made no attempt to "pair off," and in obedience to a whispered hint from Olive the young fellow devoted himself more assiduously to the elder ladies than to Miss Lincoln. He was especially attentive to her mother, she to his; and though two of the party were burdened with a portentous secret all seemed to be in high spirits and unapprehensive of impending trouble.

"There! That is our house, or rather the house we live in," said Mrs. Lincoln, as they emerged from a clump of trees which for the last few minutes had obscured the view.

" And you call it? " asked Mrs. Prince.

" The Pines."

A red brick house with a tiled roof, mellowed with age, many-gabled, and built on a hillside. Above it, terraced gardens and shrubberies, and, higher still, a dark pine wood. A little to the left a break in the cliffs and an almost land-locked cove, with fishing boats drawn up on the beach, and a small yacht riding at anchor.

" How lovely! " exclaimed Mrs. Prince with effusion. " Edward said Whitebeach was nice, but I had no idea it was so charming as this."

" Oh, yes, it is very nice and lovely, also lonely, not to say dull," observed Mrs. Lincoln dryly. " For my part, I like a little society. At present the place seems to be inhabited chiefly by women. Except the fisher folk and Mr. Oldbury, the Rector, we don't see a man in a blue moon. I am sorry Edward could not come with you. But he will be here to-morrow, you say? "

" Yes, and I hope early—if he can get away. He is de-tained by town's business, which he cannot possibly do by deputy—and he always puts business before pleasure."

" And quite right, too. It is the way to get on. By-the-bye, I hope he has found time to prepare the deed of appoint-ment."

" Oh dear, yes. Charlie has it in his bag. It can be signed to-morrow."

" There is no hurry. It will do any time before the gentle-men go, and I hope they will stay as long as they can. As for you, Mrs. Prince, I shall keep you for a fortnight, at least —longer, if your sons can spare you."

Mrs. Prince, whose cue it was to be "all things " to Mrs. Lincoln, smiled pleasantly and said she would be very glad— if her hostess could do with her.

" Do with you," exclaimed Mrs. Lincoln. " I shall be grateful to you. Why, we are sometimes so dull that I have sometimes thought of advertising for a brace of rattles."

Mrs. Prince turned pale. Rattles suggested burglars.

" Rattles! Yes, it is very lonely here, as you say. But I should think night catches and electric bells would be a better protection than rattles."

"Bless you! I didn't mean wooden rattles. I meant a brace of lively American girls who could go on talking till further orders, play and sing whenever they were asked, take a hand at whist, and make themselves generally useful and always agreeable."

Whereupon everybody laughed, but Charlie's laugh was forced, and he felt sure it sounded hollow. The mention of the deed had sent his spirits down to zero again, and for a few minutes thereafter he was so sombre and silent that Olive asked him, as he helped her over a stile, what he was dreaming about.

"You," he whispered, and truly, for the question which most troubled him was what she would say when he told her (if he did tell her) that he must decline to become her mother's trustee.

Olive, smiling archly, suggested that if thinking about her made him look so dismal he had better think about something else, on which Charlie laughed, as in duty bound, and pulling himself together, made a not unsuccessful effort to look pleasant.

When they reached the house luncheon was ready. The meal over, Mrs. Lincoln suggested that Mrs. Prince should lie down for a while.

"I am sure you must be tired," she said; "and when you are rested we will go out for a drive. What will you do, Charlie?"

"Explore."

"You mean look round the place," added Mrs. Lincoln, after a moment's thought. "But you won't know—— However, I dare say Olive will go with you—will you, Olive?"

"Certainly, mother."

"You must not be long, though. I have ordered the carriage for three o'clock."

Mrs. Lincoln did not make this proposal very heartily; but hospitality has its duties; she could not do the honors herself without missing her afternoon nap, and it was only for once in a way. Edward, when he came, would act as a check on Charlie's amatory hankerings, if he entertained any, and she was beginning to think that her apprehensions on this score had been groundless.

After Olive had taken her lover through the greenhouses and round the garden, both behaving the while as discreetly as if they were under their mothers' eyes, she piloted him by devious paths towards the pine wood, first bidding him mark well the way, so that he might find it another time unguided.

" But why ? Where are we going ? " he asked.

" You will see."

Presently they reached a quickthorn hedge, dense, high, and apparently impenetrable ; but gliding behind a fir tree with wide-spreading boughs Olive slipped through an almost invisible gap, and Charlie, following, found himself in a broad walk, hemmed in between the hedge and a high wall, hidden under a century's growth of ivy, and carpeted with mossy turf. At one end of the walk was an arbor, at the other, a tiny pool, white with water-lilies.

" Now we can talk," said Olive.

Charlie put his arm round her waist and——

" I didn't mean that (laughing). However, nobody ever comes here but me. Mother does not know of it ; besides, she objects to climbing the hill. I did not find it out until we had been here a month, and then by accident. You have no idea how weirdly beautiful it looks by moonlight. But the gardeners—Mr. Marsh keeps the gardens up, you know— won't come near the place if they can help, especially after dark."

" Why ? "

" They wouldn't tell you if you asked them. They wouldn't tell me. So I got one of the maids to find out. They think it is haunted. They are superstitious, rustics generally are, I fancy, especially when they live near the sea, but I am not in the least, are you ? "

" No ; but why should it be haunted ? "

" Well, there are two stories ; one has it that, long ago, a former owner of the property hanged himself to one of the trees hereabout ; another, that he was drowned while boating off Thornby Point, for which cause his disembodied spirit is supposed to revisit the glimpses of the moon, and has been seen on this very spot within the last four years. At least, so they say. And what do you suppose they used to call this beauti- ful glade ? 'Dead Man's Walk !' Wasn't it too horrid ! *Mais nous avons changé tout cela.*"

" What do they call it now ? "

" What should you think ? The Fairies' Tryst. Are you an early riser, Charlie ? "

"Well, not very, but I can be, you know. Why?"

"Because—early morning is the pleasantest part of the day at this time of the year. All is so fresh and bright, and the birds are singing and the rabbits hopping about, and that. I often come here about seven or eight. I daresay I shall be here to-morrow morning and on Monday."

"I am sure I shall. I like to hear the birds sing and see the rabbits hop about, and all that."

"Don't tease; if you do you will only have the rabbits and the birds to keep you company. There are three or four ways of getting here, which is fortunate, for we must not be seen coming together or following each other. Didn't you observe that mother rather hesitated to let me show you round the garden? Close to the pool is a door in the wall, opening into a path which brings you to the bottom of the carriage drive; and behind the arbor is another path leading to the boathouse and the cove."

"I shall go round by the cove."

"Do. Then nobody can suspect, and on Monday morning we might come another way. And now we must return, or we shall outstay our leave, and then mother would think— what we don't want her to think—at present."

CHAPTER XXVI.

THE FAIRIES' TRYST.

CHARLIE hesitated no longer. He would neither play the hypocrite with Olive nor deceive her mother by accepting a bogus trust. For the others, being already committed, there was some excuse; for him, with his father's warning ringing in his ears, none. He was, moreover, absolutely certain, his brother to the contrary notwithstanding, that Mrs. Lincoln would both give them time and keep their secret; and it might be that his refusal to sign the deed would compel them to deal frankly with her.

It would be very painful, of course—another scene with his mother, another quarrel with Ned—but nothing could be more painful than the agonies of doubt which he had lately endured, and anything were better than participating in an act of which he should never be able to think without shame and remorse.

In the improbable event of Olive on the following day speaking of the trust, or referring to the deed, he would tell her all that he was at liberty to disclose—otherwise not until Monday morning. For her sake it was better to keep her in the bliss of ignorance so long as might be; for his own, to put off the portentous communication to the last moment. After telling Olive he would announce his decision to Ned and his mother, and then—the deluge.

The second meeting at the Fairies' Tryst went off as Charlie expected. Olive made no mention of the trust. Why should she? She regarded the affair as settled; the brothers had agreed to act, and they had only to execute the deed which Charlie had brought in his bag. After a delightful *tête-à-tête* the lovers returned to the house by different ways, and when he strode carelessly into the breakfast-room she was pouring out a cup of tea for his mother.

He had been down at the Cove, he said; Mrs. Lincoln

hoped he enjoyed his walk, to which he answered that he had enjoyed himself immensely, and Olive from behind the tea urn gave him so roguish a glance that it was all he could do to keep his countenance.

Late in the day Edward came, and he had so much to say, and the two matrons made so much of him, and Olive deemed it to be politic to be so civil to him (by way of lulling her mother's suspicions) that Charlie had to fall rather into the background, not unwillingly, for as the day wore on he thought more and more of the ordeal before him and its possible issues, and wondered wistfully what the next forty-eight hours would bring forth.

After Edward had been flattered and refreshed, there was a walk down to the cove and an inspection of Mr. Marsh's yawl, which he had placed at Mrs. Lincoln's disposal; and at that lady's suggestion it was agreed that on Monday her daughter should go out for a sail, with Edward for captain and Charlie for crew. Both knew how to sail a boat, but the elder was supposed to be the more skilful sailor of the two.

Sunday was spent in going to church, rambling in the grounds, and sauntering by the sea-shore. At night a little concert of sacred music, in which Edward who had a voice like a corn crake, was conceited enough to think that he distinguished himself; then, all to bed. To Charlie's relief, for there is nothing more fatiguing than trying to look happy when you feel miserable, and as the critical moment drew near his uneasiness increased. All day he had been oppressed with gloomy forebodings, and for a long time wooed sleep in vain. Wakening at six and finding further sleep impossible, he rose, donned his clothes, and going softly downstairs slipped out by a side door.

Now, it so fell out that Edward, happening at the same time to open his bedroom window, to let in the fresh morning air, spied his brother wending down the avenue.

This made Edward put on his considering cap. "What," he asked himself, "can be Charlie's object in rising so early? At home he stops in bed till the last moment." And his naturally sharp wits being still further sharpened by curiosity and suspicion he was not long in coming to the conclusion that Charlie's object was Olive—that they had planned a matutinal meeting, and he was on his way to the *rendezvous*.

" If I could only catch them ! " muttered Edward between his set teeth.

It was too late to see whither Charlie went ; but if he were right in his surmise Olive would presently be making her way in the same direction (Charlie would naturally start first) and her he might shadow. So Edward hastily dressed, keeping watch the while from his windows, which looked south and west respectively, and commanded several exits. After watching for nearly an hour he was rewarded for his diligence. Miss Lincoln, wearing a sun-bonnet and garden gloves, and armed with a light spud, crossed the lawn ; and, as it might appear, made straight for the pine wood. Three minutes later Edward was on her track, at a respectable distance, however, and dodging behind shrubs and bushes to avoid being seen.

After a short, albeit exciting, chase, he reached the quick-thorn hedge ; and there the pursuit ended, for though he could have sworn that Olive was not a score of yards ahead of him, and he had caught a glimpse of her gown only a moment previously, he was completely baffled. The quarry had vanished without leaving a trace behind.

Edward looked hard at the hedge. It was as strong and impervious as a stone wall. No animal less ponderous than an elephant could break through it, none less active than a deer leap over it. He reconnoitred it from one end to the other, made several wide casts, and after loitering about a long time retraced his steps, foiled and discomfited, and wild with jealousy and rage, for though he had failed to catch the lovers in *flagrante delicto* he had not a shadow of doubt that they were together—somewhere.

When Olive, unaware of the danger she had so narrowly escaped, slipped through the opening, which Edward had fortunately overlooked, Charlie received her in his arms and greeted her even more tenderly than usual. Who could tell when or whether he should have the chance again ?

" How kind of you to come ! " he said. " Was the coast clear ? Have you any news ? "

" Quite. I did not see even a gardener. Yes, I have news, a letter—whom do you think from ? And a message for you."

" I have no idea."

" From Cousin Paul. It came yesterday. He writes from

Nevada City, California. This is the message (producing the letter). I will read it. Listen. ' Tell your (a word I cannot make out, but I know he means you) that the impossible has happened. I have come across Mark Darnley— more, I have taken him in hand and he is doing well. I gave him the message. It brought tears to his eyes, and he was very quiet and down for a long time afterwards ; he would like anybody who takes an interest in him to know that he has kept straight ever since he came to this country ; and he thinks that before long his family will hear something to his advantage. I think so, too. When are you going to bring your Prince to America ? He would make his fortune out here. He is the right sort. I shall never forget the wonderful way in which he made your horse turn a somersault over that fence.'

"Dear old Paul ! I should like to see him again. Who is this Mark Darnley, and why did you send him a message ? "

"Well, it's rather a secret, but you can keep one."

"Try me."

"Mark Darnley is my brother Jack. As you may have heard, Jack was a sad scapegrace and a sore trouble to my father and mother. He behaved so badly, in fact, that it was impossible for him to remain in England : and Ned and I got him away to America. Knowing he had gone West, I asked your cousin to keep a look-out for him, without, of course, saying he was my brother, though I fancy, from the tone of his letter, that he guesses or has been told the truth."

"Why does he go by the name of Darnley ? "

" To throw the police off his track. He deserted from the army ; and there was a hue and cry after him."

"How dreadful ! But he is doing well now, and from what Paul says, I am sure he is very sorry and penitent."

"He has need to be. When I think of the trouble he has caused ! However, the less said about Jack the better. It is a painful subject—and I have something to tell you, darling, something which has been on my mind since I came here. I am very sorry, for I fear it will make you as unhappy as it has made me—but there is no help for it."

"What is it ? " asked Olive anxiously.

" I shall have to decline being your mother's trustee."

" You are surely joking," she said, eyeing him with bewildered gaze.

"Do I look as if I were joking?"

In truth, he looked more like a man who is about to be executed, or going in for a competitive examination.

"But why? What has happened?"

"That is the worst of it. I am not at liberty to say."

"Not at liberty to say, not at liberty to tell me!" she exclaimed hotly, disengaging herself from his embrace. "I thought we were to have no secrets from each other. Is this the return for my love? Is this ——"

"Don't be so hasty, Olive. Let me explain."

"What can you explain? Will you tell me why you refuse to do this very small favor for my mother, which you said you esteemed an honor? Will you tell me, yes or no?"

"Do have a little patience with me, Olive. I cannot answer yes or no. You may be sure I would if I could—right willingly. Some time you shall know all. But for the present my lips are sealed—much against my own will. Believe me, darling, that if I could tell you without breaking my word I would not hesitate a moment."

"Breaking your word, indeed! Why, you are breaking it now. Didn't you write to my mother that you would accept the appointment with pleasure? Haven't you protested over and over again that you would do whatever I asked you, and never keep aught back from me?"

Olive spoke with great heat and indignant gesture. She was touched in her pride, and felt as if her love were contemned. The idea of making Charlie a trustee was entirely hers. It was she who had suggested it to her mother, and persuaded her to discard Mr. Marsh. Her lover's refusal to act was both a breach of faith and an affront to her mother and herself.

"It is all over between us," she continued after a short pause. "As we have not been formally engaged there is no engagement to break off. And we never shall be engaged. I cannot give my love to a man who slights my mother, and refuses me his confidence."

"Don't say that, Olive. For God's sake don't say that. You will break my heart. If you knew how sorely I have been tried you would pity me instead of blaming me. I am striving to do right under terrible pressure to do wrong. You don't want me to do wrong, and I should do if——"

Here poor Charlie, who was deeply moved, nearly broke

down, and in her heart Olive began to relent. But her temper
was still high, and her pride would not let her show signs of
yielding.

" It cannot be right to slight my mother or wrong to give
me your confidence—if you really love me," she said coldly.
" However, you will do as you think best. I shall return your
letters before you leave ; you can send mine when you get
home."

And then she turned on her heel and went down by the
arbor ; but as she thought of her lover's distress and recalled
his pathetic appeal pity conquered pride, and, once out of
sight, she stopped frequently and listened eagerly, hoping to
hear his well-known footsteps, and ready to throw herself into
his arms and ask his forgiveness for her hasty words.

But Charlie, ignorant of the vagaries of maidens' minds, and
believing that Olive had said her last words, remained for a
while in gloomy meditation, and then left the Tryst by the
gap in the hedge.

Near the house he fell in with Edward.

" You were up betimes this morning," said the latter. " I
saw you go down the avenue soon after six."

" Did you ? " answered Charlie absently, and walked on.
Then, as if suddenly remembering something, he stopped
short. " Look here, Ned," he said, " I may as well tell you
now as later. I am not going to execute that deed unless
Mrs. Lincoln is told."

" Nonsense ! you consented."

" No, I didn't. I admit that mother made me hesitate ; but
I did not consent, and I never shall. That you may make
up your mind to."

Edward felt disposed to use strong language ; but, remembering the failure of his former attempt at browbeating, he
kept his temper, observing quietly that he felt sure his
brother would think better of it before the day was over.

" No, I shall not," was the answer.

" You must tell mother yourself, then ; I won't."

" Very well ; I shall tell her when we return from our
cruise."

Edward smiled derisively. In a contest with his mother
Charlie was sure to come off second best. There would be
another scene, ending, as before, in his discomfiture, and the
deed would be signed.

" It is past eight (looking at his watch). Let us go in to breakfast, or we shall not be off before the tide ebbs."

The brothers entered the breakfast-room with the ladies. Charlie glanced at Olive; though pale and heavy-eyed she was calm and composed, and as alert as usual.

" You are not looking very bright this morning," said her mother. " The sail will do you good."

" I am not going to sail."

" Why ? "

" I don't feel like it."

" Have you a headache ? "

" Yes, I have a headache."

" In that case you had better stop at home and keep quiet. You will go all the same, of course (addressing the brothers)."

" I think so. What do you say, Charlie ? " asked Edward of his brother.

Charlie did not care for a sail with his brother for sole companion, he feared they might quarrel, and wanted to be alone—but as he could not well refuse to go because Olive was not going, answered listlessly, and not very graciously: " Yes, let us go."

" When shall we expect you back ? " asked Mrs. Lincoln, and Edward (who evidently intended to " boss the show ") replied :

" That depends a good deal on wind and weather. About three o'clock, I should say. We shall go a few miles out, and if it keeps calm do a little line fishing."

" At any rate, you will be back in time for afternoon tea ? "

" Certainly. At the very latest."

14

CHAPTER XXVII.

A CATASTROPHE.

Olive's head ached a little, her heart a good deal. Conscience told her that she had been unkind, using in her anger words which, the more she thought of them, the harsher they seemed. She knew Charlie's loyalty and worth and how deeply he loved her ; only for good reason and because he had no alternative would he do aught either to give her umbrage or affront her mother. What was it ? Why had he given his word not to execute the deed (for in this sense she construed his explanation), which only two days before he had been quite willing to execute, or he would not have brought it with him ? Had she been less impetuous and more forbearing, he might have given her a clue to the mystery without actually breaking the promise he had so strangely given. By her own act she was left completely in the dark.

Instead of keeping quiet, as her mother had bidden her, Olive roamed restlessly about the grounds in rueful mood, longing continually for Charlie's return, in order that she might let him know by sign or word that he was forgiven and she repentant, and arrange for a meeting on the morrow.

After luncheon Olive, with a book in one hand and a sunshade in the other, strolled towards the shrubberies, as if seeking a shady corner where she might sit down and read ; then, as if changing her mind, or following out a preconceived plan, she doubled and made for the Fairies' Tryst. It was the quietest spot she knew, and she wanted to be alone with her thoughts. Sitting down in the arbor, Olive opened her book, and her resolve to make it up with Charlie having somewhat tranquilized her mind, she actually succeeded in reading a few pages with understanding. But soon her thoughts wandered once more, and finding it impossible to sit still, she laid the book down and turned with pensive mien into the path leading to the Cove.

"Olive!"

The girl started and stopped short. It seemed as if somebody were calling her name a long way off. Yes. There it was again—"Olive!" faint, yet distinct, as if wafted by the breeze from over the sea. Greatly wondering, but quite on the alert, she walked slowly down the path.

Charlie! Of course. Who else could it be? Who but he would call her name in that soft, low voice?

And there he was in the path, coming to meet her.

"Back already!" she cried, hastening towards him. "I did not expect you so soon."

But even as she spoke he was gone—as suddenly and swiftly as though he had sunk into the ground, or melted into the air.

Thinking he was teasing her she ran to the spot where she had last seen him, peering into the bushes and calling his name. But her summons was unheeded, her eyes sought for him in vain; he had vanished utterly. It was very strange.

And then, feeling faint and bewildered, she leant against a tree and tried to compose herself and collect her thoughts. If it had not been for the call she might have thought that Charlie wanted to avoid her; but if he did, why was he there alone? And the manner of his disappearance was so creepily uncanny. One moment there, the next nowhere—gone without turning his head or making a sign. Olive had protested to her lover that she was not superstitious, and was probably no more so than most folks; yet she had read stories of wraiths and doubles, and now strange thoughts assailed her and a great fear came over her. But not for long; in a few minutes she was herself again, and laughing at her own folly.

"It was Charlie himself—of course it was—why should I doubt it? Anyway, I'll soon find out," a resolve that showed she was not quite so sure as she tried to believe.

In twenty minutes she was at the Cove. Two or three boatmen were loitering about, with their hands in their pockets and their pipes in their mouths.

"Is the yawl back, Job?" she asked one of them.

"Not yet; and I don't see her coming, neither" (shading his eyes with his hands and looking seaward).

It was all Olive could do to maintain her composure, and feeling that she must say something, yet not knowing what, she rather foolishly asked the man, who had a sour temper, and made a point of always looking at the dark side, when he thought the yawl would be back.

" That is more than I can tell you, Miss Lincoln," he said with a shrug of his shoulders. " It depends so much how far the gentlemen have gone, what sort of sailors they are, and what sort of weather they make. I've seen boats go out as has never come back."

Olive turned pale."

" You surely don't think they are in any danger ? " she asked.

" No, miss, I cannot say as I do think so ; the yawl is a good sea boat, the wind is fair and the weather fine. But there's no telling ; the sea is always treacherous, and we have as much weather on this coast as anywhere I've bin to, and I've bin well-nigh everywhere. As like as not it'll be blowing half-a-gale before sundown."

" Would half-a-gale be very bad ? "

" Not as bad as a hout-and-houter, nor yet three-parts of one, miss."

Olive turned away and wended homeward—by the road, not the footpath and the Fairies' Tryst.

It was not Charlie she had seen, then, after all. At any rate, not Charlie in the body, and as she did not believe in apparitions and knew nothing of telepathy, she fell back on optical illusions, about which she had lately read a paper in *Chambers's Miscellany*. Nothing was more probable than that the shadowy likeness of her lover which she had seen in the path was the coinage of her imagination. The meeting in the morning, the quarrel, Charlie's departure, the loneliness of the Fairies' Tryst and its associations; all these favored the evolution of mental phantasmagoria. Yes, there could be no doubt about it ; the figure she had seen and the voice she had heard were illusions ; an opinion in which she was confirmed by a re-perusal of the article in *Chambers's Miscellany*. Nevertheless, and in spite of herself, doubts still lingered in Olive's mind, and as the hour when the brothers had promised to return drew near her uneasiness increased. They might be back at three or four ; they were sure to be back at five. Every time the clock struck she counted the strokes, and when it went five and there was still no sign of them, her anxiety deepened into alarm.

" They are surely very late," she said to her mother.

"Oh, I don't know. When men go out fishing they lose count of time. They are perhaps having good sport and don't like to leave off; or the wind may be contrary. Let us have tea, they are sure to be back by dinner-time."

Again Olive was comforted, but only for a while. At six o'clock her suspense grew unbearable, and not liking to make another visit to the Cove she took a field-glass and went to a part of the grounds which commanded a view of the sea. Several boats were visible, any one of which might be the yawl; this cheered her; she was also glad to see that the old sailor's forebodings as to the weather were not being fulfilled. True, the boats were tossing about a bit, and there was a lively breeze, but nothing like a gale, or even half-a-gale, and as the yawl was a good sea boat and Edward a skilful boatman—to say nothing of Charlie—it was hardly conceivable that they could have met with any mishap. Her mother was no doubt right; they had either gone further than they intended or were catching so many fish that they did not like to leave off.

Olive shut up her glass, and on returning to the house found her mother at the front door, gazing seaward and looking vexed.

"I see nothing of them," she said, testily. "Whatever can they be doing? If they are not here soon the dinner will be quite spoiled. Let us walk down the avenue, and see whether they are coming."

Olive acquiesced. It was a winding avenue, and as they rounded the first turn two men were visible in the distance, coming towards them.

"Why, there they are," exclaimed Mrs. Lincoln.

"Two men, at any rate," returned Olive, with assumed indifference.

"Yes, Edward and Charlie. No, it isn't. Edward and somebody else. Who is he? Your eyes are younger than mine."

"Job, the boatman," said Olive, and for the second time that day a great fear came over her.

"Charlie is behind, no doubt; he will be here presently. I am very glad; there will be no need to keep dinner back more than ten minutes or so. Here they come. Well, you are late, I was just saying.—Why, what? Whatever is the matter?"

Edward was deadly pale, his eyes were red, as if he had been weeping! he was all of a tremble, his knees bent as he walked, and the old sailor looked portentously grave.

"Whatever is the matter?" she repeated. "Where is Charlie?"

"He—I—mean—Charlie——" stammered Edward, wiping the sweat from his brow, and leaning on Job for support. "He is——"

"Dead," said Olive in an intense whisper, looking into his eyes, her hands tightly clenched, her face ghastly.

"Who says so? How do you know? How does anybody know?" returned Edward, bending his head, as if to avoid her gaze.

"I can see it in your face."

"What has happened? Tell us right away, for Heaven's sake," exclaimed Mrs. Lincoln, who was too agitated to notice her daughter's still greater agitation. "What has happened? Where is Charlie?"

"There has been an accident. A very sad, inexplicable accident," said Edward, pulling himself together and speaking more coherently. "When we were a few miles out—south of Thornby Point—the wind fell off and we began fishing, and did pretty well, but after a while it grew very hot, and Charlie proposed that we should bathe. All this time we had been drifting further south and were a longish way from land. I agreed, of course, but as I am not much of a swimmer I said I would keep close to the boat, and I warned Charlie not to go too far away; the tide being on the turn and the yawl beginning to drift. 'All right,' he said, 'I'll not lose sight of you,' and then he dived over the port side and swam away. A few minutes afterwards I went into the water on the starboard side, and stayed in, perhaps, a quarter of an hour or twenty minutes, keeping close to the boat, which continued to drift, and floating on my back nearly all the time. The first thing I did when I got into the boat was to look for Charlie. To my horror, I could see nothing of him; even through my glass, a very powerful one that we had taken with us, I could not make him out. Then I shouted, again and again, but no answer came. . . . When I last saw him—just before I went into the water myself—he was going away from the land, but whether he had continued in that direction I could not tell—it was not likely that he would keep straight

on ; yet I feared that, with his swimming and the boat drifting, we were so far apart that he could not see me, so I made
sail and stood out to sea, then tacked, then lay to, and tacked
again, and so continued a long time, all the while keeping a
sharp lookout, and making as much noise as I could. At
last, I fell in with a fishing-smack, and, hailing her, told the
crew what had happened. They lent me a boy to help sail
the yawl ; and we both cruised about fully three hours, until,
in fact, as night was coming on and the wind rising, the
smack's people wouldn't stay with me any longer ; they said
it was no use."

"And they was right," put in Job ; "if you had stood there,
on and off, to the Judgment-day, you wouldn't have found
him. He was gone long afore you fell in with the smack—
ten to one afore you missed him. It was cramp—that's what
it was—and when a man is seized with cramp he just gives a
shriek and goes down like a stone. As like as not, however,
the body will be washed ashore or picked up."

"Did you hear any cry, Edward?" asked Mrs. Lincoln.

"Hear any cry? Oh, Mrs. Lincoln, what do you take me
for? Do you think that if I had heard a cry I wouldn't have
gone to him?"

"Of course you would. I beg your pardon. I did not
know what I was saying. What a terrible misfortune. Poor
Charlie! I fear it is as you say, Job ; he must have been
seized with cramp. God help his poor mother. Who will
break it to her? Olive!"

But Olive was gone. She had heard enough ; her worst
forebodings were realized, and, unable longer to control her
feelings, she had stolen away to her own room.

"Would you break it to her, Mrs. Lincoln?" asked Edward with bated breath, and in a broken voice. "I . . .
don't feel as if I could. The suspense and agony of the last
few hours have quite unmanned me, and I am physically exhausted. I should be eternally obliged."

It was not a pleasant thing to do, and rather in the line of
his duty than hers ; nevertheless Mrs. Lincoln gave a prompt,
albeit somewhat reluctant, assent to the proposal.

"Very well," she said, "but you must be at hand in case
she wants you. No wonder you are so overcome, but you
will have to keep up for your poor mother's sake. Go into
the house and get a glass of wine while I speak to her."

Mrs. Lincoln, though a good woman, was not good at beating about the bush; it was her habit to go straight to the point, and she broke the bad news in such a fashion as to make Mrs. Prince imagine that she had been bereft of both her sons by the same stroke.

"Dear friend," she began, "I have been asked to tell you something that it will grieve you sorely to hear. A great misfortune has happened. But He who tempers the wind to the shorn lamb will give you strength to bear it. The yawl——'

"I know what you mean. . . . . Oh my God, that it should come to this! My sin has found me out; my cup is full. Both gone, both gone!" cried Mrs. Prince, frantically, and then swooned.

Mrs. Lincoln applied restoratives, and when the stricken woman recovered consciousness explained what had really befallen, laying stress on the fact that though Charlie was missing he might not be drowned, that there was room for hope.

But Mrs. Prince refused to be comforted.

"You don't think so yourself, I can see you don't," she said. "Room for hope! Oh, that I could think so! My poor boy is gone, gone forever. He was the apple of his father's eye. Leonard and Charlie both gone! And Jack I shall never see again. Ah me!"

And then she fell a-weeping, and asked for Edward, and when he came Mrs. Lincoln left them together.

He looked much less distraught than he had done a short time previously, thanks, probably, to the wine—a good deal more than a glass—which he had just drank. His mother assailed him with passionate upbraidings. Why had he gone boating? Why did he take Charlie with him? Why did he let Charlie bathe? Why didn't he stay all night looking for the poor boy?

Edward was very patient with her, either listening in gloomy silence or answering gently and reasonably. Then she said it was a judgment—that, if they had hearkened to Charlie's advice and disclosed the secret of the broken trust to Mrs. Lincoln and offered to make restitution, he would not have died; adding, "And now we shall be obliged to tell her."

"Your grief is affecting your memory, mother, and no

wonder; the broken trust has nothing to do with our going out in the yawl or bathing."

"It was reckless beyond measure to bathe from an open boat so far from land, and neither of you a strong swimmer. Oh, why didn't Olive go with you? If she had you wouldn't have been able to bathe."

"Anyhow, Olive not going with us had nothing to do with the trust; while as for our recklessness, as you call it, if Charlie had done as I wanted him and kept near the boat, he would be here now. He went too far and sank from exhaustion before he could get back—or was seized with cramp, as Job thinks. And you are mistaken about the secret; there is no need to disclose it—now."

"I don't understand you. Do speak plainly. I am quite dazed. As the poor boy is dead, and cannot be your co-trustee, we shall be obliged to tell Mrs. Lincoln, and all the sacrifices we have made will go for nothing."

"Not unless you like. We should have been obliged to tell her if this had not happened. Charlie told me before we set out, and repeated emphatically in the boat—else I should scarce have believed him—that nothing would induce him, not even your entreaties, to sign the deed without imparting all the facts to Mrs. Lincoln."

"Did he, really? After his promise, too. Still, I don't think he would have persisted in his refusal when it came to the point. And now, you say?"

"Charlie is in the policy. The company will have no excuse for refusing to pay this time."

"I thought you had surrendered the policy."

"Not yet. We were in treaty, but the transaction was not completed, and now, of course, will not be."

"You will get the money, then?"

"Yes."

"The price of your brother's life."

Edward started as if he had been stung; and his face, which had regained some of its wonted color, became ashen gray.

"The price of my brother's life, mother," he exclaimed in a voice tremulous with emotion. "Do you think—do you mean that I, that I——" And then, as if his feelings were too much for him, he leaned back in his chair and covered his face with his hands.

" I did not mean to accuse you, dear, but the thought struck me; it seems to be so dreadful to be talking about this money, as if we regarded it in some sort as an equivalent for our poor lost boy."

" I never said so."

" You spoke of both in the same breath. But let it pass. . . . Do you think there is any chance of the body being recovered ? " she asked faintly.

" The fishermen say there is, and I shall offer a reward."

" Do. Do everything possible. If he isn't laid in consecrated ground I think it will kill me, and now, dear, leave me to myself. I shall be better alone."

When Mrs. Lincoln left her friend she went to her daughter. Olive's abrupt disappearance from the avenue had rekindled her suspicions and put her on the track of a painful discovery. She found the girl lying on her bed, indulging in a passionate outburst of grief.

" My poor child, what is this ? " she asked tenderly, taking Olive in her arms. " You loved him ? "

For a while Olive did not answer; then stifling her sobs and lifting her head, she said tremulously and with quivering lips :—

" Yes, mother. Charlie was very dear to me, and we had agreed to be engaged—with your consent—when we were a little older. He was so good and noble, mother, and he loved me, and I——"

" You did not consider yourself engaged, then ? "

" No, I wouldn't be engaged until I could tell you . . . and it would not have been right so soon after Mr. Prince's death."

" Does anybody know of this ? "

" Nobody. We kept it quite to ourselves."

To Olive's great relief, her mother asked no further questions, and instead of blaming her, or finding fault with Charlie, as she had feared, did all she could to soothe and console her.

It was agreed between them that the quasi-engagement should be kept an absolute secret, even from Mrs. Prince, and to this end Olive promised that she would " keep up," as her mother phrased it, and not betray herself by a display of inordinate grief.

" You know, darling, it would not be seemly to sorrow openly for a man to whom you were not openly engaged," said Mrs. Lincoln to Olive, and then to herself : " It was only children's love after all ; she will soon get over it."

CHAPTER XXVIII.

A SUMMONS FROM THE SEA.

IT is a trite adage, yet true withal, that adverse fortune and strokes of ill-luck are seldom quite so bad as they seem. As we sit by the fireside on a winter's night, and the storm howls without, we think with a pitying shudder of the poor wayfarer who is exposed to the fury of the blast. But the wayfarer himself is probably neither cast down nor appalled. With bent head and teeth hard set he battles on to his journey's end, knowing that at the worst it cannot be far off.

In the same way, when a neighbor or a friend is visited by a calamity so crushing that it hardly seems possible for him to survive it, he lives on, and after a time (however he may suffer in secret) appears very little the worse. The wind is tempered to the shorn lamb oftener than we suppose.

Charles Prince's death was a dire shock to Olive Lincoln; it pained her all the more that she had parted from him in anger, while she knew, or imagined she knew, that his last thought was of her, for now she firmly believed, that the voice she had heard in the Fairies' Tryst was his voice, the figure she had seen his wraith. It seemed as though the light of her life were gone out, and that she should never know happiness again. But broken hearts are rarer in reality than in romance; a middle-aged matron, bereft of her husband, is much more likely to be inconsolable than a maiden in her teens bereft of her lover, and we know that widows do not always refuse to be comforted. Olive grieved deeply for Charlie; the wound was slow to heal, and for many weeks she could not think of him without a heartache, yet she was too young to despair and too hopeful to pine, and so comported herself—"behaved so nobly," as her mother put it —that nobody guessed that Charlie had been more to her than a highly esteemed friend, and the time came when she found consolation for her sorrow in a nobler passion than love for a man.

Even Edward was deceived. " A case of flirtation on one side and calf-love on the other," he thought to himself, and drew therefrom an augury favorable to his hopes.

As for Mrs. Prince, her preoccupation about the broken trust, the deception which she had so long practised, her passionate eagerness to shield the family honor from the breath of scandal at whatever cost, and the morbid pride which was her ruling motive blunted her motherly, as it had blunted her wifely, love. True, she mourned for her lost son, yet her grief was rendered less acute, tolerable even, by the thought that his death would enable her to make good her husband's default, and keep all knowledge of the fatal secret from a censorious world. Her sense of relief from the strain of anxiety was almost as great as the pain of her sorrow, a fact of which she was fully conscious, and whereof in her heart she felt bitterly ashamed ; and the ever-recurring thought that the course advised by Charlie—a frank confession to Mrs. Lincoln—was still the right thing to do, and that she had not the courage to do it, added to her humiliation. The subject was so painful, indeed, that between Edward and herself it was tacitly ignored. Charlie they could not help sometimes talking about ; but reference to the secret was religiously avoided, and trust matters were mentioned only when absolutely necessary, and as briefly as possible.

Two days after the catastrophe Edward and his mother returned to Peele. Mrs. Lincoln would have had her stay longer, but Mrs. Prince pleaded a yearning for home, quite natural in the circumstances, and insisted on going back with her son. And she had another motive for hurrying away. Her friend's presence had become painful to her, it kept her in mind of her lost boy and the broken trust, and her nerves being unstrung she was in mortal dread lest she should say or do something which might betray the secret or give a clue to her thoughts.

Charlie's death, coming so soon after his father's, naturally made a sensation at Peele, and general sympathy was shown for the bereaved family. Cards were left by the score, but Mrs. Prince shut herself in her room, and for several days refused to see even her most intimate friends.

Before leaving Whitebeach Edward made it known that he would pay fifty pounds for the finding of his brother's body, and arranged with a local coastguard officer to send him instant information of its recovery—if it should be recovered.

His next proceeding was to advise the secretary of the Ægis of Charlie's death. He said nothing about the consequent rupture of the negotiation for the surrender of the policy. That was a matter of course.

Edward awaited Mr. Cutter's answer with some anxiety, for he was not so sure of getting the money quickly as he had led his mother to believe; and, Charlie being dead, Mrs. Lincoln might appoint another trustee at once, though, as yet, she had expressed no such intention, and he had been careful not to moot the subject. As it happened, Mrs. Lincoln meant to appoint Mr. Marsh, and only refrained from informing Edward of her decision out of a feeling of delicacy. It would not be nice, she thought, to trouble him about business so soon after poor Charlie's death.

The Secretary's answer came in due course. It was short and dry. He said how sorry he was to hear of Mr. Charles Prince's death, and that he had taken note of his correspondent's communication, and would lay it before his directors.

This meant that the company would not pay the sum due under the policy until they had received satisfactory proof of Charlie's decease, proof of which, in the circumstances, it was not easy to furnish. Edward could only say that, to the best of his belief, his brother had perished, and point out that, in view of the facts, no other theory was tenable. As, however, he had not seen him drown, it was open to the company to hold a different opinion; and, though they must pay eventually, they could procrastinate so long as to put Edward in a serious predicament. And it would be as impolite to show eagerness as to affect indifference; in the one case they might think that he had urgent need of the money, in the other, that he had so little confidence in the justice of his claim that he hesitated to urge it.

Altogether Edward Prince found himself in an embarrassing position. If the body were found his difficulties would of course be at an end; the proof of Charlie's decease would be complete; but that was a piece of good fortune on which (though he had done his best to bring it to pass) it would not be safe to count.

His final decision was to delay further action for a few days. Mrs. Lincoln had fortunately said nothing further about the appointment of another trustee, and even when he did receive her instructions in the matter he need not carry them out at once.

It was probably these perplexities, or the shock of Charlie's death, or the two causes combined, which made Edward so nervous at this time. Did anybody accost him abruptly he would start and turn pale. A knock at his door put him in a shake, and when a telegram was brought to him he would let it lie on the table until the bearer left the room, and then open it with tremulous fingers. Once, as he was walking up the street, absorbed in thought, a friend laid his hand on Edward's shoulder. For a minute or two he seemed like to faint. His knees knocked together, his face became almost ghastly, and he staggered as if he were going to fall.

" How poor Charlie's death has taken hold of Ned Prince!" said the friend afterwards to another friend. " And no wonder. It must have been a terrible experience. I never saw a man so changed."

All his other friends ascribed Edward's nervousness to the same cause—all save Lillywhite, who was watching him closely, partly on general principles, partly because he had conceived certain doubts.

The old clerk felt Charlie's death deeply, and in the manner of it, as related by Edward, there was something which struck him as being strange, if not suspicious. The younger brother, albeit a fair, was by no means a powerful swimmer, and being, moreover, out of practice, it was not likely that in the open sea he would venture far from an unanchored and possibly drifting boat, especially with Edward's warning ringing in his ears. Lillywhite gave him credit for better sense. It was also noteworthy that Edward discussed the incident like one repeating a lesson learned by rote, and when questioned on the subject showed irritation.

On the other hand, if the story were not true, how far was it false and what had really happened?

Here Lillywhite was baffled. Two or three theories suggested themselves, but none of them quite fitted the facts or was sufficiently probable for acceptance.

Edward unquestionably gained by his brother's death. It had rid him of a rival, and would enable him to reinstate

Mrs. Lincoln's trust fund—to the Prince family almost a matter of life and death. Hence there was a strong motive for foul play.

Lillywhite did not stop to consider whether Edward was capable of foul play, which in this instance meant, of course, compassing his brother's death. The old clerk was naturally cynical. In the law courts and elsewhere he had seen a good deal of the seamy side of life, and it was a common saying of his that, after Jonathan Salmon, he could believe anybody capable of anything. Thirty years previously Salmon had been one of the most prominent and respected inhabitants of Peele. A Quaker of the old type, forward in every good work, energetic in well doing, of a probity beyond doubt, he died in the odor of sanctity and amid a chorus of lamentations. But hardly had he been laid in the ground than it was discovered that for the greater part of his life he had been systematically defrauding a savings bank, of which he was the principal trustee. His defalcations reached a total of seventy thousand pounds.

So Lillywhite had some warrant for his cynicism; and he held that it could not be predicted with certainty of any man that his integrity would hold out against great temptations or severe pressure.

Edward Prince was just as likely to commit a murder as Jonathan Salmon had been to rob a savings bank, a crime quite as bad as murder. It was, however, doubtful whether he had the nerve to do anything so desperate, and whether, even though he had, he would consider the probable profit commensurate with the appalling risk. Moreover, he was physically weaker and less agile than Charlie, and though he might shoot or stab him unawares, the body, if found—and the finding was at least possible—would be damning evidence against him.

"No," said Lillywhite to himself, after long pondering. "I don't think it is a case of fratricide. The motive isn't sufficient. Also he lacks the courage; and to give the devil his due, I don't think he is wicked enough. But then why is he so nervous and restless? Grief? No, grief doesn't take that shape. Besides, I doubt whether he does grieve. There was never much love lost between them, and he has fifteen thousand reasons for not fretting."

And then Lillywhite considered another hypothesis. Was

it a scheme to defraud the insurance company? Nothing would be easier than for Edward to put Charlie ashore (disguised, say, as a sailor) in some out-of-the-way place, and then pretend he had been accidentally drowned.

In his heart the clerk did not think that Charlie would lend himself to so nefarious a scheme. Yet there was no telling. He was of a generous, confiding nature, easily led (if you took him on the right side), his mother and Edward were masterful and in desperate straits, and it was just conceivable that under pressure and to save his father's name from dishonor he might have consented to efface himself and commit a fraud. Only just, however, and when Lillywhite remembered that Charlie could not efface himself without sacrificing Olive Lincoln he perceived that it was not conceivable at all. Another objection to the theory was the fact that up to the time of his leaving Peele Charlie knew nothing of the breach of trust. Only the day before he went they were talking of his appointment as Mrs. Lincoln's trustee, when Lillywhite (by way of sounding him) observed that the office of trustee was always thankless and often hazardous.

"Not in this instance," answered the young fellow gaily. "I regard the appointment as an honor; and as for hazard, what hazard can there be when every shilling of the trust fund is in Consols?"

It was simply impossible that in two days and in a strange house Charlie could be persuaded to abandon his sweetheart, his country, and his name, and condemn himself to a life-long exile.

"That theory won't wash either, not a bit," was Lillywhite's conclusion, and but for the strangeness of Edward's demeanor since the occurrence he would have been disposed to regard his account of it as true.

Edward's manner was less that of a man suffering from grief or remorse than of one who was in a chronic state of apprehension and fear.

The "office" was once concerned in the defence of some poachers, who were accused of killing the keeper, and the "office" (meaning thereby the managing clerk) got them off. After their acquittal Lillywhite had a long talk with the ringleader, who frankly admitted that it was he who had struck the fatal blow, and he vividly described his sensations between the affray and his arrest. He hoped (vainly as it turned

out) that by staying quietly at home he should escape suspicion. But his nerves were always on edge. If the door
opened he would nearly jump out of his skin, if he heard
footsteps during the night he would break into a cold sweat,
if anybody touched him unawares he felt like to drop, and he
protested that until he found himself "in quod," he did not
know a moment's peace. It was not conscience that made a
coward of him (in his moral code the killing of a keeper was
no crime), it was fear, and after his acquittal the man was as
serene as a saint.

Edward Prince's symptoms so far resembled the poacher's as
to suggest that they proceeded from a similar cause. This
was the somewhat abortive outcome of Lillywhite's pon-
derings. Time might bring a solution of the enigma. For
the present all he could do was to keep his eye on Edward
and await developments.

Meanwhile, he had done a little stroke of business which
greatly pleased him.

So soon as Olive rallied a little from the shock of Charlie's
death, she bethought her of the letters which in her anger
she had asked him to return. They contained nothing of
which she had any reason to be ashamed, but much that she
would not like anybody else, especially Edward, to read. She
knew that Lillywhite had been in Charlie's confidence, and
believed he was a man whom she might safely trust. So she
wrote a guarded though pathetic little missive, beseeching
him, if he could to get the letters which she had written to
"Mr. Charles," and send them to her as soon as possible.
It was an extreme course, and only adopted because it seemed
the lesser of two evils.

Lillywhite, on his part, accepted the commission with pleasure and performed it with alacrity. He opened Charlie's
desk with a key—one of a score borrowed from the locksmith
—found the letters, and forwarded them to Miss Lincoln by
return of post, together with one of his own, in which he felici-
tated himself on having it in his power to serve her, assured
her of his sympathy, and protested (without much exaggera-
tion) that he had loved Mr. Charles as his own son.

Olive answered with a graceful letter of thanks, and the old
clerk felt that he had scored again. He had placed Miss
Lincoln under an obligation, added to his store of secrets,
and secured two letters which might come in useful.

So it came to pass that when Edward Prince returned from Whitebeach, and looked over his brother's papers, he found, to his surprise, and rather to his disappointment, nothing relating to Olive, from which he rashly inferred that Charlie had cared so little for his sweetheart that he had not taken the trouble to preserve her letters.

Edward never guessed that they had been purloined, and the incident was quickly forgotten ; but, being naturally acute and morbidly sensitive, he was not long in perceiving that Lillywhite was watching him—with suspicion. The idea, besides making him angry, increased his nervousness, and he resolved, when he had got the insurance money and replaced the misappropriated stock, to give his managing clerk the sack.

"The old villain knows a good deal—a good deal too much," he thought one day as he sat at his desk moodily despondent. "Suspects rather, for his knowledge is not susceptible of proof, and I don't think he could hurt me ; nobody would believe him, and now Charlie is——"

Here Edward's reflections were interrupted by a knock at the door, whereat he started violently.

"Hang it ! " he muttered. "Shall I never get over this confounded nervousness. If I could only make sure—— Come in ! "

It was Lillywhite with a telegram.

"Why didn't you let one of the boys bring it ?" asked Edward crossly. "Your time is too valuable to be carrying telegrams about."

"I wanted to speak to you about that matter of Ardwick's, so I thought I might as well bring you the despatch," returned Lillywhite deferentially.

Edward, changing countenance in spite of himself, opened the telegram with hesitating fingers. After reading it twice he drew a long breath.

"I must go to Whitebeach by the next train," he said, handing the message to Lillywhite. It ran thus—

"A body, supposed to be your brother's, has been found by some fishermen. You had better come at once."

CHAPTER XXIX.

A NARROW SHAVE.

LILLYWHITE was a man of feelings : his expressive nose changed color, and he wiped his eyes with a huge bandana pocket-handkerchief. The recovery of the body seemed to bring the fact of Charlie's death more home to him and make it more terrible. "God bless me!" he exclaimed. " Why, it is nearly a month since the accident. I had given up all hope."

"So had I—nearly. However, you see what they say. Scholes must take the dog-cart to Holmcroft and fetch me some things ; and I shall want money. Here is a check for eighty pounds ; get sixty in small notes and twenty in gold. I offered a reward of fifty pounds and there will be other expenses. Stay! What was it you wanted to ask me about ? "

" That matter of Ardwick's."

" Does he make any definite offer ? "

"Yes, twenty down and the balance by equal monthly instalments."

"Accept it. One moment (writing). Let Scholes give this note to my mother."

When Lillywhite was gone Edward went to his bookcase, took out of it a work on medical jurisprudence, and turning to the chapter on " Drowning," studied it with close attention for half-an-hour. Then, leaning back in his chair he covered his face with his hands and shuddered, murmuring : —" It has to be done. I must go through with it, must, must. To shirk it would give rise to damaging suspicions, and if the body be identified as his the Ægis must pay up at once, and that danger will be out of the way and off my mind."

Here there was another knock at the door. Edward roused himself, wiped the perspiration from his face, and bade the knocker come in. It was Lillywhite again.

"I have sent Scholes and been to the bank, and here is the money," he said, going up to the desk.

Edward, who had been momentarily oblivious of the book, closed it hurriedly and pushed the volume aside ; yet not before Lillywhite had noted the heading of the open page :— "Found dead."

"Can I do anything more for you, sir?" he asked, as he counted out the notes and gold.

"I don't think so. Yes, call at the Town Hall and tell the Mayor where I am gone ; but ask him to keep it to himself for the present, or the *Mercury* people will be sending a reporter down, and those are fellows I hate."

"Very well, sir."

Lillywhite left the room, musing.

"Found dead," he thought. "Very likely, I should say. They were sure to find the body—or some body—at that price. Fifty pounds is a fortune for a Whitebeach fisherman. And is a body recognizable after three or four weeks' immerson ? I must have a look at that book when he is gone. No wonder he is upset. But why does he look so scared ? It should be a satisfaction to him, and I know it will be to his mother to have the poor lad decently buried, to say nothing of getting the insurance money now instead of waiting for another month or two. Gad ! he did look scared and no mistake. That telegram might have been a ghost, and he has not got over it yet. Queer, very queer."

Three hours later Edward Prince was at Whitebeach. He had telegraphed to Job, the old fisherman, to meet him at the station, and the two walked together by the fields to the Wheat Sheaf, a little inn by the seashore, where Edward proposed to put up. The body had been recovered by Job and two of his mates, with whom he would have to share the reward. As the boatman described the finding of the body (on a sandbank off Thornby Point) and its appearance in the bluntest of language, sparing no detail, Mr. Prince became painfully affected and bade him peremptorily to stop : nor was conversation resumed until he had fortified himself with a stiff glass of the Wheat Sheaf's brandy.

Job had no doubt whatever as to the body being Mr, Charles's. He never forgot a face, and though the "poor young gentleman" was naturally much altered, anybody could "tell him." His mates were equally sure. The

coroner had been notified and was going to hold the
inquest on the following day. The body lay at the coastguard station—would Mr. Prince like to see it?

There was nothing in the world that Edward wanted less
to see, but as the seeing was a necessity and hesitation
might engender suspicion he overcame his repugnance and
signified his assent. After steadying his nerves with another
drink, and, standing a glass of rum for Job, he went to the
place in question and was shown by the officer on duty into
the room, where his brother's remains were laid.

The ordeal was almost more than Edward could bear.
He paused at the threshold several seconds, then went forward, visibly trembling and leaning against the wall for
support. After gazing at the ghastly sight for a few minutes
like one fascinated, he crept, with bent head, from the room.

" It do look bad, that's sure. It's changed a good deal for
the worse since yesterday, isn't it, Mr. Rentoul?" said Job.

" It is, indeed. They always do on exposure to the air.
The salt water acts as a preservative."

" Ay, ay, a sort of pickle, I've heard say. I felt sure as
it 'ud turned up sooner or later. I've known 'em washed
ashore two months arter. I was the first to spot it, aground
on the Horse Bank at low tide. You can see the waves
breaking over it now, sir; about two miles west o' th' Point."

But Edward, who still looked and felt very queer, neither
answered nor turned his head. As they returned to the inn,
Job asked whether Mr. Prince did not think that he and his
mate had earned the reward.

" I'll tell you that after the inquest," answered Edward,
who was recovering his composure.

" What has that to do with it?"

"The jury may decide that the body is not my brother's?"

" Not unless you swears as it isn't. Me and my mates, we
know as it is. We saw him afore the change set in; and
you know it too, though he does look different. Don't you,
now?"

" Oh, yes, I think it is my poor brother's body—certainly."

"Of course you do. So does everybody in these parts.
Let me see, didn't you say as he went into the water stark
naked?"

" I did."

" Well, he was found so. That's another proof, and you

may take your davy as the jury will say as you and me says."

"In that case you will get the reward right away. I have it with me" (tapping his pocket).

Old Job proved a true prophet. On the following day the coroner's jury viewed the body—Edward, to his great discomfort, being present—and heard the evidence. The local medical practitioner said the body was that of a person who had been drowned, and remained in the water from twenty to thirty days, and gave minute particulars touching his probable height and age, the color of his eyes and hair and the rest. Job and his two mates described the finding of the body, which they recognized at once as that of Mr. Charles Prince. It was quite without clothes and the face was very little changed. Edward gave his account of the way in which his brother lost his life, and said that to the best of his belief the body which they had viewed was that of Charles Prince.

In this sense the jury rendered their verdict, and when the necessary formalities had been observed the body was placed at the disposal of the relatives, and Job and his mates received their reward.

After telegraphing to his mother and Lillywhite, and making such arrangements as the circumstances required, Edward returned to Peele. He did not call at the Pines. The Lincolns were in London. When their guests were gone the loneliness and associations of the place became unbearable. Mrs. Lincoln moped, and Olive, despite heroic efforts to "keep up," began to droop. As she could not go out without being continually reminded of Charlie and his terrible end she stayed in, and though she never complained, her mother could see that the girl suffered—how much she never knew. The wound was deeper than she supposed, and while they remained at Whitebeach was unlikely to heal. The sooner they got away the better. So one morning at breakfast, Mrs. Lincoln, after observing that if she stayed there longer she should go melancholy mad, said she had made up her mind to start for London that very day, and told her daughter to pack up "right away." Her idea was to keep Olive from brooding, and when they got to town she called on all the people she knew and accepted all the invitations she received, and went in generally for all the gaieties that were going on. To Olive this was repugnant; her mood was not gay. She would much rather have been allowed to brood in peace; but as her lover's death had tamed her high spirits and impaired her power of resistance, and she knew that her mother meant kindly, she submitted passively, though often reluctantly, to her guidance. And Mrs. Lincoln's management was so far good that it distracted Olive's thoughts, took her out of herself, and little by little dulled the sharpness of her sorrow.

Among other friends whom they met in London was Mr. Marsh, who had just returned from the Continent. In her usual straightforward way Mrs. Lincoln asked him to be her second trustee. At the outset he demurred, on the ground that her settled fortune being invested in England she had better choose somebody who was sure to remain in the country, and he was not sure; but when she pointed out that as the money was in consols, and had to stay in consols, and as Edward Prince attended to all the details, there was really nothing in the world for him to do except sign a deed, he consented—stipulating, however, that a draft of the instrument in question, together with the deed of settlement, should be submitted to his own solicitor. Mr. Marsh had every confidence in Mr. Prince, but, as he aptly observed, business was business, and he made it a rule never to sign an important document without taking legal advice.

To this condition Mrs. Lincoln gave a willing assent, and wrote straightway to Edward Prince, advising him what she had done, and that he would presently receive a communication from Mr. Marsh's solicitor, as, in effect, he did, a few days later. Mr. Bunch, the gentleman in question, acting on instructions received from his client, asked for a draft of the proposed deed of appointment, together with a statement of the precise amount of Mrs. Lincoln's fortune and the manner of its investment.

This letter gave Edward a bad quarter of an hour. As yet, though he had told Mrs. Lincoln (no witness being present) that her fortune was still invested in Government stock, he had not committed himself to the assertion in writing. So far, he had been guilty of no offence more serious than a *suppressio veri* (the lie, being incapable of proof, did not count), and, to make a positively false statement under his own hand, besides being dangerous, would do violence to his

legal conscience.   Wherefore he wrote a polite letter to Mr.
Bunch, to the effect that owing to the tragical death of his
brother (of which his correspondent might have heard), he
was for the moment quite unable to attend to business, but
as soon after the funeral as possible the matter should have
his attention.

Edward believed that this would keep Mr. Bunch quiet for
a few days, probably for two or three weeks, or until Mrs.
Lincoln (to whom he forwarded a copy of his letter) moved
Mr. Marsh to further inquiry.

The funeral was conducted very quietly, only a few of the
more intimate friends of the family being invited, and as the
lead coffin had been soldered up at Whitebeach, none of
them saw the body.   Seeing that the body had been nearly
a month in the water the soldering was absolutely necessary,
explained Edward, and when his mother expressed a wish to
take a last look at the poor boy, he said significantly, that
if she wished to retain a pleasant recollection of him she had
better not, and the subject dropped.

Nobody saw in the proceeding anything strange—save
Lillywhite, who, collating it with certain facts whereof he
alone was cognizant, regarded it as suspicious, and by way
of settling his doubts—or confirming them, as the case
might be—betook himself on the following Saturday to
Whitebeach, put up at the Wheat Sheaf, foregathered with
Job and a few of his fellows, drank and "stood" a good
many glasses of rum, and the next evening returned to Peele
with an aching head, yet well content withal, for he had acquired information which gave him something to think about
and might prove useful.

Meanwhile, Edward Prince had written a second letter to
the Assurance Company, in which he enclosed documentary
evidence of his brother's death and inquired, rather peremptorily when it would suit them to pay the amount due under
the policy.

By return of post came a highly-satisfactory reply from
Mr. Cutter.   His directors had passed the claim, and at the
end of the current month a check for fifteen thousand
pounds would be at Mr. Prince's disposal, as surviving partner in the firm, according to the conditions of the policy.

At the same time Edward received a letter from Mr. Bunch
asking when he might expect the draft of the deed of appoint-

ment, as promised. His client was going on a journey and would like to have the business settled as soon as possible. Edward, now as prompt as he had previously been dilatory, sent Mr. Bunch the document by return of post, and intimated that as soon as Mr. Marsh signified his approval of the draft he would have it engrossed; and the Government stock in which the trust fund was invested, now standing in his name and his mother's should be transferred to Mr. Marsh and himself.

"A narrow shave," thought Edward as he signed the letter, "a very narrow shave. I could not have put them off more than another week, or a fortnight at the outside."

"Thank God!" exclaimed his mother fervently, when he told her that the broken trust had been reinstated and there was nothing to fear. "Thank God! It seems almost providential, don't you think so, dear?"

Her son made no answer; he doubted whether Providence had any hand in the affair; and to do Mrs. Prince justice, she was just then thinking less of Charlie's death than imminent danger narrowly escaped and a husband's name saved from dishonor; while Edward's thoughts were of a bright day and a sunlit sea, a boat gliding before the wind, two brothers fiercely wrangling and——

"You shiver dear, don't you feel well?" asked his mother anxiously.

"I have got a little chill, I think—perhaps a drop of brandy——"

And with that he went to the sideboard, filled a large wine glass with cognac and drank it neat.

CHAPTER XXX.

LILLYWHITE LEARNS ANOTHER SECRET.

THINGS seldom fall out as we anticipate ; provisions, like friends, are apt to prove untrue, and even when the wish fathered by the thought comes to pass the result does not always harmonize with our hopes.   Edward Prince and his mother had escaped a great danger by the skin of their teeth, they had shot the rapids and were floating down stream in smooth water and fair weather.   Yet they were not happy. Released from incessant preoccupation and impending peril, and having leisure for thought, Mrs. Prince began to count the cost of her deliverance—years of corroding care, two precious lives, an abiding sense of remorse and a lonely old age.   This was not quite logical.   Edward had assured her, and she could not gainsay, that the broken trust was not even remotely responsible for Charlie's death, and she was continually assuring herself that she had acted for the best and the means were justified by the end.   But the human mind is as little ruled by logic as life itself, and Mrs. Prince could no more help connecting Charlie's death with her husband's offence than hush " the still small voice," when in the watches of the night it accused her of having been his evil genius and the indirect cause of his death.

And Edward, though he no longer trembled and turned pale when a friend tapped him on the shoulder, was not the man he had been.   Some people said he was a better man, and in the sense that his manners were softer and he bore himself less arrogantly than of yore this was true.   He was also more sensitive ; the mere mention of his brother's name sufficing to make him change countenance, and cause him acute distress, from which most people concluded that the two had been devotedly attached to each other.

In addition to qualms of conscience (if he were troubled with any) Edward had two serious preoccupations.   One was

Lillywhite. He would fain have sent the old clerk away. But as yet he did not dare. True, Lillywhite, although he knew a great deal, could prove nothing, and a discharged employé, who told tales " out of doors," was discredited by the very fact. All the same, Edward did not want people's tongues to be set wagging about him and his affairs so soon after Charlie's death ; and Lillywhite had been so long in the office, was so popular with clients, and so well known in the town, that it would be impolitic to dismiss him without good cause or plausible pretext, and at present he had neither. So, though it fretted him to be continually under the observation of a man who already knew too much, and had a wonderful capacity for ferreting out secrets, there was nothing for it but to bide his time and wait for an opportunity of getting rid of him.

His other preoccupation was Olive, whom he probably loved with a passion which surprised even himself, and whom on merely money grounds it was still well worth his while to marry. She was a fine girl, and would make a wife to be proud of ; and well dowered, too. Topper, Sandboy, and Perrywinkle, urged by Mr. Jump, had pushed on the winding-up of the Chancery suit so energetically that it was going to be ended much sooner than anybody had thought possible, and matters were so far advanced that Edward could form a pretty shrewd guess as to the value of the salvage. There would be a thousand a year for Olive, when she was of age, and after her mother's death an additional fifteen hundred—not enough to make the girl a great heiress, yet more than enough to make her a very good match.

Edward never went to town that he did not call on the Lincolns, by whom he was always welcomed, and whom he naturally did his best to please—of course, with special reference to Miss Lincoln—and not without success. He looked so careworn, his manner was so quiet and subdued, and on the rare occasions when Charlie's name was mentioned showed so much emotion that Olive was moved to compassion. True, she had never liked Edward, and he had not always been as good to Charlie as he might have been. All the same, he was Charlie's brother and sorrowed for him, and on that ground alone had a right to her sympathy and respect. Whereupon it fell out that at this time Olive was kinder to Edward Prince than she had ever been before, thereby unwittingly confirming him in the belief that he might win her love.

One day he brought the ladies an invitation from his mother to spend a few weeks with them at Holmcroft—if they did not mind being very quiet, for though several months were gone since Charlie's death, Mrs. Prince still led a secluded life, neither entertaining nor "going out." But she should be delighted to see her old friends, and felt sure that a visit from them would do her good.

"And we want something to cheer us up," added Edward plaintively. "We are frightfully dull now at Holmcroft. I don't think I should be exaggerating if I said dismal—so different from what it used to be."

Mrs. Lincoln said she would leave it to Olive. The summer was nearly over, and for her own part she should be glad to spend a few days at Holmcroft before they went on the Continent, and there were certain business matters arising out of the Chancery suit which could perhaps be dealt with quite as conveniently at Peele as in London.

Here Edward observed that in the course of the ensuing month the suit would probably come to an end, and that in the meantime he should have frequent occasion to consult Mrs. Lincoln.

"All the more reason for accepting your mother's kind invitation. What do you say, Olive?"

"Certainly, let us go," returned Olive with seeming cheerfulness, though she would rather not have gone, knowing that the visit would revive painful memories, and be more of a trial than a pleasure, but her mother evidently desired to go, and it would have been ungracious to refuse Mrs. Prince's invitation.

So Edward went home, if not exactly exuberant, better in spirits than he had felt for some time. Olive's kindness and ready acceptance of his mother's invitation were distinctly encouraging; and if a favorable occasion should present itself during her stay it might be well to put the momentous question which he had resolved to ask. But he would have to mind what he was about, and look before he leaped. It was not very long since "the accident," and besides exposing him to a rebuff a premature declaration might be fatal to his hopes. Olive had a strong will, and if she once said "no" it would not be easy to persuade her to say "yes."

Anyhow, her presence would brighten the house, and it needed brightening. At the best, his mother was not a lively companion, and sometimes she kept her room two or three days running. One night, shortly before his last visit to London, he had dined alone, his mother being indisposed, and after the butler had left him to himself Edward leaned back in his chair and thought of the past and of the home and the family as they had been in days gone by. In imagination he saw his father at the head of the table, and heard his hearty laugh as he told a merry tale. Jack had come down from Liverpool for the Christmas holidays, and opposite to him sat Charlie, full of health and high spirits. It was all as objectively real as if they had been there in the flesh, and he was about to make an observation, when a piteous cry rang in his ears : "Ned ! Ned !" and the bright face before him changed into the hideous semblance of the thing he had seen in the coastguard station at Whitebeach. Edward, who had fallen into a doze, awoke groaning, his hair standing on end and his face streaming with perspiration.

After this, whenever his mother could not dine with him, he dined at Peele, and, taking papers home with him, wrought far into the night. If he could help it he would never be alone, and work was the best substitute for company.

Mrs. Prince, on the other hand, did not seem to care for company, and only invited the Lincolns for her son's sake and to afford him an opportunity of paying his court to Olive ; for though she had latterly given little thought to her old match-making project she wanted to see him happily married, and knew that he had set his heart on marrying Miss Lincoln.

Olive's presence brightened the house, as Edward had expected, for the girl was fair to see, but she contributed far less to its gaiety than her mother, who bustled about continually, and did all she could to rouse her hostess from her torpor and gloom—kept her in talk, made Olive read to them, went out with her in the pony carriage. Edward played the part of host to perfection, came home early, was affable at breakfast and urbane at dinner, read to the ladies afterwards, or made up a rubber, as they preferred, and was assiduously attentive to Mrs. Lincoln and her daughter, especially the daughter.

"How much he is changed—and improved—quite another man, I declare," observed Mrs. Lincoln more than once.

" Sorrow sours some people, it has softened Edward Prince."

" Yes," answered Olive listlessly, " he is very much nicer than he used to be."

Occasionally Mrs. Prince put a good word in for Edward, saying what a good son he was, how well the office was thriving under his admirable management, doing better than it had ever done before, and how highly people spoke of him.

But these laudations bored Olive more than they served her would-be swain ; they reminded her, too, that though he might be a good son he had not always been a kind brother. All the same, Edward flattered himself that his attentions were telling, yet before " trying his luck" he looked for an opportunity of making a little more sure as to the precise effect which they had produced in Olive's mind.

The opportunity came, as opportunities always do to those who know how to wait. She had made some casual remark about Holmcroft being lonely.

" Lonely ! You may well say so ; more, it is dull, deadly dull. So different from what it used to be," he answered with a heart-rending sigh and a woebegone look. " My mother is very good—the best woman in the world, I sometimes think—and bears up wonderfully, as you see ; but at her age, and after all that has happened, you cannot expect her to be very cheerful, and going into society or even receiving visitors—unless they are old friends, like you and your mother—is really beyond her strength. I want somebody nearer my own age in the house, some bright presence—Miss Lincoln."

" Your mother should have a companion—or you might marry."

A more impulsive man would have tried his luck there and then. But Edward Prince, being neither impulsive nor a fool, well knew that if Olive had divined the significance of his words, the observation would not have been made; and her manner was so unconcerned and void of self-consciousness as to render it evident that, as yet, she had not even so much as thought of him as a possible *prétendant*.

" A very good idea ; I'll speak to my mother about it," he replied, with a somewhat constrained smile. " As for my marrying, a good deal would depend on whom I married, don't you think ? "

" Everything, I should say."

And then, as if she did not find the subject interesting, Olive took up a book, which she had laid down a few minutes previously and went on with her reading. Yet, though the had failed, Edward was not discouraged. He believed that the rather broad hints he had dropped would bear fruit, and that the next time he tried a similar experiment the result would be more satisfactory.

A few days after this conversation, Olive, on her way through the fields to Peele, fell in with Lillywhite, who had been to a neighboring farm on office business. She was glad to see the old fellow, and spoke to him kindly. After exchanging greetings they walked on together.

" It was very good of you to send me those letters, Mr. Lillywhite. You rendered me a great service," she said frankly.

" How can I thank——"

" Don't mention it. You lay me under an obligation by allowing me to render you a service, and pray consider me always at your service. I am yours to command, both for your own sake and that of poor Mr. Charles."

Olive's eyes filled with tears.

" Oh, wasn't it terrible ! " she murmured. " Even yet can I hardly realize that—he is not here."

" You are not the only one who misses him, Miss Lincoln. Everybody at Peele misses him, I think. And the office isn't the same. He was always so bright and cheery—like sunshine in the place—and kind to everybody."

Olive liked to hear Charlie praised by one who knew him so well, yet it distressed her to talk about him, and for a minute or two they walked on in silence. But she had something to ask Lillywhite, painful though it might be. Charlie's refusal to act as her mother's trustee was still a mystery to which she had not found a clue. The clerk might be able to help her to one.

" I can trust you, Mr. Lillywhite," she said, in a tone which implied that she meant, " Can I trust you ? "

" Absolutely, Miss Lincoln. Hundreds have done, and not one has ever had occasion to regret having trusted Andrew Lillywhite. With a secret ? " (dropping his voice to a whisper.)

" Yes. The last time I ever talked with Mr. Charles— it was only an hour or two before he set out on the fatal excursion from which he never returned—he said that he

should have to decline becoming one of my mother's trustees
—why, he could not tell me."

"But he had agreed. He told me that he considered it an
honor. He drafted the deed of appointment himself, and
took it with him to Whitebeach."

"That makes the refusal all the more inexplicable."

"Of course it does. And he gave you no reason?"

"No, only that he couldn't without breaking his word;
and he seemed very much distressed."

"Very much distressed was he? God bless me! It is
very strange. I was never more surprised in my life. To
think that Mr. Charles should refuse to act as your mother's
trustee!"

"He had not actually refused, but he said he would have
to."

"Ah!"

"I see how it is," he thought. "Ned told him all, under a
pledge of secrecy, and the brave, honest lad refused to become trustee to a fraud. It's as clear as daylight, and looks
bad for his brother, damnably bad."

But he had no intention of enlightening Olive. The old
fellow hoarded secrets as a miser hoards gold pieces, and
parted with them as reluctantly. Moreover, if he told Olive,
and she told her mother, there would be the deuce to pay,
and he should lose his hold over Edward.

"I thought you might have some idea," said Olive, after
another spell of silence.

"Not the least, Miss Olive, not the least. In fact, I am
quite flabbergasted. However, I suppose you have not mentioned aught of this to anybody else—Mr. Prince, for example."

"Certainly not. How could I?"

"Oh, yes, of course. I was not thinking. I beg pardon
for asking such a foolish question. You are quite right, it
is a safe principle to keep things to yourself. And between
ourselves, I rather doubt, you know, that Mr. Prince was—
ah—very warmly attached to his brother."

"I have had similar doubts myself. But he seems to feel
Charlie's death very much. His lips quiver at the mere
mention of his brother's name."

"Well, when you have not been as kind to a person as
you might have been, and that person goes over to the great

majority, it would be strange if you did not feel it—and appearances are deceptive sometimes, Miss Lincoln."

"And you really cannot think of any clue to this mystery, Mr. Lillywhite?"

"Not yet. It has come upon me so suddenly. But I will put on my considering cap—people are pleased to say that I am good at guessing secrets—and if I find anything out I shall let you know. And if I can serve you in any way let me know. But don't write to the office, please. Here is my private address (producing a card) and as I am a bachelor you may write without reserve."

"Why more so than if you were married?"

"Do you think if I had a wife my letters would be sacred? Never tell a husband anything you don't want the wife to know."

"Nor a wife anything you don't want her husband to know, I suppose?"

"That is not so sure. I have heard of such a thing as a woman having secrets from her husband."

"I am afraid you are somewhat of a cynic, Mr. Lillywhite."

"And if I am—forty-five years in lawyers' offices is enough to make a saint cynical—and you know that the Old Book says: 'The human heart is deceitful above all things and desperately wicked.' I don't go any further than that. We are nearly at Peele, Miss Lincoln."

"You think we had better separate."

"It would be as well. Somebody might inform Mr. Prince that we had been seen in conversation, and being of a curious turn he might want to know what we were talking about and that might lead to complications. One cannot be too cautious."

"You are right. I will linger in this green meadow a few minutes while you go on. Good-bye, Mr. Lillywhite. Thank you so much."

"Yours to command, Miss Lincoln. If I can be of any use don't fail to let me know. Good-bye."

So they shook hands and parted—not to meet again until Mr. Lillywhite had made his term of service in lawyers' office a full half-century.

CHAPTER XXXI.

EDWARD TRIES HIS LUCK.

THE Lincolns stayed longer at Holmcroft than they had originally intended, partly out of a desire to please Mrs. Prince, who found their company so pleasant that she was loth to let them leave, partly because the end of the Chancery suit was longer in coming than Edward had led them to expect—and Mrs. Lincoln wanted to see the end before going abroad. He laid the blame on Perrywinkle, while Perrywinkle, in answer to the urgings of Mr. Jump, who never let him alone, laid the blame on Prince.

Perrywinkle was right. Edward, who no more wanted his guests to go than his mother did, and had persuaded Mrs. Lincoln that it would be prejudicial to her interests to leave England before the business was wound up, procrastinated unconscionably, driving Perrywinkle wild, and making the usually placid Mr. Jump mad, by suggesting imaginary difficulties and raising points that were not relevant to the issue.

But everything is fair in love and war, and Edward was deeper in love than ever; the more he saw of Olive the better he liked her, and the longer she stayed the stronger grew his desire for her to stay altogether. Her mere presence sufficed to chase away the dark phantoms which so often haunted his mind, and he looked forward with dismay to the time when he should be left alone with his mother. Yet though Olive was so necessary to his happiness—rather because she was so necessary—he hesitated more than ever to ask her to decide his fate. The result might be her immediate departure from Holmcroft. And he could not read her. Her manner and speech were not unkind, but whether her real feeling for him was more or less than kind he was unable to determine.

The fact was that Olive had altered. Charlie's death, the necessity of hiding her feelings and seeming unconcerned though her heart was heavy, the habit of introspection to which this state of things gave rise, and her sojourn in London, had developed her character more than as many years of ordinary country life would have done. The light-hearted girl with laughing eyes was become a self-contained young woman, whose refined and thoughtful face no longer reflected every passing emotion.

If Edward Prince had understood this, or even vaguely surmised the true cause of the change which he had not failed to note, he could have been under no misapprehension as to her sentiments, nor thought of speaking to her of love while she still mourned for his brother.

When his device for detaining his guests had been in operation something less than a month there came a letter from Mr. Jump to Mrs. Lincoln, complaining of Mr. Prince's procrastination and of the unnecessary delays which he was interposing to the conclusion of the suit. Mr. Jump feared that unless the business were settled "right away," as per arrangement, it would have to be fought out in the Law Courts, in which case there would not be a "red cent" for any of them.

Mrs. Lincoln handed this letter to her solicitor.

"It is really too bad," she exclaimed. "Those Perrywinkle people won't hurry up at all. They have got a good thing and mean to stick to it to the last minute, and now try to make out that the fault lies with you. I wonder Mr. Jump can be so blind. How shall I answer him?"

"Don't answer at all. Leave it to me. I'll write him on your behalf."

"Do! and be sure you tell him the truth."

"The game is nearly played out," thought Edward. "However, by speaking Jump fair and promising largely I may keep it going another month."

But on the following day there came another letter, which brought matters to an immediate crisis. It was from America, and informed Mrs. Lincoln that her uncle Amos, a gentleman who lived in Vermont, desired greatly to see her, and as he was old and feeble and obviously failing, it was desirable for her (if she were minded to comply with his request) to come as soon as might be.

"I shall go, of course," said Mrs. Lincoln, after she had imparted the purport of the communication to Mrs. Prince and her son. "Uncle Amos is my father's only surviving brother, and I should never forgive myself if I did not see him before he died. You must put that business through within the next ten days, Edward. I'll write to Mr. Jump myself, and ask him as a personal favor to stir Perrywinkle up. Anyhow, I shall write to-day to engage passages in the Cunarder which sails next Saturday week."

" Do you propose to take Olive with you ? "

" Of course I do. You surely weren't thinking I should leave her behind. Why, she hasn't seen her native land for ten years or more. If she stops in Europe much longer she will forget she is an American."

It was a great blow for Edward Prince. Mrs. Lincoln's original plan had been to winter in the Riviera, return to England in the spring, and make a trip to America at a period which she described indifferently as " later on" and " later in the year," meaning thereby the year next ensuing. The Riviera was not so far away that Edward could not have found an excuse for a journey thither, either before or after Christmas, and Mrs. Lincoln had promised to make another visit to Holmcroft before going to America.

But in America Olive would be quite out of reach ; heaven only knew when or whether he should see her again, and it could not be expected that a girl so good-looking and hand-somely dowered would be without suitors or remain long un-married. It was clear, therefore, that if he desired to win her he must speak quickly.

In the meantime he would try to better his chances with the daughter by obliging the mother in the matter of the law-suit. He told Mrs. Lincoln that he should make the arrange-ment of her affairs his sole business until he had brought it to a satisfactory conclusion. He would go to London by the night mail, see both Perrywinkle and Jump, and insist on the compromise being forthwith carried out in its integrity ; and he thought he could guarantee that the settlement would be completed before her departure.

Mrs. Lincoln seemed greatly pleased ; and when he re-turned from London two days later, with a pile of papers, and informed her that when she had executed them the suit would not only be ended, but every detail arranged, so that she might leave with an easy mind, he received earnest thanks as well from Olive as her mother.

" It is very good of you to give so much time to our affairs when you are so busy," said Olive, warmly.

"Good! I should think so," added Mrs. Lincoln, heartily. "Nobody else would have taken so much trouble, and I don't think there is another lawyer in the kingdom who could have put the business through so soon and saved so much out of the fire. You should go to America, Edward. We want men like you, who are both honest and capable. You would make a fortune; you might be anything you like."

Edward heard this with a grave face—whatever he may have felt—and the thought crossed his mind that to win Olive he would even go to the land where honest and capable men, like himself, were so much in request.

The Lincolns were to leave Peele on the following Friday morning, *en route* for Liverpool; and on the Thursday evening, Olive, having finished her packing, took a turn in the garden. Holmcroft looked charming. The setting sun, shining through a fantastically shaped mass of diaphanous cloud, bathed the old house, with its tiled roof, high gables and ivy-mantled chimney-stacks, in a flood of crimson light; the kine were lowing in the fields, and crowds of cawing rooks coming home to roost in the tall elms down by the fish-pond. Yes, Holmcroft was a dear old place, and so pleasant and peaceful withal, that it seemed as though all who lived there should be happy. Yet none of them—none of those we know—were happy. At the best, parting is not a time of joy, and Olive was as sorry to leave Holmcroft as she had been to leave All Hallows.

The two places, and the neighborhood of Peele, were associated with the chief events of her life, hallowed to her by memories which she should never forget. She was going to a land which, though her own and a land to be proud of, she only just remembered, which at first would seem very strange to her, and where, albeit she had many kinsfolk, she had no friends.

What had the future in store for her? Would it ever be her lot to revisit the fair country where she had known so much, both of joy and sorrow? And then there came to Olive's memory the pathetic lines:

> "And the stately ships go on
> To their haven under the hill;
> But oh for the touch of a vanished hand,
> And the sound of a voice that is still.

Break, break, break,
At the foot of thy crags, oh, Sea,
But the tender grace of a day that is dead
Will never come back to me."

Slowly, and in pensive mood, Olive walked down the avenue. On reaching the spot where Mr. and Mrs. Prince had parted on the day which proved to be the most momentous of their lives, she turned and began to retrace her steps, and was presently overtaken by Edward, who looked fagged and anxious, as if he had had a hard day's work ; for which reason, and because she remembered only just then that he had lately been very pleasant, and deserved well, both of her mother and herself, she returned his greeting so graciously and sympathetically that he felt quite encouraged.

" To-morrow you go," he said softly. " This is your last night at Holmcroft. You are doubtless pleased to think you will so soon see your native land."

" I suppose I ought to be. One's country is one's country, after all, but I have got to like England, and I am not sure whether the pain of leaving it won't be greater than the pleasure of returning to America."

" But you will come back ? "

" Who can tell ? I may find work to do there. So far, I have lived only for myself. Yes, I am very sorry to leave Holmcroft. I never stay long at a place that I don't get attached to it, though I have been such a rolling stone ; and everybody here has been so kind to us—your father and mother and—yourself (she had nearly said Charlie). We shall never, never forget our dear friends at Holmcroft."

" I am glad to hear you say so. And I shall never forget you. It is no use, I cannot keep it back," he exclaimed, passionately. " Olive, dear Olive, don't you see that I love you, aye, the very ground you tread on ? Don't think ill of me—I did not mean—if you had not been going away I should not have spoken to you of love so soon after my father's death—and Charlie's——"

" Ah, my poor boy ! Why did you leave him to perish ? "

This terrible question, provoked by the startling suddenness of Edward's avowal, and his mention of Charlie's name in the same breath, voiced a thought she had conceived at the time of his death and afterwards put aside as unjust, the thought that had Edward done for his brother what Charlie, in like circumstances, had done for him, her lover might have been saved. But the words were no sooner spoken than she bitterly rued them.

She had both betrayed herself and made a charge she could not justify, for which, indeed, she had absolutely no excuse. Their effect on Edward frightened her. He leaned against a tree, pale and trembling, and with lips convulsively twitching.

"Why do you say that? Good God, what do you mean?" he cried hoarsely.

"I beg your pardon, I am very sorry. I did not know what I said—I did not mean to hurt you—but you surprised me so much—speaking of love, and Charlie only just dead—that I spoke impulsively and uncharitably. It was wrong and I beg your pardon."

"Only just dead! Why, it is five months since—and I had no idea you felt his death so much," returned Edward pulling himself together.

"Yes. I felt it very much. We were play-fellows, and had always been such good friends."

"But now that you know my feelings, how dearly I love you, cannot you give me some hope? We both loved Charlie, we both mourn for him; a common sorrow is a bond of sympathy."

"Give you some hope! That means encouragement to believe that some day I may return your love?"

"Yes, that is all I ask. I will wait—yea, I will serve for you as long as Jacob served for Rachel. For heaven's sake, Olive, don't leave me without hope."

He pleaded so earnestly and looked so pitiful that Olive was touched, and regretted more than ever the cruel words which she had just spoken.

"How can I hold out hopes that I know can never be realized? It would be wrong," she said wistfully.

"But perhaps in a year or two, or even in three or four."

"How can I tell what my feelings will be three or four years hence? But I doubt whether they will alter much. If I know myself I shall never love any man."

"Well, will you promise that while you are in America you will not engage yourself?"

"By what right?" demanded Olive, indignantly.

"I beg your pardon. I forgot myself. I was presuming too much," quoth Edward, humbly.

"You have no right to make such a request. But I owe you reparation for the hasty words I spoke just now, and gratitude for your honest and able management of my mother's affairs ; and if it be any satisfaction to you I may say that I shall certainly not engage myself to anybody until I have revisited England and seen Holmcroft again."

"You are very good," murmured Edward, who was in a humor to be thankful for small mercies. "And you forgive me, do you not? We are friends?"

Olive gave him her hand, Edward raised it respectfully to his lips, and the two walked silently towards the house.

CHAPTER XXXII.

FROM JACK.

For three or four days after the departure of his guests
Edward Prince's mind was in a continual turmoil. He could
think of nothing but Olive. One moment he accused her
of being a heartless flirt, the next himself of being a fool.
Why should he be so infatuated about one particular young
woman? There were others quite as good, whom he could
have for the asking. And he was conscious of having cut
a ridiculous figure; he had been soft, absurdly soft, even to
the extent of thanking her with "whispered humbleness" for
a promise that amounted to nothing—which she might either
deny or evade. He should have spoken sooner, and been
bolder and more importunate. Olive was a girl who needed
to be "stood up to" and mastered; yet he had trembled in
her presence and let her terrorize him by the mere mention
of Charlie's name.

Was it to be ever thus? Was Charlie, alive or dead, to be
always in his way?

"Why did you leave him to perish?"

Who could have put so absurd an idea into her head?

True, she had apologized, and explained that she had not
meant it, but why had she said it? Was it possible that anybody else thought the same—that people were whispering to
each other behind his back the question which, as Olive protested, had sprung unbidden from her lips?

The thought was horror.

But no! He should have heard, and Olive would not have
been so kind; she was not the girl to let a man whom she
considered capable of committing murder kiss her hand; and
Mrs. Lincoln believed in him as entirely as she had believed
in his father. Why torment himself with a baseless fear?
Yet, try as he might, he could neither hypnotize his conscience
nor dismiss Olive from his mind.

His mother saw that he was unhappy and surmised the cause. Had he said anything to Olive, she asked.

Edward told her what had passed (except, of course, the outburst about his brother).

"Do you think she cared for Charlie?"

"I am sure she did."

"I have suspected as much, myself. Well, in that case I do not see why you need be so despondent. Olive is not one of those frivolous girls who love lightly and forget quickly. It seems to me, that considering the circumstances she has given you as much encouragement as you could expect, and if you will only have patience all will be well. If she had not had a very kindly feeling for you she would not have promised to keep herself free until she sees you again. And they will not stay long in America. England is become their second home, and Mrs. Lincoln as good as said that she prefers this country to their own. The Lincolns will be here again next year, mark me if they are not, and if you play your cards properly Olive will be yours."

Though Edward did not quite take all this as gospel, there was clearly something in it, and he felt distinctly encouraged thereby. But he found his chief solace in work, to which he applied himself with redoubled diligence, since whether he won Olive or not he was resolved to win a fortune. And there was every likelihood that he would succeed; he made money in ways that his father never thought of and which, though he had thought of them, he would have disdained to adopt, and Edward's outgoings being very much less than his father's had been, he had a large surplus income, which he knew how to turn to good account.

And presently he had a windfall, as startling and unexpected as a dividend on a written-off bad debt, or a return of over-paid duty from the Income Tax Commissioners. One morning, while they were at breakfast, Mrs. Prince received a letter, from which, as she opened it, a piece of paper fell, and fluttered to the floor. Edward picked it up. It was a first of exchange on Brown, Shipley, and Co., for two thousand pounds, drawn by an American bank in favor of Mrs. Dorothy Prince.

Mystified beyond measure, he glanced at his mother, and saw in her face a surprise greater than his own, and other feelings—bewilderment, incredulity, doubt, gladness—seemed to be struggling for the mastery.

" Oh, Edward ! " she cried, as she turned the last page and looked at the signature.

" What is it ? Whom is it from ? "

" It is—I can hardly believe it—it is from Jack. Do you hear ? It is from Jack. My boy ! My boy, whom I thought was dead or worse than dead. And he is doing well and sends money, and will send more, make full restitution, he says. Oh, such a letter, so loving and penitent."

Her voice was broken with emotion, and tears were streaming down her cheeks.

" Let me see it."

" After I have read it again. I must read it again. Oh, my dear Jack ! "

When Mrs. Prince had read the letter a second time she handed it to Edward. It was, as she had said, loving and penitent. Jack had heard of his father's death (he did not say how) and expressed bitter regret that he had not been a better son, and deep contrition for his past misconduct, which, he felt sure, must have embittered both his father's life and her own. Then he spoke of his last visit to Holmcroft, told how he had seen them at prayers and heard his mother mention his name, and how he had vowed that they should never hear of him again unless it were something good. This vow, with God's help, he had been enabled to fulfill. Paul Coniston, for whose acquaintance he was indebted to " dear old Charlie," had put him in the way of good things, and he was engaged in a profitable mining enterprise, out of which he expected to make a fortune. If he succeeded he would repay every penny he owed the family, and as a beginning enclosed a draft for two thousand pounds. When he first went to America he called himself Mark Darnley ; but not liking to sail under false colors he had resumed his true name and would try to do it as much honor in the future as he had done it dishonor in the past. He ended by entreating his mother to forgive him for the sorrow he had caused her and the wrong he had done, sent his love to Ned and Charlie, and said what pleasure it would give him to have a few lines from them now and then. But for their help God only knew what would have become of him.

It was a manly, straightforward letter, yet humble and contrite withal, in parts pathethic, and touched Edward more deeply than he had been touched for a long time. It galled him, too, for he felt that the despised Jack was behaving with a magnanimity of which he himself was incapable.

"Who would have thought it?" he said, returning the letter to his mother.

"Yes, who would have thought it? It is like one returning from the dead. I had mourned him as lost, hoped even never to hear of him again. And now! Thank God, thank God! If your father could only have known, and poor Charlie! You see he does not know of Charlie's death. How noble of him to send this money. But he need not send any more, Edward, we don't want it."

"It is not so much a question whether we want it as whether he ought to pay it. Think how much he cost father from first to last. What with insurance premiums, interest and one thing and another, more than twenty thousand pounds. But for him you and I should be much better off now, and it is evident, from the tone of the letter, that it will be a satisfaction to him to discharge the debt. I would let him pay it if I were you, and then, if you like, you can return him something, or take it into account when you make your will."

"Well, perhaps you are right. All the same, I cannot quite reconcile myself to taking so much money from Jack when we don't need it. I shall write to him by the next mail; so will you, won't you? You have got the draft, I think?"

Edward said he had got the draft and would write to Jack. He knew that whatever money his mother received would come to him. They had a common purse, and she never either asked for receipts or demanded an account of his stewardship. Before the month was out the two thousand pounds, temporarily advanced to an impecunious, albeit solvent, client, was yielding increase at the rate of two hundred a year."

Jack's resurrection raised Mrs. Prince's spirits as much as Charlie's death had depressed them. Besides gratifying her maternal love it gave her a new interest in life. The prodigal of whom she had once been so bitterly ashamed was become an occasion of pride. Edward had suggested the expediency of "keeping it quiet," but Mrs. Prince could not help mentioning to one or two friends (in strict confidence) how well her eldest son was doing; and a day or two later it was rumored in Peele that John Prince, who had been so long under a cloud, was making " a pile " in California, and sending money home for investment.

About the same time Edward found something for which he had long looked in vain—a pretext for getting rid of Lillywhite—or, rather, Lillywhite found it for him.

Nobody who looked at the managing clerk's nose, and it certainly invited observation, was likely to mistake him for a teetotaller; on the other hand, nobody could justly accuse him of being intemperate, and when he said, and he was rather fond of saying it, that nobody had ever seen him the worse for liquor, nobody could contradict him. His favorite tipple was port " of character " tawny, crusted, and old-bottled ; but as wine of this class (and he would have naught inferior) " came expensive," he could seldom indulge in it, and limited his allowance to a pint with his Sunday dinner. At other times he quenched his thirst with a certain brew of old ale locally known as "ramjam."

One day a client, also a connoisseur of old port, whom he had helped to make an excellent bargain, took Lillywhite to luncheon at the Old Bull and gave him *carte blanche* in the matter of wine. Lillywhite ordered two bottles of Croft's old tawny, at a guinea a bottle, and saw that they got them.

" What do you say to another ? " asked the client when these had been drunk. " There isn't a headache in a hogs-head of it."

Lillywhite nodded assent. He knew that he was wanted at the office, but the offer was too good to be refused. He might never have such a chance again.

" I'll fetch it myself," quoth he ; " these waiter fellows are not to be trusted."

" All right, old man ; and, I say, you may as well bring two while you are about it."

Lillywhite brought two. An hour later he left the client very much asleep on the sofa, and toddled off to the office, feeling as if his nose were on fire and his tongue had been turned into a Bologna sausage.

"The governor wants you ; he has asked for you several times," said one of the clerks.

Lillywhite walked confidently, and as steadily as he knew how, into his employer's room.

" You have been a long time at your lunch, I think. It is

past three. When is this writ of Picton's returnable?" asked Edward sharply.

"Ask your grandmother, young man," said Lillywhite, as he reeled into a chair.

"Why, you are—you have been drinking."

"Which I have, dear boy. Croft's tawny, twenty years in bottle; but only two bottles and not a headache in a hogshead of it, as Drinkwater says—only two bottles, two only, two for him, and two for me, at a guinea a bottle. Any advance on a guinea a bottle, any advance on twenty-one shillings for Croft's old tawny? Going, going, gone!"

And Lillywhite brought his fist down on Edward's table with a bang that capsized the inkstand and sent his papers flying all over the place.

"This is shameful, utterly disgraceful; a man of your age too!" he exclaimed indignantly. "You must go home at once. I'll send for a cab."

"All right, I'll go," said Lillywhite, who had just wit enough left to know that he was making a fool of himself. "I'll go. I go, thou goest, he goes. We go, ye or you go, they go. Two negatives destroy one another, or are equivalent to an affirmative, as Hickory, dickory dock, the cow jumped over the clock. O blessed shade of Lindley Murray!"

"Will you go, please? The cab is at the door. Jones will see you home."

"Certainly. Of course. I'll go—over the water and over the lea and over the water to Charlie. I would if he wasn't under water, poor, dear boy. Lord, how I hate water. Ta-ta, Ned, ta-ta!"

"The old ruffian. Why, he is as drunk as a fiddler's sow," muttered Edward wrathfully. "But I have him on the hip this time. To-morrow he goes."

The morrow came, and with it Lillywhite, penitent, seedy, and ashamed. So soon as Mr. Prince arrived he went into the latter's room and offered a frank apology for his wandering from the path of sobriety, and, above all, for appearing in such a state at the office.

"I am very sorry," he said; "at my time of life I ought to have known better. My head isn't what it used to be. I cannot drink two bottles of port with impunity, as I could when you came of age. However, I know now. Nothing of the sort ever happened before, and it shall never happen again."

"I'll take care it does not," returned Edward emphatically —"at any rate, in this office. Even your long services cannot atone for so grave an offence, to say nothing of your gross insults to myself. Our relations must cease, Mr. Lillywhite. Here is a check for three months' salary; you are only entitled to a month's."

"What! Do you mean to say that for a single offence, the first in thirty years, you are going to send me away with a quarter's salary?"

"I do. Such an offence it is impossible to overlook."

"Have you considered what the consequences will be, Mr. Prince?"

"One consequence will be that I shall engage a managing-clerk who will not come to the office drunk."

"And another that before the week is out all Peele will know that your father played hanky-panky tricks with Mrs. Lincoln's fortune, and that you and your mother, as his executors, were parties to the fraud."

"If you make any such villainous statement, Lillywhite, I'll have you laid by the heels and prosecuted for slander."

"It isn't a slander; it's true."

"You cannot prove it. Mrs. Lincoln's money is in Consols, and the papers are in that safe. I can show them to anybody."

"The Bank of England keeps books, I suppose. It will be easy to show that your father sold out fifteen thousand pounds' worth of stock the week after your brother ran away from Liverpool, and that you bought the same amount with the insurance money. And there is something else."

"What?"

"Charlie, like the honest lad he was, refused to be your co-trustee; he wouldn't be a party to the fraud."

This was a knock-down blow for Edward, and it was all he could do to maintain his self-possession.

"I deny it; it is not true," he said hotly.

"It is true enough. All the same, I am not prepared to say that I can prove it. But that isn't all. There is still something else——"

"Well?"

" That body you brought up from Whitebeach and laid in the family vault is not Charlie's."

" Man, you lie ! It is his body."

" I can prove different. You swore at the inquest that your brother dived into the water naked. The body found on the Horse Bank was clothed. In the fob was a watch with a name on it—and it is in my fob now."

Edward leaned back in his chair, pale and trembling.

" Well, how is it to be ? Have I to go ? " asked Lillywhite, after an interlude of silence.

" Those rascally boatmen must have deceived me," observed Edward, in a low voice. " However, as you have been here such a long time, and that, we'll say no more about it. Let bygones be bygones."

And with that he tore up the check and threw the fragments into the fire, and Lillywhite, smiling sardonically and wagging his great nose, went back to his desk.

CHAPTER XXXIII.

OLIVE'S RESOLVE.

WHILE Mrs. Lincoln went to Vermont, Olive stayed with the Oldburys, at Roxbury, a suburb of Boston. Hosea Oldbury was her father's first cousin, whose only unmarried daughter, Naomi, had been at All Hallows a few years previously, and Olive was warmly welcomed and made much of. The Oldburys came of an old Puritan stock, and one of the family heirlooms and treasures was a Bible, which the first of the name to settle in New England had brought with him from Old England, in the year in which Oliver Cromwell died.

Mr. Oldbury was a gentleman of something past sixty, with a rugged and powerful, yet not unkindly face; his wife, a dear old lady with beautiful brown eyes and snow-white hair, and so genial and loving withal, that Olive had not been long in the house before she felt as if she had known "Cousin Rachel" all her life.

The habits of the family were as regular as clockwork. They began the day early. Breakfast at half-past seven to the minute. Near Mr. Oldbury's plate was a Bible, from which, before beginning the meal, he read a few verses; then he said a short extempore prayer. At eight he went to his business in the city, and was not seen again until evening. During the day the ladies attended to many matters which, among English people of a similar class, are generally left to servants. The domestic establishment consisted of a couple of Irish helps, who seemed to need a good deal of looking after. In the first week after her arrival Olive made calls with Naomi and renewed her acquaintance with friends and kinsfolk she only dimly remembered, and who seemed surprised that the little girl whom they remembered had developed into a self-possessed young woman with an English accent. Other distractions were going "down town" on shopping expeditions and attending an occasional lecture; of more

worldly amusements there was never so much as a question,
and Olive learnt from Naomi that her parents took life much
too seriously to approve of theatre-going and party-giving.

One night Cousin Hosea put down his book and asked
her abruptly what she thought of slavery.

" In the abstract ? " demanded Olive, who was rather surprised at the seeming irrelevancy of the question.

" As it exists in—this land of freedom."

" I never saw a slave.   But I don't like slavery, if that is
what you mean.   I have read things about it in the English
papers and books that made me feel ashamed of being an
American—or would have done if I could have been sure
they were true.   My father used to say they were not true ;
that slavery was not nearly so bad a thing as people made out,
and that it could not be abolished without breaking up the
Union."

" So your father was against abolition ? "

" Yes, but solely on that ground."

" He did not think slavery right ? "

" I am sure he did not.   I heard him say so more than
once."

" Then he was a time-server.   He set expediency before
right and justice."

Olive fired up.

" Cousin Hosea, what are you saying?   My father a time-
server ! " she exclaimed.

" Your father was a merchant.   Suppose two of his partners, two out of five, let us say, had been high-handed robbers, and he had refused to dissolve partnership with them on
the ground that doing so would break up the firm.   How
would you characterize such an excuse ? "

" I see what you mean.   But isn't that rather begging the
question ?   Southern people are not robbers."

" Slave-holders are, and the Southern people, and many of
the Northern people, I am sorry to say, are their active and
zealous accomplices.   Robbers and worse than robbers, aye,
murderers.   What crime can be more heinous than holding
millions of our fellow-creatures in bitter bondage ?   I say nothing about cruelty.   Allow that they are no worse used than
cattle and horses.   But they are bought and sold like cattle :
wives are separated from their husbands, mothers from their
children ; it is forbidden to teach colored people to read,

lest their yearning for freedom should haply be increased; they are not allowed to give evidence in a court of justice, which means that they do not enjoy the protection of the law, and may be scourged and even murdered with impunity. They have no more rights than dumb animals. The Southern States have established a censorship of the Press. Northern newspapers and books are opened in the Post-office—with the sanction of the Government—and abolition literature is rigidly suppressed. Abolitionists who dare to travel further south than the confines of Pennsylvania are almost sure to find a bloody grave. And yet there are people who look on the Constitution as the Israelites of old looked on the Ark of the Covenant, and this Union as the Holy of Holies. Olive, the constitution is a fraud and a lie; the Union is a covenant with death, an agreement with the devil. Oh, Lord God, how long, how long? . . . . It may not be in my time, yet the time must surely come when the Almighty will mete out to this nation a punishment as terrible as her sin. 'For my sword shall be bathed in blood; behold it shall come down in Idumea, and upon the people of my curse to judgment.'"

Mr. Oldbury spoke like one inspired. His face was all aglow, his eyes shone with prophetic fire, his hands were uplifted, and his voice trembled with indignation and wrath.

He was still denouncing the wickedness of slave-holders and the covenant with death, and Olive listening with rapt attention, for her cousin's earnestness made him strangely eloquent, when the door opened and Mrs. Oldbury, coming softly into the room, laid her hand on his shoulder.

"They are come," she said.

Her husband's voice was hushed in a moment, and his face resumed its wonted expression.

"Pray excuse me, Olive," he observed quietly. "When I get to talking about slavery I am apt to forget myself—and everybody else—I will see them at once. Would you like to come, Olive? It will be an experience for you."

Olive followed her cousin into the next room, where were two women, one, middle-aged and plainly dressed, with a worn, resolute, and watchful face. Her companion was so closely cloaked and veiled that it was impossible to guess either her age or condition.

"Thank God you are arrived safely," said Mr. Oldbury. "Had you any difficulty?"

"Not the least. But as the vessel was behind her time and I had to wait, and I am known to be connected with the underground railroad, we may have been observed and followed. We must try to get her away before daylight."

"Poor dear! Let me help you off with your cloak and bonnet. You are among friends, and for the moment, at least, out of danger."

While she spoke Mrs. Oldbury doffed the mysterious stranger's cloak, revealing to Olive's astonished gaze a young girl as tall and shapely as herself, with a face no less winsome than her own—complexion, a rich olive tint; regular features, brilliant teeth, large dark eyes and jet black hair, rippling over a forehead low and broad.

"Who is she? What has she done?" demanded Olive.

"A fugitive slave, and if she is recaptured will be punished for the crime of running away by being sent back to servitude, and all that servitude implies for a young girl so attractive."

"But she must not be taken; you will not let her be taken,, Cousin Hosea."

"I will not give this poor child up, even though I have to keep her here at the peril of my own liberty. You have been away from this land of freedom so long that you may not know that the penalty of refusal to surrender a fugitive slave to the officers of the law is six months' imprisonment and a thousand dollars fine. Yes, that is what we are come to. The grandsons and great-grandsons of men who defied the might of England, and resisted to the death the attempt of a stupid English king to put a paltry tax on their tea, not only connive at slavery but act as slave-catchers. But I am a man of peace, and open resistance, besides being ineffectual, would be inexpedient. It is the old story, I suppose, Mrs. Sage" (glancing significantly at the fugitive).

"Yes—at any rate, substantially."

"What is the story?" asked Olive eagerly.

"Well, you see she belonged to a family in Virginia. She had nothing to complain of in the way of treatment. You had a kind master, hadn't you, Ruth?"

"Oh yes; and a kind mistress, and the young ladies— all were kind."

"She was a house servant, nurse, young ladies' maid, and so forth. She got a smattering of education, too, has an excellent ear for music, and can play on the piano anything she hears. And I daresay, so long as Mr. Fellowes, her master, lived, Ruth was as happy as the day was long. But a few weeks ago he died, and, his estate being heavily encumbered, the executors were obliged to dispose of all the more valuable of the slaves—among them Ruth."

" But a young girl cannot be very valuable."

" Being young—and good-looking—is exactly what makes her valuable. You don't understand the South, Miss Lincoln. There are men who would give three or four thousand dollars for Ruth. But the ladies of the family, knowing what her fate would be, connived at her escape. One of our friends took her to Norfolk and got her on board a small trading vessel, which arrived here yesterday."

" I may tell you, Olive—if you have not guessed it already —that this house is a station on the underground railroad, of which Mrs. Sage is a most efficient and devoted officer. But now to the question immediately before us. How shall we deal with this poor child ? There is sure to be a hue and cry after her."

" Of course, there is ; and as I said just now, I fear we have been observed, probably followed. A very sharp look-out is kept here just now for fugitive slaves. She ought to be on the way to Canada before this time to-morrow night, but she is too young and unsophisticated to travel alone. Never been on a railroad in her life."

" Can you go with her, Mrs. Sage ? "

" Not very well. Those people from Baltimore I told you about are on the way, and should be here or at Fall River —I shall know which to-morrow—in the course of the week."

" And you must be on the spot to look after them. I would let Naomi go, only she is rather ailing just now."

" But I am not ailing. I will go with her," broke in Olive impetuously.

" You are very kind, but the journey is long and not without risk—at any rate, of unpleasantness, if an attempt should be made to capture the girl."

" Never mind the risk. Besides, we can disguise her. I will give her some of my own clothes, and she shall travel as my maid. Where shall I take her ? "

" They generally go to Toronto, where we have kind friends

who look after them.   But it will be quite enough if you see
her as far as Buffalo."

"I will go with her all the way.   Something might happen
after I left her, and then I should never forgive myself."

And so it was arranged.   Olive and her charge left Boston
by an early morning train, furnished by Cousin Hosea with
a few back numbers of the *Liberator* and some other anti-
slavery literature to read on the way.   They went right
through, without stopping even at Niagara, and reached their
destination in due course without adventure, either pleasant
or otherwise.

Nobody troubled them.   Nevertheless it was a memorable
journey for both.   The octoroon was going from a house of
bondage to a land of liberty, an event in her life she was not
likely to forget ; and before they parted Olive made a resolve
which had far-reaching results.   Ruth was frank and com-
municative, and her story, told in detail as they sped northward, moved Olive deeply.   When quite a child the girl had
become her young mistresses' playmate ; afterwards, their
companion and maid.   She described her life, and told how
happy they all were, until Massa Fellowes was killed in a
duel.   And then a great terror came over them, for the slaves
seemed to know by instinct that the estate would be sold and
themselves dispersed to the four winds of heaven.   Mothers
went about weeping and wringing their hands ; two or three
of the men ran away and were brought back, tied with ropes.
Slave dealers came to look at them, and Ruth was several
times inspected and examined, as one examines a horse.
One night Missy Mary took her aside and told her that somebody had agreed to pay the price demanded by the executors,
and that unless she went at once she would be taken away
the next day by her new master.   There was not even time
for Ruth to see her mother, and she reached Norfolk, disguised
as an old woman, making as if she were crippled with rheuma-
tism, only an hour before the schooner sailed.

The poor girl had no hope of seeing her mother and her
sisters and brothers again, could not even communicate with
them, would never know what was become of them ; while
the slave-holding power prevailed ; might never revisit the land
of her birth.

"And yet she is as much an American as I am, and nearly
as white," thought Olive.

Olive left her *protegée* with the friends designated by Mr. Oldbury, gave them a sum of money to be used for her benefit, and offered to send more if need were. But they had no doubt they should be able to find Ruth a good place, and in effect, as Olive afterwards heard, they did.

When she returned to Roxbury and gave an account of her journey, Mr. Oldbury expressed great satisfaction, and said she had begun well.

" And as I have begun I mean to go on," Olive returned earnestly. " So far, I have lived only for myself. For the future I shall try to do something for others. When I think of my own lot and that of this poor girl, and thousands of others still more unfortunate, my blood boils, and I am almost ashamed of myself for being so well off."

"You have decided to become an abolitionist, then ? "

" I have. I know that I can do very little ; but I shall do it with all my heart and all my strength. Will you help me and put me in the way, Cousin Hosea ? "

" Right willingly. We want to enlist the young and ardent. Theirs is the future. It is through the young, not through the middle-aged and old, that we can raise the moral standard of the nation and insure the downfall of slavery, or the casting out of the States where it prevails. And you can do much, very much. Your mere adhesion to the cause will be a great encouragement. And the Divine Ruler of the world has ordained that we cannot help others without helping ourselves—albeit this should not count as a motive. To contend for truth, and justice, and humanity, is serving God ; acquiescence in wrong for peace's sake, or, in the name of political expediency, is serving the devil. You have chosen the better part, Olive."

Olive thought the same ; but her mother did not. When Mrs. Lincoln returned from Vermont and learnt that her daughter had become a Garrisonite she was ill-pleased. Like the majority of Northern people, she regarded the Union pretty much as devout Roman Catholics regard the Papacy. It was too precious a thing to be imperilled for any number of blacks.

" Let us argue the point," quoth Cousin Hosea, and then, asking her a few insidious questions and receiving guileless answers, and being a practised disputant and having the better cause, he had no difficulty in confuting her out of her own mouth.

If freedom were good and slavery bad, it followed that whatever made for the promotion of the one and the suppression of the other must also be good. If the Constitution sanctioned involuntary servitude, so much the worse for the Constitution. When Mrs. Lincoln tried to get out of the dilemma by suggesting that however good freedom might be for whites the colored people were not fit for it, Mr. Oldbury invited Olive to tell the story of Ruth's escape, which she did with so much feeling that her mother was quite touched —and silenced.

As Cousin Hosea observed, a system which allowed the white fathers of colored children to sell their offspring into slavery was indefensible—at any rate, by a mother.

Thenceforth Olive had her own way. She threw herself into the contest with characteristic ardor, and, as Mr. Oldbury protested, made herself wonderfully useful. She took an active part in running the underground railroad and the production and circulation of anti-slavery literature, went into Georgia to plan an escape at a time when the Government of Georgia was offering a prize of five thousand dollars for the production of Lloyd Garrison's body, and attended anti-slavery meetings, some of which were attacked by pro-slavery mobs and often violently dispersed.

For in those days abolitionists were only a degree less unpopular in the North than in the South. Their aims were derided as visionary and themselves denounced as traitors, and Olive Lincoln shared in the contumely and ridicule with which they were assailed.

CHAPTER XXXIV.

OLIVE'S VOW.

" DEAR ! dear ! Only to think of it," said Mrs. Briscoe, pensively. " Only to think of it ! We came with the idea of returning to Europe right away, and five years are gone by and here we are still, and I am actually married again and you are not married at all, nor likely to be so far as I can see ; and Mr. Marsh has sold The Pines and bought All Hallows, and wants us to pay him a visit. I don't see how I can go, though. Your father-in-law cannot leave his business, and it would not be nice for me to leave him all alone, and only just married. Fact is, he won't hear of it. But you had better go, Olive. You need a change ; everybody says how ill you are looking."

" All the same, mother, I don't feel like going away just now. I doubt whether it is my duty. My work lies here."

" It is your duty to keep yourself in health, I suppose. You won't do much good if you fall into a decline ; and your work, as you call it, will keep. I fear it is like trying to wash a blackamoor white, labor in vain. Abolition does not seem any nearer than it did five years since ; and I question whether it will be any nearer five years hence."

The signs of the times, as they appeared to a plain under-standing, justified Mrs. Briscoe's forecast. The cause was making way, yet abolitionists were still an insignificant minority. Even the political party which called itself Re-publican, and was supposed to favor emancipation, did not propose to do more than prohibit the extension of slavery into new territories ; their Convention had affirmed " the right of each State to order and control its own domestic in-stitutions according to its own judgment exclusively," which obviously meant that where involuntary servitude existed it would be maintained, since not even the most sanguine im-agined that any Southern State would abolish slavery on its

own motion. The sole hope of uncompromising abolitionists was that the North would purge itself of complicity
in the sin of slaveholding by seceding from the South.

"I dare say a change would do me good. I don't feel very
strong," answered Olive, "and it would be a real pleasure to
have a run in Europe, and see the old place once more. But
I don't mean to go until the campaign is over. Abraham
Lincoln has said that if slavery is not wrong, nothing is wrong.
I cannot help thinking that his election would be a hopeful
sign, if nothing else. Who knows that it might not be the
beginning of the end? Anyhow, I shall stop and see it
through."

"As you like, dear. All the same, I don't think you are
wise. Excitement, and running to and fro, and going to
stormy meetings, and writing, and what not, are wearing you
out; and you need a thorough change. A voyage to Europe
and a few months at All Hallows would set you up."

During Olive's sojourn in Boston she had received and
refused several offers of marriage, from which some of her
friends inferred that she meant to remain single all her life
long. But when asked by her mother whether this were true
she protested that she had made no such resolve.

"Mr. Right is not come yet, I suppose?" observed Mrs.
Briscoe inquiringly.

"Yes, that's it; Mr. Right is not come yet," repeated
Olive, smiling.

This set her mother wondering whether Edward Prince
would prove to be the right man. He also was still single,
and never remitted her dividends without asking to be kindly
remembered to Miss Lincoln, an attention which Miss Lincoln never omitted to acknowledge and reciprocate; and
Mrs. Briscoe hoped that when her daughter got to a country
where there were neither underground railroads nor Presiden-
tial elections she might find time to fall in love and marry.
Wifely duties would be incompatible with rescuing slaves, an
occupation which (for a woman) Mrs. Briscoe (who was a
very lukewarm abolitionist) did not in her heart approve.

But the events that followed the election of Abraham Lincoln were so momentous and exciting that not until after his
inauguration could Olive be prevailed upon to seek the rest
which her mother had prescribed and the eminent physician
whom she had consulted deemed absolutely necessary. With-

out it, he said, her health would be utterly and irretrievably ruined.

"You will come back as soon as you are well enough," said Mr. Oldbury, when she made her *p.p.c.* call. "The Cause cannot afford to lose one of its most promising recruits."

"You may be sure I shall."

"And single?"

"Single! I doubt whether I shall ever marry; and I vow that I will marry no man who is less devoted to the Cause than I am myself, and has not proved his devotion by his deeds; nor even then until the war is over and the victory won."

"This is a great vow, Olive," observed Mr. Oldbury, seriously. "Do you realize its gravity?"

"Fully, and please God I shall keep it."

So it came to pass that, while her country was resounding with the din of arms, and North and South were engaging in fratricidal strife, Olive Lincoln was constrained to betake herself for a season to other climes.

After a short stay in London, where she consulted a specialist in chest diseases, she went on to All Hallows. Mr. Marsh had made few alterations; outwardly, everything was the same, but all the old faces were gone, and the difference between then and now struck a chill to Olive's heart, and made her feel more of a stranger in her old home than she would have felt in a strange house. As she wandered about the grounds, long dormant memories, the ghosts of the past, thronged into her mind. She thought of her father, whose place knew him no more, and whose death had caused so much confusion and led to so many changes. She went to the grove where Charlie and she held their first tryst, and marked the fence over which he and Daisy had turned the somersault that so frightened her and amused Cousin Paul.

Poor Daisy. What had become of her? And Charlie! What a sad fate was his, and how, in her girlish way, she had loved him. Yes, she was a girl in those days, and he a boy . . . . Her one romance. It might have happened in another life—or a dream—so vague and shadowy and far back did it seem. . . Her mother had hinted a wish that she might find "Mr. Right" in England. That would be impossible, even though she had made no vow. To marry an Englishman and settle in England while her country was distracted with civil war, and the fate of the Union hung in the balance, were treason as base as that of a soldier who deserts his post on the eve of a battle.

Her ideal was a chivalrous American soldier, like-minded with herself, able and willing to do the cause yeoman service, whom she could trust absolutely and love without reserve.

Had she said this to her mother, that matter-of-fact lady would have laughed and said, "Don't you wish you may get him?"

Strangely enough (yet, considering her age and temperament, naturally enough) Olive, while thinking she had done with romance, was dreaming of a nonsuch Mr. Right, an abolitionist Bayard, *sans peur et sans reproche.*

One of the first of her old friends to call on her at All-Hallows was Edward Prince. Olive thought he was improved. He had broadened out somewhat, his face was fuller, his manner more dignified and urbane than of yore.

He had the air of a prosperous man, whose position is assured. Since Charlie's death the world had gone well with him.

Jack had insisted on discharging the whole of his indebtedness to his father's estate, and by lending these and other moneys to needy clients at high rates of interest for short periods, Edward doubled the ordinary profits of the office, and as his outgoings were moderate he was in a fair way for making a fortune. He also meant in no long time to represent his fellow burgesses in the Commons House of Parliament, to which end he was cultivating popularity as a fine art, a fact that had doubtless something to do with his more courtly manner.

Certain fears and nervous tremors, which had once beset him were so remote as to be remembered only on occasions, and a few months before Olive's return he had felt himself strong enough to dismiss Lillywhite, whose presence in the office was always an unpleasant reminder, and whose place Edward wanted for a less self-willed and more energetic managing clerk.

When the old clerk repeated his threats Edward laughed.

"What can you do?" he asked. "My father has been dead more than six years; it is more than five since Mrs.

Briscoe's trust fund was made good. If you blabbed nobody would believe you, and I should probably prosecute you, though I doubt whether anything you may say could hurt me. Rather the reverse, in fact. Wouldn't it tell in my favor that, like a dutiful son, I met all my father's obligations. And nobody has suffered. Jack has paid the Liverpool people to the last penny. As for the other matter, can you prove, or begin to prove, after this lapse of time, that the body found at Whitebeach was not my brother's—and what earthly difference would it make though you did? The Ægis people were bound to pay up sooner or later, and if they had made any bother, I should have forced them to presume the death by an action-at-law. All the same, I don't want my private affairs to be made the town's talk, and I'll make it worth your while to keep a still tongue. You shall have a year's salary and the Rhadamanthus agency. It will bring you in something nice, and you'll get other things. Take my advice, and don't be foolish. If we quarrel, it is you, not I, who will come off second best."

Lillywhite climbed down. He was not the man to talk for talking's sake or " blab " to his own loss. For once Edward had the better of him. It was obviously the best policy to take what he could get, and on the principle of half-a-loaf being better than no bread, he accepted the year's salary and the agency, though with an ill-grace, for he was very angry and his thoughts were bitter. It was shameful to dismiss him after thirty years' faithful service with a mere douceur and no thanks. His old master would not have treated him in that way, and if Charlie had only lived—however, there was no use crying over spilt milk. He must just nurse his wrath and bide his time, and if he did not get even with the jackanapes one of these days he would write himself down an ass.

When Olive asked Edward about Mrs. Prince he looked very grave. His mother was far from well: that was the reason she had not come with him. Meanwhile, she sent her apologies and her love, and would call as soon as she was a little stronger.

" Oh, I shall not stand on ceremony with your mother," said Olive. " I will call on her. I hope she is not seriously ill."

" Not seriously. I hope she will be better in a few days.

But she is not strong ; she has never been the same since my father and poor Charlie——"

" And no wonder. Poor Mrs. Prince! Yet how brave she was. Your mother is a woman of rare strength of character, or she would have been utterly crushed."

Olive spoke with feeling, yet quietly, and she was surprised how calmly she could refer to an event which at the time of its happening seemed like to break her heart.

" Yes, my mother is a woman in a thousand. But I fear you will find her changed. Peele is also changed—though quite in a different manner—for the better."

" How so ? "

The military authorities have established a camp—which means a collection of wooden huts—on Warcock Heath. The town is alive with red coats, and the officers are quite a social acquisition—very nice fellows, some of them, and seen a lot of service."

" I dare say," said Olive indifferently. The camp at Warcock Heath did not interest her much. " Is Mr. Lillywhite still with you ? "

" No, he has left me and set up for himself."

" As a solicitor ? "

" No ; he is agent to the Rhadamanthus Insurance Company, an appointment I got for him, and he has other agencies."

" That means he is getting on, I suppose ? I am very glad. I have a great respect for Mr. Lillywhite."

Edward looked at his watch and muttered something about an engagement. He had heard so many people say that they had a great respect for Mr. Lillywhite that he was getting rather tired of it.

" Kindly tell your mother that I shall call on her as soon as possible, probably to-morrow," added Olive, as her visitor took his leave, smiling urbanely, yet inwardly much disappointed. The bright, impulsive, rosy-cheeked girl who had once captivated his fancy was become an elderly young woman with sunken cheeks, a sallow skin, a generally limp appearance and a listless manner. She had not even seemed particularly rejoiced to see him, and there was nothing in her speech or bearing to encourage the hope that she had remained single for his sake. But she had deteriorated so much that this conclusion was less mortifying than it otherwise might have been, the more especially as his passion was on the wane. Few are the loves that survive in their integrity an absence of five years.

When his mother inquired how Olive was looking he answered dryly: "Quite Americanized and terribly gone off. But as she is going to call, you will be able to judge for yourself."

Whereupon it came to pass that when Miss Lincoln called at Holmcroft on the following day her worn face and delicate looks occasioned no great surprise.

"She is evidently out of health," Mrs. Prince thought, "and when people are out of health they cannot be expected to look their best."

Mrs. Prince was herself conscious of not looking well, and Olive was painfully impressed by the change for the worse in her friend's face. It was not merely that she looked much older; the gloved right hand, and a slight distortion of the same side of her face, rendered it only too evident that she had lately been visited with a stroke of paralysis. She was also garrulous, often repeating herself and confusing events and persons in a way which showed that her failing health had affected her memory.

After they had exchanged a few common-places, Mrs. Prince made Olive almost jump out of her chair by saying, *apropos* of nothing, that she had lately received a letter from Charlie, and that he was coming home.

"A letter from Charlie!" exclaimed Olive.

"Yes; he is in America. Didn't you know?"

"Good heavens, Mrs. Prince! What are you saying? Charlie was—drowned."

"Did I say Charlie? I meant Jack. Ah, poor Charlie, he was drowned, as you say, and is buried in the family vault, and we put up a handsome tablet to his memory in the church. I meant Jack. You never knew my eldest son, I think. He was a little wild in his younger days, and we had to pay his debts, which were very heavy, to save the credit of the family. But he went to your country, my dear, and made money, and has paid back every penny, every penny. I wanted him to pay us a visit, and, but for this dreadful war, he would have done. Dear boy, I should like to see him."

"How does the war prevent him from coming?"

"They wanted him to accept a commission—he once served

in the British army and knows about drill, and that—and he thought it his duty, you know. But he says the war will soon be over and then he will come. I hope so, for I don't think I shall be long here, and I should so like to see him before I go."

" Do you mean that he has accepted a commission in the Federal army ? "

" Yes, he is for the North. I don't see why an Englishman should fight either for the North or the South. But he has become quite an American, and says the Union must be maintained. He considers it his duty, you know. I confess that I don't understand it. Fighting to maintain a Union seems to me like a contradiction in terms. However, Jack thinks differently. I suppose you did not meet him in America. You and he used to be great friends, and went hunting together. I am sure he would have been glad to see you."

" You forget, Mrs. Prince ; I never saw your eldest son."

"Never saw Jack ! I beg your pardon, dear, I meant Charlie. Poor boy ! He lies in the family vault with his father and five generations of Princes. It is an old family, and not one of them ever did a dishonorable action ; and my son Edward is as highly esteemed in the town of Peele as his father was, and one of your mother's trustees. Charlie would have been the other if he had lived. He promised your mother, and the Princes always keep their word. Yes, it was him you went hunting with, and I sometimes thought —Shall you hunt next season, dear ? You used to be very fond of it, you and Charlie."

Olive grasped eagerly at this chance of changing the subject.

" Perhaps I shall, a little, if I regain my health," said she. " Sir George Somerton, the eminent specialist, you know, said that I ought to take riding exercise, but only a little at a time, and that I must on no account overtax my strength. And I shall have to go away in November, perhaps also in December, the neighborhood of Peele being at that time rather foggy, as you know."

" Where do you think you shall go ? "

" Probably to Torquay."

" Sir George Somerton ! Torquay ? It is a case of lungs, then ? "

" That is what they feared in Boston. But Sir George

says my lungs are quite sound, and with rest and care I shall
recover my usual health. Yes, I should certainly like a few
weeks' hunting ; but it must not be more, for when I am well
enough to hunt I shall be well enough to go home."

" You intend to return to America, then ? "

" Certainly, and as soon as I prudently can. This is no
time for Americans who love their country to be away from
it—save under compulsion."

" But women don't fight. What can you do ? "

" I shall go as nurse into one of the military hospitals at
Washington—or wherever else I can be most useful."

" I think you would do a good deal better to stay in England. However, if you do go, and should meet poor
Charlie——"

" Charlie ! "

" Dear, dear, what am I saying ? I mean Jack. If you
should see Jack—and it is possible you may, you know—give
him my love and blessing, and say that he has my full and
free forgiveness. He knows it already ; but it may be a comfort to him to have it repeated by one who has heard it from
his mother's lips, and I find writing very difficult (glancing
at the gloved hand). Not that he did anything very bad.
Like many another young man he was led away by evil companions. But he has nobly atoned for his faults, and now,
as you see, he makes duty his ruling motive, even to the
peril of his life. . . . . I have had great trials, as you know,
Olive, and trials equally great of which nobody knows ; they
have ruined my health and made me prematurely old. I am
only a little past sixty ; and but for Jack's redemption and
his dear letters I do not think I should have lived so long.
I wish I might be allowed to see him before I go. But that
is in the hands of God. . . . I must show you Jack's likeness,
he sent it to me a year ago."

From the drawer of a secretaire which stood near, Mrs.
Prince took a leather case and handed it to Olive. It contained the daguerrotype of a man in the prime of life, with a
flowing beard, blue eyes, and a face in which she recognized
a decided family resemblance to his father and Charlie.

" You could tell him if you saw him ? " inquired Mrs.
Prince, " and, as he said he might be ordered to Washington,
you might see him."

" Certainly ; it is a good face, and easy to be remembered ;

and, whatever Jack may have done amiss long ago, you have the consolation of knowing that he is doing right now. He is upholding a great and just cause, and I am sure he will do his duty."

"Of course ; he is a Prince ; and he was always reckless and daring. . . . God bless you, dear. You will come and see me again. Tell Mrs. Marsh I shall call as soon as I am a little stronger."

"Of course, I shall come and see you again," returned Olive, as cheerfully as she could, for her thoughts were sad ; and several times during the ensuing months she called at Holmcroft and had long talks with the old lady, generally of the same trying sort as the first. Early in November Olive went to Torquay. Shortly after her arrival there she heard, with great regret, but without surprise, that Mrs. Prince had had another stroke, which she survived only a few days.

CHAPTER XXXV.

AN OLD ACQUAINTANCE.

In January Olive was back at All Hallows, looking better and feeling stronger, yet not in the best of spirits. Mrs. Prince's death had evoked unhappy memories, and the condition of things at home caused her the keenest anxiety. So far from showing any signs of yielding, the South were more defiant than ever. The people of the North seemed resolved to restore the Union at whatever cost of treasure and life; the President was calling for more troops; Paul Coniston and nearly all the young men she knew were at the front, and even Mr. Seward, the Secretary of State, had ceased predicting that the rebellion would be crushed in sixty days. The governing and writing classes in England openly sympathized with the South; a great English statesman avowed his belief that Jefferson Davis had made a nation, the leading journal protested that the Union was as dead as the Heptarchy; and so bravely did the Confederates bear themselves that even those who least sympathized with their cause could not help admiring their courage; the enemies of the Union rejoiced and many of its best friends began to despair of the Republic.

Among the few who rightly discerned the character of the conflict and foresaw its issue was Cousin Hosea.

"Although the avowed object of the North," he wrote, "is simply and solely the restoration of the Union, people are beginning to see that only through abolition can that object be achieved. I have reason to believe that this is the President's opinion, and that ere long he will decree emancipation as a measure of war. The end will be the defeat of the rebellion and the restoration of the Union, but only after great suffering and bloodshed, God's judgment on the nation for its sin and the sole means whereby it can be purged thereof."

All this redoubled Olive's anxiety to go home, and only Sir George Somerton's assurance, that if she returned before her strength was fully restored and the winter well over she would lose all the good she had gained, induced her to prolong her stay.

"Ride, hunt, walk, live in the open air as much as you can," said he, "and in May or June you can go back with a quiet mind—so far as your health is concerned."

So Olive, fortified by her physician's advice, and herself nothing loth, took once more to hunting.

Mr. Marsh, who, though he did not himself ride to hounds, kept up the style of a country gentleman, placed his stud at her disposal, and two days after her return from Torquay gave a hunt breakfast, at which were many guests whom she met for the first time and several well-remembered faces. Yet some which she remembered and one which she should never forget were absent, and she thought sadly of times gone by. But when the feasting was over and she went outside and mounted the gallant gray provided for her by her host, and mingled in the gay and picturesque throng of equestriennes and cavaliers, and the master gave the signal for a move, and the huntsman rode by at the head of his pack, touching his cap and crying, "Hounds, please, gentlemen!" Olive felt again the sacred joy which only faithful devotees of Diana can know.

The weather, too, was propitious. A southerly wind and a cloudy sky proclaimed a hunting morning, and the knowing ones said the "going would be good," which meant that the turf was neither too hard to be springy nor so moist as to be spongy. But foxes were somewhat scarce, and it was not until one o'clock that a ringing view hallo from the first whip and a series of blasts from the huntsman's horn informed the impatient field that a reynard of the right sort had gone away.

And then they had a glorious scamper. Olive threw her troubles to the wind, forgot both North and South, Federals and Confederates, forgot everything save that she was riding a gallant horse, and hounds were running fast and free to a breast-high scent. The gray knew his business so well that Olive needed only to sit still and let him go. He took a line of his own from the start, and never seemed happy unless he was in the same field with the hounds.

After an hour's run, diversified only by two or three momentary checks, the fox took refuge in a hollow tree, from which it was impossible to dislodge him. While the hounds were baying round the spot where he had vanished, most of the men dismounted to ease their horses and stretch their legs, while two or three ladies, who had ridden straight and were well up, profited by the opportunity to shake out their skirts and adjust their hats and tresses. Lydia Spankaway, one of the chosen few, kindly informed Olive that her hair was down. As Olive was putting it to rights she dropped her whip, whereupon two men, who were near, good-humoredly contended for the honor of picking it up. Olive, smiling, thanked them " very much," and after a remark about the run, they sauntered a few yards further and joined in conversation with two or three others, who, like themselves, had a decidedly military air.

" You are highly honored, Miss Lincoln," observed Lydia.

" Highly honored ! How ? "

" In having your whip picked up by a hero. Those are the two famous captains of the Red Hussars."

" I must plead ignorance. I never heard of these gentlemen before."

" I was forgetting you had been away. The Red Hussars have just returned from India, where they greatly distinguished themselves in the mutiny. The two captains are Locksley—he picked up your whip—and Revel, both Victoria Cross men and inseparable friends—they have fought side by side in I don't know how many battles."

" They look as if they had been in the wars ; their faces are—a caution."

" Yes, the Pandies and the tigers have spoilt their beauty for them. One of Captain Locksley's cheeks is scarred with a sabre cut, the other blued with gunpowder. He led a charge on a battery, and after receiving several wounds and killing half a dozen Pandies was blown up by the explosion of an ammunition wagon. That is what disfigured his face and injured his eyes. As you see, he wears tinted glasses. Revel's face was disfigured and his ear torn off in a tussle with a tiger. He is a great shikaree and has killed twenty man-eaters to his own gun."

" You seem to know a good deal about them."

" I heard it from their Colonel, Ethelstan. He is a friend

of Teddy's and called the other day. Very fine fellows both of them. Did you notice how straight they rode in the run? Captain Locksley was first over the brook. If I were not a hunting woman——"

"You would not object to one of the captains as a husband, I suppose? Which would you prefer?"

"It would be about even betting, I think. Revel is rich, and Locksley, though a ranker, is a gentleman. He enlisted because he could not afford to buy a commission, and won his promotion and his cross by reckless bravery."

"Then you would naturally prefer him. The man who rises from the rank is surely more to be admired than the man who inherits a fortune and buys a commission."

"Well, I daresay you are right, and as I have plenty of money of my own the lack of fortune would not be an objection if I meant marrying—and he asked me. But I have noticed that matrimony and hunting don't go well together, and I prefer hunting. Yet any woman that way inclined would be glad to marry either. Perhaps you would like one of them yourself!"

"After you, Lydia," said Olive laughing. "When you have made up your mind to marry the tiger-slayer—for I really think you are rather gone on him—I may condescend to take the hero with the tinted spectacles. Where do these gentlemen live—at the camp?"

"I think only the subalterns live in camp. The other officers—at any rate, the married ones—live in the town. But, I say, we must be off. The hounds are gone to draw Shadow Bushes; and it's always a sure find. Come along."

Whereupon Miss Spankaway gathered up her reins, touched her horse with her heel and went off at a canter. Olive would have followed; but hunting is hard work, even when you are in tip-top condition, and she was not in tip-top condition; she felt tired, and remembering her doctor's injunction not to overtax her strength and that she was nearly a dozen miles from home, reluctantly turned her horse's head thitherward.

An hour's steady walking, alternated with an occasional canter on the turfy side of the road, brought her to the outskirts of Peele and within a mile of Warcock Heath. As she rode down a lane bordered with gaunt old-fashioned roomy cottages and small villas, each set in a " garden fair," whom should she see standing at the gate of one of them, solemnly smoking a huge meerschaum pipe, but Mr. Lillywhite.

Olive stopped and spoke to him. The old fellow, who seemed greatly pleased, acknowledged her greeting by wagging his expressive nose and exhibiting his scalp lock.

" Is this your house ? " she asked.

" Yes, it is my dwelling-place," he answered, regarding the cottage with some complacency. " We call it the Wigwam. Rather large for an old bachelor with one servant ; but at present I have a lodger who occupies two of my rooms. You may have heard of him. Captain Locksley, of the Red Hussars."

" I heard of him to-day for the first time, and saw him ; he was out hunting. So he is your lodger."

" Yes. We are very handy for the camp ; and the Captain is not considered sufficiently recovered from the effects of the Indian climate and his wounds to live in a draughty hut. A very quiet gentleman, though he is such a fire-eater. Nothing he seems to like less than talking about himself or his exploits—and he gives no trouble. His soldier servant waits on him. Great changes, Miss Lincoln, great changes. Only two Princes left, and one of them in America. Very sad about poor Mrs. Prince. I didn't think she would go so soon —only sixty-three."

" Only ! I consider sixty-three rather a good age."

" You wouldn't if you were seventy-one, Miss Lincoln. Mrs. Prince was a woman of sound constitution ; and but for her troubles might have lived to be ninety. They say that some time before she died she got rather queer, and was always harping on the respectability of the Prince family and saying that there was never a Prince who did a dishonorable action since the world began."

" Yes, I heard her talk in that way myself."

" Poor old lady, I daresay she believed it."

" Believed it ! Why shouldn't she ? Perhaps you are thinking of Jack. I am afraid he was a sad scapegrace— once ; but as you probably know, he has honorably discharged all his debts, and joined the Federal army ! out of a sense of loyalty to his adopted country. A man who does that cannot be really bad, and Mrs. Prince might well be proud of him."

"That's true, and badly as Jack behaved I always thought he was more weak than wicked. All the same, when people protest so much it makes one fancy there is something behind; and there are worse men in the world than John Prince. Have you seen Mr. Edward—Mr. Prince, I should say, since you came back?"

"Several times; but not since I returned from Torquay. I thought him improved—he isn't so thin as he used to be, and more genial. By-the-bye, he told me that you had set up on your own account and were doing well. I was very glad to hear it."

"He said that, did he? Well, I am not doing badly—but I owe no thanks to him for it. However, perhaps he does not think so. Can I offer you anything, Miss Lincoln—a glass of sherry?"

"No, thank you; I must be going home. I am very tired, and my horse will be taking cold if I stay longer;" and after shaking hands with the old man and expressing the wish that they might meet again Olive resumed her journey, pondering the while what he had said and wondering what he had meant. That he meant something she felt sure. Mr. Lillywhite was not given to talk at random and she had heard of his passion for gathering and garnering secrets.

His words pointed to a mystery. "Something behind," and the collocation of the remark that there were worse men in the world than John Prince with the inquiry about Edward had not escaped her observation. But he could not be alluding to Edward. Edward was a man of spotless reputation, and his honest and able management of her mother's affairs deserved their gratitude and had won their respect. Moreover, Lillywhite had evidently a feeling against him and was therefore not altogether a trustworthy witness. Could he mean Charlie? Impossible! Charlie had a high sense of honor, and he and Lillywhite were fast friends.

And yet—why had Charlie broken his promise to become her mother's trustee and declared that he was unable to give a reason for his refusal? What was the nature of the pledge which sealed his lips, and to whom had he given it? Had Mrs. Prince known, did Edward know aught of this? Perhaps Lillywhite did, but she felt that not even to gratify her curiosity could she confide to him, or any other body, what had passed between her lover and herself on the day of his death. If Lillywhite had any revelation to make it must be spontaneous. She should never ask him.

" I have given her something to think about," chuckled the old fellow, as Olive rode away. " Being a woman she naturally won't rest until she knows all. The next time we meet I'll pique her curiosity a bit more. Aye, aye, Ned, I know your little game and I'll spoil it ; and show you up into the bargain, you scoundrel. You'll bring an action against me for slander, will you ? We shall see, we shall see."

CHAPTER XXXVI.

THE TWO CAPTAINS.

ALTHOUGH Olive awoke next morning with a few aches and pains they soon passed away, and she felt all the better for her day's hunting. When Edward called in the afternoon he was surprised to find her looking so well—plumper in body and brighter in face, her sallowness gone, her color returning, her eyes sparkling with animation; and she smiled and talked in a way that reminded her visitor of old times, and made him rue on the spot his resolution to think no more about the " minx," as he had lately called her in his mind.

" How well you are looking," he said. " Torquay has done you a lot of good."

" Torquay and yesterday's hunting. We had a splendid run, and I was out in the open air all day."

" Hunting, were you? If I had known you were going out I would have gone too; though I seldom hunt now. I have not the time, and I was never such a Nimrod as——"

(Here Edward paused and his face clouded. He had nearly said " Charlie," and Olive, ascribing the pause to emotion evoked by painful memories, gave him a look of sympathy and pity.)

" I was never such a Nimrod as some people—and only hunted, as you hunted to-day, for the benefit of my health."

" Oh, but I enjoy it immensely, and if I lived in England I am afraid I should hunt even though it were not good for my health. Yet, although you pretend not to care much for the sport, you used to like it, and I have seen you ride very well indeed."

" You are pleased to say so," said Edward, with a gratified smile.

" It is quite true. Do you remember that time Mr. Vayle's harriers found a fox in the forest and we ran him to the King George ? And——"

This was dangerous ground, which Olive perceiving, hesi-

tated, thereby making matters worse. The observation called
Charlie to mind, as also the rather sorry part played by Edward on the eventful day in question ; and it was a relief to
both when Mrs. Marsh, a dear, albeit absent-minded, old lady,
whose hearing was not what it had been, interposed with a
remark about the weather. But no sooner was this suggestive
topic threshed out than she asked her guest, *apropos* to nothing in particular, how long it was since his brother died.

"Poor young man," she added, "I shall never forget how
shocked we were when we heard of it. How long since, did
you say ? "

"Nearly six years," returned Edward, with a sigh and a
look appropriate to the occasion ; but inwardly he was furious.
"Hang Charlie!" he thought. "When will people have
done talking about him ? "

"Six years! Dear, dear! How time flies! Why, it
seems only the other day. It was very terrible ; but it must
have been a great satisfaction to you that his body was
found and laid in consecrated ground. I don't think,
though, that your poor mother ever got over it ; and no
wonder. I remember——"

What the good lady remembered was never known to those
present ; for even as she spoke her footman opened the door
and announced two visitors :—

"Captain Locksley and Captain Revel of the Red Hussars."

Mrs. Marsh, who had already made the gentleman's acquaintance, introduced the new-comers to Olive and Edward,
on which Captain Revel observed that they had had the
pleasure of meeting Miss Lincoln in the hunting-field, complimented her on the boldness of her riding and the cleverness
of her horse, and asked whether she had learned to ride in
England or America.

"Oh, she learnt here," said Mrs. Marsh, again unwittingly
putting her foot in it. "She learnt here, and had a very
good teacher, Mr. Prince's brother, one of the best riders in
the hunt. They used to go out together regularly. Poor
fellow, we were talking about him only just now. He was
drowned six years ago, almost within sight of the Pines, a
place we used to have at Whitebeach, while on a visit to
Mrs. and Miss Lincoln, who were staying there. You were
bathing, weren't you, Mr. Prince ? "

"We were bathing," said Edward, nearly inarticulate with rage, yet constrained by politeness to bottle up his wrath and look merely grave, while Olive, deeply pained by this ripping open of old wounds, and feeling for Edward, had much ado to preserve her composure.

"They were bathing," resumed Mrs. Marsh, "and the younger brother was swept away by the tide and they did not find his body for a month or more. It was very sad, I could never bear the Pines afterwards. That was why we sold it and came to live at All Hallows."

"It must have been, as you say, very sad. A younger brother of mine was drowned pretty much in the same way many years ago," remarked Captain Revel, sympathetically; and then, inferring from Edward's silence and the gloom of his countenance, that the subject was distasteful to him, asked Miss Lincoln how she had enjoyed the run and when she was going out again.

Olive gave a suitable answer, and by way of getting as far away from Charlie as possible, asked the captain how he liked India and how long he had been there. Revel replied that he had been in India eight or nine years, and liked it very well, only it was so full of sorrowful memories for him that he did not think he should care to return.

"You mean——"

"I lost so many dear friends there—killed in battle, murdered by mutineers, died of hardship and exposure."

"Yes, that must have been a terrible time. The incidents of the Mutiny were followed with intense interest in America, especially the march of Havelock to the relief of Lucknow. Did you know Havelock?"

"No, but Captain Locksley did. He was with him in Persia, and took part in the march. We were not in the same regiment then; our first meeting was at the second leaguer of Lucknow."

"And you were actually with Havelock?" exclaimed Olive turning eagerly to Locksley, who had so far taken no part in the conversation. "You were actually with Havelock, and knew him, and took part in that heroic march, about which I have read?"

"I was with Havelock, certainly—and knew him so far as a sergeant—that was my rank at the time—can be said to know his general."

" And you were through it all ? "

" Well, I was in every engagement between the 7th of July, when we set out from Allahabad, to the 20th of September, when we forced our way into Lucknow."

" Nine battles in less than three months," observed Revel, " warm work that, Miss Lincoln, and won 'em all too. Or was it ten, Locksley ? "

" Ten, reckoning the fighting at Lucknow."

" Won't you tell us all about it, Captain Locksley ? " asked Olive softly. " Do, please ! I never thought to meet anybody who had been with Havelock."

" Tell you all about it ? " returned Locksley with a smile. " That is rather a large order, Miss Lincoln."

" Well, then, something about it, what you saw and did yourself."

Thus entreated the Captain could not refuse ; and begining with some degree of hesitation and in a low and rather husky voice, but warming to his work as he went, he told the story of that glorious and ever memorable campaign, of swift marches though a country swarming with foes, under a sun so fierce that on some days it slew as many as bayonet and bullet, of fights in which the odds against the English were fifty to one, of the fine generalship of the leader and the constancy and courage of the men, of their rage and disappointment on discovering that the women and children, whom they had fought so heroically to rescue, had been foully murdered, of the advance on Lucknow, the desperate struggle to reach the Residency, and the joy of the beleaguered garrison and their wives and little ones, whom Havelock was just in time to save from the fate that had befallen the prisoners at Cawnpore.

Olive hung breathless on his words, her cheeks flushed, her beautiful eyes alternately glowing with excitement and filling with tears.

" Thank you, Captain Locksley," she said warmly when he had told his tale. " I hope that in this hour of her trial my country will find Generals as able as Havelock, and soldiers as brave and devoted as those who followed him from victory to victory."

" I have no doubt she will," returned Captain Revel. " Americans have never shown want of pluck, and we are all of the same race. But which America do you mean, North or South ?"

" The North, of course. You surely did not think I meant the South ; the South are in rebellion," exclaimed Olive indignantly.

" So were the Colonies once, both North and South, and quite right, too."

" But the Colonies were fighting for freedom."

" So are the South now. And they are the weaker party, and one naturally sympathizes with the weaker party."

" I don't quite see the force of that," remarked Locksley quietly. " The mutineers were the weaker party or we should not have beaten them ; and when that Ghazi went for you on the Kalpi road you did not spare him because he was the smaller man."

" Besides, the only freedom the South are fighting for is the freedom to hold colored people in slavery," said Olive.

" I don't think slavery has anything whatever to do with it," said Captain Revel.

" Don't you ? I will prove to you that it has."

Olive left the room and presently returned with a little book, from which she read the Ordinance of Secession of the State of South Carolina, wherein the meddling of the people of the North with the involuntary servitude of the South was given as the cause and justification of secession.

" Well, I don't think that slavery is half a bad thing," said Revel doggedly. " I daresay those black people are a good deal better off as slaves than they would be as free men."

" If you think slavery is right I have nothing more to say," returned Olive coldly.

" He does not, Miss Lincoln," said Locksley. " He detests it just as much as you do. Like the traditional British soldier he never knows when he is beaten ; that is all. For I am as sure that you had the best of the argument as that the North have the better cause. The Southern people distinctly say that they are fighting in vindication of their right to hold men as slaves. If I felt sure that the Northerners were fighting to free the slaves they should have my warmest sympathy."

" They are. Wait only a little while, and you will have certain proof," said Olive with her sweetest smile, for she felt deeply grateful to him for siding with her, and defending the cause she had so much at heart.

After accepting an invitation to dinner for the following week, the three guests left at the same time, but separated outside, Edward Prince driving to Peele, while the two captains walked back to their quarters.

" A fine girl—young woman rather—that Miss Lincoln," observed Captain Revel to Captain Locksley, as they went along. " Her face is both comely and intelligent. She is clever, too. How she bowled me over with that Ordinance of Secession. And I like the way she stuck up for her country."

" Yes, she is clever," said the other absently.

" I never saw such a fellow as you, Locksley. You don't seem to care for the sex at all. I think Miss Lincoln inspired you, though, and your account of Havelock's campaign quite took her by storm. Why shouldn't you marry her, old man ?"

" More likely you."

" I am not a marrying man."

" Anyhow, you are rich, and can afford to keep a wife. I cannot."

" You will not need to keep her, my dear fellow. Lilly-white says she has twelve or fourteen hundred a year. And when you return to India you are sure to get a good appointment ; or, perhaps, a general you'll be."

" Small chance of that, I think."

" Oh, I don't know ; things much more unlikely have happened. You seem hipped, what's the matter ?"

" That girl's questions awakened sorrowful memories."

" Old comrades gone out ! Ah, yes, what a lot of fine fellows sleep their last sleep over there. When I think—but it is better not to think ; we cannot bring them back. Have a weed."

Locksley took a cigar from his friend's case, and the two captains went on their way, smoking pensively.

Meanwhile, Mrs. Marsh and Olive were talking about them —naturally.

" They are rather alike, aren't they? Do you think they are related ? " asked the elder.

" The two captains ? " said Olive, rousing herself from a fit of abstraction into which she had fallen when their visitors were gone.

" Yes."

" I should not wonder ; they appear to be great friends ; and now you mention it, there is a certain resemblance between them. They are the same height and build, both have tawny beards and hair, both are slightly bald, both burnt brick-red with the sun. But these are not family resemblances, and what with their faces being disfigured, and Captain Locksley's tinted spectacles, it is impossible to tell whether they are alike or not."

" He was blown up wasn't he ? "

" Yes, by the explosion of an ammunition wagon. I feel sorry for Captain Locksley. He looks like a man who has suffered."

" I should think so, indeed. Look at his poor face. They say he was nearly blinded. I wonder he was not killed."

" I did not mean personal suffering. We soon forget physical suffering. He looks like a man who has had some deep sorrow."

" He may have lost somebody who was dear to him in India. I read in the papers of a man whose wife was killed by that wretch, Nana Sahib."

" Had Captain Locksley a wife ? "

" I am not aware. It is only an idea."

" I should like to know his story. I think it would be worth hearing."

" Perhaps he will tell it us when we become better acquainted; they are coming to dinner next week, you know, and I hope we shall make good friends of them. I think they are interesting, don't you ? "

" Very," said Olive, and she thought, though she did not say so, "especially Captain Locksley."

CHAPTER XXXVII.

EDWARD SHOWS HIS TEETH.

THE dinner was a great success. To it came as well as Locksley and Revel, Colonel Ethelstan and Major Phillips, all of the Red Hussars, Edward Prince, and several others. The colonel and the major had campaigned in many lands, and were capital company. The talk was lively and entertaining, the theme for the most part, as was natural in the circumstances, being war. The two captains were asked by the host and entreated by the hostess to tell how they won their Victoria Crosses, but as both were of a retiring disposition (except before the enemy) and disliked to talk about themselves, the task was undertaken by Colonel Ethelstan, who acquitted himself to admiration, telling the story, or, rather, stories with a good deal of dramatic effect, yet in excellent taste, and while extolling their bravery as it deserved, taking care not to do violence to their modesty.

Nevertheless, the two captains did not seem quite to like it, and first one and then the other made an attempt to belittle his exploits.

"Any fellow's glad to win the Cross, that goes without saying," quoth Locksley; "and there are men who have risked their lives over and over again to get it, and failed from no fault of their own. Luck has quite as much to do with it as bravery. I sometimes think the most heroic things men do are never heard of. I once saw a private soldier, whose leg had been shattered by a musket ball, crawl fifty yards under fire and back, to fetch water for a comrade who was worse wounded than himself. That was a pluckier feat than leading a forlorn hope."

"What a noble deed! Why didn't you recommend him for the Cross?" asked somebody.

"I am afraid my recommendation would not have been of much use. Besides, I did not know his name."

"But couldn't you have got to know it?"

" Not very well.   I was otherwise occupied just then.

" How ?" inquired Olive.

" My horse was shot under me, and I was under him."

" Were you hurt ?"

" A little.   Nothing very serious."

" I thought General Havelock had no cavalry ! " said Miss Spankaway.

"At first he had not.   I was in the infantry at the time, but a scratch troop was organized, to which, as I could ride, and knew something of cavalry drill, I was temporarily attached.   Afterwards I joined the Red Hussars."

" How came you to know cavalry drill ? " demanded Miss Spankaway, who liked to know everything about everybody.

" I was once in the Yeomanry Cavalry."

" Indeed !   My brother has a troop in the Yeomanry. What regiment did you belong to ? "

Instead of answering, Captain Locksley addressed an observation to the lady on his right, from which the irrepressible Lydia inferred that he had not heard her question, Olive that he resented it—and rightly—as an impertinence.

Afterwards, in the drawing-room, the two captains (whom the ladies had been meanwhile discussing) were still the centres of attraction.   One young woman asked Revel whether it was true that a tigress had bitten off the greater part of his left ear.

" Not exactly," said Revel laughing, " if she had bitten off my ear I am afraid my head would have gone too."

And then he told how Locksley and himself had once been so foolish as to go tiger hunting afoot ; how he had shot a tigress without killing her, whereupon the maddened creature struck him down with her paw, dreadfully lacerating his head, one side of his face, and his shoulder, and how, but for Captain Locksley, who ran up in the nick of time and shot the tigress dead with his revolver (not daring to use his rifle lest he should kill his friend) it would have been all up with Captain Revel.

All this was so satisfactory to the master and mistress of the house that they expressed a strong desire to see as much of their military guests as possible, and Mr. Marsh gave them the run of his coverts, and asked them to rabbit-shooting and luncheon on the following Saturday.

Edward Prince, who had been so completely eclipsed that, as he subsequently remarked, " he could not get a word in edgeways," was probably the only guest present on the occasion who did not consider that the dinner went off well, or who, when he assured Mr. Marsh that he was indebted to him for a very pleasant evening, said more than the truth. But Edward always hated to play second-fiddle, and he did not admire the rather off-hand way in which, as he thought, the military gentlemen (especially Captain Locksley) treated a person of his importance ; neither, if the truth were known, did he regard with approval the interest that Olive obviously took in the two captains. For in spite of himself the embers of the old passion were flaming afresh, and he was only withheld from making a second proposal by fear of meeting with a second rebuff.

Two days later the two captains made the usual call, and spent an agreeable half-hour with Mrs. Marsh and Miss Lincoln. At the rabbit-shooting they met Olive again ; afterwards, at All Hallows, in the hunting-field and elsewhere, they met often, and soon became good friends.

Edward Prince also sometimes went a-hunting, but his growing importance and increasing girth had not improved his nerve, and when hounds went away he was generally left in the rear ; and Revel, seeing that his friend and Olive rather liked each other's company, lost no opportunity of leaving them *tête-à-tête*, a condition in which, especially during the " hack home," when the day was over, they not unfrequently found themselves.

The more Olive saw of Locksley the more she was confirmed in her theory that he had known trouble, and that his mind was haunted by sorrowful memories. He was often pensive, sometimes answering her questions at random, and although he would talk about his Indian experiences, he never, by any chance, referred to his previous life in England, or wherever else it might have been spent, or spoke of his family.

Once she led up to the subject, and said something about " his people."

" I have no people," he answered bitterly, and in a tone which precluded further questioning.

This mystery piqued Olive's curiosity—the stories she had heard of his bravery and of the chivalrous exploit that had won for him the Victoria Cross, together with the fact that he had risen from the ranks and achieved distinction by his own unaided efforts, had already gained her warm admiration, and there was an indefinable something in his personality or his manner that she found singularly attractive. She was also deeply grateful to the captain for his espousal of the Northern cause. Since their first conversation he had made a thorough study of the question at issue between North and South, and when, as often happened, people whom they met abused the North and expressed the hope and belief that Dixie would win, he always took Olive's side, and so potently withal that they had generally the best of it.

Edward Prince was quick to notice the growing intimacy between Miss Lincoln and Captain Locksley ; it roused his jealousy and provoked his anger, and in the end caused him to risk the rebuff which he so much dreaded. For although his passion was less ardent than of yore, he could not bear the idea of a mere ranker, a penniless soldier of adventure, succeeding where he himself had failed. And he did not like the man ; Locksley had never called at Holmcroft; when Edward asked him to dinner he pleaded a previous engagement, and showed no desire to cultivate his society. Moreover, as the result of cautious inquiries, made of the captain's comrades, Edward came to the conclusion that Locksley had either done something that would not bear the light, or belonged to a family of which he was ashamed. All that his brother officers knew of his antecedents was that that he had enlisted in the Royal Roothing Regiment shortly before the outbreak of the Mutiny and the regiment's departure for India, that his military record was excellent in every respect, his rapid promotion being as much due to soldierly smartness and the intelligent performance of ordinary duties as to gallantry in action and coolness under fire. He had won golden opinions all round, and was popular in his regiment, yet he never spoke of his family, and it was an open secret that he had no resources save his pay. On the other hand, he was evidently a gentleman ; Locksley was a good name. A man might live on his pay in India, and he intended to exchange into a regiment on the roster for that country or already there, an operation by which he would probably gain something. Meanwhile Captain Revel, a rich man, whose life he had twice saved, and who generally mounted him for the field, would take care that his friend did not want for the sinews of war. It was, indeed, rumored in the regiment that he had made a settlement on Locksley.

On the whole, not a bad report ; but as Edward had a low opinion of human nature, and no love for Captain Locksley, he made sure that there was something shady in the gentleman's antecedents. People had been known to enlist in order to escape from their creditors, or to avoid a criminal prosecution. At the best, Locksley was a mere soldier of fortune : and should Olive refuse Edward, and Locksley be the cause, it would be the former's duty, as her mother's trustee, to warn her of the risk she incurred in giving her affection to a man of whom so little was known.

Calling one day at All Hallows, shortly after he had thus resolved, Edward found Olive alone. It was a chance not to be missed. He opened the siege very cleverly, and pleaded his cause in a manly, straightforward way, which, in more propitious circumstances, might have been successful. Beginning by reminding her of their last interview at Holmcroft, when she promised not to engage herself to anybody else until she returned to England, he thanked her warmly for having kept her word, and protested that he loved her as much as ever ; that, come what might, he should never love any other woman. If she asked him to wait longer, he would wait longer ; he would serve for her as long and as loyally as Jacob served for Rachel. If she refused him, she would condemn him to a life of wretchedness. But she would not ; she could not have the heart to refuse a man who had loved her so devotedly, and had waited for her so patiently and so long.

Edward deserved credit. He did his proposing admirably, and though he told several thumping lies he was really in earnest, and pleaded so eloquently, and Olive reflected so long before she made answer, that he felt sure it would be favorable.

" I am very sorry," she said at length, in a low voice, " very sorry ; but it is impossible."

The words struck a chill to Edward's heart.

" Why impossible ? " he asked in a voice tremulous with vexation and disappointment.

" For several reasons. Though I have a great respect for you, Mr. Prince, and your able management of my mother's affairs merits my warmest gratitude, I have not that feeling for you that a woman should have for the man whom she engages to marry."

"The feeling would come in time, Olive; I am sure it would."

"I don't think so."

And then by way of softening the blow, she added that there was another reason why she could not accept his offer. She had made a resolution and given a promise neither to engage herself nor to marry until the Union was restored and the cause of freedom had triumphed.

This roused all Edward's ire. His sympathies were with the South; albeit, knowing Olive's views, he had not made much parade of his own; he was terribly annoyed at being refused a second time, and thought in his anger that the reasons she assigned for her refusal were mere subterfuge.

"Is that your last word?" he asked hoarsely.

"It is."

"Then let me say that I don't believe you. Making a vow indeed! If you don't marry until the North has triumphed you will never marry. It is the South, not the North, which is destined to triumph. You prefer another—you prefer to me, a man of means and position and family, a mere adventurer and fortune-hunter, who comes from nobody knows where, who has neither connections nor kindred. But let him beware. I will find out whether the police don't know something of him. If it costs me every shilling I possess I will unmask that man."

Before Olive, speechless with surprise and indignation, could find words to answer this furious outburst, Edward was gone.

CHAPTER XXXVIII.

OLIVE LEARNS A SECRET.

EDWARD PRINCE was keenly alive to the fact that in giving way to his passion he had made a serious mistake. It generally is a mistake to lose your temper. His had worsened with the improvement in his ordinary manner. Since his father's death and his mother's decadence there had been nobody to withstand him; opposition enraged, complaisance propitiated him. When rubbed the right way he was as bland as Oily Gammon, but rub him the wrong way and he would almost certainly give you the rough side of his tongue.

When you have made a mistake the best thing is to repair it as quickly as you can, and though Edward was still very angry with Olive (on whom he mentally laid all the blame of his own fault, for had she not provoked him to anger?) he did not want to break with her altogether, or have it known that they had quarrelled, so on reaching his office he sent her a letter of apology, written in his best style. He was fully conscious, he said, how badly he had behaved, and felt bitterly ashamed of having so far forgotten himself as to speak rudely to her, whom he respected and esteemed above all living women. Indeed, it was that very love which had caused him to err so grievously; her rejection of his suit had simply driven him frantic, and he knew not what he said. Would she try to forget it, accept the expression of his deepest contrition as an atonement for his offence, and do him the great favor of not mentioning " this most deplorable incident to any third person ? "

Olive had no intention of mentioning the incident to any third person; but she was exceedingly angry—so much so, indeed, that she did not deign to answer Edward's letter, and though the next time they met she acknowledged his greeting she showed no desire to renew their friendship. For his outburst of temper had not merely wounded her; it had revived old doubts as to his sincerity, doubts whereof his handsome conduct to her mother and kindness to herself had made her oblivious. She wondered which was the true Edward—the suave gentleman who smiled and postured, and protested his love, or the ruffian, who had rated and insulted her for rejecting his suit—with a decided disposition to think the worst of him, despite his professions of penitence.

Edward's allusions to Captain Locksley annoyed her even more than his abuse of herself, and she deeply regretted that, instead of replying with a direct negative, she had given him a soft answer and assigned reasons for her refusal. It was like casting pearls before swine. And, what was worse, he had come very near guessing the truth. Olive liked Captain Locksley so well that she was beginning to fear she might end by liking him too well, and in certain eventualities forget her promise to Mr. Oldbury, and forego her design of returning to America in the early summer, to take part, so far as a woman might, in the struggle for the restoration of the Union and the abolition of slavery. She thought none the worse of Locksley for Edward Prince's insinuations—rather the better, indeed. What though his antecedents were obscure, and he never spoke of his family and seldom of himself? He had doubtless good reason for his reticence ; and did not the fact that all that was known of him being good imply that what was unknown was equally good? A man of high courage and noble nature cannot be otherwise than honorable and brave ; those who knew Locksley the best esteemed him the most; and he had proved himself to be a chivalrous soldier and a devoted friend. If he were only an American, and, above all, an American soldier !

A few days later Olive had something else to think about. Walking one morning in the neighborhood of All Hallows, she fell in with Lillywhite—not entirely by accident ; the old fellow had been seeking an opportunity " to have a word with her " for some time.

Olive spoke to him kindly and asked after his health. Lilly-white thanked her and protested that he never felt better, that he was sounder in wind, limb and eyesight than many a man thirty years his junior. Then he inquired, rather significantly, as Olive thought, whether she saw much of Mr. Prince.

" He calls at All Hallows sometimes, and I meet him occasionally when I go out," returned Olive.

" The old lady died intestate, didn't she ? "

" I have heard so; but I really know nothing of his affairs."

" She did, which means that Edward gets everything. It is precious little he'll hand over to Jack. She must have saved a nice penny, and there was a pretty heavy policy, too."

" On her life ? "

" Yes. When poor Charlie died Edward got a fine haul —fifteen thousand, and his mother insured her life for five thousand. He has, of course, got that money ; and one way and another I dare say he is worth not far from fifty thousand pounds—to say nothing of his practice. He is a prosperous man and a proud, Miss Lincoln. But pride sometimes goes before a fall."

Olive, who did not quite like the turn the talk was taking, looked at her watch.

" One moment, Miss Lincoln, I have something to tell you, or, rather, something I should like to tell you, provided I have your assurance that in no circumstances will you give me as your authority—if you should think fit to mention it— as to which you can exercise your discretion."

" Does it concern Mr. Prince ? For, to speak candidly, I have no particular desire to hear anything about him."

" In a certain sense it does concern Mr. Prince. But it also concerns everybody else who had a respect for his brother and deplores his death."

Olive started and turned pale.

" You mean Charlie. What about him ? "

" That I propose to tell you—on the conditions I have named."

" I accept them. I give you my word that I will not mention your name in connection with what you may tell me," exclaimed Olive eagerly. Was it possible that she was about to learn the secret which Charlie at their last interview had refused to reveal ?

" Prepare yourself for a surprise," said the old fellow. And then he paused, not from indecision, but because he hated to part with a secret hardly less than a miser hates to part with his treasure.

" Prepare yourself for a great surprise," he repeated. " The body found off Whitebeach, and laid in yonder church-yard (pointing towards Peele) is not Charles Prince's body."

"Not Charlie's body! Not Charlie's body!" gasped Olive. "What do you mean, Mr. Lillywhite? Say at once what you mean."

"Simply what I said. The body supposed to be Charles's is not his body."

"Good Heavens, don't torture me in this way. Can it be possible that he is—not dead?"

"I am afraid he is—though for a while I thought—— Yes, there cannot be the slightest doubt that he was drowned."

"Then why on earth do you say that the body found at Whitebeach and buried at Peele was not his body?"

Lillywhite set forth in detail the facts on which he had based his judgment; showed her the watch which was found in the dead man's fob, and told her how he had ascertained his name. When a man buys a watch he generally keeps it, and a watchmaker generally knows the name of the customer to whom he sells a good time-keeper. The watch in question bore the name of a London maker and a number, and when, some time after the disaster at Whitebeach, Lillywhite went to London, he took the watch with him, and succeeded in tracing it to its previous possessor. The maker, a wholesale man, sold it to a dealer in the Commercial Road, who, as his books disclosed, sold it in turn to Mr. Thomas Lindale, second officer of the Orpheus, a ship then lying in the East India Dock. With this information nothing was easier than to find out the address of the owners, upon whom Lillywhite waited, and ascertained (without, of course, disclosing his object in making the inquiry) that, some four or five weeks before the body declared to be Charles Prince's was found on the sandbank, Thomas Lindale had been washed overboard one dark night during a heavy gale in the channel.

The chain of evidence seemed complete.

Nevertheless Olive was still unconvinced.

"But the body was identified as Charlie's; his brother and several people were sure it was Charlie's," she urged.

"If you had known and read about as many cases of mistaken identity as I have, nothing in that line would surprise you," returned Lillywhite quietly. "And just think how difficult must be the identification of a body that has been knocking about in salt water for four or five weeks."

"Still—do you suppose that Mr. Prince had any suspicion that this body was not Charlie's?"

" Suspicion ! He knew, I told him myself—after the funeral, of course."

" But did he know before ? "

" That I cannot tell you. He said he had been deceived by the fishermen, which is likely enough."

" Did you tell anybody else ? "

" No. Edward would have been very angry if I had, and he was my employer. Besides, what would have been the good ? I could not have restored Charlie to life ; it would have made a terrible scandal, and for the rest it is not my way to tell tales out of doors."

" Why have you told me, then ? "

" Because you are going back to America ; we may never meet again, and considering your relations—how friendly you and Charlie were, I mean—it seemed to me that you should know."

This was not strictly true ; but Mr. Lillywhite could be very diplomatic on occasions. He had a theory that no woman could keep a secret, and he felt sure that the startling information which he had just given to Miss Lincoln would be imparted—of course, in strict confidence—to somebody else, and so passed on until it became the common talk of Peele—without compromising him, since after her promise it would be impossible for Miss Lincoln to give him as her authority. Edward Prince would know, naturally, and Lillywhite wanted him to know. It was the ex-clerk's revenge for his dismissal, and if the story, with a few additions, reached the ears of the Ægis people, so much the better. A little later on he should whisper a few other things in the same ear ; but for the present he could not bring himself to say more, wherefore, when Olive, after a minute's reflection, asked whether it was possible that Mr. Prince had any object to serve in so readily assuming that " the body " was his brother's body, Lillywhite answered dryly :

" 'Pon my soul, Miss Lincoln, that is more than I can say. It is so easy to make a bad guess about motives ; and Mr. Prince is one of those men whose motives are almost past finding out."

" I am very much obliged to you, Mr. Lillywhite. I am sure you mean nothing but kindness," said Olive, pathetically. " All the same, it would have been better for my peace of mind if you had kept the secret locked up in your own breast."

Then they parted, Lillywhite felicitating himself on his astuteness; Olive with mind perturbed, and a prey to dark suspicions and painful doubts. Had Lillywhite been less circumstantial and precise she would have discredited his story utterly. It seemed more probable that he should be wrong than that Edward should make the terrible mistake which Lillywhite imputed to him. On the other hand, the old man could have no interest in inventing the story; and the watch was a *pièce de conviction* whose significance it was impossible to ignore: for if Edward's account of the manner of his brother's death were true, Charlie surely did not go into the water clothed and wearing his watch. Besides, it was not his watch; she knew it; and Job, the boatman, had brought it to the Pines with his other things.

If Edward's account were true! And why shouldn't it be true? It was beyond a doubt that Charlie was drowned while bathing, as Edward had told. And then there came back to her the thought, born of her grief and rejected in her cooler moments—the thought that had he made a more strenuous effort he might have saved his brother's life. Unless Lillywhite were an unmitigated scoundrel and liar, Edward had kept something back. If he were capable of concealing the fact that the body supposed to be Charlie's was that of an unknown sailor, he was capable—of what?

The elder brother had been jealous of the younger, and she had proof the other day that he could be violent, that he was little better than a ruffian with a veneer of politeness. Olive shuddered at the dire yet formless suspicions which forced themselves into her mind, like shadowy phantoms of the night. They were terrible; impossible, unspeakable, and with a great effort she chased them away. How she wished that Lillywhite had either held his peace or told her more; and that he knew more and could throw light on that other mystery which had given her so much concern she had no doubt whatever.

CHAPTER XXXIX.

"THOSE EYES."

THE interview with Lillywhite happened on a certain Wednesday in the month of March. On the following Tuesday the Marshes gave a dinner party, to which were invited, as usual, all the officers of the Red Hussars, then at Warcook Heath; and all—save Captain Locksley—came. "A touch of liver," explained Captain Revel, had compelled his friend at the last moment, *malgré lui*, and greatly to his regret, to stay behind. In India Locksley had had malarial fever, from the effects of which he still occasionally suffered. It was nothing serious, however, and before the end of the week he would be fit for duty and the field.

Olive said she was sorry. She might have said disappointed, for despite Lillywhite's revelations and her own anxieties she had still a thought to spare for the mysterious captain, and would have been pleased to see him. On the other hand, it was a relief, and, in some measure, a consolation, to find that Edward Prince was also among the absentees. Instead of him came a note, asking that he might be excused, on the ground of a sudden engagement and pressing business. Olive surmised correctly that the true reason was reluctance to meet her so soon after their last parting, and fear that her disdainful silence implied an intention on her part to disregard his prayer to let bygones be bygones. But, whatever the cause, his absence was satisfactory. She would have found it hard to treat him as a friend, and to treat him otherwise might attract attention and provoke inquiries.

The hostess wanted to make a musical evening of it, and when the gentlemen joined the ladies after dinner, singing was going on. Colonel Ethelstan, on being asked by Mrs. Marsh to sing, kindly consented, but instead of the rollicking soldier's song, which all were expecting, he sang, "Oh, no, we never mention her; her name is never heard," in so lugubrious a voice as to make everybody feel melancholy. Next, a lady sang an even more dismal sounding song in Italian, which nobody understood, whereupon Mrs. Marsh, in despair, appealed to Captain Revel.

"You look as if you could sing, Captain Revel," she said, in a whisper, "cannot you give us something—if possible, something lively. Those sentimental songs are very nice, but they are not exhilarating."

"I will do my best," quoth Revel modestly. "What do you say to a rattling hunting song?"

"Just the thing, by all means; thank you very much."

The captain sat down at the piano, which he played passably well, and, after striking a few notes, began:

"I've as nice a little hunter as e'er you'd wish to see,
So high she lifts her forefoot, so proudly bends her knee;
Her fiery head and nostrils red assert her noble blood;
Her girth is deep, and hocks she has that send her through the mud.
My gallant little hunter, my dashing little bay."

"Now see her at the covert side, responsive to my hand,
While other horses fret and fume, how quietly she'll stand;
But when hounds proclaim a find, and for'ard is the cry,
She'll fling the dirt behind her, and o'er the pastures fly.
My gallant little hunter, my dashing little bay."

"The scent is good, the pace is fast, the crowd's soon left behind;
A minute's check, a view hallo, and onward like the wind;
At a rotten bank and yawning ditch the funkers turn away;
The best thing, quoth the master, we've had this many a day.
Oh my noble little hunter, my dashing little bay."

"Good heavens! Miss Lincoln is fainting," exclaimed somebody.

Whereupon there was a cry for brandy and sal volatile, the singing stopped, the women fluttered round a limp figure on an ottoman, and the men asked each other what had befallen. But the sensation lasted only a few seconds; thanks to the prompt opening of a window, Olive came to as quickly as she went off.

"It's the heat of the room," said one.

"She's not very strong; rather consumptive, you know," whispered another. "She flushed, turned pale and went off. A very bad sign, I should say. Her friends should send her to Madeira or the Riviera."

"Hadn't you better take a turn in the garden and get a breath of fresh air?" suggested Mr. Marsh.

Olive smile gratefully, accepted her host's arm, and, saying she would be back presently, left the room.

When she was gone, Captain Revel, at Mrs. Marsh's request, began his song afresh and finished it, little thinking that it had anything to do with Miss Lincoln's faint. But for her the song was like a bolt out of a blue sky. She knew every word of it; Charlie and herself had spent hours in adapting it; the air was the same, and Revel's voice so closely resembled Charlie's that it was like a voice from the dead. How had this man from India learnt what was known only to Charlie and herself? The shock and surprise coming so soon after Lillywhite's strange tale were too much for her. It sent the blood back to her heart, and for a few seconds she lost consciousness, a lapse which those present ascribed to every cause but the right one.

After a short absence she returned to the drawing-room, looking somewhat pale, indeed, yet cheerful and composed, and, in answer to Mrs. Marsh's anxious inquiries, protested that she felt quite well again.

"It must have been the heat," said the elder lady.

"Yes, it must have been the heat," replied Olive, and then she sought an opportunity of asking Revel where he had learnt the song; but, as during the rest of the evening she found no opportunity of speaking to him privately, she decided to wait for a more propitious occasion.

"Hunting is nearly over, Miss Lincoln," said Revel, shortly before he and his brother officers took their leave. "We must make the best of the few days that are left to us. There is a near meet on Friday. I suppose you'll be out?"

"That is my intention, all being well."

"So, I think, will Captain Locksley. He is sure to be fit by then, and I want him to ride a horse I bought last week at Tatt's, a regular flyer, they say he is."

Olive would have gone if only on the off chance of being able to put the question which was weighing so heavily on her mind.

"Where and from whom had Revel heard Charlie's song?" she asked herself again and again, asked herself until her head ached and her brain was in a whirl.

Friday came, and Olive went. The day was, fortunately,

fine ; but even bad weather would have failed to keep her at
home.

Among the first to greet her at the meet were the two captains. Locksley rode a powerful blood chestnut, so hot that
a less consummate horseman would have found it hard to
control him.

The Master of the Riversdale Hunt was the soul of
punctuality, and, at a few minutes after eleven, the hounds
began to draw a covert, which, albeit a sure find, was large,
and difficult to get away from. Moreover, the morning being
windless, nobody had any precise idea on which side the fox
would break. A part of the field stayed outside, another
division went into the wood, and took post in the central
ride. Captain Locksley, whose horse the throng and cries
were exciting almost past holding, discreetly slipped into a
cross ride, "far from the madding crowd."

Olive, perceiving that Captain Revel was so far ahead of
the others that she might speak to him without being overheard, rode up to him.

" I hope you are none the worse for your faint," quoth he.

" Not in the least, thank you."

" The heat of the room, I suppose ? "

" I think so ; the opening of the window revived me at
once."

" We had a very pleasant evening. I say, how well that
little Miss Bravo sings ! "

" Yes, she has a splendid voice. But I think the song that
gave the most satisfaction was yours, Captain Revel."

" It was more the words and the air than my singing, then.
But it is a rattling song. ' My Little Hunter,' we call it."

" Is it in print ? I should like to have a copy."

" Oh, no. It isn't in print. I learnt it——"

" Tally-ho ! Gone away ! " hallooed a voice at the extremity
of the covert.

" For'ard, for'ard, hark, for'ard, away ! " shouted the master, who was behind them. " Gallop like blazes ; they are
outside, and running like mad."

Question time was clearly past ; Olive's query remained
unanswered. The horses, as eager as their riders, raced
wildly for the top of the wood ; and the more impatient, dis-
daining an open gate, took the boundary fence in their
stride.

The hounds were two fields ahead ; only the huntsman and one other with them. The other was Captain Locksley.

Then there was riding in hot haste to "catch up," crowding at gaps and craning at big places. Several men "went muckers" at the second fence, and soon the field became widely scattered and portentously thinned. Olive, whose veteran hunter neither faltered in his gallop nor funked at his jumps, held steadily on in the wake of the flying pack, drawing ever nearer to Captain Locksley and the huntsman, who were still leading. Revel had taken a line of his own.

And so for nearly half-an-hour, when they came to a brook, whose rotten banks and ugly "take-off" would have baulked a stag.

"No crossing here, Miss Lincoln," said Locksley. "But, unless I am mistaken, we shall find a ride and a bridge beyond that plantation to our right. I'll show you the way."

Olive followed, wondering at his knowledge of the country. He seemed to know it better than some people who had hunted in it all their lives.

It was easy to jump into the plantation, but difficult to force a way through it, so thick were the trees. As the captain stooped to avoid a branch his spectacles were plucked off by a twig. Olive caught them as they fell.

"Here are your glasses!" she said, when they were out of the wood.

Their eyes met.

Locksley's face, divested of its disguise, was entirely changed.

"Those eyes! Good God, those eyes!"

Olive reeled in her saddle, and with difficulty suppressed a scream. It all came to her like a revelation. Lillywhite's story, the hunting-song, Locksley's knowledge of the country, his admission that he had served in the yeomanry cavalry, his bold riding, and, above all, those eyes.

"You are Charlie Prince," she gasped.

"Yes; but no more just now, for our old love's sake. Another time," returned the captain, hurriedly, as he replaced his tinted glasses.

"Where are the hounds?" demanded the master (a welter weight), as he crashed through the plantation on his elephantine steed, snapping young trees as if they were willow wands. "There goes Quickly's horse. How the deuce has he got to 'em? This way, Miss Lincoln, they are running through the spinney."

On they go again, but, fortunately for those whose horses are beginning to flag, not quite so fast as at first.

Olive rides automatically, feeling as though she were in a dream. Had her horse been less clever and steady, and Locksley, who continued to gallop by her side, less watchful, she would have come to grief several times.

After another half-hour they come to a grassy lane, bounded by a bank which, though a fair jump, is a big "drop" on the further side.

Locksley, wanting to see Olive fairly over, bids her go first, whereupon the knowing gray tops the bank and slips into the lane with the agility of a cat. But the chestnut, naturally impetuous, and irritated by being held back, rushes blindly, jumps wildly, pitches on his head, and rolls over on his side. The next moment he is on his legs again; but the captain lies where he fell, motionless and limp, his face streaked with blood.

The chestnut in rising has struck him on the head.

Olive screams, and two men, who have got into the lane at an easier place, come to her call. Both dismount, and while one of them raises the prostrate man's head the other pours brandy down his throat.

Without effect. Locksley still lies motionless and limp.

" It's a bad case, I fear," says one.

" It looks so," assents the other. " He has got a terrible gash on the head. See how it bleeds."

" What shall we do? "

" Tie his head up with a pocket-handkerchief; take him to that farmhouse there, and send for a doctor."

By this time two or three more men, and a couple of laborers from an adjacent field have come up to see what is the matter and offer their help. A gate is lifted from its hinges, covered with coats and used as a litter. Meanwhile one of the horsemen gallops off for a surgeon, who lives in a village three miles away.

The farmhouse is fortunately near, and the farmer's wife, a kindly soul, who when she hears what has happened, gladly receives the wounded man into her house, and lets him be laid on her parlor sofa. Olive's courage rises to the occasion; she sees what she ought to do and does it promptly.

"I am a friend of Captain Locksley's," she says to the farmer's wife. "I will take charge of him till the doctor comes. We don't want all these people here; the quieter he is kept the better."

The hint served; gentlemen and laborers promptly withdrew; but not before Olive had asked the former, if they met Captain Revel, to send him straightway to Marle's Farm. This done, she set to work; got water and a sponge, washed Locksley's wound, rebandaged his head, and made him as comfortable as circumstances permitted. Then she sat watching him and wondering, her mind at times positively reeling under the weight of the unanswerable questionings suggested by the startling discoveries of the last few days, and above all, of that day.

It was Charlie beyond a doubt. He had admitted it; and now, as he lay there, with eyes uncovered, and she studied in detail the well-remembered features, and recalled what she had heard of the obscurity of Captain Locksley's antecedents, and his silence as to his past and his kindred, she marvelled that she did not recognize him at an earlier stage of their acquaintance. But this was an *ex post facto* judgment. As a matter of fact, it would have been marvellous if she had recognized him sooner. When you have the best reason for believing that a man is dead and buried, you do not expect to meet him in the flesh, and, in the event of your seeing anybody like him, the resemblance is ascribed to a blind chance or a freak of nature—anything but a resurrection. Moreover, Charlie was so much changed that, when he wore his tinted spectacles, his own mother would not have known him; and neither his brother, nor Olive, nor Lillywhite, nor any other of his old Peele friends had recognized him. Even his voice—and voices dwell long in the memory—was altered—either from the explosion or the relaxing effect of the Indian climate on his throat.

Yet though Olive knew that Locksley was her old love, she could not conceive how he had been saved from drowning and found his way to India; and why Edward had buried another body in his stead. Edward either knew that his brother was alive, and that Locksley and Charlie were the same, or he did not.

If it were a plot contrived by the brothers, how had Charlie been persuaded to drop his identity, renounce his inheritance,

leave his mother and herself without a word of farewell?
True, she had treated him unkindly; but Charlie was neither
heartless nor a lunatic, and surely none save a lunatic would
make so great a sacrifice for so light a cause.

And if it were not a plot, if Edward and Lillywhite believed
Charlie to be dead, what then? That was the question, a
question which the longer Olive pondered it, the harder it
seemed, and he who alone could clear up the mystery lay like
one in very truth dead, and might never. . . . The thought
was madness. He must recover, must, must. . . . Would
the doctor never come?

Olive was roused from her reverie by the clatter of hoofs
on the road, and presently Captain Revel appeared.

"This is a bad business," he said sorrowfully, regarding
his unconscious friend, "a very bad business. And all my
fault. I should not have let him ride the chestnut. He is
too hot for this country. We want horses that can creep as
well as fly. I don't think it is anything very serious, though.
It looks like a case of concussion of the brain. The doctor
will be here presently. I passed through the village where
he lives. He is coming in his trap as fast as he can. I out-
paced him. . . . . How good of you to stay with Locksley!
He will be very grateful when he knows. Wheels. There
he is. Now we shall know the worst. I do hope it isn't a
fracture."

As Revel spoke, the surgeon came in. He was a man of
few words; and without wasting any time removed the bandage and carefully examined the wound, which still bled profusely.

"It's a nasty cut, and narrowly missed being fatal," he
said at length.

"Is it a fracture?" asked Revel anxiously.

"No, a superficial scalp wound and severe concussion of
the brain. He will probably remain unconscious for several
days; but I daresay we can pull him through—if all goes well."

When the doctor had stopped the hemorrhage and stitched
up the wound, he asked Revel whether he proposed to keep
Captain Locksley at the farmhouse or take him to his own.

"Take him to his own, if it can be done safely. We have
ambulances at the camp."

"The ambulance, by all means. How soon can you have
it here?"

" In less than two hours. I will go at once, and send off an ambulance with one of our hospital orderlies and Captain Locksley's servant, and then return. Shall you remain here ? "

"Certainly ; and see my patient safely home."

Olive inquired whether she could be of any further use, adding that if she could she would be glad to stay. The doctor thought not, and suggested that the best thing she could do was to take a glass of wine and go home quietly. He saw that the shock and the strain had been almost too much for her strength.

Olive took the glass of wine and left with Captain Revel, whose road and her own lay for some miles together.

" Am I to conclude that you think there is danger, doctor ? " demanded the captain before he went away.

" Concussion is never free from danger ; and we may have complications. We are pretty sure to have inflammatory fever ; but Captain Locksley is young, and as I said before, I hope for the best," was the cautious answer.

CHAPTER XL.

ANOTHER DISAPPOINTMENT.

LOCKSLEY remained unconscious for the greater part of a week; then inflammatory fever and delirium supervened; and his convalescence was slow. But Miss Lincoln heard of him often—sometimes through Revel: and several times a week Mrs. Marsh sent a servant to inquire how it fared with the gallant captain.

One day when he was quite out of danger and in his right mind, Olive had a visit from Lillywhite. His ostensible reason was to convey Captain Locksley's thanks to Miss Lincoln for the kindness and attention she had shown him at the time of his accident, but this was merely a pretext: the message might just as well have been sent by Revel.

After Lillywhite had given her an account of his lodger's condition, and observed that it would be several months before he was fully recovered, her visitor said abruptly :—

"You know who he is?"

Olive nodded assent.

"He told me so; and he is very anxious that you should keep the knowledge to yourself—for the present."

"I have not told anybody, nor shall I, until I see him. I suppose you have known all along?"

"No. Only since the accident. When he was delirious he said things that gave me the idea, and then by putting two and two together I saw how it was, And I am really humiliated to think that I, who had fancied myself rather clever at finding things out, should have had Charles Prince in my house for months without discovering his secret. But though I knew that it was not his body that lay in the family vault, I did not doubt that he was drowned: and that, I suppose, accounts for my blindness."

"Do you think Edward knows?"

"Not a bit of it. He could not sleep in his bed if he did. I saw him in Peele yesterday. He was all smiles, greeted me affably, and looked uncommonly well satisfied with himself. Do you know, I don't think he greatly regrets the accident which has befallen Captain Locksley."

Olive reddened with indignation, and, probably, another feeling.

"But what does it all mean?" she asked. "How could Charlie escape drowning without his brother's knowledge, and having escaped why, instead of returning to Whitebeach or Peele, did he take another name and enlist; and, above all, why did Edward commit the unspeakable atrocity of burying as Charlie's a body that was not Charlie's?"

"That is more than I can say. As yet, Charles has told me very little. He is too weak for much talk. I suspect many things, and, I daresay, have formed a pretty accurate guess as to how it came about. But, as I have no certain knowledge, and could not say what I suspect without bringing a very serious charge against a certain person, I think you will have to wait until Captain Locksley can tell you himself."

"You mean that you won't tell me."

"Don't put it in that way, I beseech you," said Lillywhite plaintively. "I would do anything in reason to oblige a lady, indeed I would; especially a lady for whom I have so great a regard as yourself. But this secret is not mine. Moreover, as I don't know all the facts I may be quite wrong; and it would be much better and pleasanter for you to hear the story from the fountain-head; and I am sure the captain would be ill-pleased if I tried to anticipate him."

"But how is it to be managed? I cannot call on Captain Locksley alone."

"Mrs. Marsh might come with you."

"Then we should not be alone."

"Why, when he is a little better should not Mrs. Marsh ask him to spend a few days at All Hallows?"

"I am afraid I could not well propose anything of the sort without exciting suspicion."

"Well, you get Mrs. Marsh to call with you—or without you, and I'll manage the rest. She is a kind-hearted lady, and only needs a hint. Have you mentioned to anybody what I told you about the wrong body being buried?"

"How could I without giving my authority? Besides, it would have made such a talk."

"Humph ! There is at least one woman who can keep a secret," thought Lillywhite. "And it's just as well; we'll punish that jackanapes another way, and more effectually."

"Have you any word for the captain, Miss Lincoln ? " he asked.

"Say how glad we are that he is getting on so well, and that we hope he will soon be quite strong. And give him this," (taking a forget-me-not from a vase of flowers on the table).

So Olive had to possess her soul in patience longer than she liked or had anticipated, which was all the more provoking as she had given Mr. Oldbury cause to believe that she would be back in Boston before June, and already the hawthorn was beginning to bloom, the perfume of violets and primroses was in the air, and the woods at eve were melodious with the songs of thrushes and nightingales. Springtide was in all its glory and summer advancing with flying feet.

Yet until the mystery of Charlie's disappearance should be solved and himself restored to health she really could not leave England. She was as determined as ever to return to America, but a month more or less would make no great difference. Wherefore she informed her cousin that circumstances had arisen which might detain her where she was until July.

"I hear that Captain Locksley continues to mend ; he is downstairs," said Mrs. Marsh to Olive, one day about a fortnight after Lillywhite's visit.

"I am very glad. Shall you call? Do you think he is strong enough to receive visitors ? "

"Why not? He is strong enough to come dowstairs."

"Very well. We will call to-morrow. I have a great respect for Captain Locksley."

So on the morrow the ladies were driven to Woodbine Cottage, as Lillywhite called his dwelling. They found him at work in the garden.

"How is the captain? " inquired Mrs. Marsh.

"Getting on nicely, thank you. Still very weak, though, and I fear it will be a long time before he fully regains his strength. He wants a change, and I was thinking whether I might take the liberty of making a suggestion to Mrs. Marsh ? "

"What is it? I am sure if I can be of any use I shall be very glad."

" I was thinking that a few days at All Hallows would do him a power of good. The situation is so breezy, the gardens so spacious, and the view so fine——"

"A very good idea, Mr. Lillywhite. I am obliged to you for mentioning it, I shall certainly ask him. Can we see him, or——?"

Lillywhite showed them into the cottage. They found the sick man sitting near the window basking in the sunshine.

At the sight of them his face lighted up with smiles, and he thanked Mrs. Marsh warmly for her visit ; Olive, less profusely, but the glance which he gave her was more expressive than words, and went to her heart. She thought he was looking less unlike his old self—perhaps because confinement in the house had robbed his face of much of the bronze tinge it had acquired in India, yet the resemblance was still so remote as to render it unlikely that anybody less sharp-sighted than herself would recognize him.

After Locksley's guests had congratulated him on his recovery and talked about the accident and other matters, Mrs. Marsh asked him to make a long visit to All Hallows whenever he was well enough. Locksley protested that nothing would give him so much pleasure ; but so soon as he was fit to travel, which would be in about a week, the doctor said he must go to Brighton for at least a month. Sea air and sea bathing would do him all the good in the world. When he came back from Brighton he had to go to Captain Revel's people in Surrey ; but that visit he could put off for a while, and in the meantime should be delighted to profit by Mrs. Marsh's invitation.

This proposal pleased Mrs. Marsh, and it was agreed that Captain Locksley should make his visit to All Hallows on his return from Brighton. Olive was disappointed : she would have to wait at least another month for the satisfaction of her curiosity, and defer even longer her departure for America. What would Cousin Hosea say ? Yet she could not blame Charlie. As the doctor had ordered him to go to Brighton ; and the sea air and salt water would do him so much good, go he must, and the sooner the better. And, after all, five or six weeks are not an eternity ; the

year was still young, and she would be back in Boston before the fall. All the same, Olive felt that she was not being
altogether faithful to the spirit of her promise and her vow,
that her allegiance to the cause was wavering ; and she
began to look forward to her cousin's letters with less of
desire than of apprehension.

July was drawing to a close when Captain Locksley came
to All Hallows, looking all the better for his sojourn at the
seaside, yet not fully recovered, for his health had been so
much impaired by the Indian climate, the hardships of cam-
paigning and malarial fever, that the nervous shock occasioned by his accident had well-nigh finished him.

Olive and he had no need to contrive stolen interviews.
The man of the house spent much of his time in London ;
and Mrs. Marsh, a late riser, was seldom seen by her guests
before noon.

"I must leave you to entertain Captain Locksley in the
mornings, dear," she had said to Olive before his coming.

Olive made no objection to this arrangement—and she did
not think Charlie would.

CHAPTER XLI.

CAPTAIN LOCKSLEY'S CONFESSION.

THE next morning Captain Locksley and Miss Lincoln
took a walk through the grounds. At first neither had much
to say, for their thoughts were busy and their hearts full.
Charlie led the way to their old trysting-place and invited
her to sit down on a rustic bench under the wide-spreading
branches of a noble chestnut tree.

"You want to hear my confession, I suppose?" said he.

"Call it what you like. I am dying to know why you went
so mysteriously away, leaving us all in the belief that you were
dead. Perhaps you can justify it, but in the absence of
explanation it seems very strange, and, as regards your
mother, cruel."

"Ah, yes, my poor mother! When I think of her—however, you shall know all, and then you can judge how far I
am to blame. Fortunately, I can tell you without breaking
my word, for Lillywhite has divined, and told me, what I
had promised not to reveal."

"You are talking in riddles."

"Wait a minute. I must begin at the beginning. We
quarrelled at Whitebeach because my lips were sealed as to
the cause of my refusal to become one of your mother's trustees."

"Don't say we quarrelled. Say, rather, that I was unkind.
I should have trusted you. You said you could not tell without breaking your word."

"I had been entrapped into giving my word. All the
same, a man's word should be sacred. What I promised not
to reveal was, that under great stress, and urged by my
mother, my father used your mother's trust money to make
good my brother Jack's embezzlements at Liverpool, and
save him from prosecution and penal servitude." And then
Charlie told her all the reader knows, touching lightly on his
father's fault, and laying perhaps exaggerated emphasis on

the efforts his father had made to repair the wrong he had done.

Olive did not deem the fault very heinous.

"I am sure your father meant honestly," she said. "I still believe he was one of the best men I ever knew; if he had lived all had been well; and but for that unfortunate landing on the Spanish Main the money would have been amply secured. I don't think a bit worse of him, Charlie. But why, after his death, didn't your mother and Edward tell us all? I am sure my mother would have kept the secret and given them time to pay the money."

"That is what I urged them to do. I don't want to speak ill of my mother. Nobody could have a better mother, and she had many noble qualities. But she was proud, and set what she called the honor and credit of the family above every other consideration. . . . Well, as I was saying just now, I had a second time refused to accept the trustee-ship, unless your mother were told how matters stood; then, after another quarrel, Ned climbed down; we became friends again and went out for the sail in which you were to have borne us company. After a while the subject was renewed, and Ned did his utmost to persuade me to fall in with his views. It was a great deal easier to withstand his arguments than my mother's entreaties. I gave him a flat refusal. Then he said unpleasant things; we both grew very angry, and he threatened to throw me out of the boat. I simply laughed and dared him to try. This made him still more angry, and he said something about you——"

"What? Don't keep anything back, please," said Olive, seeing that he hesitated.

"He said he could see what I was up to—charged me with intending to curry favor with you and your mother by telling what I had promised to keep secret, 'as if Olive would have anything to do with the son of the man who had defrauded her mother.' This maddened me almost past bearing, and I told him, among other things, that if he were not my brother I would serve him as he had threatened to serve me."

"After that he shut up, and for nearly an hour, neither of us said a word. Then he came the old dodge, climbed down, said how sorry he was for losing his temper and asked my pardon. He had been so sorely tried. Mother was so masterful. If his advice had been taken, things would not have come to such a pass. For his own part, he did not care a great deal whether the whole thing came out or not: but he should like to keep father's memory free from reproach, and so forth. This touched me, and I said, 'All right, Ned, let bygones be bygones,' and we talked the whole horrid thing over again, discussed the expediency of making a confidant of your mother, whether our mother liked it or not, without, however, coming to any definite conclusion.

"By this time it was very hot, and as the wind had fallen, and the water was smooth, I proposed a swim. Ned said he would rather not just then; also, that it would not be wise for both of us to leave the boat, but if I liked he would take care of it while I bathed. To this I agreed, and while I undressed he lowered the mainsail.

"The water was like the day, warm, and the swim was enjoyable—for a while. Sometimes I would go ahead as fast as I could, then, when I got out of breath, float lazily on the rippling sea, looking up into the blue sky and thinking of you. I had been in the water perhaps half an hour when the wind began to rise, and it struck me that I had better be making for the boat. Treading water, I looked round, and to my horror saw that she was sailing away from me. With a great shout I swam after her as hard as I could. I shouted again and again, frantically, desperately. Ned must both have heard and seen me—I could see him—but the more I shouted the faster the boat seemed to go. Still I struggled on until utterly exhausted I was forced to turn on my back and let wind and waves take me whither they would. By this time the boat was a mere speck, and as I could not see land, I had no idea in what direction I was drifting.

"What I felt just then words cannot tell. Ned's cruel desertion cut me to the soul. He had left me to perish, hoping I should perish. It would have been more merciful and less base if he had stabbed me to the heart or blown out my brains. I called to him again, though I knew he would not hear; I called to you though I knew you could not help."

"I heard you," said Olive.

"You heard me! But how?"

Olive told him, and Charlie, taking her hand, continued his story.

"All the same I was determined not to give in; for though

I could only swim a few strokes now and then, and getting
back to land was quite out of the question, there was always
the off chance of my being picked up by a home-returning
fishing smack or a passing ship. I saw several in the distance, but all were too far away either to see me or hear a
hail. After a while I fell in with a broken oar. It saved
my life. Without it I must have gone under. Thus I drifted
about for hours, growing ever more exhausted and less hopeful, my eyes so sore with the salt water that I could hardly
see; and worse still, my mind began to wander. I saw
strange things, and it was only with a great effort that I
could realize where I was and what had happened. Yet I
knew that the end could not be far off. But it did not
trouble me. Exhaustion had conquered fear.

"How long this went on I cannot tell. All I know is that
I was roused from my apathy by the sound of voices. Clear-
ing my eyes from the water I looked up and saw, looming
above me, what looked like the hull of a big ship. The sight
rekindled my love of life. But when I tried to answer the
shouts my voice gave forth no sound, I could only wave one
of my arms. Then the people on the ship hove to, lowered
the boat and took me on board. It was hours before I could
give an account of myself. I told them—well, not the whole
truth—merely that while I bathed my boat drifted away, and
being unable to overtake her I drifted away too. I gave
myself the first name that came into my head—Locksley—
probably because a few days previously I had been reading
Tennyson's Locksley Hall. And it seemed appropriate :—

> "'Howsoever these things be, a long farewell to Locksley Hall,
> Now for me the woods may wither, now for me the roof tree fall,
> Comes a vapor from the margin, blackening over heath and holt,
> Cramming all the blast before it, in its breast a thunderbolt.
> Let it fall on Locksley Hall, with rain or hail or fire or snow;
> For the mighty wind arises, roaring seaward, and I go.'

"I had already resolved to go and not return to the old
place until I had made either a fortune or a name. What
else was there for me to do! My sweetheart had cast me
off."

Tears sprang into Olive's eyes.

"Oh, don't say that, Charlie," she exclaimed, reproachfully.

"At any rate, she said so, and I thought so. My mother had threatened to disown me because I refused to do a dishonorable action at her bidding; my brother had left me to die a cruel and lingering death. That was the worst. If I returned I should have to tell the story of his infamy, as, albeit for my mother's sake, and the credit of the family, I was willing to keep silence, I would not then, nor would I now, tell a single lie to shield Ned from the disgrace he so richly merits. He is not worth it.

"The ship that saved me was a brig, bound from Waterford for the Thames; the master, a warm-hearted Irishman, placed his wardrobe at my disposal, and I promised, after we reached London, to pay him for what I took. When I landed I went straight to the Tower, enlisted in a regiment on the roster for India, and paid my debt with the bounty.

"I had always desired to be a soldier, as you know, and I vowed to myself that I would either make my mark or lose my life. I think I may say that I have done the one—in a small way—and I have come very near to doing the other oftener than I can remember.

"And now, Olive, I think you know all. You have already heard how I got promoted and won the Cross, and a great deal of what befell me in India. I could easily have avoided coming into this neighborhood if I had chosen; but I yearned with an unspeakable longing to see the old place again, and learn what was become of you and how it fared with my mother and Ned. I had no fear of being recognized; and, but for Lillywhite's communication, and the song, and my spectacles falling off in the run, even you would not have recognized me, though I meant to make myself known to you and Lillywhite and Ned, and my mother—if she had lived."

"To nobody else?"

"Nobody, except Revel; he is my closest friend. You see it would be difficult to explain my disappearance and change of name without telling the story of the broken trust and Ned's treachery. And I shall retain the name of my adoption. It is the name by which I am known in the service."

"And have made illustrious. I think you are quite right. But there is one thing I cannot understand—Edward's infamous conduct. What were his motives?"

"Greed, jealousy, and revenge ; and, I daresay, dread of the disclosures which persistence in my refusal to become your mother's trustee would have rendered inevitable."

"Still, I don't quite see——"

"He had much to gain by my death. It would bring him fifteen thousand pounds from the policy on our joint lives, give him the whole of the business, the residue of my father's estate, and control over my mother's fortune. Brothers though we were, we had never been sympathetic. He was in love with you, and had discovered that you loved me."

"How ? "

"He opened one of the letters you wrote me from Geneva. Lillywhite as good as saw him do it ; he has the envelope still which Ned opened and softened, and then reclosed. I wish Lillywhite had told me at the time ; but the old fellow cannot part with a secret without a pang. Yes ; Ned had a good many reasons for wanting to get rid of me."

"Did he get the insurance money? "

"Of course. It was with the insurance money that he reinstated the broken trust."

"But won't that be bad for you, Charlie ? Won't it look as if you were implicated in the fraud."

"I doubt whether it was a fraud. Anyhow I am not implicated. Ned doubtless believes that I am dead ; and I was under no obligation to advise the company that I was alive. To tell the truth, the fact that Ned would get the insurance money did not occur to me till after I had enlisted ; and then I reflected that if I died in India the company would only have paid a little too soon, and that if I lived to come back I could compel Edward to make restitution."

"And that you will do ? "

"Certainly. Also to account for my share in my father's and mother's estates, and my share of the profits and goodwill of the business. He shall pay up to the last penny. That will punish him almost as much as exposure would."

"And when ? "

"Not just now. Probably on my return from Guildford. It will be a trying interview, and I don't feel quite up to the mark yet."

"That's true. . . . . . . Was it quite kind, do you think not to make yourself known and tell me all this sooner— when we met at All Hallows ? "

"I had no opportunity."

"You could have written."

"That might have been dangerous, and I had another reason for keeping my incognito. I fell in love with you over again."

"Oh, Charlie, had you ceased to love me?"

"Not exactly. All the same, you must remember that I thought you had cast me off, and six years' absence, you know——"

"That means you had forgotten me."

"Not at all, and I loved you again, darling, at first sight."

"Yet you did not make yourself known."

"Well, do you know (smiling), I wanted to see whether Captain Locksley could not win the heart which had once been given to Charlie Prince. Did I succeed?"

"How dare you ask such a question? It is really too bad of you," exclaimed Olive, with well-feigned indignation.

"That is no answer to my question. Tell me, now, wouldn't the captain have had a chance, even though you had not discovered that he bore another name?"

"I shall not tell you."

"Anyhow, you love me still. I have been true to you all these years, though you did cast me off."

"Cruel."

"Then you did not cast me off. So we are as we were, only a little more so. We had agreed to be engaged when you were old enough, and your mother gave her consent. You are old enough now, and your own mistress. Therefore we are really engaged, and there is nothing to do but fix the day," said Charlie, laughing pleasantly.

Olive smiled and gave him her hand.

"I doubt whether your logic is quite correct;" she said archly, "but after all you have gone through, the perils you have survived and the honors you have won, I have not the heart to controvert your arguments. I could though an I would."

"Of course you could—you can do anything you like with me—but you won't. That is enough for me. We are engaged, and now about the day?"

Olive's countenance fell. For the last half hour she had been oblivious of her promise, her vow, the cause—everything but her lover—and now like Macduff's ghost at the banquet they rose up unbidden (in her mind) and struck terror to her heart.

"Oh, Charlie, it is impossible : it cannot be," she cried.

"Cannot be! Why?"

"Because of my vow," and then she told him how it came to be made.

"Is that all? I was afraid you had promised to marry some other fellow," observed Charlie with a sigh of relief. "Don't you see that as the vow was made in ignorance of a material fact it is not binding. If you had known I was alive it would not have been made."

"Perhaps not. All the same—didn't you say just now that a man should hold his word sacred, though he may have been entrapped into giving it ; and ought not a woman's vow to be as sacred as a man's promise?"

"The cases are not analogous. My promise concerned a supposed secret, which I kept until it was imparted to me by a third person. Yours concerned your future conduct ; and in view of circumstances which have since come to light, you may disregard it with a safe conscience."

"I cannot quite see it in that light. It was essentially a promise to do my duty to my country in her present trouble. Suppose our positions were reversed. Wouldn't you come back to England and fight for her, and, if need were, die for her?"

"Women don't fight."

"They can help and encourage the men who do, nurse the wounded, and comfort those whom war has bereft of sons, fathers, and husbands. . . . . . . I love you none the less, Charlie, because I love my country and the great cause which is at stake. You have borne yourself so bravely and acted so nobly that I love you more than I did seven years ago. That was a girl's love, this is a woman's love. But I cannot, cannot forget that I am an American."

"I don't ask you to forget it. I should be very sorry. Do you know, I have sometimes thought that I should—if the rules of the service permitted—like to enter the Federal Army for a while. It would be a useful experience, and the cause is good."

"Ah, then!" exclaimed Olive, with glistening eyes.

"But you have not named the day."

" Oh, don't ask me now, dear."

" Well, think it over. You don't propose to return to America immediately ? "

" No, not immediately," returned Olive, with some hesitation.

The subject was renewed on the next day and the day after that, Charlie beseeching and arguing, and trying hard to gain his point, she resisting, yet so faintheartedly withal that he felt sure she would end by yielding.

Towards the end of the week Mr. Marsh came from London, bringing with him several visitors, whose presence in the house put an end to the lovers' private talks : and a few days later Charlie was obliged to leave for Guildford.

" I shall write," whispered Olive as he was going away.

" So shall I, and I shall be back in a fortnight."

Before the fortnight came to an end Olive had letters from America. One of them was addressed in the well-known handwriting of Cousin Hosea. Conscious of her backsliding she opened the letter in fear and trembling. But Mr. Oldbury neither wrote words of direct reproach, nor referred to the prolongation of her stay in England. On the other hand, he dwelt at length on the prospect of the war and the temper of the country, of the unflinching determination to restore the union, and of the strenuous and unexampled efforts that, to this end, were being put forth ; of the devoted men who had died on the field of battle ; of delicate young women, who were doing the work of nurses in military hospitals and following in the wake of armies to tend the wounded and the sick. The abolition of slavery in the District of Columbia, its prohibition in the territories and the offer of Congress to compensate any state which should abolish slavery, proved the nation's resolve to put away the sin which had drawn upon it God's anger and the reprobation of mankind. But in all this there was no bitterness ; he even spoke tenderly of the rebels as " our erring brethren who are fighting nobly in a bad cause."

The letter concluded thus : " I do not envy the feelings of those Americans who are absent from their country in the hour of her agony, who, as they are taking no part in the battle will have no share in the victory (a victory for the South as well as the North), and who, to the end of their days, will be haunted by the sense of having watched from afar, with cold hearts and folded hands, the most momentous struggle for human freedom of our time."

Olive read the letter in her own room. After reading it she sat a whole hour, motionless and in deep thought. Then she knelt down. When she rose from her knees her resolution was taken. She wrote the same day to Liverpool, engaging a passage to New York by the next Cunard steamer. The following day she made her preparations, and on the day of her departure, she sent Cousin Hosea's letter to Charlie, inclosing therewith a few lines from herself.

"My hesitation is at an end," she wrote. "By the time you receive this I shall be gone. My cousin's letter will inform you why I have come to this sudden resolve. I hurry away for fear lest, if I see you again I may be persuaded to relent. I am sure you will love me none the less because I love my country too well to desert her in her hour of need. When the war is over and the victory won we may meet again—if you keep in the same mind. Until then, dear Charlie, farewell, though I write the word with a faltering hand and a breaking heart.—OLIVE."

CHAPTER XLII.

EDWARD SURRENDERS.

EARLY morning. Edward Prince in his office discussing with Mr. Simpson, his managing clerk, the contents of the freshly opened letters on his desk, pretty much as his father discussed business matters with Mr. Lillywhite in days gone by.

But, for the most part, the nature of the business under discussion differed as widely from the business which the late Mr. Prince was wont to talk over with the old clerk, as the latter differed in personal appearance from his successor. Mr. Simpson was a dapper little gentleman with small features, a white face and piercing black eyes; his clothes, of the newest cut, fitted him to perfection, his hair was parted in the middle, his whiskers were beautifully curled, and he sported a flower in his buttonhole.

"Here's Walker wants his note renewed for three months, Mr. Simpson, what do you think, shall we do it?" said Edward taking up a letter.

"The security is pretty fair for a hundred and fifty, I think—a bill of sale on his stock, and a policy of insurance for five hundred, on which twenty annual premiums have been paid."

"Good! But he must plank something down—the interest in advance and legal expenses."

"He'll do that—cannot help himself. I shall insist on fifteen pounds."

"That will do. Forty per cent. isn't bad interest on a practically safe investment. Now, about Jones. He asks for a thousand pounds and wants the money to-morrow, secured by an equitable mortgage on his house and land. The security is perfect, so good, indeed, that I am surprised he does not go to the bank."

"His account is heavily overdrawn. He is afraid the bank

would want to keep the deeds as cover for the present advance."

"Then he is in a corner and squeezable. Say that he can have the money for four months, certain at one per cent. per month, and you can run him up a pretty stiff bill for expenses."

"Oh, yes, sir. That is easily done. What about Symonds? He was here just before you came, pleading for a little further delay, and talking about his wife and children."

"I have granted him delays enough, and I won't stand any nonsense. Write him that if he does not pay within ten days we shall take proceedings. There is somebody at the door; just see."

Simpson went to the door, and took from a young clerk a slip of paper on which was written: "Captain Locksley would like to see Mr. Prince."

"Captain Locksley! What can he want?" said Edward, glancing at the paper.

"Either advice or a loan, I should say," returned Simpson drily.

"On the security of his commission, I suppose. He has nothing else. Was Gubbins served with that writ yesterday?"

"Yes, sir."

"Good! Tell the gentleman I am disengaged, and shall be glad to see him."

Whereupon, exit Mr. Simpson and enter Captain Locksley, with his hat in his hand, and his tinted spectacles on his nose.

"Good-morning, captain; glad to see you: pray sit down," said Edward offering his hand.

Locksley responded with a formal bow, and sat down, looking hard the while at his brother. The latter, who hated being stared at, asked his visitor what he could do for him, to which the captain answered nothing.

"Hang the fellow, he must be deaf," thought Edward.

"What can I have the pleasure of doing for you, Captain Locksley?" he repeated.

"Don't you know me, Ned?" said Charlie removing his spectacles.

Edward's face blanched to the pallor of death, he fell back in his chair as if he had been shot, convulsively gripping the arms of it with both his hands.

After thrice essaying to speak, without producing any sound save a hoarse gurgle, he gasped :

" You are not Charlie ? "

" I am nobody else. You thought you had drowned me ? "

" I—I protest——" exclaimed Edward, wiping the sweat from his brow.

" Don't! I shouldn't believe you. You wanted me to die and left me to perish."

" I assure you, Charlie, I had no idea——"

" Come, Ned, don't add lying to your other sins. Rather thank God that though you tried to commit murder you did not succeed. You treacherously sailed away and left me to drown ; and but for a friendly oar which kept me afloat, and a passing ship which picked me up, your object would have been accomplished. I enlisted and went to India, because if I had come back I should have been constrained to make painful explanations, which, for my mother's sake—not yours —I did not want to do."

" But you call yourself Locksley. What evidence is there to show that you are Charles Prince ? " asked Edward, making a great effort to resume his ordinary manner.

" Do you doubt it ? " demanded Charlie indignantly. " If that is the line you are going to take—let me see " (rising from his chair), " the *Mercury* comes out on Saturdays. I shall see the editor at once, and by this time to-morrow all Peele will know——"

" No, no, for heaven's sake don't do anything rash," interrupted Edward. " I did not mean—I only suggested an obvious difficulty. I don't deny—I admit—yes, I admit, that you are my brother. But the shock has so upset me that I hardly know what I am saying. Does anybody else know of this ? "

" Three persons know, but every one of them—so long as I desire it—will keep the secret as religiously as I shall myself—on certain conditions. These three are Lillywhite, who is now in the general office waiting for me, my good friend and comrade, Captain Revel, and Olive Lincoln."

" Olive Lincoln ! Good heavens ! Does she know ? You told her ? "

" Naturally. We are engaged."

Edward fell back in his chair again, his face pale, his lips writhing.

Charlie watched him pitilessly.

"But she is gone to America," said Edward at length.

"That does not alter the fact. You were jealous; that is one reason why you tried to drown me. You opened a letter which you found on my desk——"

"I didn't."

"Lillywhite has the envelope which you broke open and reclosed. Shall I call him in?"

"Pray don't. Anything rather than that. You spoke of conditions—conditions on which you would keep this matter secret."

"And retain the name I bear. I suppose that would serve your purpose, though, candidly, I don't propose to do it out of consideration for you—and it is conceivable that I may have to take one or two more persons into my confidence; but not in this country."

"You are very bitter, Charlie."

"No. I am only just."

"Well, never mind that. What are your conditions?"

"That you return the fifteen thousand pounds you received from the insurance people."

"Impossible. I should have to tell them everything."

"Not at all. You would have to say that, having ascertained that, instead of being drowned, as everybody supposed, your brother was picked up by a passing ship, and left the country without communicating with his friends, you hasten to repay them the amount which you claimed and they paid in the belief that he was dead. They will be too glad to get back the money to ask questions."

"It will look very bad."

"If you wait until they find it out and make a demand it will. But if you make the offer spontaneously it will look rather well."

"But they will ask for interest."

"Why not? You have had the use of the money, and turned it to good account, too."

"No, I haven't. It went to reinstate Mrs. Lincoln's trust fund."

"Well, you have had the use of the money Jack paid. It comes to the same thing."

"Six years' interest! That will make a total of nearly twenty thousand pounds."

" I don't care, though it makes a total of thirty thousand.
Will you do it, or shall I communicate with the company?"

" I suppose I must," groaned Edward. " What else?"

" I want my share of my father's and mother's estates; and
Jack must have his share——"

" He is rich. He doesn't want it; he has written to say
so. I can show you the letter."

" In that case we shall have to divide equally. I also want
an account of my share of the profits of the office since I
went away. Our partnership has never been dissolved, remember."

" But I have done all the work; you have done nothing."

" Whose fault is that? However, though I insist on having all that is due to me I want to be scrupulously fair. You
can debit the account with the value of my personal services
for the last six years—say three thousand pounds. That will
be about fair, I think?"

Edward nodded assent, and a faint smile flickered over his
face. It was three thousand pounds saved, as it were out of
the fire. Charlie was less exacting than he had feared.

" On the other hand," resumed Charlie, " on the other
hand, there is my interest in the practice, which is quite as
much."

" Nothing of the sort. I deny it—I protest—it is not
worth half three thousand pounds."

" I think it is. Shall we have it put to arbitration? I am
quite agreeable."

" How can we without disclosing the secret? You have
the whip hand now. Have your own way."

" I will have what is right, Ned; neither more nor less.
And this is right. And there is another matter. You must
do something for Lillywhite—undertake to allow him a hundred a year as long as he lives, or buy him an annuity."

" Hang Lillywhite! This is clean ruin," exclaimed Edward
passionately. " It will take every shilling I have got. Don't
be so hard on me, Charlie."

" Don't you be so greedy, Ned. It won't take all you have
got, or anything like it. Lillywhite says that what with
money-lending and one thing and another you are making
two or three times as much as we used to make, and for the
future you will have all that to yourself. And I don't ask
for an immediate settlement. You need not approach the

Ægis people for a month, and I have no doubt they will be open to an arrangement. As for myself, all I ask is five hundred pounds down and the rest by instalments."

"Let me have a little time to consider."

"Not an hour. Why should a solvent man have time to consider whether he will pay his debts? Anyhow, my offer will not be repeated. If you refuse I shall run up to town and place myself in the hands of Topper, Sandboy, and Periwinkle."

Edward drew a deep breath and bent his head.

"I agree," he said, after a moment's reflection. "The account shall be prepared. I will settle with the Ægis a month hence: and bind myself to pay Lillywhite a hundred a year."

"When will the accounts be ready?"

"In a week. My books are well kept. If you come here this day week at this time, the accounts shall be ready, and the money, and the bond."

"Good! We may consider that business as arranged. I shall leave the details to Lillywhite. He will examine the accounts and that. But there is something else."

"Good Heavens! What?"

"You have neither expressed sorrow——"

"I am sorry, very sorry."

"I am glad to hear you say so, Ned, very glad," returned Charlie, cordially. "It is bad for brothers to be at enmity. If we cannot be friends—and I fear we never can—at any rate we need not be enemies. You are sorry, and have agreed to make amends, and I, on my part, forgive you. Here is my hand on it."

They shook hands, and Captain Locksley went his way.

For a long time after his brother was gone, Edward Prince sat with folded arms, sullenly thinking.

"Thirty-three thousand pounds?" he muttered. "Thirty-three thousand! I should not get off for a penny less; and it may be more, to say nothing of the hundred a year to Lillywhite. . . . I did not think Charlie had it in him to be so hard and sharp. But a good deal of that is Lillywhite's doing—his revenge, I suppose. I should have kept him on, and would have done if I had foreseen—but who could have foreseen? . . . Charlie will be well off, devilish well off. He has lighted on his feet again; fellows who don't

like steady work generally do.   He will have fourteen or
fifteen thousand pounds, and Olive and her money—that is
the bitterest pill of all.   He may buy as many steps as he
likes, and rise high in the service.   Oh, he may well afford
to forgive me. . . .   And I lose my chance of standing for
the borough.   I shall be too poor. . . .   Yes, I am sorry,
very sorry—that he was not drowned."

CHAPTER XLIII.

'TWIXT LOVE AND DUTY.

On a June morning, in the year 1863, a gentleman wearing a military uniform, stepped out of Willard's Hotel, Washington, and after making inquiry of another military gentleman, with an armless sleeve, who was loitering at the door, as to the whereabouts of a certain hospital, wended thitherwards.

The day was fine, and the streets were full of life and noise, and bustle. Soldiers everywhere, some in companies and squadrons, on their way to the front, or just arrived from the North or West to reinforce the garrison of the Capital ; others, mostly recruits, sauntering about, singly and in groups ; orderlies hurrying to and fro ; ammunition wagons, ambulances, gun limbers rolling sonorously over the pavement ; officers shouting their orders, sabres clashing, bayonets gleaming, horses neighing, banners flying, bugles blowing, and all the "pomp and circumstance of glorious war." Yet many—though they carried it off bravely—were under deep discouragement. The Union cause was not prospering. Fredericksburg and Chancellorsville had been fought and lost, and the fear of losing Washington was becoming greater than the hope of taking Richmond.

The officer in question surveyed the scene with an air which was alternately critical and indifferent. He had seen too much of the stern realities of war to be excited by the mere preparations for combat. After twice asking his way he reached his destination, one of the temporary frame hospitals with canvas sides, so much in vogue during the Civil War.

Passing within, the gentleman asked the dark-skinned janitor whether Miss Lincoln was in the hospital, and received an answer in the affirmative.

"I should like to see her," said the stranger.

"If you'll give me your name, and walk into the waiting-room I'll let Missy Lincoln know as you's dere."

" Take her this card."

" Yes, kernel," and the darkie went off with the card, which bore this inscription :—

" COLONEL PAUL CONISTON,
17th Illinois Bucktails."

The waiting-room was a plainly furnished parlor, with a few commonplace engravings on the walls, and a few commonplace books on the table. The " kernel " took up one of the books, glanced at the title-page and laid it down again ; then paced about the room impatiently for several minutes, then, turning a chair to one of the windows, sat down and contemplated, or seemed to contemplate, the street. While he was thus occupied the door silently opened and an eager voice exclaimed :

" Oh, Cousin Paul, I am so sorry to have kept you waiting, but I was with the doctors and could not get away sooner."

Her visitor rose from his chair and turned right about face.

" Good heavens ! You, Charlie ; you, and in that uniform ? "

" Yes, it is I, Olive, and in this uniform. And you, Olive, you are in my arms," suiting the action to the word and kissing her passionately.

" But why ? I can hardly believe. How has it come to pass ? · The porter brought me Paul Coniston's card."

" I wanted to surprise you."

" And you have succeeded. But how has it come about ? Tell me quickly. I am dying to know."

" Well I have the honor to be a major in Paul Coniston's regiment of Illinois Bucktails."

" Oh, this is agonizing. Do tell me, please. When did you leave England ? How long have you been in our army ? How was it managed ? Have you left the Red Hussars ? "

" Naturally. I could not hold the Queen's commission and Abraham Lincoln's at the same time."

" But was not that a great sacrifice to make, Charlie ? "

" It was all for love ; and what won't a man do for the woman he loves ? "

" Oh, Charlie, you make me so happy," she murmured, leaning her head on his shoulder, and looking up into his eyes, " so happy."

"Besides, it was not much of a sacrifice. The Red Hussars were ordered to London, and even with my accession of fortune I could not afford the life there—without being still more beholden to Revel than I have been and would like—though he is the best fellow in the world."

"But I am still in the dark. How was it? Begin at the beginning, and tell me everything. Do, please."

"Well, when you so cruelly deserted me——"

"Don't be unkind, dear. I did no more than my duty. You would have done the same——"

"I am not so sure about that. When you went away I was terribly disappointed, and, for a while, so angry that I resolved to think no more about you. All the same, you were always in my thoughts. I found that without you life would not be worth living: and, before you had landed in America I had decided to follow you thither, and do what I knew would please you most—fight for the cause you love so well."

"And are you really going to the front? Think of the danger, and what will become of me if——" (shuddering and clinging closer to him).

Charlie smiled.

"Wait a minute," he said. "I am not through with my story, yet. After I had arranged matters with Ned—he has made full restitution—I got an introduction to the American minister and some other people, wrote to Paul Coniston through the United States War Office, and, after sending in my papers, set sail for New York, where I arrived three months ago, and where I found a letter from your cousin, saying that he was empowered to offer me a major's commission in his own regiment. I hope to get transferred to the cavalry later on, or, perhaps, a place on some general's staff."

"Three months ago! And you never let me know."

"I had made up my mind to tell you in person, yet not before I had done something more than put on this uniform."

"And what more have you done, dear?"

"What I never did before, fought in two losing battles. However, that was no fault of the Illinois fellows, they did their duty."

"To think that you were in those terrible battles, and I didn't know it! Suppose you had been killed. Are you going back?"

"Of course. I got three days' leave with great difficulty—the war is not over by a long way."

Olive shuddered again and turned pale.

"Three days," she cried. "But why need you go back at all? You are not an American."

"I am a soldier, and must do my duty, Olive. I thought you would be pleased at my joining the Union Army."

"I am, I am so pleased that I could cry for joy. But when I think of the perils you have passed through, and the possible still greater perils to come, my heart grows faint. . . . Of course, you must return to the front. Better that than dishonor; and who am I that I should enjoy an immunity from suffering and anxiety in this time of trial? How will it end, Charlie? These repeated defeats are very disheartening."

"In the triumph of the North and the restoration of the Union."

"Do you really think so?"

"I am sure. Providence is generally on the side of the biggest battalions. We have the biggest battalions and the best equipped, and, what is of even greater importance in such a contest as this, the sea power. For the Rebs fight so superbly and are so much better handled than our fellows, that if they had a fleet and could keep their ports open, I doubt whether, despite our greater numbers, we could conquer them. I am rather afraid they would conquer us."

"Isn't it strange that men should fight so heroically for so bad a cause?"

"Well, do you know, I have rather changed my opinion about the cause. It is true that the South are fighting for the right to hold slaves; but they are also fighting for independence. The rank and file of their armies are not slaveholders, yet they fight like demons. I had an interesting talk the other day with a little rebel colonel, whom we took prisoner. He told me that he never owned a slave, and was strongly opposed to the war from the first. But when his State went out of the Union he felt it his duty to go with it and fight in vindication of the right of secession. I believe there are a great many of his way of thinking; and though the Union must be restored and slavery suppressed, in the interest of both sections of the country, I cannot refuse the Rebs a certain measure of sympathy. Most of them are as patriotic, according to their lights, as you Northerners are according to yours. I saw those ragged heroes—some of them armed only with smooth-bore muskets—advance to the attack of an entrenched position, shouting their wild battle-cry, melting like snow under a fierce cross-fire, yet never recoiling. I felt proud that I came of the same race. I hope you Yankees will deal tenderly with them when all is over. . . . . But I am forgetting that I have a letter for you. Here it is."

"From Paul" (opening the missive). "Have you read it?"

"Of course not, nor heard it read."

"Listen! It is so like Paul. 'I felt sure that a man who could make a horse turn a somersault over a hedge, in the way your sweetheart did that time at All Hallows, would make a good soldier. And he is a good one—as good as they make 'em. He did us yeoman service at Chancellorsville. If there were more like him, and we had a strong general in supreme command, and the President would hang Halleck, I believe we should be at Richmond in a month. The Bucktails worship the little Englishman (as they call Locksley) and would go through fire and water for him. I think they would almost drink water for him, if he asked 'em. . . . I hope you will grant his request. He richly deserves it.'"

"What request? What does he mean?" asked Olive.

"I want you to name the day, darling. You will, won't you?"

"But it is impossible. You are going back to the front, and who knows when——"

"Exactly, who knows when, if not now? I have three days' leave. Why cannot we be married to-morrow?"

"To-morrow! To-morrow! And lose you the day after? Oh, Charlie!"

"It would be a great comfort, dear, to feel that you belong to me, that we belong to each other, until death."

"For pity's sake, don't put it in that way. Death, death," exclaimed Olive, in a tone of terror. "I think we had better wait—but if you wish it very much let it be as you say."

"Thank you, Olive, thank you very much," said Charlie eagerly. "You have made me very happy. And now about the preliminaries, for which we have not too much time. I suppose we shall want a license, or something of that sort."

" I suppose so. I'll put on my things, and we will go and see Mr. Stretton, our clergyman. He will tell us all about it."

The things were put on, and after a conference with the parson, arrangements were made for the marriage to take place on the following day. Then other calls were made ; Olive introduced her lover to several of her Washington friends, one of whom asked them to luncheon, another to dinner ; and after spending together the greater part of a happy day they separated, but only to meet again in the evening.

It was past eleven when Charlie, after leaving his sweetheart at the hospital, returned to his quarters.

As he entered the hotel the secretary hailed him.

" Here is a telegraphic despatch for you, Major Locksley," said he. " It came at seven o'clock. If I had known where you were I should have sent it on."

Charlie's spirits went down to zero with a run, for he feared that the message boded no good. It was from Paul Coniston, and ran thus :

" Leave cancelled. You are to report yourself here right away. The Rebs are massing for a move, and fighting may begin any moment. You have got promotion. Don't delay an hour."

" Go right away ! Not until I am married. I'll see them all hanged first," thought Charlie, as he crushed the telegram angrily in his hand. " I wish that confounded secretary had not given it to me. Twenty-four hours can make no great difference, and I am on leave. They gave me three days ; I didn't ask for more, and by heaven I'll have 'em. Poor Olive, what would she think ? "

Then, cooling down a little, he reflected that twenty-four hours might make a great deal of difference ; moreover, the order was peremptory, and a soldier's first duty is obedience. If he did not obey he would deserve to be court-martialed and cashiered. What would Olive say then ? What would his old comrades say. It was a hard case, a very hard case, hard to defer his marriage indefinitely, harder still to leave Olive without seeing her and saying farewell—the chances being about even that he should never see her again. It was out of the question to disturb her at that time of night, and the interview, besides taking time, might shake his resolution.

If he did go, and he had made up his mind to go, the sooner he went the better.

His first proceeding was to send a telegram to Paul Coniston. " Message just received, am returning right away."

Next, he wrote a brief letter to Olive, in which was enclosed her cousin's despatch. Words, he said, were powerless to describe his feelings ; he was wild with disappointment. But there was no other course, compatible with honor and soldierly duty, than immediate compliance with the order he had received. He felt sure that he was doing what she would wish him to do, and bade her be of good cheer. On the very first opportunity he should ask for another and a longer leave of absence, when he would claim the fulfillment of her promise. Meanwhile, he should write to her as often as possible and hoped she would write to him.

This letter he confided to Captain Lawton (who had lost an arm at Fredericksburg and was not yet sufficiently recovered for active duty) and, after explaining the circumstances, made him promise to give it to Miss Lincoln with his own hand early on the following morning.

Half-an-hour later Major Locksley was on his way to the headquarters of the army of the Potomac.

CHAPTER XLIV.

THE BATTLE.

THE battle of Gettysburg, which proved to be the turning point of the Civil War, had three distinct phases, or, rather, it consisted of three separate conflicts, fought on successive days. The first went in favor of the South; the second was drawn; the third ended in the repulse of the rebels and their retreat into Virginia. This event, together with the fall of Vicksburg and Port Hudson, which took place about the same time, sealed the fate of the Confederacy, and sounded the death knell of slavery on the North American continent. So far, the Southerners had been fighting for Home Rule; thenceforward they fought for existence and honor, and none the less desperately that most of them, especially the leaders, foresaw the inevitable end.

Brave men do not yield because fortune seems adverse and hope grows dim, and never were braver than the tattered and hungry veterans of the army of Virginia, whose valor and constancy won the ungrudging admiration of those who least loved the cause for which so many of them shed their blood and laid down their lives.

When Charlie reported himself at headquarters he was rewarded for his previous services and prompt return by promotion to the colonelcy of his regiment, vice Coniston, promoted to the command of a brigade.

"It was very rough on you and Olive," said Paul. "But the General insisted; and if you had not hurried up you would not have got the regiment, that's a fact. And you are none too soon. The Rebs have crossed the Rappahanock, and there will be wigs on the green before long. That's another fact."

During the month which preceded the decisive encounter, there was a good deal of promiscuous fighting, in which Locksley bore a part and went through unscathed. Neither did aught worth mentioning befall him in the first day's battle.

The tactics of the Federals were strictly defensive ; they held strong positions round Gettysburg, against which, during two long summer days, the rebels dashed themselves like a stormy ocean against a rock-bound coast, but, failing in their bold endeavor, and their ammunition being exhausted and their losses appalling, gave up the contest and withdrew to their own country.

Among the more important of the positions in question were two wooded heights, on the left of the Federal line, known respectively as Round Top and Little Round Top. On the western slope of these hills was Devil's Den, a rocky crest and glen, the scene of several fierce encounters ; and a little to the north lay Trostle's Farm, the Hougoumont of Gettysburg. Hereabouts was the hottest fighting on the second day, and could the Confederates have captured and held these "coigns of vantage," the battle had been theirs. Hereabouts, too, were posted Colonel Locksley and his Bucktails, who met the rebels with a resolution equal to their own.

It was only late in the day that the Federals realized the importance of Little Round Top, and they had no sooner occupied it with a battery and two brigades of infantry than the rebels began to climb the hill. Dodging from tree to tree, now creeping, now making a rush, they marched on, heedless alike of the hurricane of musketry, which tore great gaps in their ranks, and the hissing shell, which sent scores of them to their doom. Two Federal brigadier-generals and the officer in command of the battery were killed within a few minutes.

" Hot work this," said Charlie, whose horse had just been shot under him, to one of his captains.

The words were hardly spoken when the captain leaped in the air, then fell on his face, convulsively tearing at the grass in his death agony.

" At them with the bayonet, boys ! " shouted Locksley, pointing with his sword and leading the way.

The Bucktails answered with a cheer. Then ensued a fierce and bloody hand-to-hand struggle. Bayonet crossed bay-onet, muskets were clubbed, men dashed at each other's throats, and, locked in each other's arms, rolled down the hill. Charlie had just disarmed a rebel officer, who at the same moment was shot through the head by a Federal sergeant,

when a tall Texan went for him with his bayonet. Evading
the stroke by a rapid movement, Charlie got inside the man's
guard, and ran him through the body. His sword breaking
off short, he picked up the fallen rebel's musket and fought
with that.

Finally the Confederates were hurled down the hill, with
great slaughter, and the two Round Tops left in possession
of the Federal forces. Nevertheless, the latter on the whole
had lost ground, and at seven o'clock the position of their
left wing was decidedly precarious. The men from the South
had carried the Devil's Den and captured three guns, and
now swarmed among the woods and rocks at the base of the
Round Tops, watching for an opportunity to renew the attack.
Some of the Federal positions had been abandoned, owing to
the destruction of horses and drivers. Of the eighty-eight
horses belonging to the battery which held Trostle's Farm
only four were left alive. One loyalist division had been
simply smashed up, another was giving way, and it looked
as if the entire left wing would be rolled back.

Night drew on. Yet still the battle raged; still the combat deepened. A thick pall of smoke, illumined by incessant
flashes of blood-red flame, hung over the field; great guns
roared defiance as they threw their missiles of death into the
thick of the palpitating throng; the shrieks of maddened
horses mingled with the cries of wounded men; the ground
was slippery with blood, and strewn with the bodies of the
slain and the dying.

In that terrible fight Locksley lost a third of his regiment.
As yet, however, he had not been touched. It seemed as
though he bore a charmed life. But his time came. He had
found another charger, and was cheering his men on, when a
sudden rush of the rebels on their left flank forced them back
by sheer weight of numbers, and as misfortunes never come
singly, his horse and himself were hit at the same time.
Both went down, and the horse falling on Locksley crushed
his leg and pinned him to the ground.

Just then a regiment from another corps came up at a
run to reinforce the fighting line and an officer, observing
Charlie's perilous position, hurried to his rescue. With the
help of some of the Bucktails, who had rallied and re-formed,
he raised the horse and released his fallen rider.

"Are you much hurt?" asked the officer.

"I am hit, and I fear my leg is broken," answered Charlie, faintly. "I cannot move."

"Take him to the rear," said the officer.

He also had to be taken to the rear; for even as he gave the order a bullet struck his neck, and he fell as if dead.

This was one of the last episodes of the second day's battle. As night closed in the rebels sullenly retired, but they were not pursued.

CHAPTER XLV.

AFTER THE BATTLE.

CHARLIE'S sudden departure was naturally a great shock for his sweetheart. But the postponement of their marriage gave her less concern than its cause—the opening of another campaign and the imminence of more fighting, which meant peril to the cause—another defeat might be fatal—and still greater peril to her lover. For *noblesse oblige;* as a Victoria Cross man he had a reputation to maintain, and would, she felt sure, be ever in the thick of danger, and the forefront of the battle. What if the Federals should be vanquished and Charlie slain? Heaven forbid! She put the foreboding from her, yet ever and anon it would thrust itself forward, making her nights wretched and wringing her soul with anguish.

Often she recalled the time when she had reproached him for his seeming want of purpose, and he had confided to her his dislike of the law and regret that destiny had not made him a soldier. And now he was a soldier, fighting for the Union—and her. The thought thrilled Olive with pride. He was her hero: she had gained him for the cause, given to it what she held most precious, and if he should give to it his life, God's will be done.

And yet, and yet, would it not have been better had Charlie remained a lawyer, and he and she had married and settled down in that pleasant land across the sea, and followed those country pursuits in which they both so much delighted. . . . . No! That would have been unheroic, cowardly even, a clear evasion of duty. They had chosen the better part. When the war was over and the Union restored, and Charlie had sheathed his sword, they might revisit England, see dear old All Hallows again, and hunt with the Riversdale hounds once more. God grant it!

The hot June days went swiftly on, and each day brought news to Washington, news of mustering squadrons, of encounters with the enemy, of losses and captures, and, above all, of the steady advance northward of the rebel host. Men feared for the issue, and as the supreme moment drew near, their fears deepened. The Army of Virginia, emboldened by repeated victories, was proudly confident. Composed mainly of veterans, led by a captain of consummate ability, whose Government gave him a free hand, it was ready to go anywhere and do anything.

The Army of the Potomac, on the other hand, was discouraged by defeat, in its ranks were many green recruits, the commander-in-chief had been changed five times in ten months, and the occupant of that unenviable post had to fight both the enemy and the chief of the staff at Washington, at that time the enemy's most potent ally.

On the 1st of July it was reported that Lee had attacked Meade in a position chosen by the latter, and that a great battle had begun. The result, as telegraphed to Washington the same night, was discouraging ; the result of the second day's fighting was indecisive. All the general public could make out was that neither army had retreated.

Like thousands of other women at that time, Olive Lincoln was in an agony of apprehension and excitement. She trembled for her country and her lover. She pictured him waving his sword, leading his men to victory, and when the fight was over, receiving the victor's reward. She saw him fighting hand-to-hand against overwhelming odds, saw him faint and wounded, saw him lying stark and stiff, horses galloping over him and men trampling on his bleeding body. Then she would take courage, try to persuade herself that all was well with him and the cause ; but though she preserved her outward calm and attended to her duties in the hospital, her mind was in a continual turmoil, and she knew no rest.

On the evening of July 3d she received a telegram. It was several seconds before she could muster up courage to break the seal. It might either be a code of death or bring tidings of great joy. The sender was Paul Coniston, and this is what he said :

" Locksley wounded, though not severely. He fought nobly and won great praise. Rebs in full retreat."

" That means he is severely wounded," thought Olive.

"If he had not been he would have telegraphed himself. Paul might have said how he was. At any rate, he is alive and the victory ours. I shall go to Gettysburg right away."

She sought out Captain Lawton, with whom she had become good friends, and asked him to go with her. He consented gladly, and as soon as it was possible they set off.

It was a memorable journey. On every hand they saw sights and signs that showed the terrible character of the struggle which had been waged among the hills and dales of the Quaker State—companies of Confederate prisoners under escort, gaunt, dirty, ragged fellows, their faces still black with the smoke of battle, yet stepping jauntily and bearing themselves bravely—wounded soldiers, their heads bandaged, their arms in slings, hieing them homeward or making for Washington—shattered buildings and trampled fields.

Round about Gettysburg, houses, barns, churches, stables, were crowded with wounded, who of both armies, numbered upwards of twenty-four thousand; many of the dead still lay unburied; for in the three days' fighting nearly six thousand were sent to their last account.

Olive and her companion had great difficulty in ascertaining Colonel Locksley's whereabouts; but they eventually found him in the Lutheran Church at Gettysburg, which had been turned into a hospital.

At the door whom should she meet but Captain Revel.

"You here!" exclaimed Olive. "Have you also joined our army?"

"No, I am here merely as an observer, and a student of the art of war, temporarily attached by special favor, to the staff of a general of division. I came just in time for the shindy."

"Charlie! How is he?"

"As well as can be expected. They have extracted the bullet, and his leg is not broken, only badly contused. I don't think he is as badly hurt as he was when he had that tumble into the lane and got his head broken."

"My poor boy! He is always unlucky."

"Not a bit. The luckiest man I know. Why, he was in the very thick of it—I wish I had been there—and is sure to get his promotion, I always said he would be a general."

"Take me to him, please."

The wounded hero lay on a pallet, looking very pale and

evidently in pain; but when he saw Olive his eyes brightened, and a smile of gratitude lighted up his face.

" My poor boy ! " she murmured, and stooped and kissed him.

" How good of you to come, and so quickly. God bless you, darling," he whispered.

" How could I help coming when I knew my dear lad was wounded ? Paul said so little, and I feared he had not told me the worst."

" He had no time to say more. He is pursuing the Rebs. You see that man on the next pallet ? "

The man on the next pallet was even paler than Charlie. His eyes were shut and his neck was bandaged.

" Is he dead ? "

" No ! no ! Jack ? "

The man opened his eyes.

" Here is somebody come to see us. Somebody you have heard of. Olive Lincoln—my brother Jack."

" John Prince ? "

" Yes, the brave fellow came to my rescue when I was under my horse and could not rise, and got badly wounded for his pains."

" I am sorry I cannot offer you my hand," said Jack feebly, " but I was hit in the neck and am completely paralyzed. I cannot move a limb, and have not long to live."

" Nonsense, old man, you will pull through. Never say die."

Jack shut his eyes again.

" I have paid back every penny," he murmured, " every penny. I said they should not hear of me again unless it was something good, and I have kept my word. ' Keep me, oh, keep me, King of kings, under Thine own Almighty wings.' The old man would have forgiven me, I am sure he would—and my mother——"

Olive had a happy thought.

" Jack," she said, softly.

Jack opened his eyes.

" I have something to tell you. I saw your dear mother, not long before her death; and she charged me, if I should meet you, to say that she not only forgave you with all her heart, but was proud of you; she kept your likeness always by her, and sent you her blessing."

" Thank God ! " and he closed his eyes again, as it might seem, in silent prayer.

Then he looked up.

" I have a favor to ask of you, Olive," he said, " a last favor to a dying man."

" Oh, don't talk in that way ; I will do whatever you want."

" Charlie has told me about you and himself, of his great love for you, of the trials you have undergone, and of his late disappointment, and it would be a great comfort to me to see you married before I die."

" Now ? "

" Yes, right now. This is a church, and the clergyman was with me only a few minutes since."

" What do you think, Charlie ? " asked Olive, turning to her lover with a perplexed look.

" I think we must humor him, poor fellow. The doctors don't give much hope ; his life hangs on a thread, and I should like it immensely, Olive. You could stay with me altogether, and I should get better in no time."

" Let it be so, then. I cannot do less for the dear lad who has done so much for me."

On this Captain Revel was called into counsel and informed what had been decided.

" The very best thing you can do," quoth he, and went to fetch the parson, who, on the circumstances being explained, willingly consented to perform the ceremony.

And so in that church full of wounded men, amid scenes of suffering, and on the morrow of an epoch-making battle, Charlie and Olive were made man and wife.

When the war was over they went to England, and General Locksley and his comely wife may still be occasionally seen at the covert side in a sporting county not far from the town of Peele.

Jack Prince surprised everybody, and nobody more than himself, by getting better. After two years of suffering and helplessness, he regained the use of his limbs ; but he never regained his restive strength, and his life was not long.

THE END.